From England's highest councils to its most glamorous boudoir— Edward made his inimitable mark.

Long before Edward the Seventh became king, he defied Victorian morality and ushered in an era of unabashed opulence and sensuality. Not even the grim censure of his mother, the queen, could stop him from enjoying life and love to the utmost.

Here is the full, uncensored story of this remarkable man—the colorful and passionate story of England's prince and king.

Be sure to read Volume 2 of *EDWARD THE KING*—*Edward the King: Monarch among Men*—the intimate and dramatic story of the astonishing reign of Edward the Seventh.

Edward the King

Volume I
Prince of Hearts

by David Butler

PUBLISHED BY POCKET BOOKS NEW YORK

POCKET BOOKS, a Simon & Schuster division of
GULF & WESTERN CORPORATION
1230 Avenue of the Americas, New York, N.Y. 10020

Television series format and television play
scripts copyright © 1974 by ATV Network, Ltd.
This novelization copyright © 1974 by David Butler.

Published by arrangement with Futura Publications, Ltd.

ISBN: 0-671-82666-2

First Pocket Books printing September, 1976

10   9   8   7   6   5   4

Trademarks registered in the United States and other countries.

Printed in the U.S.A.

Edward the King
Prince of Hearts

Chapter

1

Major-General the Hon. Robert Bruce paced carefully across the deck of the small river steamer, his black, mirror-polished boots testing each step. The planks were drying after heavy rain and, in patches, treacherous underfoot. At the stern, the Royal Ensign hung sodden and above his head the little coloured pennants dripped on their lines like tinkers' washing. He reached the rail and stood looking back along the wake of the steamer. They had just come out of the last of the thousand islands scattered along the beginning of the St. Lawrence River and were now sailing past the north shore of Lake Ontario. To his left he could see the shore, almost monotonously picturesque, dense woods leading down to creeks and inlets at the edge of the water. A weak sun had broken through the cloud and begun to sparkle in tiny diamond points on the wet leaves of the maples and vines and mulberries, but Bruce saw none of it.

An erect, soldierly man with iron-grey hair, in full dress uniform, scarlet tunic and medals, he was schooled by discipline and temperament into not showing his feelings. But inside himself, he felt a deep sense of outrage. The whole trip to Canada had been a success, more than that, a triumph. They had visited innumerable towns and cities from St. John's, Newfoundland, to Quebec and Montreal where the Prince had opened the tubular Victoria Bridge on the Grand Trunk Railway, and Ottawa where the Prince had laid the foundation stone of the Federal Parliament building. He had honoured the Prime Ministers of Upper and Lower Canada, knighted the Speakers of both Parliament Houses in Quebec, accepted

1

loyal addresses, attended balls and receptions. In each city, the cheers had been louder, the crowds more eager and welcoming.

The Prince had made speeches, danced, flirted, been formal, royal or naturally boyish, whichever was right for that moment. He had done well—dammit, he'd done splendidly. It was the boy's first time on his own, the first time he had been exposed to the strain of a royal tour in a strange country. That he had turned curiosity into admiration, adoration even, was due solely to his own personality. In spite of the demands of the official duties, the heavy schedule, people could see he was actually enjoying himself.

Why not? It had given him a chance to get away from home. But how had he developed that charm and tact? No one could have imagined it—certainly not his parents, the Queen and the Prince Consort, who had privately doubted the wisdom of the entire visit. It was obvious they considered their eldest son a failure. Well, perhaps this trip would help to change that opinion. If it ended as it had begun.

The feeling of outrage returned. In less than half an hour, the Governor-General's steamer on which they travelled would reach its next stop, Kingston, on the north-east shore of Lake Ontario. And there in that backwoods township, the tide of public opinion could turn, all the affection and goodwill lost by one wrong move. All Newcastle's fault, the fat hangdog Secretary of State for the Colonies, with his damned, provoking, pompous diplomacy. Bruce turned at the sound of voices.

A group of men had come out of the lounge cabin onto the deck. The portly, heavy-jowled Duke of Newcastle, the elegant Lord St. Germans, Lord Steward of the Queen's Household, leaning on his cane, Colonel Grey and Major Christopher Teesdale, VC, equerries. Half hidden behind the Colonial Secretary's bulk was the slight figure of Albert Edward, Prince of Wales. Seeing him hemmed in, being lectured by Newcastle, General Bruce felt a rush of protectiveness, a genuine affection. He realised that, against all the odds, he had begun to like the lad. Two years ago when he had been appointed to his present position he would never have believed it possible, a regimental officer of the Grenadier Guards put in charge of an unwilling boy of sixteen, despaired of by his tutors, a stammering, defensive, sulky boy whom any normal parents would have written off, except for the fact that this one was destined one day to be King of England.

With the talent he had developed for taking in all his surroundings at once, the Prince had seen Bruce turn as he came out on deck and was conscious of him now, watching from the stern rail. He had noticed his expression, too, half frowning, half smiling. He could not understand it, but he was not afraid of Bruce any more, not afraid at all. When his father had introduced the tall Scot two years ago, he had warned him that he would find his new Governor strict in all matters of behaviour, dress and moral conduct, but also amiable. The Prince had been given frequent proof of the strictness. It was only in the last few months, mostly since this trip began, that he had seen any real signs of amiability. As though it had taken a distance of two thousand miles from Windsor to make Bruce see him for himself rather than through the eyes of his father. He forced his mind back to what the Duke was saying, although he already knew what had happened and that nothing could be done until they reached Kingston.

"So you see, sir, we are not certain what our reception will be like, nor indeed of the advisability, even, of landing."

"We'll cross that gangplank when we come to it, Your Grace," said St. Germans.

The Prince smiled. The dapper Lord Steward had a dry humour that he responded to, all the more so because the Duke hardly ever noticed it. They were looking at him, waiting for him to speak.

"And this is all because I called the Catholic Bishops at Quebec 'Gentlemen', instead of 'My Lords'?"

Newcastle coughed. "On my recommendation, sir. And I refuse to retract it."

"The fact remains," St. Germans said quietly, "that

3

it caused great offence. And then your attempt to explain the reason for it caused even more."

"Hang it all, how was I to know the Protestants would make an issue of that? It was to keep them quiet that I suggested a certain formality with the Bishops in the first place! Now every Orangeman from Charlottestown to Toronto is up in arms, shouting that we're kowtowing to the Papists."

"Orangemen?" the Prince asked.

"Protestant extremists, sir." St. Germans smiled. "They take as their hero King William of Orange who defeated the Irish Catholic army at the Battle of the Boyne."

"Oh, yes, King Billy. What do they hope to achieve?"

"It's rather difficult to say, sir. To keep the Catholic subjects of the Crown in a constant state of subservience, one supposes. And their lack of any practical scheme for achieving this impossible state is only matched by their fanaticism."

"And scarcely a matter for humour," Newcastle growled. "Now they're building triumphal arches decorated with their colours across every road we're to travel. They've organised protests and marches, and plan to turn every arrival of His Royal Highness at a new town into an Orange procession."

"I could not be seen to support one side, or one group, against another. If I did, this visit would drive people further apart, instead of bringing them together."

"Precisely, sir. And its whole purpose would be ruined. I have written to the Mayor and Corporation of Kingston and told them I will not tolerate any demonstrations."

"If there are, what can we do?" the Prince asked.

"Difficult to say, sir, not till we get there. But steps will be taken."

The Duke sounded angry and belligerent, and the Prince could see that St. Germans was worried. Bruce had approached them. He coughed, looking ahead, and the group turned.

The shore town of Kingston was now clearly in sight. It was larger than they had expected, in the halfway stage of development, partly a sprawling country town of wooden cabins, partly a growing commercial centre.

Stonebuilt municipal buildings, stores, warehouses and imposing, private residences on the slopes of the hills were beginning to give it a look of prosperity.

As the steamer turned in towards the quay, there seemed at first to have been no need for the earlier concern. A specially organised band was playing. The quay was crowded with townspeople carrying flags and banners. They surged forward dangerously near the edge, jostling, excited, as Bertie moved to the rail. They saw a slim, golden-haired boy of eighteen, dressed as a colonel of the 10th Hussars which made him look even younger, absurdly handsome, almost girlish. He smiled shyly and the cheers swelled, drowning out the National Anthem. But behind him the Duke of Newcastle was scowling. Amongst the banners, 'Long Live Victoria's Son', 'A.E.', 'Ich Dien', 'God Save the Queen', there were others decorated with orange rosettes and colours and many saying 'Remember 1690'.

The gangplank had been lowered; the magistrates detached themselves from the crowd in the official enclosure and came aboard to be presented and deliver their address of welcome. Although the Prince tried to put them at ease, they were nervous and subdued. St. Germans took one aside and found out why. The Mayor and representatives of the Corporation had elected to wait on the quay to present their address when the Prince came ashore. The crowd was packed with Protestant supporters just waiting for that signal to start their demonstration. There were thousands of Orangemen gathered in the town; over every road and street they had built arches in imitation of the old gate of Londonderry, hung with Orange banners and violently anti-Catholic posters. St. Germans spoke to General Bruce and the younger of the two equerries, Major Teesdale, a good-looking, serious young man, moved forward to the Prince.

He bowed. "It appears it may be some time before we go ashore, sir. Perhaps you would care to wait in your cabin."

The Prince paused. He knew he was being asked politely to withdraw but, in the circumstances, it seemed the least embarrassing solution. He smiled. "I believe

I would. I have a letter to finish and I may put my feet up for a while".

As he turned to the companionway, followed by Teesdale, he could hear the cheering falter. Then a howl of disappointment and derision went up from the Orangemen. "No Popery!" someone shouted. "Remember the Boyne!" The Prince flushed and forced himself not to look round.

In his cabin, he could still hear the ugly shouting from outside, mixed with the screaming of women. He liked his cabin, compact, bright, gleaming with brass and mahogany. He liked its very ordinariness. Here he had no pretensions, no dignity to keep up.

That reminded him. He really did have a letter to finish. It lay open on the green leather of the desk. It was to his parents and he had been trying to finish it for days. He sat at the desk, making himself ignore the rhythmic chanting that had started on the quay. As he read through what he had written, he knew his father would not be pleased. He expected a letter to be half scientific treatise and half social document, with comments, facts and figures. The only facts he had remembered were that the new tubular Victoria Bridge, named after his mother, was a mile and three quarters in length, had twenty-four spans and a total, painted surface of thirty-two acres. He had copied that from the official programme.

How could he tell them about the other things? The absurd pride he had felt in driving home the last, silver rivet, the way the workmen had crowded round, boasting about their achievement in their strange accent. The children at St. John, New Brunswick, who were to sing the National Anthem and scatter flowers in his path but got so excited that they sang out of time and threw the flowers all over him. The sharp, dizzying tang of his first cigar and the girl with dark eyes and a torn dress showing her shoulders, standing in a field of ripe grain, who blew him a kiss on his way to Fredericton. The Iroquois wardance and a thousand lumbermen in dark red tunics paddling downstream to meet him in

6

painted, birchbark canoes. And, most of all, the timbershoot at Ottawa Falls.

He smiled, remembering how the Duke and the Governor-General had squashed him between them for safety sitting on a raised plank above the great raft of logs as it swooped and plunged down the steep, artificial channel. The raft had moved so slowly towards the wooden-sided shoot, heavy and clumsy, then quickening until it quivered suddenly all along its length and leapt off over the edge, rushing down the side of the falls at terrifying, exhilarating speed. He had laughed with the lumbermen guiding it, when it flopped on to its first straight run and a spuming torrent swept over the raft beneath their feet, before it dipped and shot downwards again. When it reached its last straight drop of four feet and landed with a spine-jarring crash that sent waves fountaining up on either side and wallowed till the water reached their knees, before sailing out into the calm centre of the river below the falls, he had wished the shoot had taken twice as long. The Duke of Newcastle had looked uncomfortably sick.

How could he tell them, his parents who were so remote? He read the plain, short letter again. There was nothing he knew how to add. Giving up, he wrote at the bottom, 'As ever, your loving son—Bertie'. He pushed his chair back and put his feet up on the desk. He smiled, remembering the pretty farmgirl with dark eyes.

Bruce stood at the top of the gangplank and watched as the Duke and Lord St. Germans left the Mayor's group to stride back through a chorus of catcalls and angry jeering. He wished he had a company, half a company of Guards with him. They'd run that mob off the quayside in ten minutes. And clear the town in an hour.

Newcastle returned with the Mayor's promise to tear down the arches and disperse the mob. At the threat that the Prince would not land, he had capitulated and undertaken to cancel the demonstration. He would present himself on board in the morning with his address of welcome. The steamer moved out from the quay and the royal party stayed on board for the night.

In the morning, however, the situation was worse. The Mayor had been offended by the Duke's high-handed manner and the extremists on the Corporation, during a long night of whisky and fiery eloquence, worked themselves up into a state of defiance. At first light, the Mayor sent a message that the Prince would be given a welcome if he came ashore and led an Orange Walk, otherwise he could go to hell and take his lackeys with him.

The Duke of Newcastle was speechless. In all his years of dealing with the Colonies, he had never imagined such an insult to a royal visitor and, through him, to the Queen. The text of the message was softened before it was relayed to Bertie but he could see very easily what it meant. The situation was deadlocked.

'I had hoped it would be handled a little more tactfully,' he said. 'If the the situation had been explained to them rather than orders given . . . What happens if they will not see reason?'

The Duke had stiffened. The whole responsibility for the State Visit was his, althought the Prince was its figurehead, and he did not accept criticism. 'As I have said, sir, steps will be taken.'

St. Germans, Bruce and the Canadian members of the entourage were increasingly worried. Bertie looked round them, waiting for one of them to suggest a solution. The longer they stayed here, the more embarrassing and the more insulting it became. In his troubled dealings with his parents, Bertie had learnt the lesson that confrontation, whenever possible, should be avoided.

'Since their conditions are unacceptable and you will not allow me to land,' he said hesitantly, 'and since they do not want to come aboard, the only answer would seem to be to leave. Before any further damage is done.'

It was, indeed, the only answer, as even Newcastle could see. With very bad grace he ordered the gangplank up and the captain to proceed. The jubilant Orangemen on the quay, certain, until now, that they had won, stared in disbelief. Some of them ran forward, shouting and the band struck up a ragged version of the Marseillaise, the French revolutionary song. But by that time Bertie was standing at the offshore rail. He had tried not to let them see how disturbed he was. Although the Duke made all the decisions according to his own rigid opinions, if anything went wrong with the tour, he knew that his parents would blame him. They would think that, somehow, it was his fault. He was looking out over the sparkling waters of the lake. And over there—no, that must be an island—but beyond that was America, where he would be in exactly two weeks' time. More cities, more people and not his own. If he failed with his own people, what could he hope for there?

Toronto made up for everything. Indignation over the insult turned the normal enthusiasm of the crowds into a massive demonstration of loyalty to the Queen and affection for the Prince. The memory of Kingston was blotted out by receptions, levees and a gaslit ball that set a new standard for extravagance. There were days of sightseeing, opening buildings and laying foundation stones and, at last, Bertie found himself at Niagara. On his first night, the great falls were turned into a cascade of crystal and silver with hundreds of Bengal lights burning behind the main falls and others, under Table Rock, sparkling on the waters of the Horseshoe Cataract and making the clouds of blown spray into a luminous haze.

On the next day he watched, breathlessly, as the Frenchman, Blondin, crossed the space below the falls on a rope, one thousand two hundred feet in just under half an hour. The short wiry man with a waxed moustache and pointed beard, wearing a skin-tight woollen vest and drawers, rested once or twice on the way over, turned somersaults and spun on the rope like a squirrel in a cage. It was an astonishing performance and, with the Prince of Wales watching, one that could make him famous in a day. He followed up the single crossing by another in which he carried his agent across on his back, with his feet in special stirrups that hung from Blondin's shoulders. His last crossing he made on stilts which were strapped to his legs and forked at the end. Once he dropped without warning onto the rope and the spectators screamed in horror, but he explained later he had only sat down to rest. Bertie was waiting for him when he reached the enclosure. He congratulated him and begged him not to do any more, the excitement had been too intense. Blondin assured him there was no danger and offered to carry Bertie across on his shoulders to prove it. It was too tempting and, to the dismay of the watching dignitaries, Bertie accepted at once.

Bruce categorically refused to give his permission. No argument would make him change his mind. The idea of the Prince of Wales sitting on the back of a Frenchman, balanced on a rope three hundred feet above the Niagara Falls, was unthinkable. Laughing, but disappointed, Bertie shook hands with Blondin and the little man walked home to his wife and children with his stilts and balancing pole over his shoulder and on to fortune.

Bertie crossed over into America more conventionally in a riverboat, five days later.

If his trip to Canada had begun as a success and ended as a triumph, America for Bertie began as a triumph and ended as a conquest. He was never to forget his reception in the United States.

Reporters from the major newspapers had followed his tour with interest so far and there was great excitement throughout the country. The reaction at the first place he visited, Detroit, should have given them an indication of what was to follow. The whole town and river was specially illuminated and the civic officials led out a crowd of thirty thousand to cheer him. By the time he reached Chicago, the crowd had trebled, and the roads into the city were blocked with people coming to see him. He rested for a few days after Chicago, living in a small cabin out on the prairie at Dwight's Station, shooting quail and rabbits and prairie fowl. Then on to St. Louis.

He was travelling incognito, as Lord Renfrew, a student, but it was impossible to keep it up. The vast crowds who waited to see him would not be put off with a mere Baron when they knew they had the Prince of Wales. His picture was everywhere, every move reported, every expression noted. The loose jackets with unmatching trousers, which his mother disapproved of but which he found comfortable, became the rage. His shy smile, blue eyes and charm turned the heads of staunchy Republican ladies. It was said he would consider himself lucky if he escaped being nominated as President before he left for home.

The fever to see him, to shake hands or just to glimpse him as his carriage forced its slow way through the crowds, doubled at each stop. Cincinnati, Pittsburg, Harrisburg and Baltimore, Maryland, where he was escorted in a procession through streets hung with flags that made a final nonsense of his incognito. And at last to Washington, where he was formally welcomed by the Secretary of State to the sound of artillery salutes.

In Washington, he stayed at the White House with the dignified, cultured old President, James Buchanan. That night there was a State Banquet and the hostess was beautiful, dark-haired, Harriet Lane, the President's niece. She was the first young woman Bertie had met for more than a few minutes on the entire tour and they became friends at once. She showed him the Capitol and the Houses of Congress, taught him ten pin bowling, sat with him at dinner and held his arm during the firework display that ended the second day. She was the most envied woman in America.

The next morning, they sailed with President Buchanan in a revenue cutter down the Potomac to Mount Vernon. They stood bareheaded at the tomb of George Washington while a marine band played the dirge from 'Il Trovatore'. The report that the descendant of George the Third had honoured the grave of the first American, converted the last sceptics. He planted a chestnut sapling at the side of the tomb before visiting Washington's house, then danced with Harriet on deck on the way back.

It was hard for him to leave Washington and the President's niece would gladly have kept him longer,

11

but he had other places to see. Richmond, Virginia, Petersburg and Philadelphia where he talked to the prisoners in the model penitentiary and the good manners of his hosts let him walk in the streets without being jostled and stared at. When he went that evening to hear Madame Patti at the Academy of Music, the audience rose to its feet and sang 'God Save the Queen'.

He was still moved by that memory when he sailed from Perth Amboy on the steamer *Harriet Lane* for New York and received a welcome such as had never been given to anyone before. Wearing his colonel's uniform, he arrived at the Battery to the thunder of saluting cannons and cheering. He reviewed six thousand militia massed in Castle Garden, then took his place in an open barouche drawn by six black horses, beside the Mayor of New York, Fernando Wood. With an escort of cavalry, he rode along Broadway to the Fifth Avenue Hotel where he was to stay, a Broadway filled with people on either side for over a mile, sidewalks, windows, rooftops, all crowded, half a million people come to cheer the Prince and the Queen, flags waving, handkerchiefs fluttering, flowers, cheers, and confetti.

New York surpassed itself, and continued to do so. His rooms at the Fifth Avenue were the most comfortable he had ever seen, far more so than Buckingham Palace or Windsor Castle. At a ball given for him at the Academy of Music by New York Society, three thousand guests had invitations. Nearly the same number again, offended at not being invited, forced their way into the hall, gentlemen in evening dress, ladies in crinolines and elaborate coiffures, so many that the temporary ballroom floor which had been built for the occasion gave way and dropped three feet into the pit. No one was injured and the floor was repaired while Bertie had supper. Afterwards, he danced every dance and his only regret was that his partners had to be socially prominent matrons, starting with the wife of the State Governor, rather than the eager girls who stood on chairs in the lower galleries to see him.

The following night, six thousand men of the New York Fire Department, in their uniforms of red tunics and gleaming brass helmets, and their engines decorated with lamps, flags and flowers, paraded past him as he stood on the balcony of his hotel. Ingenious new limelight burned in the lamps behind powerful reflectors that turned the rays into pencils of white flame. Each brigade was preceded by its own band and every fireman carried a blazing torch. Many of them had Roman candles which they lit when they came in sight of the hotel, sending globes of coloured lights spluttering up into the night sky. Bertie stood on his balcony, flushed and excited, saluting each brigade as it came past to the sound of the cheering of the crowds which, incredibly, had almost doubled.

His ears, still ringing, he visited West Point, Bunker's Hill, Albany and Boston, which nearly matched New York. He met Longfellow and Emerson and danced till dawn at the most elegant and colourful ball of the whole tour. He regretted the shortness of time he was allowed to spend at Harvard. He took the train for Portland, Maine, and at last sailed out to the line-of-battleship *Hero* for the voyage to England.

In his spacious cabin with its leather chairs, hanging silver candelabras and cabinets made out of timbers from Nelson's *Victory*, he had three weeks to gather his thoughts, to remember that he was only eighteen and that, at home, things would be very different.

Chapter
2

"When I had the honour of addressing your Majesty in June last, I confidently predicted a cordial welcome for the Prince of Wales throughout this country, should he pay us a visit on his return from Canada to England. What was then prophecy has now become history. He has been everywhere received with enthusiasm, and this is attributable not only to the very high regard entertained for your Majesty, but also to his own noble and manly bearing. Dignified, frank, and affable . . . In our domestic circle he won all hearts. I shall ever cherish the warmest wishes for his welfare.

The visit of the Prince to the tomb of Washington, and the simple but solemn ceremonies at this consecrated spot, will become an historic event, and cannot fail to exert a happy influence on the kindred people of the two countries.

With my respectful regards for the Prince Consort, I remain your Majesty's friend and obedient servant,

James Buchanan."
'Washington, 6th October. 1860.'

Victoria had read the letter twice. As she put it down, she caught sight of the cast of Bertie's hand when he was a baby that lay on the front edge of her desk, next to one of Vicky's, the Princess Royal. For a moment, she saw them as they had been then, small, naked and wriggling, like pink-skinned frogs, and gave a faint shudder of revulsion. Small children were so ugly. Of course, then they went through a period when they were really very endearing, like puppies, but later they became problems again.

She frowned as she looked at the letter lying in front of her. At forty-one, she had lost all trace of the girlish prettiness that had so charmed her first Ministers. Her cheeks had grown pouchy, bulging out on either side of her nose, emphasising her receding chin. Her eyes were still clear and bright blue but her hair had grown darker and was drawn back severly from a strict centre parting to a bun covered with a black lace bow. Her short figure had thickened and although that had perfected the line of the white shoulders of which she was so proud, they were now kept covered by high-necked dresses, in permanent deference to Albert's wishes. His

14

idea on dress had been formed in Germany when he was a boy and he was very strict on the subject of modesty.

She looked to the side where Albert sat working at his desk which had been placed by her orders next to hers. The desks were identical except that the bust of the Prince Consort which stood on the far corner of hers was replaced by a bust of the Queen on his. He was absorbed, writing quickly, reducing a report of many pages, on the probable results of the occupation of the port of Tientsin by units of the British navy, to a single page memorandum. Victoria had never fully grasped the Chinese question and the memorandum was for her to study before meeting her Foreign Secretary. It was important that she understood the necessity for the establishment of a firm peace with China, ensuring the freedom of trade in the port and the safety of its British residents. Watching him, Victoria felt that secret, warm glow which so often emptied her mind of everything else when she thought of him, from the moment when she had first seen him as a man, tall and slim in the Quadrangle of Windsor Castle almost exactly twenty-one years before. From that day they had never been apart, and the fact that such a being was her husband and father of her children was incontestable proof to Victoria of the beneficence of Divine Providence.

The light from the tall windows behind picked out with gold the fair, curled hair above his ears and glowed in his full sidewhiskers. With a slight start of surprise, Victoria suddenly realised how far his hair had receded. It only made his brow more lofty, his expression more noble. His moustache, grown to add dignity to his youth, was now heavier and his dear face lined with care and study. Everything about him was heavier but it only made him all the more handsome, so solid, comforting, working tirelessly on her behalf. And their people's. She had resisted the temptation to reach out and touch him, not to demand affection and attention, merely to feel that strength, that warm reality for herself.

Sensing her, Albert looked up. It always gave Victoria a moment's unease when he caught her looking at him, a tinge of guilt as though her thoughts had been impure when his clear, blue eyes, so like her own, turned to her.

'Have you read President Buchanan's letter?' she asked. He shook his head and she passed him the letter from her desk.

He read it quickly, frowning slightly in the same way she had. Like her, he read it twice to make sure of what it said.

'It appears that Bertie's tour has been a triumph. "Dignified, frank and affable . . ." '

'It doesn't sound like Bertie at all.'

'Not the one I know,' Albert murmured and placed the disturbing letter down squarely on his desk to cover the memorandum. He could see that behind Victoria's apparently normal interest there was a spreading disquiet. She had hesitated for a long time before finally consenting to the tour. In anything concerning her sovereignty she was apt to be jealous. It had taken some years before she would accept that her husband, even, could stand beside her without diminishing her, by attracting to himself some of the devotion that was due to her alone. Only the certainty that their son would be felt in some way to be inadequate had finally convinced her to give her consent. She was certain he would be welcome but, somehow, that welcome should show how much more they longed for his mother. Now there was this letter . . .

'What's happened? How has he won such opinions?'

'They have been carried away,' Albert decided. 'The natural affection and demonstration of loyalty with which people greeted your representative has made them believe it was due to Bertie, himself.'

'Do you think that's it?'

'Buchanan says so, here. The enthusiasm was due partly to our son's bearing, but in the main to the high regard which, even in America, they entertain you.'

Victoria's agitation stilled. 'Of course. Yes, of course. I am very grateful to them for being so kind to Bertie. I shall write to Washington and say how deeply touched I am by the many signs of affection towards me which his presence called forth.'

Albert smiled. 'I think you should.' He was perfectly sincere. He had reason to remember vividly his wife's jealousy when she felt that another was receiving the affection which loyalty owed only to her, but he was not being diplomatic. It simply occurred to neither of them that some at least of the adulation which had turned Bertie's tour into a triumphal progress might be due to qualities in him which they had not suspected. Albert was fond of his eldest son, but he was a disappointment. With what high hopes his education had been planned from the earliest years and how bitter to realise that he fell far short of that moral and intellectual height, that steadfast application and sureness of purpose which had been expected to him.

'I can scarcely believe he'll soon be home,' Victoria said.

Yes, he has been away a long time. And through many excitements. We must make sure he does not expect them to become a habit.'

If Bertie had hoped that through absence and reports of his triumph the attitude of his parents to him had changed, he was soon to be disabused. Contrary winds and stormy seas caused fears for his safety and delayed his return but the moment he landed in Plymouth, he travelled as quickly as possible to Windsor. As his carriage rattled up the hill from the station that November evening, past the high, grey, battlemented walls, he craned his neck for a glimpse of the lights shining in the windows of the Round Tower rising above the mound built by William the Conqueror on the west side of the Quadrangle. He felt a rush of love and affection for his family, a longing to see them and a real sense of pride at coming home, for once, as a success.

The first to greet him was his younger brother, Prince Alfred. Affie, a slight, likable boy of sixteen, was home for a few days from his spell of training in the navy. Still in his midshipman's uniform, he rushed down the stone stairs and hugged Bertie excitedly, overjoyed to see him, wanting to hear everything at once. Bertie at last had someone who would understand and, as they

17

climbed back up and hurried along the corridors to the family sitting room, told him in a rush about Blondin and the Indians and the watershoot and the New York Fire Brigade, until Affie's eyes were shining with admiration and envy. He knew exactly how Bertie must have felt when Bruce had refused permission for him to ride on Blondin's shoulders, but was pleased that the General was turning out to be not such a bad old stick. Affie was avid for descriptions of the Red Indians, Algonquins, Iroquois and Chippewas whom Bertie had met and to whom he had given medals bearing the Great Queen's Portrait. The idea of their mother's picture hanging on a red man's chest among the feathers and beads and buffalo teeth amused Affie enormously.

Victoria found herself genuinely delighted to have Bertie home. She hugged and kissed him, exclaiming how well and handsome he looked. Albert smiled and hugged him, too. Bertie had meant to be different with them, to be open and friendly. He felt different since his trip, much more confident and at ease, but seeing them as they had always been, unchanged themselves, put a kind of constraint on him and he did not know how to begin.

'So you had a successful trip,' Victoria said.

'I can't begin to tell you. There's so much.'

Victoria smiled. 'Everyone writes very well of you.'

Bertie smiled from her to his father.

Albert frowned slightly. 'But you must not let it go to your head. If you were accepted and applauded, it was not due to you, but solely to your mother's position.'

The excited words and the warmth died in Bertie.

'Any kindness you were shown was because your mother is Queen of England.'

'Yes, Papa.'

Looking at him, Victoria could see that he was hurt. It had perhaps not been necessary to apply the corrective quite so abruptly, nor so soon, although it was for Bertie's own good. She could see that Albert had realised that too, but the words had been said.

'Yet you really deserve the highest praise, all the more since you have never been spared any reproof.'

18

She laid her hand on his arm approvingly and he smiled to her, grateful.

'We really have missed you, Bertie'.

'And I you, Mama. I was longing to see you and tell you all the—But we were held up by storms.'

'Yes, that is especially unfortunate,' Albert said. 'It has made you miss half the Michaelmas term at Oxford. You will return to Christ Church and try to catch up, as soon as you have recovered from your journey.'

In later years, Bertie could never think of Oxford with any real affection. He had looked forward to university as a means of escape into the world but he had not been allowed to live in college, nor even to belong to any particular one. Apart from a few lectures at Christ Church, the rest of his studies consisted of a series of courses prepared by chosen professors and delivered to him at Frewin Hall off Cornmarket Street, where he was installed with General and Mrs. Bruce and his equerries. All he saw of his fellow students were groups of young men who bowed, removing their mortar boards as he crossed Tom Quad, or stood respectfully when he entered the cathedral in the morning for college prayers. Apart from that, there were dinners given at Frewin Hall to heads of Houses and undergraduates, vetted for brilliance and moral rectitude, whose conversation was bound to be instructive and edifying. There were Union debates, Commemoration in the Sheldonian Theatre and bumping races on the river at which Bertie was always a spectator, although he longed to join in. His only release was an occasional shooting party and hunting with neighbouring packs of hounds. He rode well and began to be popular among the young men who formed the Bullingdon Club and hunted with the Pytchley, but that was discouraged. His father had decreed that Oxford was to be considered solely as a place of study. Quite clearly, time spent on recreation or unimproving conversation was time wasted.

Bertie realised that during the Christmas vacation, however daunting the thought, he would have to appeal to his father. After Christmas he would be moving to

Cambridge. The Prince Consort felt that his son could not spend time at one university without spending a corresponding time at the other, thus showing impartiality, and Bertie was determined that the lonelieness of his life at Oxford would not be repeated. During his stay in the New World, Bertie had found he had a talent for making friends, or at least putting people at their ease so that they could behave naturally when they were with him. He desperately wanted the companionship of younger people who would neither talk down to him nor wait deferentially for him to start every subject in a conversation. He had never had a great taste for books or for abstract learning. He wanted to know more about life.

Christmas was one of the best times, with parties and entertainments, dressing up and decorations. The little Christmas trees which Albert had sent for from the woods round his boyhood home at Rosenau, one for the private sitting room and another for the terrace, had become such a feature that other people now put up their own trees in imitation. The one in the sitting room was prettiest hung with tiny bells and lanterns and presents for everyone. The whole family had gathered at Windsor, except Vicky who was expecting her second child now in Prussia. Her first, Willy, was quite the most adorable baby ever except for his poor, little left arm which had been damaged at birth, but Victoria was furious at her daughter having another so soon. She had counselled her to wait at least a year between babies. 'But,' as she told her mother, 'after all, it is not we women who decide these things.'

The Duchess of Kent, Victoria's mother, laughed. A plump and attractive old lady, who still wore her hair in bunches of ribboned ringlets on either side of her head, she remembered saying exactly the same thing to Victoria. But Albert had proved more vigorous or her daughter more seductive than anyone supposed. The Duchess had grown wise and contented after a stormy and ambitious life. The young widow of the Prince of Leiningen, she had married Edward, Duke of Kent, during the scramble of the sons of George the Third to produce an heir. Widowed again, she had devoted her life to protecting and developing their daughter, Victoria, until the inevitable time when she became Queen. The Duchess had expected to be Regent for her eighteen-year-old daughter, with power over all those who had slighted them for so long, and fell out with Victoria when she announced that she would rule alone. She was even more rigorously excluded three years later when Albert made himself master of his household and sole adviser to his wife. Mother and daughter had only recently become reconciled through a long and painful illness from which the Duchess had now fully recovered, except for an ache in her left arm which secretly troubled her. They were in the sitting room, watching the younger royal children who squatted on the floor, trying to teach their baby sister Beatrice how to play Snakes and Ladders.

'What, Mama?' Victoria asked crossly.

'I was just thinking—nine grandchildren of which the youngest is only three, and now the great grandchildren arrive.' After all those years in England, she still spoke with a thick, German accent. 'The years pass so quickly. And now little Alice is to be married.'

That was one of the reasons Victoria was so cross with Vicky. She had written to her eldest daughter, the Princess Royal, now Princess of Prussia, frequently, reminding her that Alice was nearly seventeen and a husband must be found for her. A Protestant German prince preferably, and not another Prussian. Vicky's husband, Fritz, was a dear and sensible young man but the country would not stand for another Prussian. They had grown so arrogant of late. Vicky had been too busy with her new son and the affairs of her own position to devote the amount of time her mother thought was due and necessary. Now, however, everything was happily settled with the betrothal of Alice to Prince Louis of Hesse.

Prince Louis was skating with Alice and Bertie and some of the younger gentlemen-in-waiting on the frozen

21

pond at Frogmore. A plump, amiable young man with a silky moustache and an earnest expression, he did not skate well. Bertie had helped him up several times already and when Louis sat again with a crash that shook the whole surface of the pond, Bertie went into hoots of laughter. He fully expected to see Louis' bottom stuck fast in a hole in the ice. Alice pretended not to notice so that her fiancé would not be embarrassed. An intelligent, narrow-faced girl with fine eyes, she thought privately that Bertie was laughing a little too loudly. Yet he was her favourite brother. Ever since that day long ago when they were children and she had been sent to bed without any supper. He had crept through all the dark corridors of Osborne to her room, terrified of being discovered, with a piece of cake he had saved from tea.

A gentleman-in-waiting was helping Louis to the side and Alice skated over to Bertie.

'Is he all right?'

'He said his pride was bruised.' Alice laughed despite herself. Mama would have been shocked but Bertie had a way of saying such things. He was smiling to her.

'Happy, Alice?'

She nodded. He took her arm and they began a slow circuit of the pond, moving easily side by side. She did not have to tell him how much she was in love. He could see it in the way she looked at the faintly ridiculous Louis. It was an emotion he could not understand, although he recognised it.

'How long is Louis to be here?'

'He has to rejoin his regiment next month.'

'You'll miss him.'

Alice slowed and stopped, turning to her brother. 'Wait till you find someone. You'll be the next.'

'No, not me,' Bertie said. Alice looked at him in surprise. He was so very definite and, at this moment, she could not believe that everyone did not wish to be in love. 'It's different for you. You'll be going abroad. But I'll have to stay here whatever happens. I'd only be changing one cage for another. I don't intend to get married before I've begun to live.'

Albert was working on a pile of despatches in the study. It was a difficult period for him. Italy was struggling towards national unity and in the north fighting to free herself from Austria. Albert had many relatives in the Austrian court but he was Prince Consort of Great Britain. And Britain must always champion those nations which thirst for freedom, he wrote, injustice and honour.

For some time past he had heard the piano playing through the connecting doors to the sitting room. That would be Alice back from her skating. None of the others played so well. Now there was added to it shrieks of laughter and the shouting laugh which he recognised as Bertie's. It really was intolerable while he was trying to work. He rose and made for the sitting room.

They were all here, except Louis who had gone to change his wet clothes. The youngest children sat in a ring near the fireplace with little Beatrice, Baby. Bertie was standing by Alice at the piano and Victoria sat on the sofa next to the Duchess of Kent. They were all laughing and made no attempt to stop when Albert came in.

'There is so much noise in here I can hardly work!'

Victoria could tell that he was annoyed and called out sharply, 'Children, not so loud!'

They fell silent and looked round at their father, but they were still smiling. Albert was intrigued. His most attractive quality was that he adored children. He found their innocence and their high spirits irresistible. When he was with them, it was the only time he could relax.

'Why were you laughing so loudly, anyway?'

'It was Baby, Papa,' said Louise, at twelve, the prettiest and most talented of the little girls. 'We told her she must go to bed. And she said she couldn't, as she had to write to her nephew.'

Albert laughed with a sudden wholeheartedness that surprised them, and the children joined in.

'That's better,' said the Duchess. 'Now why don't you stop whatever you're doing and join us?'

'Tea will be served soon,' Victoria said.

'Oh, do Papa!' the children shouted. 'Do join us!'

After the briefest of hesitations, Albert gave in. He

could put off writing to Palmerston for another day. 'Oh, very well, since I'm obviously not going to be left in peace to work.' He smiled and moved towards the children. Bertie straightened from beside the piano and stepped forward.

'Father—'

'Yes?'

'Alice says Louis is to rejoin his regiment next month.'

Albert was exasperated, knowing immediately what was coming. 'Not the Army again! I have told you it is not possible—unmöglich! Neither your Mother nor I intend that you should make a career in the Services. In any case you know you are to go to Cambridge next term.'

Bertie stood his ground. 'At least at Cambridge, let me stay in college.'

'We have had this out before. If you stay in college, you will become too familiar. You are bound to make acquaintances, some of which may develop into friendships. I assure you they can only embarrass you in later life. Now why must you spoil a good party?' He left Bertie and moved to the children.

Bertie watched his father kneel on the floor and begin a little hopping dance on his knees, holding Beatrice's hands, to make the children laugh. He remembered how he, too, had adored him when he was a child. Nothing he said was too simple for his father not to be fascinated by it, but now he never listened to what Bertie thought or wished. Cambridge, he knew, would be just like Oxford. The subject was closed.

But Cambridge turned out to be very different. The house taken for him was Madingley Hall, in a village about three miles outside town. The intention was that he would be more secluded and Bruce could keep him under stricter observation, but the distance from town made it inconvenient for him to return on days when he attended lectures at Trinity College. He spent the waiting time in the rooms of the Master or walking with one of his equerries. A lecture of Charles Kingsley's, the author and historian, one day finished early. The great man had wound himself up to a peroration of such eloquence and emotion that, although it was premature, he could not continue without anticlimax and Bertie found himself crossing the quadrangle of Trinity on his own. None of his equerries was in sight. He acknowledged the usual groups of undergraduates who stopped and bowed as he passed. In one of the groups was a young man who bowed and then smiled in such an engaging way that Bertie involuntarily paused and smiled back. He was about Bertie's age, tall, good-looking, with a frank, open face.

'Charles Carrington, sir.'

He made no move to walk on. Bertie was not quite sure what to do. Perhaps he should shake hands? 'We are f-fellow students,' he said lamely.

Carrington smiled. 'Yes, My rooms are just up there.'

'Really?' Bertie glanced at the gatehouse. There was still no equerry in sight. 'I have never been in-uh-in . . .'

Carrington hesitated. 'Perhaps you'd care to see them, sir?'

Carrington's rooms were small and cluttered, with recessed, leaded windows. Books and clothes lay scattered on the sofa and on the one good armchair. There was an inscribed oar hanging over the fireplace and an opened bottle of wine stood by a box of tin cigars on the table. Bertie found it fascinating. Carrington was a little embarrassed. He had never really thought the Prince would take him up on it and the place was a mess.

'It's frightfully untidy, I'm afraid. This is the study—and there's a small bedroom through there.'

He was about to fling his cloak and mortarboard on top of the dresser, when he stopped himself. He hung them for once on the hook behind the door. The Prince was wandering round the room, looking at it as if it were something rich and rare. Very polite of him, Carrington thought. It gave him time to clear the armchair and shift some books and a top hat from the sofa. He dumped them behind it. The Prince was turning.

'You have this all to yourself?'

'Yes.'

'And you can entertain here?'

Carrington smiled. 'Well, yes.'

'You are lucky.'

Carrington was sure the Prince sounded envious but it was hardly likely. 'You have a whole house, sir.'

'But I also have a Governor who doesn't approve of visitors and who clocks me in and out.'

'I see.' The Prince was obviously envious or he wouldn't have said so much. How old was he? Nineteen? He hadn't changed at all. 'We have met before, you know.'

Bertie was surprised. He was usually very good at placing people.

'I was one of a group of boys from Eton who were sent to play with you and your brother at Windsor.'

Bertie remembered the agony of that experiment. Mr. Gibbs, his tutor, had decided that the princes lacked companionship with boys of their own age. He had convinced Prince Albert that it might benefit Bertie. After all, he dominated his brothers and sisters easily as the eldest. Meeting other boys might show him how far he really was behind and waken 'a healthy spirit of emulation'. Bertie and Affie had waited for the moment when their father and Mr. Gibbs would leave them alone in the park with the Eton boys with a mixture of fear and anticipation. They wanted to make friends but did not know how. Their father had stressed to them that they must, on no account, behave familiarly and the meeting had been awkward for both sides.

'Carrington? . . . Of course! We ran a race.'

Carrington smiled. 'Nearly.'

'Oh, yes. We wrestled and—' All at once, he saw it clearly. He had wanted so much to impress the other boys that, when Carrington would not let him win, he had knocked him down. He laughed. Carrington was relieved. The Prince seemed to be quite a good sort. A little too pretty, but a good sort. 'I was a frightful little brute in those days. What a small world!'

'It is indeed,' Carrington agreed. 'I thought you had a hard life, even then.'

Bertie was not exactly sure how to take that. He realised his father would have thought it familiar but, when Carrington invited him to sit, he accepted gladly, taking the armchair. He found his new acquaintance's frankness refreshing. Already he felt quite at home in this dingy, cramped room which he so envied. He refused a glass of wine but accepted a cigar to his host's surprise.

'It's a habit I picked up in Canada. I'm afraid I like it—though my parents don't approve at all.'

When he had collected his anxious equerry and returned to Madingley Hall, Bertie broached the subject of rooms in College to his Governor. Bruce could see the inconvenience of having nowhere to rest between lectures and when Bertie pointed out that they might be used for private study during the day, extra tutorials even, became fairly enthusiastic. He was sure the Prince Consort could not reasonably object.

The Prince Consort had much more on his mind than the vexed question of his son's rooms in college. The Prime Minister, Lord Palmerston, had asked for an audience on an urgent matter. Victoria and Albert saw him in the Blue Closet at Windsor which the Queen had used for meetings with her Ministers from the beginning. Palmerston at seventy-three was no longer the dashing, impetuous statesman who fluttered the hearts of the ladies and trumpeted the challenge of Britain's arms across Europe. At his best only gingerbeer, Disraeli had said, and not champagne, but he was still a dandy, wise, witty, the people's darling and, most important, now with the confidence of the Queen. He was serious as he advanced towards them and bowed, more soberly dressed than usual in a dark grey frockcoat and lavender stock.

'What is this urgent matter, Lord Palmerston? Italy again?'

'Not this time, Your Majesty. Nor the Emperor Louis Napoleon. Not even Mr. Gladstone's Budget.' He smiled briefly, then grew serious. 'A matter that may have more far-reaching consequences than any of them.'

'Yes?'

'We have heard for some time of unrest in America. A trickle of southern states seceding from the Union. Now that trickle has become a flood—Florida, Georgia, Alabama and Texas among others. They have proclaimed themselves the Confederate States of America with one Jefferson Davis as their President.'

Victoria's first thought was for the ageing, kindly President Buchanan.

'What will it mean?'

'In my opinion, inevitably—civil war in America.'

Albert's mind had leapt ahead to the practical problems involved. He knew that Pam would not have spared the time at this crisis merely to give them information. 'Will the Southern States expect us to support them?'

Palmerston was impressed. The Prince Consort was always so quick to understand. If only half his colleagues had the same ability to grasp essentials. They should appoint the Prince as a permanent, ex-officio member of Cabinet and be done with it. Victoria and Albert were waiting.

'They certainly cannot survive without us, sir. The problem will be—are they rebels, or should Her Majesty's Government recognise them as a new nation?'

Chapter
3

For Bertie, his first two terms at Cambridge were developing as the most enjoyable period of his life so far. He did spare a thought for his Yankee friends, disturbed to think that war should scar those rich plains and peaceful valleys. However, as he told Professor Kingsley, from what he had seen of the industrial power of the North, the South would surely not attempt to challenge them. His chief delight was that the sympathetic

Warden of Trinity had made over a set of rooms to him for his personal use, so far with no objection from Bruce. Carrington had become a friend and, with his new confidence, he was making more. He joined the Volunteer Rifle Corps and became President of the Amateur Dramatic Club, forcing the Heads of Colleges to recognise it officially for the first time, and he hunted whenever he had the chance.

Through hunting, he became friendly with another undergraduate, Nathaniel Rothschild, Natty, of the banking family. It was his first real acquaintance with a Jewish person and he found it stimulating. Natty told the most amusing stories he had ever heard and was certainly the richest young man he knew.

One day when they had been out riding, Natty and he were lounging in Carrington's rooms, waiting for Charlie to pour out a refreshing concoction of iced sherry and soda, which he had learnt from a cousin who served in India and called Sherry Pawnee. Bertie had complimented Natty on his horses. Natty always had the finest mount in the Drag.

Charlie laughed and said, 'No one can compete with him. The Rothschilds have the best stables in England.'

'I'd like to see them sometime,' Bertie said.

Natty was looking at him strangely. 'I'd be honoured to show them to you, if you would visit us.'

Bertie thought about it. He knew his parents would not care for it but he was fond of Natty and prejudice, in the circumstances, was ridiculous. Besides, he'd like to see the stables. 'As soon as I'm free to choose, I will. I promise you.'

'It will be an honour to my family, sir.' Bertie could see that Natty was moved and he was slightly uncomfortable. It wasn't an honour, it was only natural between friends. Charlie brought their glasses.

'By the bye,' he said, 'one or two of us are thinking of going up to Town tonight.'

Bertie was surprised. All the way to London?

'There's a little music hall in Holborn. Nothing pretentious. We thought we'd go there, meet some amusing company and have a bite to eat.'

Natty smiled. 'A night on the town.'

Bertie knew what he meant. It had never occurred to him before, but of course it was perfectly possible to get on a train and be in London in just over an hour. It sounded exciting and he envied them.

'We wondered if you'd care to join us?' Carrington asked.

'I've never done anything like that.'

'Then why don't you, for once?'

'It's very discreet,' Natty assured him.

Bertie was tempted. An impromptu night out, with no formality. He had heard about the music halls, like smoking concerts where you could drink and enjoy yourself with good company. And where they allowed women. Perfectly respectable really, most of them. It would be an adventure, but there were too many drawbacks.

'They don't allow me much money.'

'That's no problem,' Natty laughed.

'No, no, I wish I could—but General Bruce would never let me go.'

All the way home and all through supper, Bertie thought about it. They had told him where they were going in case he changed his mind. The more he thought about it, the more tempted he was. Finally, alone with his books, he could think of nothing else. He could imagine his friends laughing, already on the train. Harmless and pleasant, Charlie said, just fun. Some of the fellows make a beeline for the women, but we keep away from all that. Much safer. It was not the women that scared Bertie, not even Bruce. It was something much more simple that his friends had not considered. Bertie had never been anywhere on his own, that meant without an equerry or servant in attendance, and he certainly could not take either Teesdale or his valet. The mere thought of it was frightening yet, by the time General Bruce bade him goodnight and set out for his evening's walk, Bertie had made up his mind. He would despise himself if he did not do what any other young man of his age could do freely. He slipped out of the silent house, walked quickly to Cambridge Station and, with some excitement, bought a return ticket to London.

When the train pulled out, he could scarcely believe what he had done. The feeling of excitement became almost unbearable. He had made a free decision for the first time in his life and here he was, sitting in an ordinary railway compartment with perfectly ordinary people. Purely by accident he had chosen a smoking compartment. He took a cigar from his case and an elderly gentleman sitting opposite cleared his throat ostentatiously. Bertie asked him politely if he minded and the old gentleman grumbled, 'Do what you like.' He had only wanted to be asked. Bertie lit his cigar and smiled. He was doing what he liked and it felt good. He almost laughed out loud. Carrington had described in detail the pleasures of the evening. He doubted if it was always quite so innocent as they claimed, but he had no intention of finding out. He had already made up his mind. He would spend exactly an hour with them and then return to Cambridge. He would not let Natty pay for him and to stay any longer might be dangerous. Meanwhile, he was having just as much pleasure sitting here, unnoticed and unrecognised.

When the train reached its terminus in London, he jumped on to the platform and strode briskly for the barrier. He handed in the correct half of the ticket and moved through. He did not notice the two men who had followed him and closed in on either side until they gripped his arms. One of them nodded to the Station Master who had been hovering nervously near the barrier in his tailcoat and top hat.

The other said to Bertie, "No fuss, sir, if you please." They were burly men in dark clothes and bowler hats. When the first shock was over, Bertie recognised them both with a sickening lurch of the stomach. They were day servants, footmen from Buckingham Palace in their walking out clothes.

They marched him smartly out of the station and into a hansom cab without anything more being said. Bertie had managed to compose himself by the time they turned into the Mall but, when they reached Buckingham Palace and hurried him up the great stairs, along the corridors and into the small, red Audience Room, his heart was beating so wildly that he could feel it against the constriction of his chest. He found himself face to face with his father.

Albert was in a deadly, almost uncontrollable, rage, tight with anger. 'How could you?! How could a son of mine stoop to anything so base?'

'I've done nothing.' Bertie stammered.

'Nothing! You have been guilty of the most flagrant breach of confidence and shown yourself a prey to debauchery. Where were you going?'

'Only to dinner.'

'With whom?'

'. . . With friends.'

Albert stared at him, his pale blue eyes grown almost colourless. 'I can well imagine such friends. How often have you done this before?'

'It was the first time.' Bertie felt so humiliated he could hardly speak. He had to fight to stop himself stammering as he had done when he was a child.

'You expect me to believe that?'

'I swear it!'

Albert considered him. If he was capable of this, he was capable of lying. But that was one sin he had never committed before. He always owned up.

'Then I am grateful for the vigilance of your Governor, or Heaven knows what might have happened.'

General Bruce had returned from his walk to find Bertie gone. He had waited for him and then, becoming anxious, traced his movements as far as the station. The man in the ticket office remembered the fairhaired, young man in a dark, loose jacket with velvet revers and a high-necked, matching waistcoat over check trousers. He had seemed excited and did not know the cost of a ticket to London. With great presence of mind, Bruce had immediately telegraphed the Palace.

Part, at least, of Albert's fears were calmed. If this were indeed the first time, then his son was not yet fully lost. It was a terror of the Prince Consort's, the one consideration that had made him hesitate before accepting Victoria's proposal of marriage, that squalid, scandalous behaviour of her family. The Kings of

Hanover become Kings of England and their children of both sexes had behaved as though driven by demons of moral destruction. No hint of scandal had ever been attached to Victoria, but she was light-minded and given to girlish frivolity. It had taken him many years to convince her that strict devotion to duty and the highest moral tone were the only way to rescue the monarchy from the depths to which its reputation had been lowered. His fear was always that the blood of the Hanovers might show in one of their children and all his work be undone. He had considered Bertie safe, and now this.

'To think I should have to send servants to apprehend my own son!' He paced away, agitated, but he could still see Bertie in the mirror above the ornate, marble fireplace. 'Do you wish to cause your mother the deepest distress? To bring shame on your family?'

'Of course not.'

Albert swung round. 'I thought if I'd failed to make you a scholar, at least I had turned you into a gentleman. And yet at a time when people look to the Throne, as never before, set an example for honesty and morality, you seek deliberately to destroy its character and reputation.'

Bertie knew his father was being unjust, but he had no defence. Anything he said would be taken as insolence.

'You were sent to Cambridge to work, not to study vice!' At least he had improved in one respect. He did not cry or whimper any more. He stood there, turning his hat in his hands, flushed and guilty. For a fleeting moment, Albert wondered what could have made him behave like this. 'Are you not happy there?'

Bertie was silent.

'Well if you are not happy studying, what else do you think you can do?'

Faced with a direct question, Bertie could not stop himself any more from stammering. 'I—All I w-want is to please you. But at University, all my life, it's been like being in p-prison. If only I could do something useful. If I had some aim in life.'

'Such as?' Albert asked coldly.

'I've begged you to let me join the army.'

'I have said no repeatedly and given you my reasons. You are incapable of thinking of anything but your own selfish desires. You will be sent back to Cambridge under escort.'

Bertie stared at him, horrified.

'Under escort,' Albert repeated. 'And you will apologize to General Bruce. He has allowed you a measure of freedom of late—and see how you have abused him. You will ask his forgiveness.'

Bertie could not speak. He knew there was no point in saying anything, anyway. His only hope lay in complete submission to his father. He nodded. As Albert still waited, he said very quietly, 'Yes.'

'Upon his report, your future depends. Until you have shown yourself thoroughly penitent and reformed, you will go nowhere and see no one without his permission. I myself shall take a closer personal care of your behaviour.'

'Yes, Father.'

Albert turned away. He moved beyond the range of the mirror and appeared to be looking at a Gainsborough landscape that hung in front of him on the dark red wall.

'Now get out. I can't bear the sight of you.'

Bertie returned to Cambridge by rail, sitting between the two servants from the Palace. Bruce and Teesdale met him in silence at the station barrier and drove him back to Madingley Hall in the Phaeton. Nothing was said until Bertie was in his room. He apologized to Bruce who nodded acceptance and wished him a gruff good night.

But Bertie was not entirely without friends. One unexpected ally was Palmerston who had been impressed by the reports of his tour of North Africa and also increasingly worried by the obvious strain under which the Prince Consort was suffering. He brought the subject up at their next interview by suggesting that the Prince of Wales might take over some of the lesser royal duties. Albert told him it was out of the question.

'With respect, sir,' Palmerston said, 'you are already gravely overworked. Surely the Prince could carry out some of the purely ceremonial duties?'

'Lord Palmerston, I will not expose him to society yet. And more important, I will not expose society to him.'

Palmerston could see that he was determined, for reasons at which he could only guess. Though surely not, in this case, the natural antipathy of the ruler for the heir. The boy was too inexperienced and submissive to have royal ambitions. 'I believe he is keen to serve in the army?'

Albert sighed. 'He likes the idea of uniforms. But service in the army would show discrimination against the navy, which must be avoided.'

'Quite so, sir.' Palmerston allowed himself the merest trace of a smile. There were occasions when the Prince Consort's scrupulous sense of fairness seemed a trifle overdone.

'To return to the American question—the new President of the Union, Lincoln, is, I believe, a fine man.'

'But he has been unable to prevent his people rushing into war.'

'I do not think he would wish to do so,' Palmerston said. 'America is now two nations, totally divided.'

'Surely the Southern States cannot hope to win?'

'They are well led and know they are fighting for survival. Already they have had their first success, the capture of Fort Sumter. Other states are bound to join them.' He shrugged. Albert silently agreed with him. It was an appalling business.

'We have still left undecided, sir, the question of whether we are to recognise the Confederacy. It is dangerous. But we must also consider that a large part of our trade is with the Cotton producers of the South. I would welcome your advice.'

Albert considered for a long moment, then rose and moved away. Palmerston rose, too, thinking that the Prince Consort had refused to make such a difficult decision and he was being dismissed. After all, he must know that Britain had been at war with the American states twice in less than a hundred years. The wrong decision now could mean war again. At best, commitment to either side would antagonise the other. Albert was turning. It was a subject over which he had already thought long and deeply.

'I think we must recognise them. Not to do so would be dishonest and unrealistic,' he said slowly. 'But at the same time, we must not be influenced by the necessities of trade. We must not give them aid and comfort. Great Britain cannot support a nation whose principal reason for existence is the defence of slavery. That is the opinion of Her Majesty—and of myself.'

Palmerston honoured the man. Prig he might be, bigoted in many ways, but he was a damn fine statesman. He bowed. 'And I believe it is the opinion of the majority of your people. If I may use your words, sir, they shall become the opinion of my Government.'

Another ally was the aged Duchess of Kent. Bertie's grandmother was weakening physically. Her eyesight was failing and the fingers of her painful left hand growing stiff. Her doctors had told her it might be cancer of the bone. Victoria wanted her to have it examined but the Duchess refused to let anyone cut her up. She suspected she would not have to bear the pain for much longer. She was quite resigned to leaving a world that was becoming increasingly ugly, with steam engines, and railway trains making it smaller every day. The March of Progress, Albert called it. She preferred open carriages and a suitable distance between places so that you knew you had been somewhere when you arrived. She would not be sorry to go but, before she did, she wanted to do something for Bertie.

Privately, she thought that Albert had always been far too hard on the boy, expecting too much of him, trying to make him into a miniature professor at the age of seven and having him beaten when he did not turn into a genius overnight. Which Heaven forbid. He couldn't see then that he'd turned the boy right against books and learning, and he couldn't see it now. She knew Victoria was fond enough of her son but she saw him through Albert's eyes and, like him, had written him off as a failure. She asked after her grandson one day when Victoria and Albert had driven over to Frogmore to visit.

Albert's brows contracted. He had enough concerns without being reminded of Bertie. 'Bruce says he is suitably chastened. He's even made some progress. But—' He shrugged. If only Vicky had been born a boy.

'My greatest fear is that something might happen to me,' Victoria said. 'I dread the thought of him becoming King. His only hope would be to put himself entirely in Albert's hands.'

'I think perhaps you underestimate him,' the Duchess said.

'Oh, he tries hard,' Victoria explained. 'But he has no staying power. We just don't know what to do about him.'

It was the cue the Duchess had been waiting for. 'It's simple. Marry him off as soon as possible. He won't get out of that. The right wife will settle him down.'

Victoria looked at her in astonishment. 'Do you think it would work, Mama?'

'It always does. You were a forward little miss before your marriage—now look at you.'

She smiled at Victoria's involuntary flash of indignation. One of the few benefits of growing old was that she could occasionally remind her daughter of the days when she was not perfect.

Albert has seen the possibilities at once. It was a solution, but there were difficulties. 'We couldn't merely tell him whom his is to marry, like the girls. He would have to have a choice.'

'Of course,' The Duchess smiled. 'Make a list of all the available princesses—from fourteen to thirty. It'll give him something to think about.' She could see that Victoria was becoming excited. As for Albert, he had not rejected the idea outright, so that meant he would consider it in his careful manner. 'And why don't you let him go into the army?' she asked him.

Albert stiffened and she hoped she had not gone too far too soon.

'Nothing permanent,' she explained. 'Let him do some training since he's so set on it. The discipline will do him good. And prepare him for marriage.'

Victoria clapped her hands, delighted. 'Oh, yes, Mama! Why didn't you suggest it before?'

'Because you never asked me. I'm not just a silly old woman, you know.'

She shook her ringlets under her lace cap and sat back, smoothing the shawl round her shoulders. Then she chuckled. Victoria laughed back and Albert smiled to see them so happy together. Perhaps he should have urged the reconciliation between them earlier. Even he was surprised by how close they had again become in such a short time.

The days passed for Bertie like the end of a prison sentence. Superficially free, his every movement was watched, his conduct noted and a report on his behaviour sent weekly to his father. He missed his new friends greatly and it hurt him to have to acknowledge them only by the briefest of nods in passing, but he was not by nature a rebel and he genuinely wished for a reconciliation with his father. Bruce had completely forgiven him and eased his surveillance to the extent of letting him hunt again and attend meetings of the Rifle Corps. He had no desire to be unduly hard on the boy when he could tell he was trying his best to behave as correctly as the Prince Consort wished. He even stopped objecting to him smoking after dinner, which surprised Bertie.

He would have been even more surprised at a conversation which took place one day when his father had descended on Madingley Hall to confer with the General. He was asked to leave the study, presumably to let the Governor deliver a verbal report on his conduct without embarrassment.

When the door closed behind him, Bruce smiled. 'I was delighted to get your letter, sir.' Albert had written to tell him he was debating the effect that a short period in the army might have on his son. 'In the Prince's case it would not merely fulfill an ambition, but the discipline and strict attention to duty could only benefit him.'

Albert had not expected Bruce to be quite so enthusiastic.

'A period of intensive training. Of course, for the Prince of Wales it would have to be the best available.' Bruce smiled. 'I hesitate to suggest my old regiment. But the Grenadiers *are* the best. With the added advantage that Your Royal Highness is regimental colonel.'

Albert smiled briefly. 'Yes. That still leaves the question of moral example.'

Bruce hesitated. 'I would not recommend the London Barracks.'

'Certainly not,' Albert agreed. 'Nor, from what I have heard, Aldershot. It's as natural for young officers there to keep a woman as to keep a horse.'

'Unfortunately, true, sir. But there is no risk of that with the Prince. He is still completely innocent.' Albert was certain of that, too, but it troubled him. 'Have you thought when you would like the training to begin, sir?'

Albert shook his head. 'Oh, nothing is certain yet. The final decision remains with Her Majesty.'

It was a polite fiction. Bruce realised he had been too direct. The Prince Consort would not be rushed into changing his mind.

Tragedy made the decision for them. Shortly after an agonising operation for an abscess in her arm, the Duchess of Kent died, with Victoria holding her hand. After her mother's death, Victoria found in her effects so many signs of the deep love her mother had borne her, even during the long period of their estrangement, that she was overcome with feelings of grief. In her grief, her health suffered and she had a nervous collapse. All she could think of was her childhood when her mother slept in her room to protect her, of how she had spurned her at her accession and refused to have her back until these recent years. Even Albert could not comfort her. He was too busy to devote the necessary time and, in some respects, she associated him with the rejection. Only Alice among her children could calm her, spending long

39

hours holding her, talking to her quietly and listening to her sobbed self-reproaches.

Bertie, like Affie, came home for the funeral. He felt his grandmother's death deeply but not visibly enough for Victoria. In her state, she wanted mourning to be continued indefinitely and the thought of his being at Windsor all summer, laughing in a room down the corridor or playing games as if the death of the Duchess had not ended true happiness forever, filled her with horror.

Bertie had been rebuked by his father several times for boisterous behaviour which added to his mother's distress so, when summoned to the study, he expected another lecture on the correct attitude of mourning. Instead he was handed a copy of a letter. It said: 'Her Majesty the Queen having directed that His Royal Highness the Prince of Wales is to proceed to Ireland for the purpose of acquiring military instruction, His Royal Highness will join the Curragh Division on the staff, and will be attached for the purpose of drill to the First Battalion Grenadier Guards.'

He looked at his father, for a moment, unable to speak.

Albert smiled. 'It's what you wanted. You'll go as a staff colonel.'

'Yes,' Bertie said. 'Yes, only—' Albert looked up sharply. "I wanted to start as a subaltern and work my way up.'

Albert relaxed. He was afraid that Bertie had conceived some new ambition. Instead, it was only a romantic illusion.

'You will receive a subaltern's training to start with.'

'But I'm to go as a colonel. I've no idea of the duties. The other officers may resent me.'

Albert was exasperated. In a moment he would cancel the whole thing.

'No one expects you to know anything! You realise it is only for ten weeks? After that, we may have other plans for you.' He softened. After all, the boy was naturally anxious. It would be different from anything he had previously known.

'Now don't worry. You will wear a colonel's uniform

as befits your station, but you will be treated just like any other junior officer.'

Bertie was relieved. He had dreamt for years of proving himself in the army, by his own efforts. And it had to be genuine, he did not want favours. Still, he doubted if his position would ever let him be really accepted. In a month, he would find out.

Chapter
4

Alix loved riding. She often thought it was the only time she was really happy. She sometimes felt that about dancing or playing the piano, but riding was her first love. Especially when she did not have to sit tall and formal, sidesaddle. Alone in the park, like now, she could throw her legs over her horse and gallop as she chose, feeling the beautiful animal moving under her, spurning the ground or soaring clear into the air over hedges and fences, like a swallow.

She knew she was already late for tea. And she knew what her mother would say if she could see her now, with her dress pulled up on either side showing her slim bare legs above her boots and her long, auburn hair shaken loose and streaming behind her in the sunlight, but she could not go back. Not just yet. Some way ahead of her down the slope lay the old, fallen trunk of a tree, quite overgrown with ferns and tiny, white roses. A year ago it had seemed impossibly high. Now she set her horse at it, raced down the long slope and cleared it in one easy leap, to land with a shock and a bound forward that made her laugh with sheer joy. She cantered on to make one last circuit of the lake.

When she arrived at the Yellow Palace, out of breath

and dishevelled, the housekeeper told her to use the back stairs and to hurry.

The Yellow Palace was scarcely a palace at all. Rather, a charming, old house in a pleasant, little street that ran down from the Amalienborg Square in Copenhagen. Alix lived there with her many brothers and sisters and her mother. Her father, too, when he was not away on exercises, for he was a serving officer in the Danish army. They had very little money to spare for luxuries but the family was close and friendly and they made their own amusements. Alix shared a bedroom at the top of the house with her younger sister, Minny. It was her favourite room, fairly small but decorated in bright blue, with a window let into the sloping roof that seemed to catch all the sun. There were two single beds at right angles to each other and a painted chest of drawers. Apart from that there was only space for one chair and a clothes press.

When Alix reached her bedroom, Minny was fastening the pearl buttons up the front of her best dress. She was an attractive, vivid, darkhaired girl of fourteen.

'Where have you been, Alix?' she asked urgently. 'Mama's been looking for you. We're late already.'

Alix was already pulling her blouse free of the waistband of her skirt. 'I know,' she said. She sat on her bed, tugged off one of her riding boots and dropped it on the floor. 'What does she want us to wear?'

'Anything—so long as we're down in five minutes.'

Minny was at the mirror on the chest of drawers, combing her hair, worn short with a mass of curls over the ears. Alix pulled off the other boot and dragged the blouse over her head without undoing it.

'Get me a dress, will you, Minny?'

Minny moved to open the press. Alix dropped the blouse and rose to look at herself in the mirror. She pushed up her long, tousled hair, made a despairing face and let it fall again. She would have to make do with a ribbon. Minny had taken a pale green dress from the press and was watching her. She envied Alix's height and the fact that her figure had begun to show. It was not fair that Alix had a bosom already, little cones just nudging out the front of her chemise. Anyway, she's two years older. When I'm her age mine'll be much bigger, she thought. Alix had begun to undo her skirt.

'Is this green one all right?' Minny asked.

'I think the sleeve's torn,' Alix said. Minny laughed. Alix pulled her skirt up again. 'Just give me a jacket. I'll wear this skirt.'

Minny hung the dress back in the press. Alix was combing her hair.

'Who's coming to tea, anyway?'

'The wife of the new British Minister.'

'British?' Alix made a face. 'Oh, bother!'

Minny brought her a brown jacket. 'Why?'

'They never send anyone very important to Denmark. And they're always so polite and formal.' She gave up and dropped the comb back on the dresser. 'I suppose they're just not interested in us.'

Wally Paget, the wife of the British Minister, was not quite what Alix expected. An attractive, young woman in her early twenties, very well dressed and vivacious, she had been married for less than a year and this was her husband's first appointment. She was sitting with Louise, the Princess Christian, and looked round, smiling, as the girls came into the drawing room.

'May I present my daughters, Mrs. Paget,' Princess Christian said. 'My eldest daughter, Princess Alexandra—and my second, Princess Dagmar.'

Alix and Minny curtsied. Wally thought that Dagmar, the younger, was charming, but she was chiefly impressed by Alexandra. Only sixteen, but with such carriage, slim, graceful. The brown velvet jacket over the simple, plaid skirt suited her and showed her figure to perfection. Her red-gold hair hung in two thick ringlets framing her face, a face perhaps slightly too long but so finely boned, pale ivory, with clear, innocent blue eyes. Truly enchanting.

'I'm sorry we're late, Mama,' Alix said. 'It was my fault.'

'I knew it would be,' Princess Christian laughed.

'Didn't I tell you, Mrs. Paget? Alexandra has no idea of time.'

'Oh, neither have I,' Wally said. 'Fortunately, I warned my husband before we were married, so he can't scold me.'

She smiled to the girls and they found themselves responding to this very informal ambassador's wife. Princess Christian indicated to the girls that they could serve tea. Wally watched them as Alexandra wheeled in a wooden trolley, set with tea things, cake and biscuits. Dagmar moved two small tables from a nest of tables and placed one for Wally and one for her mother. Wally looked from them to Princess Christian. She was a dignified, middle-aged woman, still slim and quietly attractive. Although her husband was heir to the throne of Denmark, Wally had heard that they lived very simply, with hardly any servants. She found them delightful.

'I had hoped to meet Prince Christian,' she said. She remembered that her hostess suffered from early deafness and repeated it louder. 'I had hoped to meet Prince Christian.'

'He is serving with his regiment,' the Princess explained. 'But he will be home at the weekend. Nowhere in Denmark is more than a day by train.'

Alix set a cup and saucer down on Wally's table. She had learnt English from her childhood nurse, but she spoke it with a marked, lilting Danish accent, as she did German and French. 'Is this your first time in Copenhagen, Mrs. Paget?' she asked.

'Yes.'

Minny brought the cake stand to Wally. She was envious of the obvious stylishness of her tangerine-coloured afternoon dress, the crescent-shaped tucks down the front of the full skirt, the hint of lace at the discreetly open neck and at the end of the tapered sleeves. And the narrow bonnet perched on her elegantly piled up coiffure must have cost a fortune.

'People say they find it very dull,' she said.

'On the contrary, Your Royal Highness. It is picturesque and quiet, but not dull.'

Princess Christian was pleased. 'You see? My daughters are convinced we are in a backwater here. They are always plaguing us to travel.'

'Only to see something of the world, Mama. Since it certainly won't come to us.'

Princess Christian sat up a little straighter. 'Now, now, now. Don't be pert.'

Alix was putting down a cup of tea for her mother. She gave her a quick warming smile, excusing Minny, and the Princess softened. She shrugged to Mrs. Paget, as if to say, you see what I have to endure? Wally smiled. She found the family more and more charming and felt a little sorry for the girls. This room with its windows that led out onto an iron balcony overlooking the street below, its grand piano and pots of pampas grass and dried ferns was pleasing enough, but hardly the right setting for royal princesses. Of course, she realised there was scarcely any Society in Copenhagen and that there was some scandal about the ageing King and a rather fast countess that made it unsuitable for them to attend the court except on very formal occasions. She determined to do what she could to help and daringly invited Princess Christian and her daughters to an afternoon party at the Legation. The Princess accepted without hesitation, for herself and Alexandra, but Minny had not yet come out and might not be able to attend.

Minny, that must be Dagmar, was evidently very put out, but Wally had the feeling that she would talk her mother round when it came to it. She could see that Alexandra was pleased. Something, however, was troubling her.

'You'll have to give us lots of warning,' she said.

'Do you have so many invitations, Your Royal Highness?'

Alix laughed. 'No. But we'll need time to make something to wear.'

For a moment, Wally was taken aback and forgot herself. 'You make your own clothes?'

'Most of them,' Alix said, quite unselfconsciously. She was sitting on a cushioned stool by the trolley. Minny perched on the edge of it beside her, was thinking already of the practical problems and determined that they would not look like country cousins. 'You'll have to describe the English fashions for us, Mrs. Paget.'

'I really don't know much about them.'

Alix was surprised. 'But you are English.'

'Only by marriage,' Wally explained. 'Until quite recently I was in Berlin, as lady-in-waiting to the Crown Princess of Prussia, the former Princess Royal of England.'

The Crown Princess Victoria was in the nursery of the Kronprinzenpalais in Berlin, trying to comfort her year-old son, Willy. He was cutting his first tooth. That was distressing enough but his crying upset his new sister, Charlotte, who should have been asleep after her feed. Willy clung to his mother, a plump girl of twenty, with a wide, round face and dark, intelligent eyes. Too serious for her age, her critics at the German court said, too interested in politics and things that should not concern a woman, especially a foreigner. Still, a devoted mother. She kissed Willy's sore cheek, stroked his weak left arm and finally managed to quieten him. She left the day nurse in charge and hurried down to the private drawingroom where she knew Fritz would be waiting.

They always had tea together at this time in the English fashion, when he could get away from his duties at the Chancellery. Although his family and their advisers laughed at him, the Crown Prince Frederick William liked to indulge his wife in small ways like this. He knew how difficult it had been for her to leave the comparatively informal family life at Windsor to come to the stiff, ceremonious court at Berlin with its jealousies and constant intrigue. And he knew how hard it was for her always to be careful what she said. Many of her ideas, pacifist and liberal, had been picked up from her father and were admirable, even desirable, but they would not do here. Fortunately, she understood, as she always did. He loved his wife very dearly.

Vicky found him standing at her desk. He knew a courier had brought a letter from her father, the Prince Consort, and had been very tempted to read it. He turned quickly, a tall, fair, gentle man in the uniform of a colonel in the Prussian Hussars. It was one of the things Vicky disliked most about her new country, so many people wearing uniforms, but she had to admit it suited Fritz. If only he had not taken to letting his whiskers grow in the style of his father, the King, sprouting out aggressively at the angles of his jaw and curving up to meet his moustache. He thought it made him look impressive and was offended when she said he looked more like a King Charles Spaniel. She hurried over to kiss him and reassure him about the children. He had not been thinking about them, but of the possible news from England. He watched her as she sat at the table to pour tea from a Dresden pot into the large, sensible cups she insisted on.

'You had a letter today,' he prompted.

'Yes, from Papa.'

'How is your mother?'

Vicky paused, thinking of what her father had written. 'He's very worried.' She knew she was her father's only confidante. Even so, she was surprised at how frankly he had written. In the first years of his marriage to Victoria, he had been shaken by the intensity of her emotions. He had seen signs of instability and could never forget that her grandfather, George the Third, died mad. She had been more in command of herself recently but was still subject to violent rages, uncontrollable jealousies and depths of grief that passed all reason. Now the extravagance of her grief at the death of the Duchess of Kent made him fear for her mind. This time, he was afraid she might not recover.

Fritz was still waiting, concerned. She set the teapot down carefully.

'She is very distressed. He wants to take her to Balmoral.'

Fritz came to sit opposite her, relieved. 'Good.' He smiled. 'You know your parents tend to overdramatise their feelings. In Scotland, she'll have peace and quiet, that is all she needs.' Vicky smiled, pretending to be reassured. 'She has lost her mother, but she still has her husband and family.'

'She's so worried about them all. Especially Bertie.'

'Poor boy.' Fritz had grown very fond of his brother-in-law. 'Does he know yet that he's going to be married?'

'No.' Vicky was glad to change the subject. She rose to fetch a sheet of paper from the desk. 'I've been making a list of princesses.'

When she turned, she saw that Fritz was laughing. 'I read it,' he said. 'You can't be serious.'

'Why not?'

He took the list from her and ran down it quickly. 'Well—Augusta of Meiningen. She's still a child, completely undeveloped. And Addy of Prussia? It's unthinkable. She's—well, you know Addy. And Marie of Altenburg—she would frighten Frankenstein.'

Vicky laughed. Fritz laid the list down beside his cup.

'As for the Danish girl. That's impossible politically.'

Vicky knew he was right. She shrugged as she sat opposite him again. 'I put them all down, just to show Mama I was trying. It's only to give Bertie something to think about.'

Fritz smiled. 'I'm sure he's in no hurry. And now he's doing what he's always wanted to, he'll have other things on his mind.'

Bertie had hoped to arrive quietly in Ireland and begin his training with the minimum of fuss, but his father arranged for him to be received in Dublin first by the Viceroy and thousands of people filled the streets to cheer him.

Still, the Curragh Camp where he was to have his training was many miles away, in a large, open plain south of Kildare, reserved for the army since the Crimean War. There would be no crowds. His heart rose as the open carriage carrying him and General Bruce came in sight of the camp. A clock tower, chapels, barrack squares, stables and rows of single-storey huts, built for the men who fought at the Sebastopol and Inkerman. Bruce saw the involuntary tensing, the flush of anticipation. How very young the boy looked in his colonel's uniform. He hoped he was not expecting too much.

When they drove up to the Headquarter's block, Bertie was dismayed to see a guard of honour of a hundred

NCOs and men drawn up in front of it and the senior officers of the camp waiting to receive him, led by gruff, imposing Sir George Brown, General Officer Commanding, Ireland. He had reviewed troops before, in a lighthearted way, but now, walking down the ranks of handpicked Grenadiers in front of the men who were to be responsible for turning him into a soldier, he felt that everyone was assessing him, the very correct officers behind him, the tall privates standing rigidly to attention. He could feel the tip of his scabbard digging into his left ankle and gripped the swordhilt to steady it and sweat gathered above his eyes under the fur rim of his busby.

The senior officers were presented to him in the anteroom of the Mess, all dark wood, military prints and silver trophies. The names for once went straight out of his head as soon as each one bowed, shook hands and moved on, except for Colonel the Hon. Henry Percy, VC, who was to be his Commanding Officer. Percy was the ideal soldier, disciplined, courageous, intelligent. He was to be personally responsible for Bertie's training.

'You will be attached to the Ninth Company, sir,' he told him. 'I shall be your instructor in Company, Battalion, and Brigade drill. Your instructors in the manual and first and second positions will be Sergeant-Major Baker and Drill Sergeant Haycock.'

Bertie tried not to look completely blank. He had not understood a word.

'Perhaps you would like Colonel Percy to show you your quarters, sir?' Sir George Brown suggested.

The quarters assigned to him were some distance from the Mess, a miniature wooden house with pointed gables and a verandah in front. It contained a bedroom, sitting room, study and dining room, much larger than he had imagined. He had heard the camp was overcrowded and uncomfortable. He moved round the sitting room, liking its solid, military plainness, oil lamps, good furniture, a bust of the Duke of Wellington and an old regimental Union Jack on the wall.

49

'Your trunks arrived safely, sir.' Percy told him. 'Your batman should have unpacked by now.'

Bertie thanked him. As he stopped by the sideboard, he noticed a curving, well-smoked meerschaum pipe lying just behind a sherry tantalus. He picked it up, smiling.

Percy stiffened. 'I'm terribly sorry, sir. I-I don't know how it could have been overlooked.'

Bertie smiled. 'It must belong to the previous occupant. He'll be glad not to have lost it.' Percy took the pipe from him and glanced apologetically at Bruce who was with them.

Bertie had a sudden, anxious thought. 'I haven't turned anyone out, have I?'

'It's an honour, sir.'

'Whose quarters are these? Not yours?'

Percy had strict instructions from Bruce not to raise this subject for some reason, but he had been asked the question. 'The GOC's sir. He's sharing a Brigadier's hut nearby.'

He could see that the Prince had turned pale. He realised that, somehow, he had said just the wrong thing. General Bruce coughed discreetly, warning, and Percy took the hint.

'If you'll excuse me, sir, I have duties to attend to,' he said. 'I hope to have the honour of seeing you in the Mess later.'

The Prince had turned away. 'Yes. Yes, of course.'

When Percy bowed and left them, Bertie could not look at Bruce. He walked through into the small bedroom trying not to show how upset he was. It was childish, embarrassing, but he could not help it. He sat on the bed, wishing, not for the first time, that he came from some obscure country family. Bruce watched him from the door, understanding, surprisingly sympathetic. He knew how important it was to him to be accepted for himself.

'Why? . . .' Bertie asked. 'Why? . . .'

'His Royal Highness, your father, asked that you should be given quarters suitable for a Field Officer and Prince of the Blood.'

'But doesn't he see?' Bertie said. 'Everything has started just the way I hoped to avoid. I can never be one of them now.'

Bruce moved nearer. He had to stop himself putting his hand on Bertie's shoulder. 'I shouldn't worry too much. Colonel Percy is a first rate soldier, a VC in the Crimea.'

Bertie nodded. He admired Percy. That such a man had to treat him with respect and formality somehow made it worse.

Bruce smiled. 'He may be very respectful here and in the Mess, but on the parade ground you'll find him quite different.'

On the parade ground, Percy was a demon. He found Bertie conscientious and keen, very different from what he had expected. But at the same time nervous, easily flustered and indistinct in giving words of command. He had to remind himself that the Prince was not used to being given orders, nor having to shout commands. Quite the opposite. However, as he got to know the other junior officers training with him, he improved. His arms drill and musketry were excellent. He began to carry himself like a soldier.

Colonel Percy often thought of that first night, talking to the Prince and General Bruce. Because of their visitor, the Mess was unusually subdued. The junior officers, who normally would have played some noisy game after dinner, made uneasy groups at the far end of the ante-room. The older members drank and talked quietly, avoiding looking at the Prince. Standing with him, Percy felt awkward and tried to make light conversation to bring him into the ways of the Mess, but the Prince was only interested in learning what his duties were to be.

'My instructions are that you are to dine twice a week in the Regimental Mess, and once a week as the guest of other regiments, sir.'

'Twice a week, you will give dinner parties to senior officers,' Bruce said. 'And the remaining two evenings you will dine in your own quarters, and read or write. Always on Sundays.'

51

The Prince had nodded.

'As for your training,' Percy told him, 'you will learn the duties of every rank from ensign upwards, without spending longer than is strictly necessary at any one.'

'In that manner, you should earn promotion every fortnight, and at the end of ten weeks arrive at the command of a battalion,' Bruce explained.

The Prince's eyes had grown wider. He thought for a moment, then asked, 'Is it possible?'

Percy's smile could barely be seen. 'Theroretically, sir.' He personally considered the completion of the course highly unlikely. It was only some token, royal show of interest in the military. He had not reckoned on the Prince's determination.

'I would not like to be given promotion I had not earned.'

Percy's back straightened perceptibly. 'That would not be permitted, Your Royal Highness.'

'You may depend on the Colonel to be completely fair,' Bruce said.

The Prince had smiled, genuinely and openly, as if a pressure had lifted in him. 'That is all I ask. Thank you.'

As he moved away, Bruce murmured. 'You'll see he's very willing.'

Up till now, Percy had not thought much of his charge. It had promised to be an uncomfortable ten weeks. Now watching him move among his fellow officers, putting them at their ease with the right, apparently spontaneous words, he began to alter his opinion. Natural leadership was a quality he recognised. In less than five minutes, the Prince had the subalterns relaxed and laughing, telling him about the local hunt and where the best shooting was to be had. No, it would not do to underestimate him.

The air at Lochnager was sharp and clear. So often when they had been here before, the mountain was shrouded in thick mists or obscured by heavy, driving rain that made the coarse turf like polished ice underfoot and the stocky, highland ponies slithered dangerously on the slopes until they had to turn back. Today they had skirted the clumps of gorse and picked their way up the winding sheep tracks with ease. The slopes had welcomed them with the scent of heather and blackberries.

Oh, it was worth it, Victoria thought. She looked back, seeing the spiky peaks of the mountain stand out sharp against the pale, late afternoon sky. The bare crags below shone with an amber light and the westering sun picked out every fold and crevice. Up there, on that shoulder, they had rested while Brown unpacked the hamper and, gazing out over the wild, romantic landscape of Scotland, she had felt truly at peace for the first time since Mama died. Albert had risen excitedly, pointing to a tiny speck that circled high, high above them. It was a golden eagle, only the second they had seen since they came to Balmoral. Albert had drawn her to her feet and held her so close. His cheeks were flushed and she realised how much better he looked. He had been so tired of late. She knew they had come here for her sake but she was glad that he, too, could rest.

He was riding ahead of her now, through the trees of the old pine forest, very fine and handsome in his tweed jacket and close-fitting tartan trousers that showed the shape of his leg. His favourite among their highland servants, John Brown, was leading Victoria's pony. A tall, goodlooking man with a light fringe of beard, wearing a kilt under a short, open coat, he carried a folding rug over his shoulder and the hamper under his free arm. He had carried it all day without seeming to grow tired. He was singing under his breath as he walked, in Gaelic, quietly, like a cradle song. Victoria half closed her eyes, drowsy, listening to the gentle melody, the cry of the birds and the soft pad of the ponies' hooves on the cushioning moss and heather of the forest ground. Over them she heard the sound of water and her eyes opened with pleasure as she realised where Albert was leading them.

He had ridden out of the trees into the sunlight on the banks of a rushing stream. The Garawalt burn which

53

they had discovered on one of their first expeditions. He dismounted, and turned, smiling to her as Brown led her pony to a halt.

Brown looked up at her. 'You've lost your shawl,' he said. 'I'll go and look for it.'

'I'm sorry, Brown.' She knew it could be anywhere in the forest.

'It's no trouble,' Brown said. 'Will you be all right?'

Albert was watching them, smiling. The independent, lack of ceremony of the highlanders amused him and their natural good manners robbed it of any offence. Often when Brown spoke to her, Victoria felt very young, like a niece being taken to task by a rather severe, but protective, uncle.

'I'm sure I shall,' she said primly.

'Mind you are now. His Highness would never forgive me if you fell off.'

Brown put down the rug and hamper and walked away into the trees. Albert came to Victoria, laughing. He reached up and swung her to the ground.

'There,' he said. He was still holding her by the waist.

'Brown thinks I've grown heavier. Do you?'

'Not at all,' Albert reassured her. 'Well—perhaps just a little.'

Victoria frowned. 'You two are so alike. One of you might at least flatter me a little.'

Albert laughed and Victoria joined in. They turned together and walked to the edge of the burn above the small waterfall. Albert kissed her cheek and she laid her head on his chest, looking at the swift, dark, flowing water. He could sense the peace, the new contentment in her. The shadows were retreating.

'Liebes Fraüchen,' he murmured. 'Dear, little wife.' Leaning against him, feeling the strength of his arm round her, Victoria thought of the burn as their love and her troubles as the big, foamy bubbles the stones threw up that were gone by the time the water reached the still pool below.

Bertie was delighted to find that Carrington was at the Curragh, attached for the summer to the Fifth Company.

They were able to do some of their training together, and, through him, he made other friends, Fred Crichton, a dashing, irreverent lieutenant, Viscount Uffington and Ralph Vyner. They became a rather close group, meeting whenever possible in the Headquarters Mess after dinner.

They were laughing as Bertie told them of his latest exploit. He had been given two squads of men to drill under Colonel Percy's supervision and, somehow or other, he had managed to march them straight into each other, getting them hopelessly entangled. Percy had sorted them out and told him to begin again. He had handled one squad superbly, wheeling and counter-marching them. In fact, he had been so carried away, he forgot all about the second squad which marched right across the regimental garden and ended up, marking time, facing the wall of a hut. The men were all grinning and even Percy had laughed out loud before giving Bertie the most fearful dressing down yet.

They chuckled over their brandies and soda, which Carrington insisted on calling Brandy Pawnees, but Bertie was not nearly as carefree as he seemed. His parents had arrived in Ireland and were due to attend a parade at the camp. He had hoped to impress them by commanding a company but Percy had informed him that, although he had made a noticeable improvement, he would only be permitted to carry out a lieutenant's duites. It was especially galling since he would be wearing the uniform of a colonel.

The Queen and Prince Consort brought their older children, Prince Alfred and the Princess Alice and Helena, with them. They watched the march past in drenching rain. Affie and the girls were proud of Bertie as he marched by and saluted with his left hand, his right with the sword flashing out and down to the right. Victoria thought he looked surprisingly grown up. Although he seemed to have a tendency to grow outwards as well. The army must have been overfeeding him. After lunch in Bertie's quarters, she thanked Colonel Percy for treating him just like he would anyone else.

Albert was disappointed that he had not made greater

progress but was relatively pleased. Neither of them seemed to realise the immensity of the task he had been set and accepted his partial success as only to be expected.

They all spent the next few days together, touring Tipperary and the lakes of Killarney, so that they could be together for Albert's forty-second birthday.

Bertie returned to the camp to fill in the time before going back to Cambridge, fairly dejected. The visit of the Queen had reminded his fellow officers forcibly of his position and they tended to avoid him. He thought it was for other reasons. Then one night, Crichton and Carrington came to him as he sat alone in the Mess, nursing a cigar.

'Is there something wrong, sir?' Crichton asked.

'No,' Bertie said. 'No, it's just—Well, I didn't think anyone much wanted to talk to me.'

'Why?' Carrington asked.

'Well—I haven't exactly been a shining success.'

Carrington and Crichton sat on either side of him, leaning towards him.

'But you've done wonders,' Carrington said sincerely.

'Miracles in such a short time,' Crichton agreed.

Bertie knew they were trying to be kind. 'My parents don't think so.'

'With respect, sir,' Crichton said quietly, 'they either don't know or they've forgotten how difficult it is. All the officers—everyone's amazed. You've done two years' work in two months.'

Bertie looked up. 'Do they really say that?'

'They only wish they had a chance to show you. But the way things are—' Crichton shrugged.

Bertie felt greatly cheered, but puzzled. 'How do you mean?'

Carrington smiled. 'They'd like to give you a proper regimental party, but General Bruce put a stop to it.'

Almost without thinking, Bertie said, 'Bruce isn't here tonight. He's dining with the GOC.'

'So you'll be alone,' Carrington murmured and looked at Crichton. Crichton grinned.

'Could we use your quarters, sir?'

Bertie was excited. His disappointment at his parents' reaction disappeared in the realisation that his fellow officers had accepted him, actually liked him. Why had Bruce stopped them from showing it? He was sure he would forbid this party, too, if he heard about it, but he was to be out of the camp until late.

'Use my quarters, by all means,' he said. 'But they won't hold many.'

Crichton was rising. 'There'll only be a few of us.' He smiled. 'Come on, Charlie. See you later, sir.'

Bertie waited in his sitting room. He had never entertained on his own and was not quite sure what to expect. There was no one else in the hut, not even his batman. He laid out some glasses on the sideboard and unlocked the sherry tantalus. He found some unopened claret and half a bottle of brandy. An odd mixture, but it would have to do. There was absolutely no food. As he crossed to the bedroom to get his cigars, there was a knock at the door and it opened partly.

Crichton looked in and grinned. 'All clear?'

Bertie smiled. 'Yes.'

Crichton opened the door fully and came in. He was carrying an uncorked bottle of champagne. Uffington and Vyner followed him in, carrying two bottles each. They were in high spirits, laughing. Bertie moved forward to meet them, and stopped.

Carrington came through the door with a girl on his arm. She had dark blonde hair, with lightly rouged, high cheekbones, the reddest lips Bertie had ever seen and eyes that laughed at him as if they shared a secret. Her dress was crimson velvet, tight to the waist, then ruched with black silk over the hips. The same black lace covered the bodice and cupped her bosom. The dress was cut low, leaving her shoulders bare, and her arms down to the tops of her black, elbow-length gloves. The skin of her arms and shoulders was shining and silky. Bertie made himself look only at her face, but her eyes, bold and challenging behind a veil of demureness, disconcerted him. They were deep brown, almost black eyes, in spite of the colour of her hair. He did

57

not see that she was on her best behaviour, excited at meeting him.

Carrington smiled. 'May I present Miss Nellie Clifden?'

Bertie bowed. Nellie managed a small curtsey and stifled a giggle. Carrington was holding her elbow very tightly.

Crichton was pouring champagne at the sideboard. 'Miss Clifden is a talented singer, sir.'

Bertie was relieved. He knew she was a type of girl he had not met before and had been unable to place her. 'Really?' he said. 'I go to the opera quite often.'

'Opera?' Nellie laughed. 'I'm playing at the Palace.'

He was completely confused until Carrington explained she meant she was appearing currently at the Palace Music Hall, Dublin. They laughed and Crichton brought the champagne. They stood awkwardly, waiting for Bertie, holding their glasses.

'Well—cheers!' Nellie said.

Bertie smiled. 'Cheers.'

As they drank, a captain and two lieutenants came in with two more girls, a strawberry blonde and a brunette, and a little Irish fiddler who winked and closed the door behind him, a merry little man with a face like a crinkled red apple, in a green and white checked suit. The girls were dancers from the Olympia, as vivid and vivacious in their way as Nellie but without her style. The lieutenants had brought a full crate of champagne and the fiddler struck up to honour the corks as they popped.

Although he normally drank very little, Bertie found himself laughing and toasting Nellie whenever her glass was refilled. It seemed to have no effect on her except to heighten the two spots of colour on her cheekbones and soften her smile. He felt himself becoming flushed and told himself he would only drink the glass he was holding. Somehow, without his noticing, it was always refilled.

The fiddler had climbed on to a chair and played without stop, country jigs and reels, which Carrington and Crichton danced with the two Olympia girls, whirling

58

and spinning and lifting them up into the air. The girls squealed and laughed, kicking their legs in their flounced petticoats, and Bertie and the others stood round, laughing also and clapping their hands in time. Carrington opened the collar of his tunic because of the heat. Nellie helped Bertie to open his too, and when the fiddler struck up the latest polka, pulled him out to join the dancers. She smiled and said she'd teach him how to do it properly.

He had held a girl close in dancing before, Harriet Lane and a young Romanian Countess in Berlin who had made a set at him and been chased off by Fritz. But never so close as this. Nellie's breath smelt of violets and he could see her eyes were painted above and below, the upper lids smudged with dark paste. It made them seem larger and more striking. Her pupils were almost fully dilated and she smiled, holding him, spinning to the music. Her right hand did not rest lightly on his wrist as he was used to, but clasped his tightly, and her left arm was around him, drawing him near. He could feel her fingertips on his back through his tunic and, when they hopped after every third step, their bodies met, her breasts aganst his chest, her leg pressing between his.

When the music stopped, she still held him. Carrington flopped into an armchair, exhausted, pulling one of the girls on to his lap. She laughed and kissed him. The fiddler began to play again, more quietly, but Bertie hardly heard him. All he was conscious of was Nellie smiling to him, waiting. Waiting for him to do or say something. He realised he was aroused, embarrassingly, aggressively. He stepped back quickly, hoping she had not noticed.

He was flustered, faced with a situation he did not know how to control. Like he had been at first on the parade ground. Fortunately, none of the others were looking at them. Carrington seemed to have passed out in his chair, his girl draped over him, murmuring in his ear. Crichton and Vyner stood laughing with the other, the brunette, at the sideboard, with their backs turned. Bertie's head felt dizzy. The heat in the room was stifling. He had to get out for a moment to give himself a chance to recover.

'Excuse me,' he muttered, turning away.

'Where are you going?' Nellie asked, surprised.

'I think I'd like a cigar,' he said. 'They're in the bedroom.' Nellie smiled. 'I'll come with you.'

Bertie stumbled as they crossed the room and Nellie caught his arm. None of the others watched him go. In the bedroom, he moved to the table beside the bed where he had left his cigars. He heard a clicking noise behind him and turned. Nellie had closed the door and stood watching him, smiling.

In the sitting room, Carrington sat up in his armchair and laughed. He tickled the blonde dancer on his lap and she jumped. Crichton toasted him in champagne across the room.

The wick of the lamp in the bedroom was turned low. The frosted shade glowed with a soft, pearly incandescence. Bertie's hand reached towards it.

'Leave it like that,' Nellie whispered.

She moved towards him and her fingers slowly undid the brass buttons down the front of his tunic. She eased it from his shoulders and it dropped to the floor. His shirt was already open. The edge of the bed pressed against the backs of his knees and as she moved closer, still smiling, he sat, looking up at her. Her eyes seemed to have grown enormous.

As she leaned towards him, she shrugged her shoulders in a twisting, fluid motion. The narrow straps holding up her dress slipped down her arms and her shimmering, perfect breasts slid free of their black cups, tipped with dark fire.

Her hand was gentle, pushing him back on to the bed. 'You don't have to do anything,' she whispered. 'Just lie still.'

Chapter
5

Victoria thought of herself as being back in harness. There were whole days, weeks, in the period since her mother died which she could not remember. When the choir on Sunday sang the Duchess favourite hymn or when she saw a picture or trinket they had admired together, she could still become tearful and cling to Alice for comfort, but she had largely recovered. She saw Albert and herself as a work team, harnessed together, and she had not been pulling her weight. She liked that simile. It was very apt. Poor Albert had been forced to shoulder everything, all her duties as well as his own, on committees, commissions, councils, see her Ministers and deal with all correspondence and Affairs of State. It was too much for him. Some things she could still happily leave to him—politics, as she said, sickened her—but there were other matters which she could make her responsibility. Chief among them was the finding of a wife for Bertie.

Once more she had to rely heavily on Vicky's help, who, incredibly and against all advice, had again allowed herself to become pregnant. Three children in three years was too much, and smacked unpleasantly of the farmyard. Still, this time she had really done her best, scouring the courts of Europe and the Almanac de Gotha for all likely candidates. The results had been disappointing. For one reason or another, age, religion, unsuitability of family or sheer ugliness, the choice had narrowed to seven, and then three. Three German princesses, and even they left much to be desired. There was always the little Danish girl but, as both Albert and Fritz said, she was ruled out by the border dispute between Denmark and Prussia. It was not worth alienating the Prussians.

She was in the sitting room at Windsor with Alice when the gentleman-in-waiting brought a letter from Vicky that had just arrived by courier. Victoria read it quickly and sent Alice to fetch her father. She paced, reading it again, until Albert came in from the study. He was drawn and tired. The strain of years of overwork was telling on him. His chest and digestion were bad. Anxiety over the world situation disturbed his sleep. His advice was constantly asked and he felt guilty when he was not working. It had become an obsession.

'Albert—a letter from Vicky.'

'And that is why I am interrupted? I am trying to write, myself. To President Lincoln and Jefferson Davis.'

'What is more important?' Victoria asked him. 'Their Civil War or the marriage of our eldest son?'

Albert smiled faintly to Alice. 'That might make an interesting subject for debate.'

As always when she felt excluded, Victoria bridled. 'I, at least, am taking it seriously. She has sent us more information about the Danish girl, Alexandra. From Mrs. Paget.' Albert looked away, exasperated. 'Now what is wrong?'

'You know my opinion,' he said patiently. 'While there is trouble between Prussia and Denmark, she cannot even be considered.'

'But Alexandra sounds the most suitable of all the princesses available. You always think so much of what Vicky says. Listen.' She read Vicky's letter aloud, with emphasis. ' "You asked me whether I had anything more about the Danish beauty. Wally, who is *very* difficult to please, is in *raptures* about her. I have seen several people who all give accounts of her *beauty*, her *charm*, amiability, her frank *natural manner* and many *excellent* qualities. I thought it right to tell you all this in Bertie's interest, though I as a Prussian cannot wish Bertie should ever marry her." ' She waited for Albert's comment. 'Well?'

'Some of her relations are not entirely respectable.'

'That can scarcely be the girl's fault.'

Albert sighed. 'Oh, very well. We must ask Vicky to send us a photograph.'

'Mrs. Paget can get one,' Victoria told him. 'For all the good it will do. I've sent the other photographs to him and, so far, had absolutely no response.'

Albert snorted. 'Did you really expect one? At the moment he is too happy playing soldiers.'

Bertie was still at the Curragh, waiting to go back to Cambridge. Now that his official training was over, he had only token duties and he was enjoying life immensely. He had wanted to impress his parents so much that they would forget their objection to his staying in the army, but it was no longer so important. He had learnt a great deal since that first night.

He no longer had any tendency to stammer. He was more self-possessed and he had his long, golden hair cut shorter so that, all at once, he lost the slightly girlish look and became a handsome young man. Nellie had taught him much about himself. He had learnt about her, too. Her breath smelt of violets because her teeth were not very good and she sucked little crystallised pastilles to hide the effect. She was almost completely uneducated, except in the use of her body, and she was not a true blonde. She powdered her beautiful body instead of bathing it and the vivid, enticing red of her lips left smears on his neck and chest. She had been understanding, a priestess revealing mysteries. What had seemed so complicated and difficult, she made wonderfully simple, exciting and natural, and she had found him quick to learn, to recover, to match her inventiveness. Each time they met made the need to see her again stronger, but each time it became more difficult to arrange. Besides, he discovered she was really Carrington's girl and he was intrigued at the thought of finding one of his own, not just like her, someone as exciting but more real.

He laughed out loud as he looked at the photographs his mother had sent him. One was of a very thin girl with frizzy hair and prominent teeth. Another showed a plump princess of about thirty with a round, simpering face, in a romantic pose. The third was of Elizabeth of Wied. He knew her. Not absolutely unattractive but she did not speak, she bellowed, and had shoulders like a professional boxer. His parents' announcement of their plans for his marriage had shocked him at first, but if this was their selection, he was in no danger. As long as he had the final choice, he was safe.

He told Crichton and Carrington that night in the Mess, in confidence. They understood his reluctance perfectly. None of them wanted a wife at their age.

'What would you do, Charlie, if your parents tried to force you to marry?' he asked.

'I'd sooner be sent to the Tower,' Carrington said sincerely.

'And so would I, gentlemen,' he assured them. 'So would I.'

An invitation to dinner at Windsor Castle was a great honour. Even if it was not one of the former State banquets in the Waterloo Chamber, it was still an elaborate meal in a sumptuously regal setting with the Queen and the Prince Consort presiding at the long table filled with distinguished guests.

August Paget, British Minister in Copenhagen home on leave, was deeply conscious of the honour. He sat next to Sir James Clark, the royal physician, and opposite him was Lord John Russell, the Foreign Secretary, a short man with a high-domed forehead and sharp eyes. On the Queen's right was Viscount Palmerston. Paget felt that his invitation was probably due in part to his wife, Walburga's, friendship with the Crown Princess Victoria but, whatever the cause, if it brought him to the attention of Palmerston and Russell, it could only help his career.

Wally Paget was sitting next to Prince Albert. He had seen that she was rather overawed and, as she was so close to Vicky, was exerting himself to be charming. She noticed that he ate little and drank hardly at all. They were listening to Palmerston who was expounding on a point made by Albert that, in his opinion, the several states of Germany were bound to unite one day under the leadership of the strongest. Palmerston felt it was a pattern that would be repeated.

'The map of Europe is like a jigsaw puzzle with some of the pieces not yet in place,' he said. 'Take Denmark. She lost half her territory after the Napoleonic wars, and stands to lose more if this claim of Prussia's to Schleswig and Holstein goes through.'

Russell looked across at August Paget. 'What is the feeling over there?'

Paget was aware of everyone looking at him, even the Queen. 'The Danes are fiercely patriotic,' he said carefully. 'And will obviously grow more so, the smaller they become.'

Palmerston nodded. He would remember Paget. It was good to have a man on the spot who could sense the temper of the people. 'Surely they realise it is hopeless for them to oppose Prussia?' he murmured.

'They know it,' Paget told him. 'But they will fight with all the heroism of desperation.'

'You are all talking as if Prussia were the bully in the school playground.' Victoria's tone was disapproving. She felt it her duty to defend the country of her daughter and son-in-law, not to mention Albert's many connections in Germany.

'Very apt, ma'am,' Palmerston agreed, deliberately misunderstanding her. 'You can almost see it flexing its muscles. But I fancy His Royal Highness knows more about Prussian intentions than any of us.'

'At one time I thought I did,' Albert said seriously. 'With this new King and Government, I had hoped for a more enlightened, liberal policy, but—' he shook his head.

It was not a subject which Victoria wished discussed, not in her presence, anyway. 'Well, if the gentlemen insist on talking politics,' she declared, 'I think we ladies should leave them.'

She rose as the footman in attendance on her drew back her chair. The other ladies were rising. Wally Paget saw the Queen look at her significantly and realised the time had come for her to fulfil the reason for her invitation to Windsor.

Victoria led Wally into the private sitting room and turned. 'Now, Mrs. Paget,' she said, 'we only have a few minutes before we must rejoin the others, so speak frankly. Has my daughter written off the German girls completely for our son?'

Wally collected her thought. 'Apparently so, ma'am. With much regret.' She opened her satin evening bag. 'I have here some photographs of Princess Alexandra of Denmark.'

'At last!' Victoria waited as Wally brought out two tinted photographs. She noticed with distaste that her daughter's friend was, herself, pregnant. It must be catching, she thought. She took the photographs.

'They really are a very good likeness of Princess Alix,' Wally assured her.

'Of whom?'

'That is what they call her, ma'am.'

'Well, I don't care for it,' Victoria said. 'It is only with the greatest reluctance that we even consider her.' She looked at the photographs and saw one was of a slender, fair-skinned girl, serious and beautiful, standing with one hand on a sundial. The second had been taken nearer and showed the girl's youth, her tender smile and her clear eyes. 'You say they are like her?'

'They hardly do her justice.'

'She is indeed very lovely.' Victoria found herself impressed. 'My daughter has written some extraordinary things about her, for one so young.'

'Nothing I would not underline, ma'am.' Wally told her. 'Her manner is perfect, simply and unassuming.'

'She's not an intellectual?' Victoria asked sharply.

'Oh, far from it.'

'Good.'

Victoria looked again at the photographs. How modestly dressed the girl was. Not a trace of artifice in her smile. And with a becoming dignity. She looked round as Albert came to find her.

'Our guests, my dear,' he reminded.

'Mrs. Paget had brought these from Vicky.' She handed him the photographs and watched to see his reaction. He gazed at them for a long moment without speaking.

'You know Vicky is prone to exaggerate, but Mrs. Paget, I believe, is not. Alexandra appears to be everything we have been told.'

Albert nodded. He was thinking, if she looks like this now, how exquisite she will be in a few years' time. Bertie could not fail to be attracted.

'What a pity she is who she is,' Victoria said.

The photographs were shown to Palmerston the next morning. He was a house-guest at Windsor for the weekend and had asked for a private audience with the Queen as soon as his correspondence arrived from Downing street.

'The news from the United States is very grave, ma'am,' he informed her. 'Or should I say the Disunited States? The North appears to be losing. The Confederates are pushing ahead on all fronts.'

'So it seems that gallantry is still superior to industrial power,' Victoria said. She was not entirely displeased.

'Incredibly enough, it looks like it. Of course, it all depends on whether the Southern States can maintain sufficient supplies to support their army.' He paused. 'President Lincoln is angered by the number of British ships which beat the blockade with provisions for the South.'

'It is not official trade,' Victoria reminded him. 'They are only privateers.'

'"But what would we do if one of them were attacked?'

Victoria understood the potential danger. She signed 'It is very difficult when one's sympathies clash with one's convictions.'

'It is indeed, ma'am. And the issues are largely emotional. I am greatly indebted to the advice of the Prince Consort.'

'I wish you would let him rest,' Victoria protested. 'He has so little stamina these days. The slightest thing gets him down.'

It was then the photographs of Alexandra were produced, with the explanation that the Prince Consort was deeply distressed that his son had not picked one of the German princesses. Palmerston looked from the photographs to the Queen, surprised.

'I hadn't realised . . . Has the Prince of Wales finally chosen her?'

'It's not a question of choice, Lord Palmerston. He will have none of the others. She is the only one left.'

Bertie was shown photographs himself when he called at Windsor on the way back to Cambridge. He was grateful this girl was not one of the Germans or he would have had difficulty refusing her unseen.

Albert was watching him. 'From the photographs, I'd marry her myself,' he said.

Bertie nearly replied, it's a pity you can't. He had so nearly said it that it unnerved him. His father's reaction would have been memorable. When his mother swept in, he hoped the subject would be changed but she had come to hear his comments for herself. From her eagerness, it became blindingly clear to him that his parents had already decided. The net, which he thought had been avoided, was drawing in.

'I-I thought you were against a marriage with Denmark!'

Albert drew himself up. 'Your sister and Fritz have now met her, a carefully arranged, chance meeting. Even so, it caused a storm of protest in Prussia. Against their own interests, they gave her their absolute approval.' Bertie was staring at him.

'Do you think any of us would hesitate when it is a matter of your future happiness?'

'If she really looks like that,' Bertie muttered.

'A portrait may flatter,' Albert told him. 'Photography, I believe, cannot.'

Bertie felt the net grow tighter. His mother was watching him closely, perplexed by his caution and lack of enthusiasm after all her efforts.

'I-I couldn't decide . . . not without at least seeing her,' he said. 'And that can't be for some time. I'm going back to Cambridge tomorrow.'

'We have thought of that,' Albert smiled. 'We shall say that, to complete your course in military training, you are being sent to watch the German army manoeuvres on the Rhine.'

Bertie looked at him blankly. 'Germany?'

'You will leave next week with General Bruce, to join Vicky and Fritz. Princess Alexandra and her parents will be there at the same time.'

Bertie panicked. 'But—if she is brought to meet me, I'll be committed automatically!"

'Her parents have agreed to the meeting at our request,' Albert informed him, exasperated at last. 'Quite nobly, in my opinion. Purely to give you a chance to see their daughter and she you. You will not be committed unless you wish.'

'Princess Alexandra thinks they are only visiting relatives in Germany,' Victoria added.

Albert controlled himself, reminding himself that his son was totally inexperienced in these affairs. No wonder he was nervous. He remembered his own anxiety on the journey to this very castle from his boyhood home in Saxe-Coburg-Gotha all those years ago, knowing that if he pleased her, the young, autocratic Queen of England might ask him to become her Consort. A challenge and a great responsibility, when he was not sure he could love her. Even after their marriage, it had taken years before they reached a balance and a mutual respect. But with that respect had come understanding and love.

'The meeting will appear accidental,' he said gently, and smiled. 'She knows nothing, and expects nothing.'

The old house of Rumpenheim was set in spacious, wooded grounds in the peaceful valley of the River Main, which flowed past on its journey to the Rhine. The rambling, high-turreted house, dignified by the name, Castle Rumpenheim, had been left by the Landgrave Friedrich of Hesse-Cassel to his many children and their descendants, on condition that the whole family met there at least once every two years. The Landgrave Friedrich was Princess Christian's grandfather and the one great excitement in the life of Alix and her brothers and sisters was the holiday they spent every second year in the draughty, cluttered old house with all their equally impoverished but jolly royals and semi-royal aunts, uncles and cousins. Many matches were made at Rumpenheim, which was the intention behind the bequest, flirtations began and ended, reputations were dissected and pinned mercilessly to the walls of the drawing rooms and the children romped, battled and played devastatingly crude practical jokes.

Alix and Minny loved these holidays, the long trip by train to Frankfurt, the carriage rides, the tea parties and the games. The Aunts said that Alix would soon have to stop tomboying about the gardens with the younger children, but she was not ready to give it up yet. On that late September morning, she was playing Blind Man's Buff with Minny, their little sister, Thyra, and some of their cousins on the lawn by the white, pillared summerhouse. Minny was 'it', with a scarf tied round her head, covering her eyes. As Alix crept round one of the bushes, Minny grabbed her from nowhere and guessed, 'Alix!'

Alix suspected Minny had been peeping but she laughed and, as the other children ran giggling and shouting from hiding, let herself be blindfolded and turned round three times. While she counted up to ten, the children darted away from her. 'Come on, Alix! 'You won't catch me!' She steadied herself and moved forward. One of the older boys ran past behind her, and pulled her long curls. She gasped and started after him, laughing, but he was too fast.

She could hear some of the younger children whispering as they circled round her cautiously, keeping out of reach. After a few swift rushes and scoops that sent them scattering and shrieking, she decided to try the summerhouse. Someone always hid there. She moved stealthily towards it, her hands stretched out. Her sister Thyra, a small girl of seven with a mass of ringlets stood by the doorway, frozen, holding her breath with excitement as Alix drew nearer. Alix seemed to be passing her, feeling with her foot for the step up to the door, when she suddenly turned and grabbed. Thyra squealed.

'Who is it? . . . Charlotte?' Alix was touching her face, then felt the ringlets. 'Thyra!' she guessed and laughed, pulling off the scarf.

Thyra was indignant but excited, and giggled when the others ran up, shouting, 'Come on, Thyra! Your turn!'

As Alix slipped the scarf over Thyra's eyes and began to tie it, she heard their mother calling to her from the path. She left Minny to finish knotting the blindfold and ran to her.

Princess Christian was wearing her new, dark brown travelling costume and was unusually tense. 'Run and change,' she told Alix. 'Your father is taking us to Speyer on the ten o'clock train. To visit the cathedral.'

Alix was pleased. 'I'll tell Minny.'

'No, no, Minny is too young,' her mother said. And added, 'You are to wear your best dress.'

'The cream one?' Alix was puzzled. 'But trains are so dirty. It will be spoilt.'

'Your father wants us to look our best. We may meet the Bishop.' Princess Christian was not looking at Alix, but watching the children as the game began again. 'Hurry now.'

Alix ran off up the path. Princess Christian saw little Thyra, blindfolded, run squealing in circles while the others danced round her, but she was thinking of Alix. She was so young, and very soon there might be no more Rumpenheim for her, no more children's games.

Alix took great care on the journey and her new cream dress with the high neck and white lace pleats down the bodice was hardly even wrinkled when they arrived. She wore the lace-trimmed bonnet she had made herself to go with it. They changed trains at Heidelberg and she was excited to learn they were returning there to spend the night.

At the Cathedral of Speyer they were met by the Sacristan, who showed them round. Alix' father, Prince Christian, a vigorous, thoughtful man of middle height, with a full, soldierly moustache and soft, curling hair, appeared to listen intently as they moved slowly along the north aisle of the long, Gothic nave, but his eyes kept flicking to the side to catch glimpses of the rest of the interior through the pillars. Alix, walking behind with her mother, tried to overhear as the Sacristan explained that, here, in this very cathedral the famous assembly had taken place in 1529, which condemned the Reformation and created the term 'Protestant'.

They admired the statues behind the wall of the choir and, as they turned in to the sanctuary in front of the high altar, they came face to face with another group, led by the Bishop himself, coming in from the south aisle. With a smile of pleasure, Alix recognised the Crown Princess Victoria and her tall husband whom she had met at Strelitz a few months before. There was a reserved, young man with them, with light blue eyes and fair hair, very handsome, who bowed as she curtsied to Vicky and Fritz. Vicky introduced him as her brother, Bertie, of whom she had spoken so affectionately when they met. Alix had, of course, heard often of the Prince of Wales and was thrilled to meet him. Minny would be very envious.

The two groups expressed their delighted surprise at this happy, unexpected meeting and agreed to have lunch together. By a further coincidence, they were all staying at the same hotel in Heidelberg. Somehow or other, the older members moved off, leaving Alix with Bertie. When he gave her his arm and offered to be her guide for the rest of the visit, his voice was so low she could barely catch what he said.

And so Albert Edward, Prince of Wales, met Alexandra Caroline Marie Charlotte Louise Julia, Princess of Schleswig-Holstein-Sonderburg-Glucksburg.

Victoria and Albert waited on tenterhooks to hear the outcome of the meeting. They had returned to Balmoral for a few weeks. Every day Victoria asked anxiously, to Albert's amusement, if the courier had arrived with any letters. No telegrams could be sent as the whole affair had to be handled very discreetly in case any word of it leaked out to the Press and to the girl herself. The only letters were a page from Vicky to say the meeting had taken place and the young people appeared to like each other, as well as a disappointing note from Bertie saying the parents were pleasant and agreeable enough and the young lady very charming but he would give them his impressions later. They had to wait until he came to Balmoral.

They met him in the sitting room, its decorations designed by Prince Albert in what he conceived to be a truly Highland style, deer heads and antlers, tartan wallpaper and carpets, tartan seat covers and tartan cushions. Unkind visitors said Balmoral suffered from 'tartanitis'. Bertie had decided his tactics on the voyage north to Scotland. One sign of admiration, even of interest and he was lost. While his mother waited, almost breathless with anticipation, he told them he had enjoyed his trip, Vicky sent her love, Alexandra was quite pretty and he had not made up his mind.

Victoria gazed at him, incredulous. Love to her was something that happened at once, a thunderstroke, like her first sight of Albert. Having accepted Alexandra in her mind, she had visualised the meeting over and over again, the first hesitant smile, the delicious warmth, the quickening of the heart. And now here was her son, apparently unmoved, saying he had not made up his mind. Was she not beautiful?

'Beauty isn't everything,' Bertie told her. 'And besides, she is not as lovely as I expected. Her nose is too long and her forehead too low.'

'Her nose . . . ?,' Victoria repeated after him. 'Her forehead? . . . '

Like Victoria, Albert was distinctly annoyed. 'This is not the reaction we expected.'

'It's too important a step to decide at once,' Bertie said. 'Marry in haste, repent at leisure.'

'You will not quote proverbs at me!' Victoria snapped.

For once, Bertie did not flush or stammer. To her amazement, he shrugged. 'I'm sorry, Mama, but it sums up my feelings exactly. I have not written her off, but

I have not yet fully decided.' He bowed. 'If you'll forgive me, I think I should change for dinner.'

He moved calmly to the door and was gone before either of his parents had recovered sufficiently to prevent him. Victoria rose and stormed across the room, turning at the massive, stone fireplace. 'Not fully decided!' she exploded. 'We wait for two weeks and this is all he says.'

Albert was still watching the door, thoughtful. Something had happened to Bertie. Was it his time in the army? 'He is more in command of himself,' he murmured. 'More grown-up.'

'A little taller, that's all!' Victoria saw nothing in her son but stubbornness, ingratitude for everything she had done. 'He's incapable of any true feeling.'

'He certainly doesn't behave like a young man who's in love,' Albert agreed.

Alix was collecting the last of her belongings from the bedroom she shared with Minny. Her parents insisted on her moving into the rooms set aside for her on her sixteenth birthday. She must be serious, responsible, put away childish things and take her place in the adult world. She must begin to live like a royal princess. She did not understand. Usually her parents cared so little for show and ceremony. At last, she found out the reason.

After dinner one evening, her father asked her if she had enjoyed her visit to Germany and meeting the Prince of Wales. She laughed and said she could not believe it when she found out who he was. He had been very kind, and afterwards had sent her a photograph of himself in his colonel's uniform. Alix admired the photograph very much. She often took it out of the book of poetry in which she kept it and looked at it, remembering the real colour of those eyes, a perfect blue, lighter than her own, and the tiny curve at the corner of his mouth when he smiled his shy, almost reluctant smile. She did not know exactly why she looked at it so often and she did not tell her father.

Her mother asked her what they had talked about

when they walked round the cathedral and, later, at the ruins of the old castle of Heidelberg. Her mother had asked her several times before and her interest puzzled Alix. He had tried to explain the meaning of the carvings, although she suspected he really did not know much about them, and he had said he liked travelling and would like one day to come to Denmark.

'Did he say that?' her father asked quickly. Alix nodded.

'Well, how did he say it? Did he sound as if he really meant it—as if he wanted you to invite him?'

He seemed impatient and, at the same time, anxious. Alix did not know how to answer and turned to her mother.

'Your father is asking if you think the Prince liked you,' her mother explained gently.

'I'm not sure,' Alix said, more puzzled than ever. 'Why? Why is it so important?'

Her parents were silent. Neither of them could look at her and each was waiting for the other to speak.

'One day he will be the King of England,' Prince Christian said at last.

'Yes.'

'Whoever marries him will be the Queen of the greatest Empire the world has ever known.'

Alix gazed at her father, her eyes full of questions to which she was beginning to guess the astounding answer.

He took her hand and smiled very tenderly. 'If he cares for you,' he said. 'If you could come to care for him.'

Now Alix was packing to move to her new bedroom and sittingroom. Minny was already in her nightdress and sat cross-legged on her bed, watching as Alix took the last of her clothes from the press and folded them, laying them in a neat pile on her old bed.

'All because of the stupid Prince of Wales . . . ' Minny pouted. Alix folded the green dress with the torn sleeve and placed it on the pile. Even Minny could see she was uncertain and already, in a strange way, older.

'Do you love him?' she asked.

'I don't know.' Alix said.

She sat on her bed. She had put the photograph of Bertie in a silver locket which she wore round her neck. She opened it, seeing again that handsome, unlined face with its enigmatic smile.

'I carry his photograph with me always, now. And I look at it. And I wonder . . . '

Minny smiled. 'What it is like to be a Queen?' She leaned back against the painted, wooden head of her bed, and hugged herself, imagining. 'All those servants . . . All that power . . . '

'No, not power—not servants,' Alix said, almost to herself. 'I wonder what it's like to be in love.'

Chapter
6

Victoria had to confess herself more than a little irritated by Albert. Since their return from Balmoral, she had felt revitalised. In her depression, the smallest task had been too much for her, but now she had recovered her natural energy. She had a great talent for recuperation, while Albert gave in to everything. Bronchitis, gastric upsets, rheumatism, he complained of them all. As she grew stronger, he became weaker. It was almost perverse.

From the window of her boudoir looking south, she could see the Long Walk and the Home Park stretching into the far distance until the view was lost behind a rampart of oaks and elms, all rich browns and gold in their late autumn colours. She had merely suggested that they walk to the Home Farm for exercise and Albert had been quite sharp. Too tiring, he said. But he was not too tired to work. Work, work, work, that was all he could think of. How often she had seen him rising from her side in the sullen light before dawn, fumble for his quilted dressing-gown and creep out to his study to continue his endless notes and memorandums. No wonder he was tired. He'd be lucky to get through the winter without influenza. She had a sudden, superstitious fear of wishing it on him.

'Unberufen, unberufen,' she muttered, and touched the wood of the windowsill.

Albert had to put down his pen for a moment. His wrist felt quite numb. He flexed the fingers of his right hand. How white his knuckles were and between the stretched tendons he saw faint flecks of darker skin, mottling. A sign of age. But he was not old, only forty-two. He came here when he was twenty, over half his whole life he had now spent in England.

How much he had learnt in that time. How much he had had to learn so as not to make mistakes among these people who were so suspicious of him. They had been slow to accept him and he even slower to realise that the monarch did not rule here as in the rest of Europe. In a strange way, the most powerful nation in the world was also one of the most backward. Under his guidance Victoria had seen the urgent need for social reform, for changes in foreign policy, but even she, because of the Constitution, could only suggest and recommend, she could not order change. For him, as a foreigner, it had been infinitely more difficult. The English were independent and insular, resentful of authority. He had had to move obliquely, learning to achieve his aims by gradual means, by charm and by example. In some respects it had been humiliating, yet he had slowly come to see the strength and value of the Constitution and to admire the independence of the people. Slowly they had come to accept him.

It was all becoming easier. He almost felt English himself now. At times it was hard even to remember his boyhood home in Rosenau. Only a few details—the flowers on the wallpaper of his room, the fountains under the terrace of the little castle, the morning clamour of the birds in the green forest that lay all around, birds that he and his brother Ernest mounted and framed under glass in their own miniature museum. He could barely remember his mother, only a gentle, smiling softness torn from him when he was a child, when his harsh father sent her away. People who could remember her said he had her eyes.

He shook his head. His mind was wandering, as it did so often lately. He glanced over to see if his secretary had noticed, but Phipps was busy transcribing the notes they had made on the necessity for increasing the membership of the Horticultural Society. Albert picked up his pen and smiled. How Victoria resented his interest in gardens. She loved them herself but could not understand that delicate blooms did not just grow. People had to be encouraged to cultivate and appreciate them.

It was a point he would make in his letter to Stockmar. His old tutor had been proved right in so many things. Of course, he had not had the advantage of actually being in a position of power, but he had planned the strategy by which Albert became, first of all, the Queen's principal adviser and then the voice through which she spoke to her Government. It was the voice of reason, counselling friendship with other countries, compromise in crises and steady, carefully-considered reform at home. Both Stockmar and he had seen that this nation, so rich materially, was a cultural waste-land. Progress was inevitable and desirable, but the arts and sciences which enrich humanity should expand at the same time as industrial wealth or a desert of materialism would be created. Not only would it make for a greater division between rich and poor, a breeding ground for anarchy, but the souls of men would wither in the arid ugliness of their surroundings. Art should be free to all classes and he had set himself to sponsor and promote everything which enhanced and spiritualised the quality of life. From flowers to music, painting, sculpture, literature and architecture, all the arts and crafts capable of raising the mind and enlarging the heart of man.

Above all was science. All progress came from exploring its mysteries and applying the knowledge, the techniques learnt from it. His first real victory over the prejudice and suspicion of his new countrymen had been ten years ago with the Great Exhibition. That staggering mass of exhibits, scientific, technical and artistic, all selected and approved by him, had opened their minds to the possiblity of a richer life that could be theirs if they grasped it. The response had been overwhelming. No one laughed at his ideas any more. His scheme for the fuller education of the labouring classes had been thought impractical. Now employers began to see that it would increase skill and production, and unskilled men began to realise that it would improve their working conditions and standard of living, that education gave them a right to be heard in the affairs of their country. A deep bond was forged between Prince Albert and his people. Not even Stockmar could have foretold how proud Albert was to be acknowledged as the leader of this quarrelsome, independent, energetic, distrustful, basically conservative island race.

He thanked God daily for the opportunity he had been given and prayed to be made worthy of it. He prayed also for Victoria, and for their son. Victoria often spoke of death, convinced that she would die young. The thought of Bertie as King chilled him, what follies might be committed. He prayed that Victoria would be spared, at least until their son had a wife and children of his own to mature him.

It was coming up to the end of Bertie's time at Cambridge, only a few more weeks, and he found he was regretting it. He had never enjoyed a year so much. He even enjoyed studying and his circumstances had improved beyond recognition.

Whether it was because he was now nearly twenty or because his marriage had been discussed, General Bruce had relaxed all controls and was now more of a companion than a Governor. He proved to be charming and amusing. His brother James, the Earl of Elgin, had just been made Viceroy of India. Bertie was touched to learn that the General had turned down a post as his aide to stay with him. On one of their trips to London, Bruce took him to see the famous marbles his father had brought back from the Parthenon in Athens. Soldiers of the Turkish army of occupation had been using them for target practice. The Earl bought them, shipped them home and sold them to the British Museum for safekeeping.

The night before his birthday, Bertie had Carrington to dinner at Madingley Hall. Bruce left them alone to their cigars and brandy. Like the Prince, Carrington found Bruce had mellowed, but he was glad of the opportunity to talk freely.

He smiled. 'There's a certin young actress who wishes to be remembered to you.' Nellie was back in London and Carrington had seen her several times but she always asked after Bertie. 'She wondered if another meeting would not be possible?'

Bertie considered it. It was nearly two months since he had seen her and the thought that she was fairly near, keen and waiting, was tempting. He had been pouring brandy into two round-bellied glasses. He handed one to Carrington. 'It might be arranged.'

He toasted Carrington and they moved to sit in high-backed leather chairs by the fire. Bertie thought of his life at Cambridge. For all its pleasantness, there were certain drawbacks, some things were made very difficult. He had had no chance to find a girl of his own, although he felt the need strongly. It troubled and preoccupied him, but the thought of approaching one of the younger ladies-in-waiting or one of the simpering misses who blushed at him during his mother's Drawing Room Receptions or rested their sticky hands on his, clammy even through their gloves when they danced, alternately made him laugh and tremble at the probable reaction.

'No,' he reflected, 'lots of things should be possible when I leave Cambridge.'

'What will you do at the end of term?'

'They're talking of sending me on a tour of the Middle East. For "educational purposes". After that I've no idea, Charlie. I'd like to go back into the Guards, but they won't let me join the army—not permanently.' He frowned, imitating his father. 'It would show discrimination against the Navy—and we can't have a mutiny in the Home Fleet.'

Carrington laughed. 'Of course, you may be married. Or isn't that settled yet?'

'Not for as long as I can put it off,' Bertie told him. 'Do you seriously think I want to tie myself down? Just when I'm beginning to live for the first time? I know that one day I must have a wife, but not yet.'

'The Princess Alexandra?'

Bertie looked at him and shrugged. 'She's the most likely. But Alix is young—we both are. There's time, time, time enough for all that. That's what I can't make them understand. Tomorrow I'm going to Windsor for my birthday, and I know they'll be at me again. But I shall resist.'

'Well, in case I forget later, I'd better give you this,' Carrington said. He took a slim package wrapped in tissue paper from his inside pocket and passed it to Bertie, with unusual diffidence.

'I thought I heard you rustling.' Bertie was intrigued. He stripped off the paper and found a black leather cigarcase with silver mountings.

'It's only a small present, for your birthday.'

'It's beautiful, Charlie.'

Carrington smiled. 'I took the liberty of filling it.'

'Because I always smoke yours?' Bertie laughed and took the top off the case, sniffing the dark aroma of Havana. 'I'll have to hide this when I get home. Mama would be very upset.'

'What do you do when you want a smoke?'

'Well, I'll tell you,' Bertie said. 'I excuse myself, go along the corridor to the north-east tower, dodge the servants, find a window that faces away from the wind and blow the smoke out carefully.'

Carrington laughed.

'But from tomorrow,' Bertie promised him, 'some things will be different.'

When the Queen and Prince Consort had left Balmoral to return south, their highland servant John Brown had been sadly reluctant to see them go. He told Victoria he hoped they would all be well through the winter and return safe. And above all, that there would be no deaths in the family. The words had seemed strange then and now took on the appearance of prophecy, as typhoid struck at the royal house of Portugal where Albert's closest and dearest cousin was king.

Bertie arrived at Windsor to find his sisters dressed in black. In such a large and widespread family there was always someone to mourn, and it did not worry him unduly. He was delighted to see Affie had come for his birthday and kissed his sisters Alice and Helena. Although she was still only seventeen, Alice looked older after the heartbreaking months she had spent comforting their mother. Helena, whom they called Lenchen, the gentlest of his sisters, was growing at fifteen into a plain, retiring young woman. She adored Bertie extravagantly and could not believe he was twenty. Alice wished him many happy returns. She supposed this might be the last time they would all spend his birthday together, as by next year they would both be married. When he denied the likelihood in his case, Affie made them smile by saying, if Bertie didn't want Alexandra, he'd marry her himself.

'Why not?' he asked indignantly. 'We're the same age.'

'You've never even seen her,' Lenchen laughed.

'I've seen her photograph.'

'Well, next time you go to sea,' Bertie suggested, 'get them to sail round to Copenhagen and you can propose to her.'

Victoria stormed into the small sitting room from next door to find out why they were laughing so loudly. She was dressed in deep mourning and had not realised Bertie was there.

'Good morning, Mama,' he said, smiling. He had made up his mind to act his age from now on, to be poised and adult with her, but she saw nothing but his grey, Tweedside jacket, tan stock and checked trousers.

'Why aren't you dressed in mourning?' she asked coldly. 'Our cousin Ferdinand died two days ago of typhoid and his poor brother, King Pedro, is dying. Your father is very distressed.'

'I'm sorry. I didn't know,' Bertie apologised.

'Alice—run and find Papa,' Victoria ordered. 'Lenchen—Affie, I wish to speak to Bertie.'

Alice and Lenchen bobbed, Affie bowed, subdued, and they left the room. Bertie knew he should go and change before seeing his father, who loved the young King more like a son than a cousin and often held him up as an example.

'Be careful what you say to your father. You can be very thoughtless,' Victoria said. 'He has enough on his mind without contradictions from you.'

'Yes, Mama,' Bertie answered after a pause.

'Now, I wish you many happy returns of the day.' Victoria raised her cheek. 'Though you'll understand we cannot celebrate with any real joy.'

Bertie kissed her offered cheek, then turned quickly as Albert came in from the study. He thought he looked more grey, heavier, older than he had ever seen him.

'He has just heard. He has not had time to change,' Victoria said quickly.

Albert shook his head. All his movements seemed to have become slower. 'Macht nichts,' he muttered. 'It doesn't matter.' He forced himself to smile and hold out his hand. 'My congratulations, Bertie.'

They shook hands. Bertie had hoped his father would kiss him, hug him as he once did, but Albert moved to the fire. As he warmed himself, he said, 'I know you're reluctant to discuss it, but your marriage is too important to be left undecided. It is important for you and for the country, morally, socially and politically.'

Bertie had already rehearsed what he would say but, aware of his mother's eyes fixed on him, he could not speak.

'Both your mother and I are for it. And Alexandra's parents.' Albert went on.

'We are both still very young,' Bertie began.

Albert looked at him. 'News of your meeting has leaked out abroad. Also that there has been no proposal. It has drawn attention to Alexandra. Already the Czar of Russia has asked for her for the Czarevitch. If you do not act soon, you will lose her.'

'Yes.'

Albert smiled faintly, 'If there are only four women in the whole world you can possibly marry, you should be grateful that one of them looks like her.'

'I realise that,' Bertie said slowly. 'But I can't know my own mind after having met her for only such a short time.'

Victoria gave a panted cough of annoyance but Albert nodded. 'That is quite reasonable and proper. Another meeting can be arranged.'

'But you must clearly understand,' Victoria stated firmly, 'that it will be expressly to give you a chance to propose.'

'If not, it will be your duty to tell the young lady and her parents at once that an engagement is out of the question.' Bertie was shaken. The meeting he had asked for as a delaying tactic would put him in an impossible situation.

'Any delay would be most insulting, both to them and to us,' Victoria told him.

Bertie looked from her to his father. Albert had turned back to the fire. 'But you know I shall not force you,' he said. 'There are six weeks till the end of the year. I give you till then.'

Alix and Minny were sharing the piano stool, playing a duet together. It was a fast piece and they were laughing as their fingers kept getting mixed up.

'I know—let's play something romantic,' Minny suggested. 'Schubert.' She reached for some music stacked on top of the piano but she tugged too sharply and half the pile of sheets went fountaining on to the floor. Still laughing, the girls hurried to pick them up.

As she knelt and leant forward, the silver locket that Alix wore swung away from her. She caught it and held it, thinking suddenly of Bertie. She thought of him often and tried to remember everything about him, and to imagine what it would be like to be with him. Sometimes her thoughts gave her odd, disturbing feelings. But it was so pointless. He had only written to her twice since they met, short notes which said nothing. Her mother had questioned her again, asking her to be completely frank and tell her how she felt about him. She could see something was troubling her mother and wondered if she had had some news.

But all she would say was, 'I'm just anxious. Not all young men can make up their minds at once.'

Alix was sure there was more, that she had heard something about Bertie. Perhaps that he had chosen someone else.

Although it was late, Lord Palmerston brought the news to the Queen and the Prince Consort himself. They stood in the Blue Closet, tense, listening as he explained.

From the start of the Civil War in America, Britain had tried to maintain strict neutrality. Now something had happened that they could not let pass. The Southern States had sent two envoys to London to plead their cause and ask for assistance. They were named Mason and Slidell and they travelled with their families on a British vessel, the main steamer *Trent*. In British waters off the West Indies, the Trent was chased by a Federal cruiser, stopped at gunpoint and the envoys taken off. It was an insult to the flag and a direct violation of International Law.

'Do they realise the consequences?' Victoria asked, almost in a whisper.

'I have written at once to President Lincoln, demanding an explanation and the return of the envoys.'

'And if he does not reply?'

Palmerston drew himself up. 'Action must be taken. Already, at the first reports, excitement and anger in the country are intense.'

He spoke decisively. The sibilance which had come with age seemed to have gone from his voice. Looking at him, Albert saw not the charming old politician but the commanding figure he had once been, the vigorous statesman who had flung his challenge at every nation whose policies threatened Britain's interests and honour.

The people thought of him as their champion. He would still lead and they would follow him now.

'Promise me, Lord Palmerston,' Albert said urgently, 'you will promise me to take no positive steps until you know all the details, until you have heard from Washington. And not without consulting me.'

Palmerston hesitated. He could see the tension in Albert.

'Very well, sir, I promise.' He bowed. 'You will excuse me, I must return to London.'

Albert could tell that Victoria was excited. She stood watching the door after the Prime Minister had bowed himself out, her mind racing. She felt a horror at the possibilities, outrage at the insult and disbelief that it had been committed by the very country to which they had so recently offered friendship.

'Will it be war?' she asked him.

'Lieber Gott, not!' He stared at her. 'No, no, no. Lincoln is a man of sense. He would not risk retaliation at this time by the British Navy.'

'They must apologize,' Victoria declared. 'Fully.'

'Of course,' he said soothingly. 'But it must be handled with care. There are other ways to settle these things than to send in a gunboat.'

She followed him through into the study. He moved to his desk and stood, touching one of the red despatch boxes, one of the many that still waited for his attention. The top of the desk was covered with a profusion of books, notes, letters answered and to be answered. The work was never ending.

'What are you going to do?' Victoria asked him.

'Work for a little.'

'Oh no! You look so tired.'

Albert shrugged. For days now he had suffered from insomnia. The muscles of his neck and shoulders were tight with strain and a dull pain ached in the small of his back when he walked. Lying awake for hours in bed gave him no relief.

Victoria came to him. 'You do too much,' she said gently. 'It's my fault. I know I depend on you too much.'

Albert managed to smile. 'We are a team. Besides

I enjoy the work. If something interests me, I must see it through.'

Victoria fought down her irritation. She must not think of herself as neglected, that would be unfair. But he cared too much about too many things. She put her hand on his arm. 'Come to bed.'

'Not just yet.'

'Please, Albert,' He looked at her. Her eyes were pleading. When her voice was low and soft like this, she was like the tender, shy girl whom he had found hiding behind the mask of the imperious young Queen. 'You are always tired. Always working. We never go to bed at the same time any more.'

Albert gave in. 'Very well. I have a few things to finish, but I'll be in in a minute.'

Victoria smiled tremulously, gratefully. She reached up and, as he stooped, kissed his cheek.

Albert watched her as she moved to the door and turned to smile at him before going out. He sat at his desk and took from his waistcoat pocket the small gold key to the despatch boxes which she had given him so long ago. He reached for the top box and stopped. The hand holding the key was trembling and he felt an irresistible tiredness wash over him. Only his devotion to duty had kept him functioning. The death of his young cousins had distressed him deeply. And now this storm over the mail steamer *Trent*. He saw no hope for the future in the power-conscious, shifting alliances of Europe. The safety of the world to come lay in the friendship of the English-speaking peoples, he was convinced, principally between Great Britain and the United States, that new nation forging itself across the Atlantic which had already shown its willingness in the reception given to Bertie.

But there was nothing he could do now. He put the key back in his pocket. As he rose and crossed the study, there was a knock at the door from the corridor. The duty equerry came in with a letter on a silver salver.

'A special messenger from Germany, sir. From Baron Stockmar.'

'Thank you.' Albert took the letter. The equerry bowed

and retreated to the door, going out. Albert broke the seal and began to read as he moved towards the private apartments, wondering what his former tutor could have considered so urgent. As he read the first words, he stopped. He read the whole letter through quickly and the flush of tiredness drained from his face. As he read it again, he began to tremble.

Victoria had moved from her dressing room into the bedroom. She had already changed into her nightgown, snowy white and perfumed with lavender. She sat at her dressing table and Augusta Bruce, the General's sister, who was in attendance, unpinned her hair. It fell in glossy, brown waves to below her shoulders. Victoria passed the brush to Lady Augusta and the nighly ritual began. She partly closed her eyes at the tug and tingle as the bristles lightly brushed her scalp. It was a delicious, faintly wicked feeling.

She started and covered her bosom as the door opened. It was Albert. She smiled but could see at once that something was terribly wrong. He stood just inside the door, pale and taut, looking at her and holding a letter.

'Thank you, Augusta,' she said. 'I shan't need you any more tonight.'

Lady Augusta curtsied and moved nervously round Albert who did not acknowledge her. When the door closed, Victoria asked, 'What is it, dearest?'

Albert had to force himself to speak. He held up the letter. 'From Stockmar . . .'

'What does he say?' Victoria rose anxiously and came to him to take it, but Albert stepped away, not letting her see it.

'It's about Bertie,' he muttered. 'He writes . . . about Bertie. That son of mine . . . a son of mine . . .' Victoria did not understand. She wanted to touch him, to hold him. He looked about to collapse. 'I know now why he does not want to be married. Why he keeps putting it off.'

'Why?' she whispered.

'Stockmar heard it some weeks ago but refused to believe it until it was confirmed. Now everyone knows—everyone but us. Bertie is having an affair—with an actress. A music hall singer!'

He sat on the edge of the bed, bleak, drained now he had told her. She took the letter from his slack fingers. He did not seem to notice.

'Under the noses of his Governor and his Commanding Officer, she was smuggled into his quarters at camp, by some of his friends—to make him a man!'

Victoria sat on her dressing stool. She read the letter, avidly, horrified, the story of the nights at the Curragh burning into her mind.

Bertie was shocked to hear from Bruce that his father knew what had happened. He hardly heard anything else the General said but he could see he was stern, not so much angry, as hurt that he had been deceived. The Prince Consort himself arrived the following Monday. It was a difficult meeting.

It was as well for Bertie that time had passed since his father first heard the story. Albert's anger had cooled and he could see that his son was genuinely contrite. Bruce was also a calming influence.

He condemned what had occurred, yet he was sincerely fond of Bertie. Like Albert, he was relieved to discover that the Prince had not planned the affaire himself but was led into it almost by accident. Bertie refused to tell them who the friends were who had brought her to him. Bruce insisted that their names should be reported to the Battalion Commander, but Bertie still refused. To his surprise, his father told Bruce to make no further attempt to find them. The General bowed and left them alone.

"That, at least, I admire you for,' Albert said. 'It would have been cowardly to sacrifice those who risked themselves for you—even for such a reason.'

Bertie was silent. Albert looked at him for a long moment, seeing the strain he was under. He moved behind the desk to look out the bow window of the small sitting room. Outside, it was a cold, wet day, the trees standing gaunt in the garden of the Hall.

When he spoke again, his voice was oddly gentle. 'It is a long time since we have talked together.'

'Yes, father,' Bertie answered very quietly.

'In fact, I can't remember when we have talked. Strange that a father and son should know so little of each other.' He turned back from the window. Normally when he looked at Bertie, if he saw anything, it was a vague amalgam of a helpless, puzzle-eyed baby, a long-haired, nervous boy of ten crying over his inability to answer simple questions on history and philosophy and a malicious, lazy teenager bullying his smaller brothers and sisters. For the first time really he saw a young man of twenty, of medium height, his physique strong and well-proportioned, fair-haired, with a dusting of moustache on his upper lip and eyes that watched him, unafraid, as clear and blue as Victoria's.

'Perhaps in the past I have given you cause to resent me,' Albert said. 'I did not mean to. Everything I have done is because I love you, because I wanted you to have every advantage, every possibility of success in life. Perhaps I forgot that you also needed affection. We must try to be closer in the future. The past is past.' He looked at his son and saw that he was near to tears. Albert was glad that he did not cry or he would have wept with him. He shook his head. 'I know I need not ask you to promise never to see this woman again.'

Bertie and his father walked together in the cold and rain of the November evening and Albert told him of his dream, to see those thrones of Europe filled with a new race of enlightened rulers, joined together by family ties, the only way to make peace a reality. A start had already been made. His uncle Leopold was King of Belgium, his brother Ernest, Duke of Saxe-Coburg. Vicky and Fritz would one day be King and Queen of Prussia. Louis Napoleon of France had become a friend. It was one of the reasons he mourned so bitterly the death of Pedro of Portugal, the loss of a link in the chain. In time, Bertie would take his father's place as head of the family.

'From now on, I shall try to be more how you wish me to be,' Bertie promised him.

'That is all I ask,' Albert said. 'In our place in life, everything we do is important. We cannot live as other people. We must think always of our country, and of the example we set.'

They lost their way in the dark and the chilling rain. The walk lasted longer than they had meant but neither of them cared. They felt closer to each other than either of them had thought possible before.

Albert could not throw off the heavy cold he picked up in Cambridge. His rhematic pains became worse. Victoria longed for them to get away from the dank air of Windsor to their favourite home, Osborne, which they had built on the Isle of Wight, but the international tension made it impossible. Osborne was too far from London.

The seriousness of the crisis was spelt out to them by Palmerston and Lord John Russell. The country and all political parties were completely behind the Government in its determination not to allow the British flag to be insulted. An apology had been asked for from Washington and had so far been refused. The American attitude was aggressive and unfriendly. It was not merely an attitude. They had taken positive steps against Great Britain, sending General Scott to Paris on diplomatic business. He told the French Government that the seizure of the envoys was discussed in Cabinet at Washington and deliberately ordered, even though they knew it might lead to war with England.

Palmerston was very grave. 'He is commissioned to propose to France that she joins the Northern States in war against us, and to offer France in that case the restoration of the French Province of Canada.'

Victoria gasped. Albert looked from Palmerston to Russell, shaken.

'Has Lincoln gone mad?'

Russell shrugged. 'Perhaps not he, but some of his advisers.'

'That is why we have had to move,' Palmerston told them. 'We have sent the Brigade of Guards to Canada —with more men to follow.'

'Of course! We must be ready for them,' Victoria insisted.

Albert shook his head. 'Doesn't Lincoln realise that the French will never join them in a war against us? Apart from anything else, French sympathies are with the South.'

'Exactly, sir,' Palmerston agreed. 'They are more interested in cotton than in Canada.'

'The Federal States will find themselves alone—caught between the Confederates in the South and us in the North,' Russell said.

Palmerston was no more in favour of war than the Prince Consort. It was degrading, expensive and the least satisfactory solution. 'The irony is,' he told Russell on their journey back to Downing Street, 'if the Southern envoys *had* reached us, we would have paid them and their cause no more attention than we have in the past.'

Albert was so weak that he could not eat and when, to please Victoria, he helped her to inspect the Volunteer Corps of Eton School, he walked with difficulty, wrapped in a long fur coat. She tried to encourage him to take exercise and fresh air which old Sir James Clark recommended but he resisted her, although he still insisted on walking.

Mr. Gladstone, the Chancellor of the Exchequer, was a guest at Windsor for the weekend, with his wife. Although Albert admired Gladstone, Victoria found him difficult to like. He was a tall, still strikingly handsome man in his fifties, but the Queen thought him too radical and opinionated, even if high-principled and with a charming wife. She disliked him even more for interrupting the weekend with business when Albert should have been given a chance to rest and recover. He had brought from Lord John Russell the text of the dispatch which the Government proposed to send as an ultimatum to Washington.

When Albert read it in his study that night, he stared at Gladstone. 'We cannot send this.'

'We must, sir. We must demand the immediate release of those men and an apology from the American Government. If that is refused, our Minister has been instructed to leave Washington.'

Albert breathed out slowly. He felt feverish and his head throbbed with a constant, unrelieved headache. Victoria had said that the Government should be left to deal with this matter, but he knew the consequences would be disastrous. 'Of course, we must,' he conceded. 'But this is too strong. The Americans would see it as a direct challenge.'

'They are in the wrong.' The normally reasonable Gladstone sounded as implacable as Palmerston.

'Yet they must be given a chance to get out of it with honour,' Albert explained patiently. 'Otherwise we shall be forced into a pointless war. Even if we win, what would we do? Split America in two with the Southern States?'

Gladstone was silent. He realised that the calmness in the Prince Consort's voice was assumed but, even so, it cooled the fevour in his own mind. What had seemed so right and necessary in Cabinet now gave him doubts.

Albert saw he had gained a small advantage. 'This despatch must be rewritten, in a form that Lincoln can reasonably accept,' he finished firmly.

'The Prime Minister is determined,' Gladstone told him. 'It must leave on the packet boat tomorrow afternoon.'

'Give me till then,' Albert said.

He could not sleep. His mind raced from Lincoln to Bertie, to the children left in Portugal, to Vicky who was expecting her third child and hoping for another boy and back to Lincoln and the despatch. Lying beside him in their wide bed, Victoria felt him turn restlessly and lay silent, afraid to complain or move because Sir James had said he must not be agitated.

As light began to filter into the room, he rose and stumbled out to the study, pulling on his dressing-gown. At least he is well enough to rise, Victoria thought, and fell into an exhausted sleep. When she woke again, it was a cold, raw day. She remembered that Albert had not dressed properly and that there would probably be no fire lit in the study. She rose quickly and took her wrap.

Albert had finished his redraft of the despatch. He made a copy and locked it in the box to go to the Foreign Office. He was cold, trembling with cold and tiredness and his hand could hardly hold the pen. Although it was light, his desk lamp was still burning. He looked at his hands, trying to will them to stop shaking.

Victoria came hurrying to him. She was concerned to see how pale, how drawn he looked, and scolded him for trying to work.

'It had to be done,' he told her.

'Yes,' she said, 'yes.' She helped him up and back towards the bedroom. He was very weak.

'We could not send an ultimatum. They couldn't see that.'

'No, no, of course they couldn't.' She got him back to bed and sent for Sir James Clark and Dr. Jenner, the famous specialist.

The two doctors examined the Prince Consort. Jenner was worried. He detected fever. Sir James had tended the royal family for many years. He knew that the Prince Consort had a morbid fear of fever and was convinced that, if it ever took hold of him, he would never recover. He explained to Jenner that two of the family had just died and the Prince would be especially sensitive. It would be better, also, not to worry the Queen since it would only excite her unnecessarily. So they told Victoria there was no cause for alarm.

Albert's restlessness increased. He moved to a smaller bed, but he would not stay there. He could not sleep without ether. By day he walked about the private apartments without settling, or listened as Alice read to him. Victoria wrote to her uncle Leopold in Belgium and to Vicky to tell them there was no danger, but when Alice suggested that Bertie should be told, she refused to send for him. To her, it was all Bertie's fault. Worry about him and the cold at Cambridge had caused Albert's illness. She did not wish to see him.

Clark was soothing and promised a daily recovery,

but Albert was no better. He lay at night, sleepless, in the single bed and, during the day, on a sofa in the Blue Room. His mind began to wander. Some days he did not recognise Victoria, then he would cling to her and ask her to pray with him. She was brave, not letting him see the agony his worsening condition caused her. She felt it her duty to keep up everyone's spirits, but there were times when she broke down, despairing at how long his recovery was taking.

For many hours, Alice sat with her father. She was patient and gentle and her quiet love soothed him. She read to him or wrote letters. Once she told him she was writing to Vicky to say he was getting better.

'Don't lie to her,' Albert muttered. 'Tell her I am dying.'

Alice was in tears. He repeated, 'I am dying and I am the only one who seems to know it.'

In the morning, he was delirious. They listened as his mind wandered. 'No, it is too much! Zu stark. You must speak to the Ministers . . . What does he know? If only Stockmar were here. Er versteht alles . . .' He listened and some of the wildness went from his eyes as he smiled. 'Wie schon . . . wundershon . . . I can hear them.'

'What, Albert?' Victoria asked, her voice breaking.

'The birds—in my garden at Rosenau . . .'

When his mind was clear, he asked Alice to play his favourite hymn on the piano, 'Eine feste Burg ist unser Gott,' and to leave all the doors open so that he could hear.

Between watching over him and the short, tearful rests which the doctors forced her to take in another room, Victoria tried to handle the business and correspondence which still flooded in. Without Albert to explain it, most of it was nearly incomprehensible to her, but she coped with as much as she could so that he would not find it too great a strain to catch up when he had recovered.

Lord Palmerston reported to her that the Cabinet had accepted unanimously the Prince Consort's careful, diplomatic version of the despatch to be sent to Washington and that war had certainly been averted. The envoys had been released.

Palmerston smiled. 'It is only another proof that we should always consult His Royal Highness.'

'I have always said so,' Victoria told him.

When the Prime Minister tried to move on to other matters, Victoria begged him to consider her feelings. She could not think of anything else while her husband was so ill. Palmerston was surprised. The bulletins had only said that the Prince Consort was suffering from a mild indisposition.

'It is more—much more,' Victoria confessed. 'They said the fever would not develop, but it has!'

Palmerston could hear the pain and despair in her voice. Tearfully, she told him the days had become a hideous dream, at night she lay awake, afraid to sleep in case there was a change in her husband's condition. Already she had endured this for nearly two weeks and Jenner had said it might be another two before the feverish cold was cured. Palmerston was alarmed at the mention of fever and persuaded her to let another specialist, Dr. Watson, examine the Prince Consort. Like many others, he considered the doddering Sir James Clark and the fawning Dr. Jenner unfit to attend a sick cat.

Victoria wrote to Uncle Leopold and to Vicky to tell them that, although she had been very frightened, each day was now more cheering and that, in two or three more, Albert would be quite himself again. She was reluctant to allow Watson to examine him because he might be alarmed by a strange face and because it would certainly offend the other doctors who had been so reassuring, but she finally consented. Watson hardly needed to carry out an examination. From the moment he saw him, it was clear to him that for the past three weeks the Prince Consort had been dying of untreated typhoid. Alice had heard her father call for Bertie. Without telling her mother, she wrote to Madingley Hall. The letter she sent Bertie did not make their father's illness sound urgent but she suggested he should come home. He discussed it with Bruce and they left for London that evening. They had a leisurely dinner in town and caught a late train for Windsor, arriving at three in the morning.

As their cab reached the castle, they could not understand why all the lights were burning. Footmen and servants stood silently in the corridors. Bertie hurried to the private sitting room. It was empty but the lamps were lit. The same in his parent's drawing room and study. When they reached the anteroom to the royal bedroom, Clark stopped them from going any further. Through the door, Bertie could hear his father's tortured, laboured breathing.

All that night and the next morning and afternoon he waited. Victoria would not talk to him. Only she and Alice were allowed into the Blue Room with the doctors and the Dean of Windsor. Bertie waited, numb and shaking. The anteroom and corridor filled with officers of the Household, gentlemen and ladies-in-waiting. Bruce held Bertie's arm to support him. Finally word came that the Prince Consort would like to see his son, although the Queen had warned that it might disturb him.

Bertie went into the room with Bruce. His father's bed had been wheeled away from the wall. He lay motionless. The fever had gone, leaving him pale and calm. Bertie knelt by him and kissed his hand. Albert was too weak to speak but his eyes smiled to him. Bertie fought back his tears and moved to the foot of the bed. One by one the other children came to kiss their father's hand. The youngest were taken out again, but Lenchen stayed by Bertie.

Victoria left the room for a moment. Her grief was so intense, so unendurable, but she still did not dare let it show. Alice came for her. Albert's breathing had become ragged, but it soon quietened. As Victoria looked at him, she saw the pain ease and his face relax. With the pallor and the weight he had lost, he was again as slim and handsome as when she first saw him. She leant towards him and took his hand. He gazed up at her, puzzled, not recognising her.

'Wer . . . wer ist da?' he asked.

Victoria could not understand why she did not die herself. 'Es ist das kleine Frauchen . . . Your little wife, Albert,' she whispered.

He smiled to her, very lovingly. 'Gutes, kleines Frauchen.' His voice was as faint as the rustle of dry leaves. He moved his lips in a kiss and his hand went limp in hers.

There was a stunned, incredulous silence. Victoria kissed his forehead and gazed at him, willing him not to leave her, but he was dead. She cried out in anguish and fell to her knees by the bed, reaching for him.

'Oh, my dear darling . . . ' She crouched as if paralysed, unable to speak, not even able to weep.

Alice knelt opposite her. Lenchen and Bertie knelt at the foot of the bed. As Dean Wellesley began to mutter the prayer for the dead, Bertie trembled and covered his eyes with his hands. Like Victoria, the whole world seemed empty to him. All his sorrow was for his father whom he had so recently found, only to lose.

Chapter

7

The coffin, draped in black velvet embroidered in gold with the arms of the Queen and the Prince Consort, was borne reverently down the south aisle of St. George's Chapel, Windsor, up the long, columned nave between ranks of weeping guests and servants to the choir and the entrance to the vault which was the burial place of kings.

Bertie led the procession of royal mourners. He comforted his younger brother Arthur who was only twelve and sobbed so desperately that his whole body shook. Bertie controlled himself although, on the other side, his father's brother, Duke Ernest of Saxe-Coburg, wept unashamedly, although behind him Crown Prince Frederick of Prussia was weeping. All through the funeral service and the ceremony when the crimson coffin was uncovered and the crown of the Prince Consort and his Field-Marshal's insignia placed on it, he controlled himself, even though the voice of the Dean faltered and the Garter King-at-Arms broke down when he proclaimed the style and titles of the Prince.

In the stillness that followed, the mourners heard the swift, harsh rattle outside as the troops reversed their arms. The muffled bell began to toll, the minute guns boomed in the Long Walk and the coffin was lowered slowly into the vault. The last words were said and the symbolic earth thrown down to spatter on the crown and baton and clatter on the brass plate. As the organ played the Dead March, Bertie stepped forward to take his last look, his hands clasped tightly. Only then was he unable to bear it any longer. He hid his face in his arms and the Lord Chamberlain, Viscount Sydney, helped him from the chapel.

At first, in her grief, Victoria had kissed Bertie and held him, needed him when he promised to be everything to her for the rest of her life. But she did not believe that Albert died only of typhoid, and, as the days passed, she became more and more convinced that her inconsolable loss was Bertie's fault. She could not suffer him near her, to have to look at him.

Windsor, too, was full of hateful memories now. Before the funeral, she left for the Isle of Wight, for Osborne, the house which Albert had designed in the Italian style to be a home where they could bring up their children in peace and seclusion. From now on, it would be a memorial to his departed spirit. Nothing of his, his clothes, his pens, his books, nothing was to be touched or moved, just as she had ordered at Windsor. And she was determined that he would not rest in a vault with lesser beings. He was to have his own special mausoleum built at Frogmore, near the house in which her mother died. It had to be designed and built quickly, because she knew that she could not continue to live without him and that she would be dead herself in less than a year.

In the cold emptiness of her bed she wept, but the tears brought no relief. She had felt deep sorrow before. Now she learnt that its true depths were unimaginable. Albert had been everything to her, husband, friend, adviser, teacher and lover. She could make no decisions without him, not even choose a dress or a new pair of gloves without his approval. There was no one to explain things to her, no one to confide in. And her nights would be as comfortless as the days. Especially the nights, without his warmth, his touch, the gentle murmur of his voice. She was only forty-two and she would never know that demanding warmth, that answered need again. She longed for death. Oh, please, please take me soon, she prayed, let me follow him.

The shock was more severe because she had believed the words of reassurance. They had blinded her to the truth which even Alice had seen, days before the end. Now she reproached herself bitterly for all the times she had scolded Albert, for driving him on, for being irritated when he was slow, for her complaints when his energy and interest did not equal hers. Vicky's tender letters consoled her for moments until she remembered that her daughter's husband was still alive, that she could hold him and have his children. She thought of John Brown's prophetic words. Albert's had been the third death, and Brown must have foreseen it. And she thought of her own children, fatherless. And Bertie.

She could never forget. It was worse for her because Albert had made her promise never to reveal to their son that she knew all that had happened. She could never confront him with it. She tried to forgive him in her heart but there was no room left for forgiveness. She could see that he loved her and wanted to help her but having him constantly near her, knowing what she did, filled her with horror. She had to keep him away from her, without letting him find out why. In her misery, she realised that Albert had left her the answer. He had planned a tour of Egypt and the Holy Land for Bertie. He had wished it. That wish must be obeyed. No one could object. Bertie must leave at once.

Princess Christian of Denmark was an intelligent woman. In her younger years, she had been considered very attractive and ambitious. It was expected that she would make a brilliant match but she met her husband, Christian, at the family holiday at Rumpenheim and married him for his charm, simplicity and his gentle manners. She had never regretted it, although their life had not been easy and she had had to do without many things, especially after the children came. Because they had not been able to go out much in society, they had made their own amusements. Until they could afford tutors, Christian had given both boys and girls riding lessons and still took them for physical exercises on the lawn every Saturday morning. She had taught her daughters the piano and needlework and read with them. They were a very close family. Now that they were growing into beautiful, talented young women, all her ambitions were revived and centred in them.

She had had to control her excitement carefully when the first, cautious approach had been made by England. For Alix to marry the Prince of Wales would be the greatest match of all, but she knew there were many obstacles and she had not dared to hope for it until the meeting had been arranged at Speyer. Since then, Princess Christian had been in a quandary. There had been no word from England and, at the same time, this offer had come for Alix from Russia. Then there were these disturbing rumours about the Prince and an actress which, if they were true, might explain his reluctance to commit himself. Now his father had died and that could be another excuse for him to put off his choice of a wife for as long as possible. She had almost decided to accept the Czar's offer, except for one thing.

They had been genuinely saddened to hear of the death of the Prince Consort. Christian had said they must pray for him. He admired Albert and considered him the finest man in Europe. Alix had been very quiet. She said that Bertie had spoken of his father and was sure she would like him. Princess Christian had said nothing to her husband and daughter of the stories of Bertie's indiscretion, but she told them the latest rumour she had heard, that Victoria blamed her son for his father's death and refused even to see him. Her fear was that the Queen would also turn against his future wife.

Later that day she had passed her daughter's room and stopped at the sound of sobbing. Through the partly open door, she had seen Alix sitting on the window seat, holding the open locket with Bertie's photograph and crying. Normally Alix kept nothing from her. She had not realised how deeply she had fallen in love.

Bertie resigned himself to a cheerless tour of the Middle East. He had been allowed to choose no companions of his own. The party was led and organised by General Bruce and the whole, intended nature of the trip was set by the appointment of Dr. Stanley, Regius Professor of Ecclesiastical History at Oxford, to be its spiritual guide. Bertie wanted to travel informally, to recover from the shock of his father's death, not to have someone censoring and protecting on one hand and someone else moralising and preaching on the other. But Bruce again surprised him. In action, coping with the difficulties and hazards of travelling in wild, unfamiliar countries, he proved to be both resourceful and amusing. He knew when to be diplomatic with British and Turkish officials and when to shoulder obstructive protocol aside. He was tactful with religious sects and desert chieftains and, when actual danger threatened, he was found to have anticipated it and taken just the right precautions. Bertie felt a new respect and affection for him and Bruce became a friend.

The other surprise was Dr. Stanley. The middle-aged, intellectual professor was a deeply religious man and had no experience of royalty. Their dealings at first were stiff, and suspicious on both sides. However, after state visits to the Turkish Viceroy in Alexandria and in Cairo, Bertie had had enough of formality. A trip round the Cairo mosques and bazaars was arranged, and he shocked the Viceroy's Chamberlain by insisting on riding on a donkey. It broke the ice with Stanley who laughed and said he wished he had suggested it. Bertie set off on a well-fed beast called 'Captain Snooks' with Stanley beside him on 'Tom Sayers'. Bruce trotted behind on 'Billy'.

Stanley had travelled and studied in the Middle East. He turned out to be a fascinating guide. They visited the pyramids and the Sphinx, sailed down the Nile to the temples of Edfu, Luxor and Karnak and on to Aswan. Then back to Alexandria and to Palestine, to Jerusalem and Bethlehem and Nazareth. At Hebron, by Bruce's diplomacy, the Prince of Wales and Dr. Stanley were the first Europeans for seven hundred years to be allowed to enter the sanctuary to see the shrines of Abraham and Sarah, and the Tomb of Jacob, while the guardians prayed and begged the holy dead to forgive them. They attended the sacrifice of the sheep in the Samaritan Passover on Mount Gerizim and spent Easter by the Sea of Galilee, before riding on to Damascus and Baalbec. From Beirut, the royal yacht *Osborne* took them to Tyre and Sidon, Rhodes, Ephesus and the Golden Horn. From Constantinople they sailed to Athens and Marseilles, where they caught a special train to Paris, so that Bertie could visit Louis Napoleon and his beautiful wife, Eugenie, Emperor and Empress of France, at Versailles. During his unhappy boyhood, feeling himself unloved, he had often wished they were his parents and they treated him as if he had come home.

Victoria had been unable to stay at Osborne. Despite her grief and longing for privacy, she was the Queen. Her presence was needed, and, reluctant, protesting, she returned to Windsor although the thought of that place and its memories and of being exposed to people terrified her.

The amount of work that waited for her was immense. She had no hope of dealing with it at once. So much of it she had left to Albert, the parts which were too involved or too boring. She had not even tried to understand them, never realised the load he carried. For the past ten years he had virtually been king. Now she had to set herself again, slowly, little by little, to learn the business of government. She had one guiding light, the mass of notes and memoranda which he had left. Reading them, she was overwhelmed by the clarity of his mind, the brillance of his ideas. She vowed to preserve them. If she must live, it would be to perpetuate his thoughts and to see that all his hopes were fulfilled.

Six months after the funeral, Palmerston presented himself for an Audience in the Blue Closet. He knew it would be difficult. He respected the Queen's grief, but she delayed decisions and refused to attend meetings of the Privy Council, pleading her desolation. He was grateful to Princess Alice who had become her mother's secretary, speaking for her, writing her letters, and he felt sorry for the young Princess as she showed him in. Alice was pale, her eyes shadowed with care. As well as the work, she spent long hours comforting her mother who relived Albert's death nightly.

Palmerston thanked her and waited. The girl did wonders, and so did the Queen in the circumstances, but it was no way to run a country. The Queen had told him, herself, that she was convinced she would die within the year and had even hinted that she might abdicate before that in favour of her son. Her doctors were certainly concerned for her heatlh. His task today was to settle which of her duties the Prince of Wales should take over now. Best to get it decided before he came back from Egypt.

He bowed as the Queen came in. She was in total black, except for a widow's cap in white lace which reached a peak above her forehead, covering most of her hair. Victoria stiffened as she saw him. In all the months since the death, no one had dared to approach her not wearing mourning. In his brights, dandified clothes, his green cravat and yellow waistcoat Palmerston seemed to her to be dressed like a popinjay, deliberately heartless and disrespectful. Unaware of the effect his appearance had caused, the Prime Minister congratulated her on the success of the Prince of Wales' tour. Victoria told him he had been well received because he was her son. He smiled and agreed, pointing out that the Prince had created a very favourable impression in Egypt and Turkey, winning golden opinions, even from the Sultan. Victoria told him the Sultan would have said equally flattering things about any of her sons. Palmerston did not notice the new firmness in the Queen nor the way, at the mention of Bertie, her hands twisted the small, black handkerchief she carried. He reminded her that they were discussing the Prince of Wales and the share of the royal duties which he should take on, as she had suggested, those duties which were expected of him as Heir Apparent.

Victoria looked at him coldly. 'There are *no* duties laid down for the Heir.'

'But you said yourself, Ma'am,—' Palmerston began.

'I may have done so,' Victoria cut in. 'But I have reconsidered. I do not—*we* do not believe that our son is yet capable of taking part in government. I intend to carry out *all* my duties, as my husband would have expected—by myself.'

No further argument was possible.

Bertie arrived from Paris, fit and tanned. The Emperor and Empress had been kindly and sympathetic and the ladies of their court, the fascinating and sophisticated ladies of fashion had made much of him, wanting him to stay longer, but he had been gone for nearly half a year and he felt his mother needed him. He was worried, too, about General Bruce who had caught a fever in Constantinople and had weakened seriously on the way home. They took him to his sister Augusta's rooms in St. James Palace.

Bertie found Windsor Castle hushed and quiet, the servants still wearing mourning. He changed quickly from his travelling clothes into a black frock coat. Alice was waiting for him in the sitting room. She was so thin and drawn that he hardly recognised her. He was surprised when she told him that her marriage to Louis was to take place in spite of court mourning. He had thought it would be put off, at least for a year. Alice had thought so, too. She was devoted to her mother,

105

aware of how much help she really needed, and she was no longer certain that she wanted to marry Louis. He was charming and good-looking, but vain and, she had discovered, not very bright. Yet she had no choice, the marriage had been arranged by her father.

Her flat, unemotional acceptance troubled Bertie. He had not suffered like Alice through the months of Victoria's most violent sorrow. He had not known that every night Albert's nightgown and dressing-gown were still laid out on the bed and that his mother cried herself to sleep, holding them. He did not know how the Blue Room had been redecorated and become a shrine, with the Prince Consort's bust draped in black by the bed in which he died. He did not know that his mother was afraid to meet him, because she was unsure of how she would react.

Alice warned him that the Queen had decided to go to Coburg in Germany, to visit the scenes of Albert's boyhood. On the journey, she planned to stay with her Uncle Leopold of Belguim at his palace of Laeken. She had asked Prince and Princess Christian to meet her there with their elder daughters. Bertie was to follow her. Alice confirmed his fear. If Victoria still approved of Alexandra when she met her, he was to propose.

Bertie felt numbed. 'I'll do anything,' he muttered. 'But this is my whole life . . .'

'Please, Bertie,' Alice begged. 'Do not refuse. Don't even question. She has said—if you do not obey her in everything, she will withdraw herself from you, and never see you again.'

He found his mother in the Blue Room. In her black dress and widow's cap, she sat gazing at the white marble bust of his father on its pedestal, still and grieving. She was asking for courage. From the moment of Bertie's homecoming, she had dreaded this meeting. Bertie moved to her and bowed, thinking she had not noticed him. She rose abruptly and her instinct was to run out. She could not look at him, but felt him quite near her, as tense and uncertain as she was. He saw the deep lines of sorrow, the face sallow with suffering.

'Mama . . . ,' he said very quietly.

He stepped closer and leant down to kiss her. She turned her face away and her whole body was taut. He kissed her cheek and straightened. Victoria looked at him, unable to speak. Then the stiffness suddenly left her and she collapsed against him, her head on his chest, crying bitterly. He held her, closing his eyes.

'Mama . . .'

Five days later, General Bruce died at St. James's Palace. To Bertie, it was as if he had lost another father. To Victoria, it was another punishment, another sign of the destruction which his conduct brought to the best of those around him. Bruce had sacrificed his life for Bertie.

The following Thursday, Alice was married to Louis of Hesse-Darmstadt in a room at Windsor, prepared as a chapel. The makeshift altar stood under a portrait of her parents when they were young, surrounded by their children. Her father's brother, Ernest, gave her away. Apart from the bride and bridesmaids everyone wore full mourning. Victoria sat throughout in an armchair, shielded from the eyes of the few guests by Bertie and Affie and her two youngest sons, Arthur and the sickly Leopold. She wept piteously at losing her daughter who had been such a support to her, but comforted herself that her husband's wish had been obeyed. Alice was perfectly controlled. Tall, serious and graceful, she seemed not to hear the sobs nor see the tears of those around her making her wedding day into another funeral. Looking at her, Bertie prayed that when it was his turn to stand at the altar, he could face it with the same quiet resignation and dignity.

Leopold of Saxe-Coburg, once son-in-law to George the Fourth, and now the first King of the Belgians, was very dear to Victoria. Uncle to both her and Albert, it was he who had first brought them together. He was a thin-faced, crafty man, given in his age to wearing rather obvious, brightly coloured wigs. Under a veneer of piety and extreme correctness, he had carried out a highly successful career as a seducer and political opportunist.

He had absolutely no illusions, but he was sincerely fond of Victoria. He had gained enormous personal prestige from arranging her marriage and he hoped to continue it by promoting this marriage of her son to the pretty Danish girl.

He was in the main reception room of his exquisite palace at Laeken with Victoria and Mrs. Paget, the wife of the British Minister to Copenhagen, who was to effect the introductions. He saw how his neice trembled when Wally Paget announced that Les Danois had arrived and were waiting.

'Courage, ma chere,' he murmured, and nodded to an usher who stood by the doors at the end of the room. Leopold kissed Victoria's hand and moved to stand behind her chair. The doors opened and Prince and Princess Christian with their two elder daughters came in. Wally advanced to meet them.

Princess Christian had precedence over her husband and was presented first. She curtsied. Victoria inclined her head slightly. Albert had not approved of the family and she was determined to allow no familiarities. Prince Christian bowed and she repeated her nod. The two princesses were presented and curtsied. Victoria had forced herself not to look at Alexandra before. She had been aware of two girls, one dark and smiling, the other taller and more serious. Now the impact of the girl's beauty struck her. After a moment, she beckoned and Alix came forward alone.

Reaching Victoria's chair, she curtsied again and stayed down, not quite daring to look up at the Queen whose name and dignity were already a legend. Out of natural tact, she had come dressed in mourning with no jewellery, her hair swept back from her forehead and falling at the sides in long ringlets to her shoulders. She seemed calm and collected but her heart was beating so loudly she was afraid everyone could hear it.

Victoria was touched by the tribute of the mourning. She took Alix's chin and raised her face. Albert had said this girl was an angel. Gazing into those clear, blue, innocent eyes, Victoria could think of no other description so perfect. On the arm of the chair beside her, there

108

was a small, carved box. She opened it and took out a sprig of white heather. She gave it to Alix.

Alix did not understand, but realised instinctively that it meant something important. She hesitated, then held it against her heart. Looking up, she saw the Queen blink tears from her eyes and she smiled, quite naturally and affectionately. The corners of Victoria's mouth lifted in a tremulous, answering smile, the first since the agony of that night eight months before.

Bertie waited in a hotel room in Brussels. With him was General Sir William Knollys, a tall, dignified soldier appointed to replace Bruce, not as Governor but as Comptroller of his Household. He waited, nervous, until the Pagets arrived to tell him that the Queen had accepted Alexandra at once. She had said to Wally, 'How HE would have loved her'. Bertie resigned himself. He could see it was all decided, all he had to do was turn up at the altar.

'By no means,' Wally told him. 'The final decision is still yours. Her Majesty has let her wishes be known, but the choice must be Your Royal Highness's alone.'

Next day Bertie met Alexandra and her parents at his great-uncle's palace. It was awkward for him because now everyone knew why he was here. He found it difficult even to look at Alix. He had studied her photographs, trying to will himself into feeling something for her. Now, the photographs seemed to have no relation to this quiet girl who smiled to him but gave him no special encouragement. She was stunningly attractive, he could see that. But very reserved. It did not occur to him that she felt just as awkward as he did. Her younger sister Minny did most of the talking, rattling on about how they both longed to see the world, in her quaint English.

Uncle Leopold suggested that they all take a walk in the gardens after lunch. It was a warm, dry September day. The older people walked on ahead down the formal terraces towards the Lake. Bertie was some distance behind with Alix and Minny.

'I've never been to England,' Minny sighed.

'Then you must come. Some time,' Bertie told her. He had been hoping for a chance at last to talk to Alix alone. The longer it took, the more nervous he became, but Minny would just not leave them. She found him fascinating.

'This is the furthest we've ever traveled. And just think—you've seen France and Italy and America. And Egypt! What was it like?'

'Hot,' Bertie said tersely. Alix smiled.

King Leopold had noticed what was happening and waited for them. He shook his finger at Minny. 'So there you are! I thought you were walking with me?'

'I was just asking Bertie about his travels.'

'Well, I've seen a lot more,' Leopold chuckled. 'Come and talk to me.' He tucked Minny's arm firmly in his and walked her off.

Alix did not know Bertie well enough to laugh, but she wanted to. His seriousness stopped her. He had the same, inborn dignity as his mother and Alix hoped that he was not always so solemn. He looked very handsome, even more than she had remembered, and now that he had put on weight, was even more manly. He was motioning to her and they moved off along a path that diverged from the other. She saw that it led to steps down to a terrace of weathered stone, screened by box hedges. She had never been alone with a man before and she felt as if she were flushing. She tried to compose herself.

Bertie was watching her secretly. He had not realised just how lovely she was. Of course, she was a year older since they had last met and her figure had developed more. She wore a dress of ivory lace, tied with a blue sash at the waist. Soft ruffles at the open neck accentuated the rise of her breasts. He noticed the sprig of heather pinned above her heart. The skin of her neck was delicate and slightly golden. There was another blue ribbon in her hair, matching the colour of her eyes. And her hair in the sunlight,—why had he not realised before?—was beautiful, shining, not gold nor red, somewhere in between, like finespun copper. She made him feel clumsy.

110

He could not imagine himself touching her, but the thought excited him.

Alix had been aware of him watching her. As she glanced at him, he looked away. 'You mustn't mind Minny,' she said. 'She's just so keen to see other countries.'

Bertie coughed. 'I understand.'

'Denmark is so small and quiet, sometimes we feel the rest of the world is turning while we stand still.'

He had the impression that, somehow, she did not mind that, the smallness and the quiet. They had reached the steps and he let her walk down in front of him, watching how gracefully she moved. She was not like other girls who either flirted with him or fell tongue-tied and blushing. She was natural, unaffected. He had the sudden, uncomfortable feeling that, perhaps, that was because she was indifferent to him. Perhaps she knew other young men she preferred.

They were at the bottom of the steps. She turned to him. 'You speak English pretty well,' he told her. She smiled. The old stones of the terrace they had reached trapped the sun. Late-flowering roses in troughs round the borders scented the air. The box hedge hid them from the other members of the party who were now on some lower level. In the silence, Alix could hear the hum of bees and the song of a single thrush, clear but far away. She was holding the stem of the sprig of heather. She pulled it from the clip.

'The Queen, your mother gave me this. She said it was from Balmoral.'

Fritz had given Vicky a sprig of heather before he proposed. Victoria had wanted Bertie to continue the tradition. 'Yes, I picked it for you, myself.' Alix looked at him. It was his chance to speak, but he could not. 'I hoped it would bring you luck.'

Alix smiled gently. 'Do you think I need it?'

There was a hint of challenge in her voice, of teasing, which threw Bertie slightly, and intrigued him. He was very aware of the warmth and the perfume of the roses and the girl smiling at him. Each moment of silence between them stretched out and seemed infinite. He knew that now was his moment if it was ever to be.

'You haven't said—would you like to visit England, too?'

'Very much. It must be beautiful.'

'I believe it is,' he said. His voice was as quiet and as tense as hers. They both knew that he was skirting round the central question. 'I would very much like to show it to you. If you come, how long would you stay?'

'That would depend.'

'If you came—I should want you to stay forever.' He managed to look at her directly. She was gazing at him. He could see now that she was taut. To him, she looked uncertain and he was very afraid that she would refuse him. He did not realise that she was nearly in tears because he had at last spoken.

He took her hand, the one holding the heather. 'Alix . . . I would have liked to know you better. But there was never the chance.'

'No.'

'I am only afraid that I am not worthy of you'

Her eyes widened. 'But that is how I feel about you.'

'You must consider it carefully,' Bertie said.

Alix answered very quietly. 'I did that long ago.' She smiled and her eyes closed as he kissed her. Then they broke apart and they both laughed and discovered that neither of them was very solemn after all.

Uncle Leopold was happier at the result than anyone, next to Bertie. He waited impatiently in the private drawing room while champagne was passed round the parents and close friends like the Pagets. He saw how Bertie stood with his arm round Alix, flushed and excited, as well he might be. If only Victoria had stayed instead of going on to Coburg.

He took two glasses to the new couple. 'Happy, my boy?'

'I can't tell you how much, Uncle Leopold.'

'You'll cherish her?'

'Till the end of my life,' Bertie promised.

'Mind you do.' Leopold turned to the others. 'Your Royal Highness, Ladies and Gentlemen—since I made the match that began it all, between my niece Victoria and my nephew, the late, dearly loved Albert of Saxe-Coburg—and since I have now played matchmaker again to their son and the most beautiful princess in Europe, I feel I have the right to propose a toast.'

The others laughed.

'Bertie and Alix!'

As the toast was drunk, Alix turned in Bertie's arm and smiled to him. Already she felt part of him and could not stand the thought of their being separated, even for a day. Bertie kissed her cheek and everyone applauded. He did not know if he was in love, but he was excited by everyone's reaction and proud of having won her. And he knew that he wanted her.

Victoria took good care to keep them apart before the wedding by sending Bertie on a Mediterranean cruise with Vicky and Fritz. She meant the German influence in his life to be the strongest and did not like him associating too much with his future wife's relations. When she returned from Coburg, she informed Palmerston that the wedding would be in early March. This surprised him, as the church had objected to the wedding taking place during Lent.

'Their objection rests merely on prejudice,' she pointed out.

'Marriage is a solemn, holy act—*not* to be classed with amusements.'

Palmerston suppressed a smile and agreed with her, then was concerned to hear that Princess Alexandra had been summoned to spend a month at Osborne to learn what was expected of her before marriage. He thought that it would be an ordeal for a young girl, to feel that she was on approval, but was glad that the Queen had a new interest to take her mind off her bereavement.

Prince Christian brought Alix to the Isle of Wight at the beginning of November, but was not asked to stay. Alix had never been separated from her parents before and at first felt strange in the huge, formal house with its busts and paintings and mementoes of the Prince Consort, draped in black crepe. But she liked her new brothers and sisters. She brought warmth back to Osborne. Affie, the same age as her, was handsome and flirtatious and asked her all about her younger sisters. Lenchen, Louise and little Beatrice adored her and squealed when she showed them how to do cartwheels in the drawing room. In turn, they showed her the grounds, and the tiny house built like an Alpine chalet, the Swiss Cottage where they had learnt to cook and sew and Affie and Bertie had been taught bricklaying and gardening. They laughed when she told them her home in Denmark could be hidden in a wing of Osborne and no one would notice it. Alice was three months pregnant but came home to meet her. She found Alix charming and told her mother that Bertie was truly lucky to have won such a jewel.

Victoria was uncertain. The more she saw Alexandra, the more enchanted she was. She was modest, her sympathy was touching and unassumed, her smile irresistible. With her, she felt her heart lightened, her grief retreating, and it made her feel guilty. The girl was almost too perfect, certainly too good for Bertie. There had to be something wrong with her. She examined the well-thumbed books in Alexandra's room. They were in Danish and turned out to be religious works. She objected to Alexandra bringing any Danish ladies or servants with her. Alix did not argue. She accepted at once that it was wrong to have servants to whom she could talk in a language her husband did not understand. She criticised the way Alexandra dressed, always in skirts and jackets. Alix explained that they were more economical and easier to make, as she made many of her clothes herself. Each time she thought of this, Victoria smiled at its novelty and practicality. Yet she had to be sure.

One evening, sitting with Alexandra, Alice and Lenchen after dinner, she told her future daughter-in-law what Parliament had voted for her as pin money after the wedding.

Alix gazed at her, astonished. 'But that's five times

114

'more than my father's income for a year!' she protested. 'I could never spend all that.'

Alice and Lenchen laughed and Victoria silenced them with a look. 'I hear from Bertie that he misses you dreadfully.'

'As I do him,' Alix told her.

'That is fitting,' Victoria conceded. 'I hope you do really love him and not merely his wealth and position.

Alix was very conscious of Alice and Lenchen listening, but she had to say what she felt. 'People may think that is why, because they do not know him. But if he was a simple cowherd, I should love him just the same and would marry no one else.'

Victoria was moved. Albert's instincts had been correct. She took Alexandra's hand and pressed it. 'I have no doubts,' she said gently.

Bertie enjoyed his holiday with Vicky and Fritz. He felt closer to them because they had found Alix for him and they smiled to see how she was beginning to obsess him. Every day he thought more about her, resenting the time they were apart. Every day he wrote to her and he treasured her letters in their careful English. He was delighted to hear that his mother had decreed the ladies not to wear full mourning for the wedding, grey and white or lilac and white would do. It was a sign of how pleased she was at his choice of bride. The only disappointment was that she would not come out of mourning herself. It worried him.

The Queen's attitude worried her Government, too. As interest in the marriage and in Alexandra grew, she changed her mind again. In spite of objections from Palmerston, Russell and Gladstone, she decided that there would be no celebrations and that the wedding would be held in St. George's Chapel, Windsor. She had to be present and could not face the thought of exposing herself to crowds at St. Paul's or Westminster.

'That's far too small,' Russell protested.

'The marriage of the Prince of Wales cannot be a family affair. It concerns the whole country,' Gladstone agreed.

They were in the Prime Minister's study at Downing Street. Russell held up a copy of Punch Magazine. 'Did you see what it says here?' he asked them. ' "It seems the wedding is to take place in an obscure Berkshire village, noted only for an old castle with no sanitary arrangements." '

Palmerston chuckled. Gladstone frowned. 'If she were not the Queen, I would say Her Majesty was jealous.'

Palmerston glanced at him. Gladstone was heavy-going, but he could be peculiarly perceptive at times. 'Be that as it may,' he murmured. 'I think she underestimates the popularity of the Prince. Already his bride's photograph seems to be in every shop window in London. Her Majesty may not wish them to show their enthusiasm because of her personal loss, she may wish to keep the marriage as private as possible, but the people of Britain will not be cheated—and may surprise her.'

Chapter
8

Alix said goodbye to the Yellow Palace, to her rooms and the dear bedroom she had shared with Minny. She said goodbye to Bernstorff, the little chateau in the country her father had been given when he became heir to the throne, and to her ponies. Prince Christian had spent more than he could afford to buy her clothes to travel in and to wear on her arrival, and her old tutors and friends cried to see how lovely she was and because she was leaving. The people of Denmark loved her because she had always been one of them, unaffected and sincere, caring for the poor and the sick. In every town and village they collected money and put it together to make a dowry for her, the People's Dowry. But because she knew her country was not rich,

Alix had it made into a trust to provide dowries for girls who were poorer than herself and the people cheered, wept and came to every railway station on her way south to say farewell.

Alix had never realised how much her country loved her and at Korsor where she took ship for Kiel with her parents and brothers and sisters she cried, too, at the words of the Governor and Burgomaster at the last goodbye. They said they knew she was going from an insignificant land to marry the Prince of the greatest nation in the world. But they were proud he had come to them for his bride. They knew how much they were losing in her and only hoped that she would keep a corner of her heart for memories of Denmark.

As the Royal Yacht *Victoria and Albert* headed out from Antwerp on the last stage of the journey, she was met by an escort of British ironclads. On board, Alix's brothers and sisters were excited. Her favourite, younger brother, Willy, who was a student at a Naval College, gazed at the mighty battleships around them, enormously impressed. Thyra had to be stopped from shouting and pointing. Alix stood silent and thoughtful at the bow, remembering the country she had left, where she felt safe and loved.

Minny came to her and hugged her. 'You know, I was afraid I was going to be jealous of you,' she confessed. 'But I'm not. Not since Papa told me that, now you're to marry Bertie, the Czar's eldest son has asked for me. Isn't it funny?' She laughed. 'I hope I'll be as happy as you are.'

Alix kissed her and said, 'I'm sure of it.'

'Do you really love him?' Minny asked.

'Very much.'

Minny could see that although she smiled, something was wrong. 'What's the matter?' she whispered.

Alix was looking at the sombre battleships on the grey sea. A storm threatened and all day the sky had been overcast. Now as evening fell, it was even darker and more ominous. She shivered. 'If only I knew—I think Bertie cares for me—if only I knew his people would love me, too.'

117

At that moment they were off Flushing. As the ironclads around them crossed out of Dutch waters, lights suddenly blazed on all the yardarms. Fireworks crackled and spluttered all along their sides, whirling Catherine wheels, geysers of dazzling, white sparks, Roman candles, cascades of green and red fire, and rockets soared upwards trailing meteors of spangled flame, to burst and pepper the dark sky with miniature, coloured stars. Alix and Minny gasped and held each other. Willy shouted and the rest of the family came running as the cheers of the sailors carrying their new princess home to England rang out, clear across the water.

Alix could not know of how the people of Britain felt about their Prince. They had toasted his birth, applauded his shy smile at the Great Exhibition, grumbled at his parents' attempt to turn him into a child professor, sympathised with his wish to join the army, admired his dignity and sorrow at his great father's funeral. Now he had found a bride, young and beautiful, not from one of the stuffy, arrogant, little German courts but a descendant of the Vikings, the old, free sea rovers who were part of their own blood. For over a year there had been no state occasions, no public sign of the Queen. She could keep her mourning. Now joy and spectacle were coming back, whether she approved or not. As Palmerston had said, they would not be cheated.

The storm made the yacht and its escort shelter for the night in Margate Roads but the next day was fair and calm and they sailed on up the Thames to Gravesend. All the way up the river they were surrounded by a flotilla of decorated small craft, paddle steamers, yachts, rowing boats, filled with people who waved and cheered. The guns of the floating batteries saluted them. When they anchored off the pier at Gravesend, more warships and the Lords of the Admiralty were there to greet them. In spite of Princess Christian's chiding, the younger children crowded the portholes of the state room, describing the vast crowds on the dock, the flags, the bands, the lines of soldiers in red and gold.

Alix wore her white dress. She stood listening to the cheers and the sound of the music outside. She had never heard, never imagined anything like it at home. She still held a rolled-up scroll, an address of welcome given her by the mayor of Margate that morning. On seeing her, he had been so overcome by the unexpected honour that he could only gabble parts of his prepared speech, bowing and jerking. Alix had been sympathetic and thanked him as the first of her new countrymen to welcome her to shore. After the mayor and his party left, Willy advanced towards her smiling.

"Highness . . . ," he stammered, imitating him. 'Most welcome—auspicious . . . Such an honour . . .' He bowed and Alix hit him on the head with the rolled parchment. She smiled, remembering.

Her father was standing by the door. 'Alix,' he said, 'It's time.'

He held the door open for her. She took a deep breath and stepped out on to the main deck. The huge shout which greeted her made her stand still, her heart pounding. Her eyes gave her a confused impression of rising tiers of people, hats, Danish flags, Union Jacks, handkerchiefs waving, bunting, uniforms, yardarms manned with sailors, but she could take nothing in. So many people, such cheering. 'For me?' she wondered. 'Is all this for me? . . .' Her mother's hand on her arm steadied her and she moved forward to the rail. She bowed her thanks and her smile captivated those who saw it forever.

Three times her mother led her out and then she went below to change into the gown she was to travel in, of mauve Irish poplin with a purple velvet mantle and a white bonnet edged with rosebuds. As she finished changing, she heard another great cheer from the crowds, then silence and the band playing the National Anthem.

Bertie's special train from Windsor was late and the press of people had delayed his carriage. He leapt from it, hurried up the gangplank of the *Victoria and Albert,* past the saluting officers and onto the main deck. He looked like a bridegroom already in his grey trousers and blue frock coat. The crowd was hushed, expectant.

Groups of dignitaries were waiting on the deck to present their addresses. Bertie strode through them as he saw Alix come from the door to the stateroom. He

119

stopped and they gazed at each other for a moment. In that moment he realised that he loved her, more than he could ever hope to tell, more than he would ever have believed possible. He threw his hat behind him, took her in his arms and kissed her. And neither of them heard the delirium on the quay, the applause and the cheering.

They left the pier on a carpet of strewn flowers and drove to the station under arches of orange blossom and bunting. On the journey to London, the train slowed at every station to give the waiting crowds a glimpse of Alexandra. The terminus was at the Bricklayers' Arms Station in Southwark, which had been elaborately decorated. There were banks of raised seats for distinguished guests and a royal welcoming party waited by the red carpet, led by the Duke of Cambridge, Crown Prince Frederick of Prussia and Duke Ernest of Saxe-Coburg. The people of London had declared a holiday and outside, the streets were nearly impassable. Nothing like it had ever been seen. The noise and cheering was tumultuous. Lines of top-hatted peelers struggled to hold back the throng while squadrons of Royal Horse Guards and Life Guards forced a passage for the procession of open carriages. Alix was dismayed at first and gripped Bertie's hand tightly. Then she saw that the crowds were good-natured and laughing as they struggled and that the horsemen were smiling. Fathers held babies above their heads. Young men had girls sitting on their shoulders, all laughing and waving.

She had always thought of the English as very reserved and formal. Now she saw the real people and realised why Bertie loved them. When she lost her shyness and raised her right hand to them and smiled, the answering roar startled the carriage-horses and the outriders had to strain to hold them.

There were flags everywhere, British and Danish, wreaths and mottoes. As the carriage in which they rode with Prince and Princess Christian came past, the crowd surged forward all along the route, to gasp and cheer as Alix and Bertie smiled and waved to them. Along the Borough High Street to London Bridge, where the parapets were topped with figures of all the Danish Kings. On each side of the approach to the bridge were statues of Danish warriors carrying the national flag and bronze tripods filled with burning incense. As she looked up, Alix saw masts with her country's standard again, ravens and gilt elephants with castles on their backs. At the other end of the bridge was a colossal arch, seventy feet high, with medallions of her and Bertie, and gilded plaster groups showing Britannia welcoming her to England.

Sometimes people were so near they tried to kiss her hand. The lines of soldiers from the Honourable Artillery Company and the London Rifle Brigade that marched with them kept being broken. A man was caught in the wheels of the carriage but was saved. So many bouquets were offered that the carriage was nearly filled. The most beautiful was the one given by the Lady Mayoress at the Mansion House. In the narrower streets of Cheapside and Ludgate Hill, the cavalry had to drive a wedge through the dense crowds. Twelve thousand were packed into St. Paul's churchyard alone. And on along Fleet Street to Old Temple Bar which was covered with cloth of gold, a statue of Hymen and more tripods of perfumed incense. There responsibility for the procession passed from the City to the Duke of Buccleuch, High Steward of Westminster.

All the church bells of London were ringing. School children sang on platforms, more addresses, official greetings, flowers, banners and garlands and the unending cheers. Along the Strand, past the clubs of Pall Mall to the colourful, more fashionable crowds of Piccadilly where the windows of all the mansions were filled. Flag-decked wooden galleries had been built and stops had to be made at Cambridge House for the Prime Minister and Lady Palmerston to be presented, as well as at the houses of the other leading nobles. Through Hyde Park where a giant muster of Volunteers passed in review, round thronged Marble Arch and up Edgware Road to the Great Western Railway Station at Paddington. The twenty minute journey from Southwark had taken nearly three and a half hours, and the special saloon train, which the Earl of Caithness insisted on driving, left almost at once, cutting short more speeches and greetings.

Bertie and Alix were nearly dazed. The smiling, waving and the noise had exhausted them, but they recovered in time to be met by Arthur and Leopold and Prince Louis of Hesse on behalf of the Queen. It was dark when they reached Windsor and raining heavily. Mercifully, it shortened the speech of the Mayor and the stop at Eton College. At last, the procession trundled up to the castle where lights shone in every window and the excited princesses were waiting.

Victoria sat in her boudoir, alone, gazing at a portrait of Albert on their wedding day. She had seen Alix briefly when she arrived and welcomed her. She had been flushed and lovely and Victoria did not grudge her her happiness but it reminded her cruelly of all that she had lost. She had heard of the joy and the enthusiasm. How could her people be so heartless, so thoughtless to rejoice while her sorrow was so great? Had they forgotten already? She thought of Bertie and Alix together and her thoughts became bitter.

She looked round at a light knock. The door opened and Alix came in, alone. She had not changed from her journey. She had sensed the Queen's bitterness and, in spite of her own happiness, pitied her suffering. She came to Victoria and knelt in front of her, looking up at her, sympathetic, trusting. Victoria caught her breath, then drew Alix to her, kissing her again and again, holding her close.

On the morning of the wedding, Victoria led Bertie and Alix to the new mausoleum at Frogmore where the Prince Consort's body was now buried. The mausoleum was shaped like a Greek cross, its pillars covered with mosaics and frescoes. Under the high dome, a white marble effigy of Prince Albert lay on a sarcophagus of dark grey granite, standing on a block of black marble. They knelt for a moment in prayer. It was cold, chill and silent in the mausoleum. Alix shivered and Bertie put his arm round her as they rose. Victoria turned.

She took Bertie's right and Alix' left hand and joined them together.

'HE gives you his blessing,' she said.

The marriage was held in St. George's Chapel, where Bertie had been christened and his father first buried. But on that day it was transformed into a blaze of pageantry and colour, with the vestments of the bishops and the gold communion plate on the altar, the hanging banners of the knights of the Garter, the rich greens, scarlets and blues of the uniforms and mauve and magenta silks and velvets of the ladies.

Bertie was supported by Fritz and Duke Ernest. He wore a general's uniform with the collar and purple robes of the Garter over it. Alix was in a gown of white satin covered with Honiton lace, trimmed with silver. The bodice was tight to the waist and the full skirt was garlanded with orange blossom and myrtle. Her train was of silver watered silk and her veil of white lace topped by a wreath of orange blossoms and a coronet of diamonds. Her bridesmaids wore white silk dresses gathered up with blush roses.

Victoria wore black mourning and her white widow's cap. She watched from Catherine of Aragon's closet, high on the left of the altar, a small, private balcony. Alix began the day excitedly, awake before anyone else. Her mother had coached her with Vicky's help so that she knew exactly what to do and how to behave, but the visit to the mausoleum had unnerved her. She felt, somehow, that it was wrong to be so happy and that the Queen would never forgive her if she showed it. Bertie had been wakened by Fritz with gruff, traditional jokes and had breakfasted with him and Uncle Ernest. His father's brother had always seemed to be distant and unyielding but he turned out to be a jocular man of the world with a surprisingly risqué humour. Bertie felt as if being married was giving him entrance to a new club where the male members relaxed and showed themselves as they really were. Then, like Alix, the mausoleum had shaken him and, like her, he was aware of his mother sitting up there watching them, motionless.

She did not intend any of them to forget that Albert should have been here. When the choir began to sing the chorale he had composed, 'This day, with joyful heart and voice, To Heaven be raised a Nation's prayer,' she withdrew from sight, weeping. A long sigh went through the congregation. Bertie could feel Alix tremble beside him. He could hear his sisters sobbing, although they hid their tears in their bouquets for his sake. He began to tremble but Fritz coughed reassuringly behind him and he braced himself.

Although the Queen meant to turn the service into another memorial to her husband, the sympathy of the guests was with the bridal couple. The Royal Family grieved and remembered but the guests enjoyed the spectacle, even though there was so little room that rival duchesses were crushed together and Mr. Disraeli, the Leader of the Opposition, had to sit on his wife's lap. The men envied Bertie. Alexandra was pale but her beauty was true and delicate. Nothing they had heard about her was exaggerated. The ladies approved of how the Queen, once she had revived, sat with her eyes raised to the departed spirit of Albert, envied Alexandra's complexion, criticised the bridesmaids and admired the little princes in their highland costume. They strained to hear the responses which the Prince and his bride spoke so quietly and nervously.

During the final benediction, the Queen was again overcome and buried her face in her handkerchief. She managed to recover when Bertie and Alix joined hands, turned to her and bowed. She nodded to them, smiling, and left her balcony. Still holding hands, Bertie and Alix led the slow procession of bridesmaids and family down the aisle. Only then did the guests see his pride and the radiance of his princess bride and their hearts went out to them.

Then the bells rang out and the thunder of the guns outside was drowned in the cheers. The other bells in the town answered St. George's and were picked up in the villages across the river and the towns and cities beyond, until all the churchbells in England were ringing.

They honeymooned at Osborne. The house had unhappy memories for Bertie and its formal rooms with their mementoes reminded them of the mausoleum, but their happiness transformed it. Alix was everything that Bertie had imagined. Her beauty kept surprising him and her artless innocence made him feel experienced and protective. At last he had found a girl of his own, someone to cherish.

Vicky and Fritz joined them for a few days and became their dearest friends. Even though they were Prussians, Alix loved them for arranging the meeting that had brought Bertie and her together. Vicky explained to her that they did not agree with their Chancellor Bismarck's aggressive policy to Denmark and she honoured Fritz all the more for defying his father and standing next to her at the wedding.

Bertie would not let them become serious. 'At least, by all accounts, he'll be pleased with my nephew,' he smiled.

Alix remembered the tight-faced little boy sitting between Arthur and Leopold. He had objected to being made to wear a kilt and been rude to Thyra when she wanted to play with him.

'My son, Wilhelm,' Vicky explained. 'He behaved very badly. He picked the jewel out of his dirk and threw it right across the chapel. And when Arthur tried to stop him, he bit him on the knee.'

'A real Prussian,' Fritz murmured and they laughed.

At night in bed, snuggled next to Bertie, Alix smiled, remembering. She ran her hand down his arm, feeling the muscles which she thought would crush her, but had been so gentle. She murmured as he sat up and leant out of bed. She twisted round to see what he was doing. He was lighting a cigarette at the top of the oil lamp on the bedside table. Cigarettes were a new discovery, less satisfying but more economical than cigars. They helped him to relax.

'Bertie . . . !' She was half laughing and half shocked. She knew his mother's strict disapproval of tobacco. 'You're smoking.' He nodded, smiling, and leant back against the satin pillows, embroidered with their initials, A.E.A. 'At Osborne? . . .'

'Why not? It's our home while we're here.' He put his arm round her and drew her close. 'It was bad enough having to bring you to this museum for our honeymoon.'

'I don't mind,' she whispered.

Her head was on his shoulder. He blew softly at the fine red-gold hairs that tickled his chin. 'I know you don't, my love.' He smiled. 'But I promise our new home will be everything this one is not.'

Marlborough House had been built first by Wren for the Duke and Duchess of Marlborough. The last person to live in it was the Dowager Queen Adelaide. It stood at the end of Pall Mall near St. James's Palace, in its own grounds, and it had been acquired for Bertie when he came of age. A third storey had been added and its decorations often altered since the days of Wren, but Alix loved the redbrick house and its secluded garden, their private apartments on the first floor, the white and gold reception rooms with panels of crimson silk, gold Chinese screens, ormulu cabinets, on the ground floor. On the west staircase were portraits of Marlborough at the battle of Ramillies, on the other the battle of Malplaquet.

Drawing rooms, sitting rooms, State and private dining rooms, dressing rooms and studies, over a hundred rooms and nearly twice as many servants just to look after her and Bertie. Alix wondered if could possibly afford it, until she found out that the Prince Consort's careful management of his son's estates had made Bertie a very rich man. As well as Marlborough House, they had Sandringham in the flat, bracing county of Norfolk. The grounds there were delightful and reminded her of Bernstorff, but the house was draughty and uncomfortable and Bertie was going to have it rebuilt. Then there was Abergeldie Castle in Scotland which was just as uncomfortable and too near Balmoral. Still, it was better than actually staying *there*.

Alix thought after their short honeymoon that they would live like her parents at home, quietly, seeing only a few friends, but Bertie was too proud of her. Fashionable London was agog to meet the Princess. Victoria and Albert had never been lavish with hospitality. They had given and attended few balls and, instead of evening Courts, held afternoon Drawing Rooms for scrupulously selected guests. Society was delighted when Bertie threw open Marlborough House to a series of receptions, dinners and parties. He wanted to show Alix off and everyone to love her as he did. He watched their reactions when they were introduced and questioned Lady Macclesfield, Alix's plump Lady-of-the-Bedchamber, about people's comments.

Palmerston was a frequent guest. He enjoyed his visits and admired the Princess. He occasionally wondered why he was invited so often, until one evening he found out. The Prince led him aside. He seemed faintly embarrassed. He asked the Prime Minister's help in approaching the Queen. She had not yet given him any official work and he felt, being married, over twenty-one and heir to the throne, that it was time he did something for his country. Palmerston could see he was sincere and it impressed him. He knew, better than anyone, that the Prince Consort's death had been a national calamity of far greater importance than the public imagined and that the Queen was far from able yet to cope with the vast load of Crown business by herself. Nothing could be more desirable than the Prince taking over some of her duties. He assured him that he had already discussed it with Her Majesty and would do so again.

Yet when he raised the subject at his next Audience, the Queen shook her head. She appreciated her son's desire to help her. She could see his wife's steadying influence in that. But it was too soon after his marriage.

She was more interested when Palmerston introduced the next subject, the future of Prince Alfred. Bertie's handsome younger brother had been ill in Malta and had missed the wedding. Now he was back from sea, she saw how he escaped as often as possible from Windsor to Marlborough House. He followed his new sister-in-law about like one of her puppies.

'Yes,' she said emphatically, 'He is far too taken with

Alexandra. The sooner he is sent back to sea again, the better.'

Palmerston was thrown. 'I was referring to the offer from Greece, Ma'am.'

Greece had recently won its freedom from Turkey and its parliament had decided to elect a king. Among the favourite choices were the aged Leopold of Belgium, Duke Ernest of Saxe-Coburg and Victoria's second son.

'Out of the question!' she said. 'Albert always intended him to succeed his Uncle Ernest as Duke of Saxe-Coburg.'

'Duke Ernest may accept Greece himself, if Prince Alfred refuses.'

The Queen was scandalised. She had very definite opinions on the qualities necessary for kingship. Despite being Albert's brother, Ernest had shown that he was morally suspect. 'He would not even consider it!'

'I assure you, Ma'am, he *is* considering it,' Palmerston told her. 'If they will let him keep Coburg, with Prince Alfred as Regent.'

'To be responsible for Ernest's debts and misgovernment? Never! You must put a stop to it, Lord Palmerston,' she insisted.

'The Major Powers are pledged not to support one candidate against the other,' he reminded her.

'Then you must find someone else! We do not see Affie as a king—and will not accept Ernest!'

In their favourite drawing room at Marlborough House, Bertie and Alix were giving an informal party for a few of their closest friends. Wally Paget was there, and Charlotte Knollys, the young daughter of Bertie's Comptroller. Rather a sticky filly, he thought, but Alix liked her. Some of the other ladies were much more attractive. The Duchess of Manchester, now. Louisa dressed to show that she was a woman. She could hardly deny it, with her reputation and the number of lovers she'd been credited with. Her figure was rather full and stately, but it gave a magnificent line to her bust and shoulders. He liked rather full women with shapely arms.

128

He was amused to see how many of them had taken to wearing Alix' hairstyle, the long lovelocks which the wits had called 'Follow-me-lads'. Affie was doing just that. His eyes followed Alix all round the room. He didn't object to his wife being admired, but thought Affie should make it a little less obvious.

They were standing with Palmerston, Charles Carrington and Alix's younger brother, Willy. He murmured, 'You should try it, Affie. Find yourself a wife.'

Affie rolled his eyes. 'Why does every newly married man want to see everyone else wearing the same ball and chain?' They laughed 'I'm quite happy in the navy.'

'You're in the navy, too, aren't you, sir?' Carrington asked Willy.

Willy nodded. 'I'm a naval cadet at Copenhagen.'

'Is that where your ambitions lie?' Palmerston asked.

Willy shrugged. 'I quite like it—except for the bookwork. As a younger son, I don't have much choice.'

'Poor old Willy,' Bertie said. He found his brother-in-law bright and amusing and was concerned for his future. He looked at the Prime Minister. 'Surely we could do something for him?'

Palmerston pretended to consider Willy. 'Well—the Hellenes have voted for a monarchy. How would you like to be King of Greece?' He smiled to show that he was joking.

'Very much,' Willy assured him. 'At least, I wouldn't have to sit any more exams.'

'Well, we'll see,' Palmerston murmured. They laughed, yet Bertie could tell that something had occurred to Palmerston. The old fox had that partly withdrawn look as though an idea was turning itself over in his mind.

Before he could take it any further, Alix came to them. One of the ladies-in-waiting was at the piano, playing a waltz. Alix spun in front of them so that her dress swirled. She laughed. 'Since none of you will take the hint, I'll have to make it more obvious. Who's going to dance with me?'

Affie bowed quickly. 'May I?'

Alix curtsied. 'How gallant, Affie.' She took his arm. As she led him away, she called back over her shoulder, 'Don't keep the other ladies waiting!'

Carrington and Willy followed her and Bertie was left with Palmerston. It was what he had been waiting for, but the Prime Minister disappointed him. The Queen would not agree to any definite employment for him. For the time being, she considered his first duty to his wife. Bertie knew it was useless to protest. He hoped, however, that he would at least be kept informed.

Palmerston hesitated. 'I cannot give you details of Cabinet business without Her Majesty's permission.'

Bertie stared at him. 'Am I only to learn what's happening in the country by reading the newspapers?'

Palmerston lowered his voice. 'I was speaking officially. Unofficially . . . I'll try to send you essential information. And I shall maintain a gentle pressure on the Queen.'

Bertie controlled himself. He admired Palmerston and was grateful to him. Behind them, the dancers were laughing. Willy had just found out from Wally Paget that the old gentleman with the intrusive false teeth to whom he had been talking was the great Pam, Pilgerstein to the Germans. He would not believe it until Alix confirmed it.

Palmerston was smiling, watching them. He regretted deeply that, at his age, even the ladies were pleasures of remembrance. 'I am glad your bride has been so enthusiastically received,' he said.

Bertie was happy to change the subject. 'People adore her. We have so many invitations, if we accepted them all, we'd have no time to ourselves.'

'It would be a sacrifice,' Palmerston acknowledged. 'But one I would welcome.' Bertie did not understand. 'As time goes by, there is a growing protest against Her Majesty's self-imposed seclusion. Part of the function of the monarchy is to be seen. To show interest and approval. People feel slighted—as if the Queen considers their needs unimportant compared to her private sorrow.'

'No one works harder than she!' Bertie objected. 'Don't they know that?'

'Who can know it, except her Ministers? I'm afraid the protests will grow louder. But you can help.' Bertie was intrigued and excited. Palmerston smiled. 'You and Her Royal Highness. You cannot deputise for the Queen, without her leave. But you can be seen—as often as possible. You are the natural leaders of society. You, and only you, can bring joy and vitality back into public life after these years of mourning.'

The season which followed, in which the Prince and Princess of Wales took their place as the leaders of society, without training, without experience, was the beginning of an era. Only those who had been alive at the time of Prinny and the Regency could remember anything like it.

Glittering receptions, lavish dinners and balls each one more elegant and more splendid than the one before. Through it all moved Bertie and Alix, applauded at the Royal Academy, cheered at Covent Garden, dancing the first quadrille at the Guildhall, handsome, beautiful and untiring. Even stern judges like Gladstone and Carlyle were captivated.

It was not only fashionable London who saw them. They travelled wherever there was need for them, to visit factories and sponsor charities, lay foundation stones of hospitals and Town Halls. They opened the Orphan Asylum at Slough and the Working Men's Industrial Exhibition, inaugurated Sailors' homes and raised money for the Royal Dramatic College. Bertie was given a Doctorate at Oxford and when Alix held a Drawing Room, so many ladies attended that the queue of carriages stretched from St. James's Palace to Harley Street. Race meetings, military reviews, schools and reformatories, the crowds followed them.

The people had wanted to see their Prince and his Princess. The more they saw, the more they wanted them. The murmurs against the Queen were silenced and when Bertie spoke of her care for her country and how his ambition was to follow in the footsteps of his beloved father, however far behind, they applauded and honoured him. There were those few who complained that they did too much, that royalty should be more distant and dignified but, when they criticised the Prince or his bride, they learnt to do it in private.

The climax of the season for Bertie, the chief event of the social year, was the Officers' Ball of the Brigade of Guards. They were proud that he was one of them and the reception they gave him was so warm and genuine that his Uncle George, Duke of Cambridge and Commander-in-Chief, muttered to him, 'I wish to God your father had seen this.' Alix was radiant in a pure white crinoline, with her coronet and necklace of diamonds. He had never seen her eyes so bright. At the end of the ball, the officers formed two lines facing inwards and held up their swords to make an arch. As Bertie waltzed down the room under the glittering arch of crossed swords, gazing into Alix's eyes, he felt that at last he had proved himself, he had become what he should be.

Palmerston agreed with him. He had watched with astonishment the development over these few months. He admired the Prince's poise and self-control, the dignity that could unbend but never be lost. He saw the emergence of a remarkable talent for handling people and winning them over. It could be invaluable in diplomacy. And he saw that, while the boy was no scholar, if he heard something complicated discussed, he understood the essentials at once.

It was with high hopes that he accompanied the Prince to Windsor to present his case. The Queen received them formally in the Blue Closet and he could see at once that things would go wrong. She had not invited them to sit. He reminded the Queen of her promise to find employment for the Prince of Wales, suitable to his standing and talents.

Victoria listened in silence. Her protuberant, blue eyes were fixed on Palmerston, unblinking, expressionless. 'Am I to believe my ears?' she asked after a pause.

Bertie smiled. 'It's quite simple, Mama.'

'His Royal Highness is asking for acknowledgement

of his worth and position, and recognition of the valuable work he has done in—'

Victoria sat up sharply. 'Work! Valuable? . . . What is valuable in this whirl of amusements?'

'In the past six months,' Palmerston explained, 'the Prince has attended banquets at the Royal Academy, the Guildhall and universities, amongst others. He has presided at charities, laid the foundation stones of hospitals and public buildings, received the freedom of the cities and—'

'And plunged headlong into society! Which his Father always kept at a distance—with good reason!' They could see now the Queen was furious. She turned on Bertie. 'You go about, begging for admiration, with no care for your position. And Alexandra is the same! I am very disappointed in her.'

'We have a duty—' Bertie began.

'You have a duty to *deny* yourself amusement, in order to keep up that moral tone in society which *used* to be the pride of England! The greatest danger to the country lies in the conduct of the Higher Classes.'

'They will take their tone from me,' Bertie assured her.

'And what are you?' Victoria's voice was contemptuous. 'Nothing but a puppet running about every night for show!'

Bertie could not believe that his mother did not understand. Everything he had done was in her service. He had to make her see. 'Not just for show,' he said quietly.

'I will not be contradicted!' Victoria snapped. 'You may go.' She looked away, dismissing him. Her nostrils were pinched and her lips thin and tight.

Bertie was too shaken and hurt to trust himself to speak. He glanced at Palmerston who was gazing at the Queen, bewildered by the suddenness and vehemence of her anger. He bowed shortly and left the room.

Palmerston heard the door shut behind him. He felt like a whipped schoolboy and did not appreciate it. Waiting for the Queen to speak, he wished he were in Downing Street or that he had had the courage to leave with the Prince. At last, the Queen spoke. Her voice was curt and reproachful.

'Am I to understand that you encouraged him, Lord Palmerston? We did not expect this of you.'

Palmerston cleared his throat. 'Perhaps His Royal Highness's motives have been misinterpreted to you, Ma'am.' Victoria turned her head towards him. 'There are occasions when the presence of a member of the Royal Family is essential. In your continued absence from London—'

'Not again!' Victoria interrupted fretfully. 'I have told you—my nerves will not allow me to appear in public. And this behaviour of my son's only makes me more sick and anxious.'

'These are troubled times,' Palmerston pointed out. 'The popularity of the Prince and Princess is of great value.'

Victoria bridled. 'The country *never* was so loyal or so devoted to their Sovereign as now.'

Palmerston could see he had touched her on the raw. Surely she had heard of the protests, the shouts of Republicanism which the Prince had now silenced? But he must tread carefully. 'Still, the Prince of Wales, as your representative—'

'He is not!' Victoria broke in, infuriated. 'He does not represent me in public. That is a position to which he is not entitled! No one can represent the Sovereign but herself, or her Consort.' Her face was contorted, her eyes glaring. Palmerston had once found Prince Albert shaking after one of his wife's rages but had never experienced it himself. He almost took a step back as her voice stabbed at him again. 'He must not be regarded in that light! And how dare you suggest that he should preside at any of those Societies or Commissions in which his beloved and great father took so prominent a part?'

Palmerston was incredulous. 'He is your son, Ma'am.'

'And nothing else,' Victoria shrilled, 'unless we choose to appoint him! He will never stand beside me in his father's place! No one—no one will ever stand beside me again.'

Her voice faltered and she shivered as if cold. Palmerston realised that she was no longer seeing him. He had never believed stories of the Queen's instability before and was alarmed. Her eyes were flickering and her hands clenched and unclenched. She began to mutter to herself, then more loudly.

'Each day I feel that lost more deeply, oh, more deeply. Even the dear Baron is gone. And Uncle Leopold dying . . . All the best are taken. What will become of my poor country when I am dead? . . . And Bertie—and his wife!—are brought forward more and more.' Her voice was vicious in its jealousy. 'People cry out for them. They are not my representatives! They have not the right. You will not let them compete for popularity with *me!*'

When Bertie returned to Marlborough House, Alix could see that he was distressed and angry at his mother's treatment of him. It was quite different from what he had expected. She had sounded wild, as if she did not know what she was saying.

Alix was unhappy for him and tried to comfort him. She drew him down on to the couch beside her. 'That's it, my darling. She didn't really mean it.'

'Then why would she say it?'

'She is lost and lonely. And feels that no one loves her any more.' Bertie shook his head. Alix had thought about their relationship with the Queen. Her own father had to be careful in Denmark. 'Perhaps she is even afraid that, if people get to like you too much, they won't want her,' she suggested.

Bertie looked at her. It had genuinely never occurred to him and he did not believe it. 'How could she? She is the Queen.'

'Of course,' Alix said gently, and smiled. 'You mustn't worry. She will realise in time that she needs you.'

Bertie nodded. He did not have much confidence in his mother changing her mind.

'We mustn't let it spoil everything,' Alix said. 'It's been such a wonderful year. Our marriage—and Willy becoming King of Greece. Who'd have believed that six months ago?'

'Certainly not Willy,' Bertie said. Alix laughed and kissed his cheek.

He smiled slightly and rose, crossing towards the open door to the garden. He stopped, looking out at the table where he had sat with Palmerston before leaving for Windsor. He had been able to help Willy. He seemed able to help everyone but himself. Behind him, he heard Alix speaking.

'And we, ourselves, have something wonderful to look forward to.' He nodded, only half hearing. 'You're going to be a father.'

Alix had whispered and it took a moment for him to realise what she had said. He turned slowly. She was smiling to him, hesitant.

'You mean, you—you're—?'

'Yes,' Alix said. She did not understand. Bertie looked completely dismayed. 'Is something wrong?

'I-I've only just got used to being a husband,' he stammered.

Alix laughed and he moved back to her. He sat again beside her. 'Alix—are you sure?'

'Very sure,' she told him.

'But when—when will it be?'

She smiled. 'Oh, not for a long time yet. I've only just found out.'

He put his hands out to hold her, but touched her very gently as if she might break. She smiled to him and he laughed back, all at once feeling lightheaded and foolish and very young.

Chapter
9

Lord Granville, President of the Council, was a punctilious and dignified man. As one of the few friends of the Prince Consort, the Government asked him to approach the Queen again.

'We have to accept her seclusion,' he reported. 'If we try to force her, she is afraid for her reason. She will fulfill all the deskwork but none of the public functions. Nor will she let the Prince of Wales deputise for her.'

There was a silence in the dark, panelled Cabinet Room. The Prime Minister as usual, sat at the centre of the long table with his back to the fire, other senior Ministers spread out round him.

Gladstone's fingers drummed on the polished table. 'She must change her mind,' he declared.

Palmerston sighed. 'Easier said, Mr. Gladstone. I'll give you a hint, for when you have to deal with her. She's taken to using the royal 'We', 'Us', 'Our', at times—to show she is speaking both for herself and her late husband. When she says 'We', her opinions are not to be changed.'

'If the Queen appears to be in retirement and the Prince obviously unemployed, Disraeli will use it as a stick to beat us with,' Gladstone complained.

'He'll be too taken up with our losses from the cotton famine in the North,' Russell said. 'Conditions there are very bad. Most of our cotton came from the Southern Confederate States of America.'

Palmerston nodded. The Confederates had surrendered Vicksburg to General Grant and lost the battle of Gettysburg. It was not only a question of how long they could hold out. Gallantry was not enough after all.

'They could not survive without our support.' He paused. 'The question is now—can Denmark?'

Some of the people round the table were surprised 'It's not so serious, surely?' Gladstone asked.

'It soon may be.'

'Bismarck and King Wilhelm want a united Germany under the leadership of Prussia,' Russell explained. 'They have spent years building up their army, and now they need a quick and easy success to demonstrate its effectiveness. They have found it in the Danish provinces of Schleswig and Holstein.'

But he and Palmerston knew that the problem was much more involved, and had become dangerous for Britain. The death of fat King Frederick had brought Princess Alexandra's father to the Danish throne sooner than anyone had expected and the new King Christian was faced with a hopeless war. It was a pygmy against an armoured elephant. There was no question where British sympathy lay and, with the enormous popularity of the Princess, people were now clamouring for the Government to take sides with Denmark. Yet the Government knew that if they went to war with Prussia it would involve the rest of the German states and Austria, perhaps France, probably even the Russians. All because of two unimportant, sleepy little provinces.

'Prussia claims them,' Palmerston said. 'They only belong to Denmark to treaty, by agreement. They've been squabbling for years. Holstein's half German, Schleswig is nearly all Danish. It's a complicated situation.'

'Does anyone knew the rights of it?' Granville asked.

Palmerston pouted his lips. 'Only three people ever really understood the Schleswig-Holstein question. One was a German Professor—and he's gone mad. Another was the Prince Consort—and he's dead. The third was myself—and I've forgotten all about it.'

A ripple of laughter went round the table. Even Gladstone smiled.

'Still, we must decide out position,' Palmerston added. 'Before long, armies will be marching across Europe.'

Bertie was glad to get Alix away from Osborne after the Christmas holiday. The baby was not due for another three months but her pregnancy had not been easy. His mother blamed him for letting her run about too much, dancing and joining in games. She could not understand that if they were invited to a party, Alix would just not stay at home. She wanted to be with him.

Then there was all the excitement over her father's coronation and the demands from Prussia. Alix was violently, blindly patriotic. She was normally so cool and self-possessed, he had never imagined her capable of such anger. She had even tackled the Queen, asking her to intervene. Mama had been surprisingly sympathetic, but firm. The memoranda laid down a belief in a strong Germany and in British neutrality. She would not deviate from that.

What made it worse was that the whole family had met in December on the anniversary of the Prince Consort's death, to honour his memory. The arguments began at once. As a Prussian, it was natural for Fritz to support his own country, but to hear Vicky preaching that Germany must be allowed to achieve its destiny in Europe, trying to rationalise illegal policies, had been horrifying. Fritz and Vicky had been their dearest friends. Now they could not see that to threaten a country one tenth the size of theirs was despicable. The argument had risen to such a pitch, with everyone inevitably taking sides, that the Queen had turned on all of them, forbidding any further mention of the matter. She had been sharp with Vicky for seeming to justify war and reminded Alix that she was no longer Danish.

'Your country is now England. There was no political treaty included in your marriage,' she declared.

Alix had to submit but, as the pressure mounted on her father's small country, she became desperate.

She looked much better after a few days at Frogmore almost alone with Bertie. Lady Macclesfield had been anxious about her, thinking she looked haggard and wan. It was hard to credit that she was going to be a mother, the baby scarcely showed at all. She was alarmed when the Princess went to watch the skating on the pond but the Prince overruled her. It was good to see Alix smile again, pink-cheeked and her eyes shining after a few swift turns in the sledge. They gave a boisterous seasonal party for all the local children.

At last it was more like Christmas. It had been strained and difficult at Windsor, and gloomy at Osborne. Now in this comfortable old house, with crisp snow outside and the ponds frozen, they could begin to enjoy themselves. Alix knew that she bored him with her constant talk of Denmark and tried to keep her feelings to herself. She knew he sympathised with her, but he had learnt to accept what he could not alter. That was his way, but not hers. She would never accept the injustice done to her father's country, as she must call it now. Yet she hid her distress for Bertie's sake.

She would have been quite happy to stay quietly in Frogmore House during the day with Lady Mac but Bertie was impatient at being indoors. He and some of his gentlemen got up an ice hockey team and played five and seven-a-sides every afternoon. It absorbed him like everything else he took up, eating, politics, dancing, making love. Alix encouraged him and went to watch although it tired her.

One day, early in January, they were playing at Virginia Water. Alix bumped over to see him in a high-backed, horsedrawn sleigh. Lady Mac kept telling the footmen at the reins to drive slower, but Alix liked the rush of the fresh, cold air and the jingle of the bells. She was warmly wrapped in rugs. Bertie was happy to see her and, because she was missing the fun, took her out on the ice in a chair-sledge and raced her round the pond until they were both breathless. Lady Mac hurried to them, scolding in her concern. Alix laughed and protested, yet all the same she suddenly felt exhausted and, as Bertie pushed her to the edge, a twinge of pain nearly made her cry out.

Lady Mac saw her fingers clutch at the tartan rug and bent over her, solicitous. Alix shook her head and smiled. 'It's nothing, Mac,' she assured her. 'I'm fine.'

Lady Macclesfield insisted on taking her back to Frogmore, although Bertie was disappointed that she would miss the game. He kissed Alix and told her he would return in time for dinner. She watched him as he skated out on to the ice, driving the wooden chuck ahead with his stick and chasing after it to warm up. With his stockings rolled over his Tweed breeches and his short jacket, cap and scarf, he looked almost like a schoolboy. With all a boy's vigour and energy. Alix felt another stab of pain, more severe, and held herself tightly with both hands. Lady Macclesfield nodded to the footman and they set off for home.

By the time they reached Frogmore, it was growing dark and Alix's pains were more frequent. Lady Mac and the footman helped her through the dressing room into her bedroom. She was clinging to them.

'Fetch the nearest doctor—don't matter who,' Lady Mac told the footman. 'And get word to the Prince.'

The footman hurried out and Lady Mac sat Alix on the bed. The pain lessened as she sat and let her breathe more easily. Such pain was new to her, a cruel wrenching as if a hand squeezed her abdomen.

'What is it, Mac?' she gasped.

'Your time has come, I think. A little sooner than we expected.' Lady Mac said. Alix looked up at her, worried. It was far too soon. Lady Mac laid her back against the pillows. 'There, now. Nothing to worry about. I've had thirteen so I should know.' She smiled and Alix was reassured. Holding the older woman's hand, she relaxed and closed her eyes.

Watching her, Lady Mac felt far less confident than she appeared. The poor child looked so young and frail, and Heaven knew what complications there might be with the baby coming so much before its time. They had really been caught napping, with nothing prepared. Alix whimpered and Lady Mac patted her hand, soothing. She took stock of the situation. The royal doctors and obstetricians would have to be sent for but she could not be certain how soon they would get here. There was no nurse. She would have to get someone to sit with the Princess while she did some shopping.

Old Dr. Brown, a general practitioner in Windsor, galloped over as soon as the footman brought his message.

Lady Macclesfield had herself driven to the nearest draper's shop and brought yards of various quality flannel and rolls of cottonwool wadding. When Bertie hurried in from Virginia Water, he found her in the dressing room improvising a cradle out of a wicker basket, the flannel and cottonwood. By chance, Lord Granville had come to watch the ice hockey and he brought him with him. They were alarmed and anxious. The servant sent to fetch the Prince had not dared to interrupt till the end of the game.

Bertie went into the bedroom. The lamps were lit and Alix was in bed. He saw Dr. Brown, whom he knew, a stocky, competent man, standing beside her, sponging her forehead. She was clutching his arm.

Brown released her hand and laid it down. 'Now, you relax, Ma'am,' he told her. As he turned, he noticed Bertie and bowed.

Alix had seen him, too. She held out her arms. 'Bertie—' He hurried to her and his fingers gripped hers. He saw the pain in her eyes, although she smiled. She would not let him apologise for leaving her so long and he kissed her hands as they suddenly tightened, her fingers digging into his palms. The contractions were coming one after another.

Lady Macclesfield brought in the cradle and stood it on a table near the bed. He watched her as she moved to the fire and turned a large iron kettle that was steaming on the hob. Dr. Brown took instruments from his bag and placed them in a tin basin. He tried to set them down carefully but the tin scrape of the metal was frightening in the silence. Alix gasped again, biting her lip. Bertie felt guilty and useless. He wanted to relieve her pain, but there was no way. He looked at the quiet doctor who was half turned from them, timing the contractions by his watch.

'Is there anything I can do?'

Brown shook his head. 'I don't think so, sir.'

Bertie murmured to Alix telling her how brave she was, how well she was doing. Her lips were dry. The fire had been built up high and, with the heat and the pains, her neck and forehead were beaded with sweat.

He freed one of his hands and used the sponge to wipe her face. She smiled her thanks.

'It's too soon,' she whispered. 'Too soon . . .'

Bertie was aware of the risks and the danger, but he had to reassure her. 'No, no. It often happens.'

He glanced at Dr. Brown for confirmation. The doctor nodded. 'Oh, quite often.'

Alix pulled on his hand. 'No, I meant—you always scold me for being late.' She managed to smile and he realised that she had seen his nervousness and was trying to reassure *him*. He leant down and kissed her hot cheek. He had to close his eyes because he was afraid she would see how close he was to tears.

'With your permission, sir,' Dr. Brown said. He was taking off his coat.

Lord Granville waited anxiously in the dressing room. He desperately hoped that some other officials would arrive to share the responsibility which had been forced on him. He tried to frame some suitable words in the event of the worst happening, something comforting and well-chosen, but for once he could not organise his mind. He turned quickly as Bertie came out of the bedroom.

Bertie closed the door. 'They've just sent me out for a moment,' he explained. Away from Alix, he could let his concern show. He could see that he had been thoughtless. His mother was right, he was irresponsible and selfish.

'You mustn't blame yourself, sir,' Granville said.

Bertie moved from the door. 'I should have taken more care of her. They warned me she wasn't strong. And here we are—nothing ready.' There was no sign of the royal physicians, nor of the Home Secretary who had to be present at the birth. 'You'll have to witness it, Granville. Whatever happens.'

The words created their own pause. Granville bowed. 'Of course, sir.' He thought of the news he had brought to Virginia Waters. 'Have you told Her Royal Highness that the Prussian Army is on the Danish border?'

Bertie shook his head. 'She mustn't know. Not yet.'

Granville was relieved. Bertie sat on a chair beside the bedroom door. He felt unsteady and rested his head on his clasped hands. He had a vision of life without Alix and how empty it would be. They shared everything, all their hopes and pleasures. She was always alive, always eager for life like he was, the only person whose energy matched his, until this last month. He realised she might lose the baby, but he did not care about anything as long as she was saved. A cry, louder than the other, brought him to his feet and he hurried into the bedroom.

He was just in time to see the birth. From the door, Granville watched as Dr. Brown laid the tiny baby in a swaddling cloth made out of one of Lady Macclesfield's petticoats.

The doctor examined it, turned to the Prince and bowed. 'Both well, sir. Weight's just over three pounds, I'd say, but I believe it will live.' He smiled. 'And may I be the first to congratulate you? It's a boy.'

Lady Mac washed the baby's face and head. She brought it to Alix and placed it, wrapped in the petticoat, in the crook of her arm. It was very red, but its features were perfectly formed and it had a fine crown of hair. Bertie moved closer. All the strain had gone from Alix's face. Her skin seemed filled with light and, when she looked from baby to him, her smile grateful, loving and proud.

Bertie hardly knew how to thank the doctor and Lady Mac. He would not let himself think what might have happened without them. They assured him that the Princess had done all the work and that she was lucky to have had such a short confinement. When the royal doctors and the Home Secretary arrived two hours later, astounded to find that it was all over, Lady Mac would only allow them the shortest of examinations. The Princess must be permitted to rest.

When they had drunk the health of the new heir and gone, Bertie sneaked back in to Alix's room. She had been waiting for him. The baby was encased, all but its head, in layers of cottonwool. He lifted it very carefully from its basket and laid it by Alix. He knelt beside her and smiled to see her so happy. She was gazing at the baby, marvelling at it.

She eased the cottonwool down further from its face. 'Look, Bertie—,' she whispered. 'Our son.'

Victoria was extremely displeased to have missed the birth. It was her right to be present at the delivery of an heir and the whole proceedings had been most irregular. She travelled up at once from Osborne, but was so enchanted with her grandson that she forgave Bertie and Alix at once, although she warned them that it must not happen again without proper precautions. She objected to the names they were considering and it was finally agreed that he should be christened Albert Victor Christian Edward. The Queen happily called him Albert Victor, but at home he was always known as Eddy.

Apart from the delight in her son, it was a sad spring and summer for Alix. Prussia and Austria attacked Denmark and, although the little Danish army held out with incredible bravery for over five months, the end was never in question. By the summer, her father had lost half his country. Her recovery after the birth was affected and news of her suffering made the British people violently anti-Prussian. Bertie had tried to be unbiased for the sake of his family, but he could see, as his father had not, that Prussia would not be satisfied with being chief of the German states. She would absorb them and then seek to dominate Europe. The Prince Consort's memoranda flatly contradicted him and the Queen would not listen. Nor would the Government involve itself in a foreign war. Every effort he made to help Denmark was blocked.

The Queen believed that the Austrian Empire of Franz Josef would be a restraining, civilizing influence on the more aggressive Prussia. She was shocked when they divided Schleswig and Holstein between them. It was as if Austria had been hired by Bismarck. It made her change her attitude slightly and she began to think for herself. The memoranda had to be revised in the light of new events and, by understanding more, she began

145

to have more influence and even to enjoy the problems of statecraft. That was the time she might have drawn the Prince of Wales more into her confidence, but his attempts to affect policy on Denmark alarmed her and she was still angry with him for visiting Garibaldi when he came to London. Garibaldi's struggle was to free Italy from Austria to create a united country, and Bertie honoured him as a patriot. To the Queen he was a revolutionary. The situation was not helped by the public approving loudly of the Prince's gesture. She was very reluctant to allow Bertie and Alix to visit Copenhagen with their son. Bertie protested that Alix was entitled to let her parents see their grandson and she gave in, on condition that they travelled incognito, so as not to show too great a sympathy for Denmark, and that they visited their Prussian relations on the way home.

They were welcomed enthusiastically by the Danes, who had heard of Bertie's stand on their behalf. Danish losses in the war had been terrible but all was forgotten for a time at Alexandra's homecoming. Alix was overjoyed to be there for Minny's betrothal to the Czarevitch Nicholas of Russia. The actual ceremony they had to miss on Victoria's orders and had to move to Stockholm where, to her fury, they stayed at the King's palace instead of in a hotel. Bertie had realised that, if he wanted to achieve anything, he would have to make his own contacts. He could only do that by evolving a technique of treating his mother's commands as suggestions whenever they conflicted with his interests, and then explaining afterwards.

He had lost his political innocence. Denmark's cause seemed so just that he had assumed that everyone would naturally defend her. The bias of the Queen and the fumbling of the Government bewildered him, and the cheers for him in Copenhagen made him feel guilty because he knew how little he had been able to do. Without the backing of the Queen he was impotent. The bitterness became stronger when they met Vicky and Fritz at Cologne. Fritz wore uniform and a medal ribbon for the victory over Denmark. His final disillusionment came when he heard that Prince Gorchakov had been reported as saying to the British Ambassador to Russia, 'Well, Excellency, I discount the possibility that England could ever make war on a matter of honour.'

When he returned to London, he made peace with his mother and resumed leadership of society. Here, at least, no one could deny his right to lead. With Alexandra, he created his own empire. His tastes were its laws and an invitation to Marlborough House was the highest accolade. The clothes that Alix and he wore became fashion. After Eddy's birth, Alix began to wear her hair up, braided and looped at the back. Fashionable ladies followed her. She had a small mark on her neck, a scar left by a feverish cold when she was a girl. With her hair up, she chose highnecked dresses and, in the evenings, a velvet or jewelled collar to disguise it and the 'Alexandra choker' became essential evening wear for every well-dressed woman. Bertie developed a style of correct dress for every occasion. It was an elaborate game but one had to follow its rules to be accepted.

The Season had existed before, but under Bertie it became a ritual. There was a correct time to shoot, a correct time to go sailing or to the races, a time to be in the country and a time to go abroad. He accepted most public engagements as his duty, otherwise he expected to be entertained and stayed no longer than he found the pastime or the company amusing. He chose his friends for their wit and high spirits, friends like Carrington, for their lavish hospitality, like Christopher Sykes and the Duke of Sutherland, for their sportsmanship, like Henry Chaplin and Sir Frederick Johnstone whom he had met hunting at Oxford. Others like the three-times-married Duchess of Manchester and her lover Lord Hartington, Harty Tarty, were simply good company. In London, Alix and he were indefatigable. Their life was a whirl of parties and balls, theatres and receptions. It needed enormous stamina to keep up with them, and when Alix fell out through her second pregnancy, Bertie continued alone. With his friends he visited the music halls and discreet houses of pleasure, the cock-fights in dockland, played baccarat and bowls and, when the clubs closed, brought them home for cigars and whist till dawn. In less than a year he was known as 'The First Gentleman of Europe'.

While the public and most of the fashionable world admired him, there were some who complained of his frivolity and extravagance. Others said that he was lowering himself and his position. There were a few who felt that his way of life was a substitute for the work which had been denied him and regretted that his tireless energy was wasted. There were fewer who saw that amongst his friends were financiers like Natty Rothschild and his brothers, politicians like Dilke and Roseberry, and that amongst his guest were Gladstone, the leading Liberal when Palmerston died, and the brilliant Tory Disraeli. They did not think it strange that foreign diplomats began to visit Marlborough House to discuss their problems informally with the Prince. He had made one last attempt to be granted a key to the despatch boxes so that he could learn the business of his country. The Queen had refused. She would not trust his discretion. He had devised his own means of gathering information and the diplomats began to realise that a hint dropped at one of the Prince's parties would be passed on quickly to where it would do most good with no political strings attached. It was laborious and uncertain, often frustrating, but it was the only way left for Bertie to work.

Again, the Queen was not pleased by the premature birth of her second grandson, George. Again she was not present.

The birth marked a turning point in Bertie and Alix's lives. Up till then, he had not thought of going anywhere without her, apart from short visits to clubs and music halls and diversions to which one did not take ladies. A few weeks before the birth he went alone on a state visit to Ireland to open the Dublin International Exhibition. It was very successful and, although he missed her, he found that he enjoyed himself. For some months she was occupied with the new baby and in mourning for Minny's betrothed, the Czarevitch Nicholas, who had died suddenly of tuberculosis. Minny's heart was not broken long for the engagement was transferred to the Czar's second son, Alexander, the next Czarevitch. However, Alix had time to discover that she liked being a mother staying at home with her children.

Bertie loved her dearly, although her unpunctuality and lack of organisation exasperated him. She was late at their wedding and she was late for something nearly every day. He rose early, read his mail, went for a walk in St James's Park and was back for a second breakfast before nine. Alix rose about eleven. They still went to house parties and the theatre and spent their holidays together at Sandringham and Abergeldie for the shooting but, gradually, Bertie began to do more and accept more invitations on his own. He was still faithful to her, as Alix never doubted that he would be, yet he began to regard her more as a companion and the mother of his children than as a lover. It became increasingly difficult to resist temptation when flirtation could easily become seduction, when wives and daughters of nearly everyone he met fell in love with him and the fashionable cocottes made their availability very clear. But he loved Alix and was painfully aware of the dangers of scandal and disease.

The Queen disapproved strongly of Bertie's new mode of life, and of the character and reputation of many of his friends. Albert had never been to a music hall, they had never dined in a restaurant and visited only three or four of the leading aristocratic houses in a year. Not always so many. She censured him for not choosing his friends more wisely, for making himself too accessible, for overspending and leading a life of pleasure. The remedy was in her hands but she could not see it. Bertie loved and honoured her, yet he would not let her dictate how he and Alix should live, nor whom they should meet. She disliked most his racing and his Jewish friends. On the one hand she was afraid he would get into debt through gambling and, on the other, she heard the shocked condemnation of the old elite. Jews were not accepted, unless they were Christianised like Disraeli and even that was hard-won. The Queen loathed prejudice in any form, against race, colour or religion. She thought it best, however, to avoid embarrassing situations.

Once, when one of her ladies-in-waiting had recently become a widow and sobbed that all both of them could look forward to now was meeting their husbands again with Abraham, Victoria considered for a moment and said emphatically, 'I shall not receive Abraham.'

Bertie was totally unprejudiced. He sensed the rising tide of democracy, and he welcomed it. His father had hoped for a future where an educated working class took its share with the professional, merchant classes, a responsible aristocracy and ruler in running the country. Bertie did not believe in miracles, but he honoured any man who had proved himself, whatever his trade or profession, position or race. He even envied them.

Although he frequently disagreed with his mother, he avoided any outright clash with her again. If he could not change her mind, he saw it as his duty to obey her enough to satisfy her. His developing gift for diplomacy was useful, yet there were times when it stretched to breaking point.

One occasion was Princess Helena's marriage. The Queen believed that her daughters should be allowed to find happiness in marriage, but she was reluctant to let Lenchen go. She had become very useful as a confidante and an unofficial personal secretary. Eventually, she gave her permission, provided that a suitable German prince could be found who was prepared to live in England. The choice angered Bertie as a direct insult to Alix. Less than a year after her father had been defeated, the man chosen for Lenchen was a younger son of the family who had claimed the two provinces and begun the war. They discussed it heatedly with Affie.

Alix was also concerned for her sister-in-law. 'This marriage is wrong! Not only politically,' she assured them. 'Lenchen is a sweet girl, the kindest of your sisters. And she is being forced to marry a man she does not love. She told me, herself! He's old enough to be her father. Dull and stupid. Is that the husband you want for her?'

Bertie knew this Prince Frederick Christian 'of Schleswig-Holstein'. He was middle aged, one-eyed, half bald and slow-witted. He and Affie protested to the Queen; Alice wrote from Hesse. Their mother refused to reconsider. Finally, Bertie made up his mind to go to Windsor, to discover his sister's real feelings and, if necessary, to tackle the Queen, himself.

He found Lenchen playing the piano in the private sitting room. At nineteen, she was plain, serious and intelligent. 'I always thought I'd be the one to stay at home,' she confessed. 'When Mama told me I was to marry, I couldn't believe it. I would be free. Then when I met him . . . He was so different from what I imagined, I cried myself to sleep every night.'

The way she spoke, her resignation, upset Bertie. It reminded him of Alice. 'I'll speak to Mama,' he promised her. 'No one can force you.'

Lenchen had stopped playing. Her head was lowered 'Don't you see? They don't have to.' She was almost whispering. 'I have no illusions. No one would choose me just for myself. This is my one chance. If I refuse it—' She looked up at him, pleading for understanding.

He envisaged her life, and knew that she could see it, too. She was not like Alice. She was escaping. He put out his hand and she held it tightly, loving him. They broke apart as the door from the study opened. It was John Brown. Victoria had brought him down from Scotland to look after her ponies, as a link with the past and with Balmoral. She was so pleased with his blunt honesty and devotion to her that he was soon promoted to Personal Attendant. He wore his indoor dress of kilt, dark jacket and waistcoat.

He nodded to Bertie. 'Oh, you're in here. I'll tell the Queen.'

'Thank you, Brown,' Bertie said stiffly.

'Will you be wanting tea?' Bertie shook his head. 'Good. She's just had hers.'

Bertie watched as Brown left without any more ceremony, leaving the door to the study open. The tall Scot with his fringed beard, direct speech and manners, irritated him. 'I do not like that man,' he said.

Lenchen had risen. She glanced quickly, warningly,

at the open door. 'Mama feels safe with him here. Papa trusted him.' She moved to the door to the corridor. Victoria did not allow her unmarried daughters to be alone with a man, even their brothers. 'She mustn't find us here. Thank you, Bertie.'

Left by himself, Bertie was nervous. Recently he had opposed the Queen. Now he understood how Lenchen felt, there was little he could say. He would have to withdraw his objections to the marriage. His mother would think he was yielding to her will. Well, that wouldn't hurt.

He bowed as she limped in on Brown's arm. She had put on weight and begun to have attacks of rheumatism, but at least she had come out of the eternal black. She still wore 'her sad cap' as Baby called it but had changed into the other permissible mourning dress, deep purple with a frill of white at the neck and cuffs.

'How nice to see you,' she said. Bertie kissed her cheek when Brown had gone out. Victoria's eyes peered suspiciously round the room. 'My good Brown told me Lenchen was with you. You haven't been filling her head with nonsense?'

Bertie helped her to the sofa. He made himself smile. 'No. She was telling me how happy she is.'

Victoria settled herself and panted, pleased. 'Splendid! She's such a sensible girl. Besides, she understands the reasons for her marriage.'

'I wish I did,' Bertie said carefully. 'Alix is very hurt by it.'

Victoria's head jerked in annoyance. 'Your wife is delightful, yet she has not learnt to keep her duty to me and her private feelings separate.'

'She tried to do so, Mama,' he told her. 'She is not alone in thinking the marriage has only been arranged to buy favour with Germany.'

Victoria's mouth pursed angrily, but she forced herself to be patient. Her nerves would not stand excitement and she realised Bertie had been led astray by Alix and her relatives. He did not have the mind or character to resist.

'Fritz will one day be King of Prussia, with your sister

Vicky as his Queen,' she explained as if to a child. 'They are working to liberalise their country—as your dear father wished. Alice and her husband are pledged to help them. With Lenchen married to a third German prince, their power will be greatly strengthened.' It was the old argument, although Bertie suspected that his father would have revised his opinions if he were still alive. Victoria sighed. 'Try to remember that you are not only the son-in-law of the King of Denmark. You don't know the problems of foreign policy.'

'How can I? I've been given no chance to learn,' Bertie protested. He could see the Queen bridling, but went on. 'How can I serve you and the country properly? I cannot even talk to people seriously because they would find out within minutes that I know less than any clerk in the Government!'

He was so tense and sincere, Victoria felt herself grow sorry for him. His intentions were good, yet she remembered Albert saying he could never keep them up. She could not trust him until he proved he could be discreet. 'I realise it is difficult,' she said more gently. 'I shall consider it.'

His suspicion of Prussia was confirmed, to Victoria's horror, when Bismarck picked a quarrel with Austria over the division of Schleswig and Holstein, invaded Saxony and forced Franz Josef to declare war. Victoria begged the Prussians to stop before it was too late, but it was part of a deliberate, long-planned policy and the cumbersome, old-fashioned army of the Austrian Empire had no chance against the ruthlessly efficient machine developed by Bismarck. It was hideously complicated for the family as they had relatives on both sides. Fritz was a general in the Prussian Army and Uncle Ernest commanded a battalion. Among those in the German states allied to Austria were Victoria's cousin, the King of Hanover, Louis of Hesse-Darmstadt and Princess Alice.

In seven weeks, Austria was humiliated. As she had wanted all along, Prussia took both Schleswig and Holstein, annexed the states which had resisted and allowed

Austria to exist only as an obvious satellite with reduced territory. Two days after the last battle, Lenchen married Prince Frederick Christian whose family was now ruined. The Queen deplored bloodshed, yet welcomed the new power of Prussia. It was not the way Albert had wished it, but it was a step towards a united Germany.

She could not refuse when Bertie asked to go to St. Petersburg for Minny's wedding. The Government were in favour of it as the Czar was anxious for better relations with Britain. Alix was pregnant again and, to her despair, could not go with him. She had longed to be at her sister's wedding and to see Russia.

The Prince's reception in St. Petersburg was unlike anything he had known. He had visited Canada and America, Ireland, most of Europe and the Middle East. The journeys had either been within British territory or incognito. Here he was on his first official state visit to a foreign country. It was not merely the cheers or the hospitality which did not match London's or New York's.

He was given magnificent apartments in the New Hermitage, attached to the Winter Palace and overlooking the Neva. The Czar treated him with much honour. Minny was excited and grateful. Most of her family were too poor to come all this way. He brought loving messages from Alix and increased her prestige. The young, retiring Czarevitch Alexander, Sacha, still bewildered by inheriting his elder brother's position and fiancee, responded to him, to everyone's pleasure and they became friends. He had more or less expected all this. What he had not expected was the attitude of most of the people he met. In a country where the Czar was absolute ruler, they assumed the Prince had far greater power than he possessed. They spoke to him as though, one day, his commands would be the laws of England.

It was a heady experience and Bertie did not correct the impression. The most delightful effect was on the ladies. As well as being immensely rich and powerful, as they thought, he was so charming and good-looking. The light moustache he had grown and his heavy-lidded eyes made him seem raffish and worldly, and they shivered to think of all the mistresses he must have. The language of the Court was French which he spoke fluently. His deep, slightly guttural voice made it sound even more sensual. He soon realised they were not interested in simple, enjoyable flirtations.

The marriage was held at the Chapel Royal on his twenty-fifth birthday. At the ball which followed, he was virtually besieged. It was torture with Alix's sister there. Minny laughed and marvelled at his popularity. He spent the days sight-seeing or hunting and the evenings pretending not to understand the obvious invitations. One young, married princess began to fascinate him. Her eyes were wicked in a demure, heart-shaped face. Her hair was raven and her figure petite and exquisite. He danced with her as often as he could without causing comment. She was in the party with him on a trip to the palace of Catherine the Great at Tsarskoe Selo. Someone suggested going on to the Summer Palace at Pavlovsk to see the paintings. He found himself in a troika next to the Princess. Under her white fur hood, her eyes laughed to him. She had arranged it. A huge coverlet of bearskins was tucked round them, almost to their shoulders. As the troika jingled across the frozen countryside under the leafless trees, its runners hissing on the snow, her warmth beside him and her impudent fingers teased him out of all control.

He was glad to go on a tour of the country, but the pattern was repeated everywhere. He visited Moscow and was given rooms in the Kremlin. He went round the hospitals and reviewed the Circassian bodyguard. At a meeting with the Metropolitan Archbishop in his bare, monk's cell, he astonished his entourage and won the hearts of the Russians by kneeling and asking for the venerable old man's blessing.

The Governor of Moscow, Prince Dolgorouki, gave him a grand banquet. Afterwards, at the Prince's palace, they were entertained in the drawing room by a group of gypsies. The dancers were mostly women, not the usual disreputable vagabonds he had seen with their painted caravans by the roadside, but dusky-skinned, finely-boned true gypsies. They were as elegantly dressed as the court ladies who watched them. Their singing was wild and discordant, a memory of their origins in India, and their dancing was like the nautch, with little movement of the feet while their bodies swayed and their arms twined, now fierce and ardent, now langorous and desiring. Bertie and the others talked to them afterwards through interpreters. He was stimulated by what he had seen. The dancers seemed to symbolise all the feelings he had suppressed in St. Petersburg. One in particular, slender, haughty, with narrow, high cheekbones intrigued him. He smiled and complimented her and, as she left, she gave him the bright silk scarf she had used in her dancing. Prince Dolgorouki noticed. When Bertie wished the others goodnight and went to his rooms, he let the scarf trail through his fingers onto the table in the anteroom, remembering the girl who gave it to him. He found her waiting in his bedroom. Her dark, sinuous body gave him release and her skilled but unrestrained passion woke a sensuality in him which had been dormant.

When he returned to the Hermitage, Minny and Sacha had left on their honeymoon. The reins were off. The princess welcomed him. He accepted her invitation to dine, and a score of others. He stayed to the end of the month and proved himself more than able to keep the ladies of St. Petersburg happy.

Chapter
10

It was difficult for Bertie to adjust when he came back from Russia. He had to tell himself the experience was dreamlike and could never be repeated. The state visit had been sponsored by Benjamin Disraeli, Chancellor of the Exchequer in the new Conservative

Government, and had been a pronounced diplomatic success. However, the war with Russia in the Crimea was too recent, and as time passed, Bertie saw that the start he had made towards better relations was not followed up. The chance was wasted. And the Queen still gave him no work.

He was concerned about Alix's health. She was in the last months of her pregnancy and had an ache in the right leg which did not let her sleep properly. She missed him greatly during the six weeks he was away, their first long separation, but seemed to recover when she had him back. They filled Sandringham over Christmas with as many of their friends as they could cram in. Affie came and the two brothers experimented with growing different types of beard. Prince Alfred was making swift progress in the navy and was a popular officer. He had the same tastes as Bertie and had caused considerable scandal by his reckless affair with a married woman. He favoured a razor-trimmed, fringing beard like Abraham Lincoln. Bertie's was full, bushy and made Alix laugh. She said he looked as if he was wearing a disguise.

Christmas was hectic for them, with games and parties, informal dances and presents for all the people on the estate. The house was too cramped for everyone in spite of the alterations and they decided to have the whole place enlarged and modernised. They both liked the country and the freedom it allowed them.

Early in the New Year, Lady Macclesfield and the doctor who came to examine Alix suggested that she ought to be in London where she would have more expert medical attention. She left reluctantly. Bertie did not go with her. He was disillusioned with politics. Sitting idle in London only made him more conscious that he was a powerless, unemployed figurehead. The season from May to the end of July was enough. And the prospect of long evenings at home with Alix unwell bored him. When they could go out together or entertain their friends, there was no one he would rather be with, but enforced inactivity made him restless and irritable. He went shooting on his own grounds and his neighbours'.

157

He visited his sporting friend, the Duke of Sutherland, in Staffordshire and rode to hounds. He had never forgotten the New York Fire Brigade and was delighted to find that Sutherland had a similar enthusiasm. He lived the life of a bachelor country gentleman for a month and enjoyed it.

A letter from Lady Mac brought him to London. Alix's health was failing and she had caught a chill. General Knollys and her ladies-in-waiting were worried but she had never been really ill before and made light of it. She wore her prettiest dress and her hair loose at the sides as he liked it. Although he could see that she was weaker, her cheeks pallid, she was animated and interested in everything he had been doing.

She lay propped on a chaise longue and shifted her position occasionally in pain. Lady Macclesfield took her up to bed early. 'She bullies me, you see,' she complained.

'She loves you very dearly,' Bertie smiled. 'As we all do.'

He called briefly on Harriet Mordaunt, a childhood friend of his who had recently been married, before going on to dine with Affie and Carrington at Prince's. Affie was being sent for more navigation training on the Queen's orders. She was determined to protect him from the vices of society. They were joined by Harry Chaplin, a handsome, extravagant gambler whose stud of race-horses rivalled those of the spendthrift young Marquis of Hastings. The two were rivals in more than one field. Chaplin had been engaged to the Duke of Sutherland's beautiful daughter, Florence, 'the pocket Venus'. Shortly before the marriage, he went shopping with her one day at Marshall and Snelgrove's. While he was buying her a pair of gloves, she slipped out of the rear door to where Hastings waited for her with a carriage and a marriage licence. As a gentleman, Chaplin accepted his loss with grace but the rivalry continued on the turf. Bertie liked them both, but particularly Chaplin.

After dinner, they drove slowly down the Haymarket in a cab. Affie was fascinated by the noisy, made-up

158

women in their flashy dresses standing under the lamp posts and the others beckoning from the windows of the coffee houses. There was music from barrel organs, from pianos and bands in the ginshops. The girls laughed and traded crude compliments with the semi-swells who sauntered on the pavements, catching their arms or calling after them. The harsh gaslight washed the colour from their faces, except for the livid spots of rouge and the slash of their mouths, making them look like tawdry, painted dolls. The most appealing were the youngest, factory girls and servants, up west for a lark or to earn enough for the rent or a new pair of shoes. They walked slowly in twos and threes, giggling and daring one another, or singly down at the lower, darker end, more nervous, ashamed to be seen in their drab skirts and half capes and plain bonnets. There were dozens of them, the coy, the brazen, the beaten and the hopeful, speckled birds of passage, Carrington said. Chaplin knew some of them. You could buy yourself a whole aviary from the price of a decent bottle of claret.

Bertie would rather have the claret.

'Bought flesh is like forced meat compared to venison,' he contended.

'Both a bit high,' Carrington drawled.

On the way back, they turned up the notorious, twisting streets behind Piccadilly and Jermyn Street. The girls here were younger, some barely in their teens, but just as varied as their older sisters. It sickened Bertie, as it always did. He was not sure which he pitied most, the ones whose immature faces were arch and knowing or the others who were timid, starved with cold in the cheap little dresses in which their keepers sent them out. Some were pathetically young. Still, until they raised the age of consent from twelve, there was little one could do. The lamp posts were wider spaced here. As the cab passed, the bolder of the girls stepped out into the glare of the light, offering to climb in, smiling but ready to dart back into the shadows if it was the Law or a decoy from one of the Reform Societies.

Affie wanted to go back to Soho or, beyond Charing Cross Road, to Seven Dials, but Carrington advised against it. They would need a police guide, a couple of plain clothes officers who knew the areas. They were more or less sanctuaries for thieves, pickpockets, pimps and cutthroats. Even by daylight they were dangerous and there was no possibility of getting through them safely at night. They decided on a compromise. They cut over to Regent Street, paid off the driver on the other side of the Circus and walked up Great Windmill Street.

It felt strange to Bertie to be strolling here, among the very people who lined the pavements to cheer him. Carrington and Chaplin kept close to him on either side so that he would not be jostled. He wore his coat collar up, but had little fear of being recognised. No one was used to his beard yet. They went into the Casino Public House. It was warm and brightly lit. The mantles on the gas jets were tinted orange; the light glittered back from a whole wall and ceiling of etched mirror glass. The long horseshoe bar was crowded and they found a table on the half-landing where there were other groups of men in evening dress, so they would not be conspicuous. The waiter brought them glasses of champagne and a tray of oysters. Chaplin promised that they were an infallible aphrodisiac.

'I hope not,' Affie muttered. 'I have to get back to Windsor tonight.'

As Bertie chuckled, he caught the eye of a tall redhead who sat two tables away beyond a stucco, pink pillar. She smiled imperceptibly and looked away. She was turned in profile to him. The long line of her throat was flawless. She wore a modish dress in the new bustle style, cut fairly low. There was a teasing, artificial mole at the corner of her mouth. She was either not made up or so subtly that one could not tell. The slim throat was her best feature. Round it she wore a black velvet Alexandra choker.

Affie had noticed her, too. He nudged Chaplin. 'Is she—?'

'They all are,' Chaplin told him. 'And only the best. They spend the afternoon in Burlington Arcade and, if they haven't struck gold, come here in the evening.'

Affie swivelled to look at the tables around them and beyond the bar, seeing how many were occupied by two or three women on their own. Most of them were fashionably dressed, decorous but attractive. He saw how their eyes moved over the men at the bar and their veiled smiles when they made contact.

'It's paradise,' he breathed.

'And these are the birds of paradise,' Carrington said.

Bertie smiled at Affie's eagerness. He could feel the enticing, erotic atmosphere himself, as if the air were drugged with it. He had often come to similar places but had lost his taste for them. Although his spirits lifted with the uninhibited laughter and the sense of freedom, it was like watching a kaleidoscope. He could never really join in and only stay so long as his incognito was not broken. While Affie and Chaplin laughed, listing the tables in order of preference, he talked to Charlie Carrington. He saw the paradox in a society dedicated to public morality which allowed child prostitution, legions of street women and thieves' rookeries to exist not one hundred yards from respectable thoroughfares, not three hundred from the Mall. Westminster, itself, was one of the most areas. Carrington, who had entered Parliament as a Liberal, hid a highly-developed social conscience under his humorous mask. Normally he avoided serious topics with the Prince, honouring his need to keep outside party politics. However, this was a national matter. He explained that the rookeries existed because the police were not organised to deal with them. As long as the social conditions lasted, the slums that were the breeding ground for violence and robbery, there could be no improvement. Children and women would take to the streets as long as there were no better opportunities for them. Many were driven to it. Who could blame the thousand of others, when they saw prosperity all round them and the only alternative was skivvying or starvation?

Bertie never forgot a face. He saw one he knew on the lower level, an engineer in the Metropolitan Board of Works. He became certain when the man whispered to the girl he was with and she glanced up instinctively. She leant round to tell the girls at the table behind her. In a few more minutes, they would all be whispering and staring.

'I'm sorry, gentlemen,' he said quietly. 'I think we've been rumbled.' He felt for his wallet.

'Allow me, sir,' Carrington offered.

Bertie rose from the table and moved away, to stand with his back to the people below. He was annoyed at being chased out. He saw no reason why he should not enjoy himself like everyone else, but, if there were a scene, it would be in all the scandal sheets by morning. They printed enough without any definite facts and his younger brother being with him would make it worse. They'd have a field day, and then the black-bordered letters would pour in from Osborne. He turned impatiently and found he was standing next to the redheaded charmer. She was watching him, puzzled, clearly thinking he had been trying to work up courage to speak to her. She smiled. Bertie smiled back. She reminded him of one of the chief rivals of the princess in St. Petersburg.

'Good evening,' she murmured. Bertie hesitated. Should he speak to her or just nod and move on? The girl smiled again. 'May I be permitted to pay my addresses to you?' she asked. The oddness of the formula made him smile. The girl was more puzzled than ever. He was good-looking, obviously rich and not drunk or nancy. She had a feeling she had seen him somewhere before, not as a client.

Affie came up behind Bertie. Carrington was just finishing paying the bill. Affie looked from Bertie to the redhead who was sitting straighter, poised, so that her magnificent bust swelled above the neckline of her dress.

'Nothing would give me greater pleasure, my dear,' Bertie assured her. 'But to my great regret, I have to put my baby brother on a train.' Affie's mouth rounded, indignantly. 'It is long past his bedtime and his mama will be sitting up.' He bowed, took Affie's arm and led him out. Carrington and Chaplin both bowed to the girl, smiling, as they followed them.

Bloody Hell, she thought. Maybe I should've promised him a nice dolly with a stick of barley sugar.

Bertie was smiling when he arrived back at Marlborough House. They had seen Affie to Paddington, then gone on to White's Club. He won over forty pounds at baccarat. If he knew where the redheaded one lived, he would have sent it to her. Anonymously, of course. He would like to have talked to her. Being candid with himself, he admitted he would like to have done much more. But the memory of Nelly Clifden's boasting and the trouble it had caused haunted him. You could not expect members of her profession to be discreet. Hartington said she should have had 'By Appointment' tattooed on her bum. He had pretended to be outraged, but it still amused him.

The clock was striking three as he crossed the hall. One of the footmen took his hat and overcoat and he crossed into the drawing room to pour himself a brandy nightcap. Sir William Knollys was sitting by the fire and rose as he came in.

'Her Royal Highness expected you back before this, sir,' he said. His tone was disapproving.

Bertie fought down his irritation. Part of Knollys's position was to be a watchdog for the Queen. So far he had behaved more like a courtier than a censor and Bertie took care not to alienate him.

'I had things to do,' he growled.

As he moved towards the sideboard, he heard the door open again and turned. It was Dr. Gull, a leading practitioner, tall and distinguished. He bowed stiffly. Bertie could not understand why he was here at this time.

'Come in, Doctor,' he said. 'Were you sent for?'

'Dr. Gull has been here for the last four hours,' Knollys told him. Bertie was reaching for a cigar. He paused.

'I'm afraid Her Royal Highness has taken a turn for the worse, sir,' Gull reported. 'The inflammation in her hip and leg has increased.'

'What is it?' Bertie asked.

'I suspect rheumatic fever. Serious enough in itself,

and in her present condition—' He stopped, unwilling to go on.

Bertie was numb. 'Will she lose the baby?'

'Not necessarily,' Gull said slowly. 'But it will undoubtedly once again be premature. She is already in great pain. He paused. 'She would not even take a sleeping draught in case she was asleep when you returned.'

Bertie knew, then, why Knollys had been so distant.

Alix was in bed, restless and feverish. The joints of her knees and ankles ached and her whole body perspired. Lady Macclesfield was trying to smooth her forehead with a damp cloth. She stepped back when Bertie hurried in. He came to the bed and crouched beside it. He had been warned that Alix should not be touched. Alix made herself stop shaking. She smiled at him.

'My darling—I had no idea,' Bertie apologised. 'Is it very bad?'

Alix panted. 'I can—I can bear it when you're here,' she faltered. She smiled again and bit her lip.

Lady Mac took a small glass of opiate from the dressing-table and gave it to Bertie, in silence. He nodded and turned to Alix. 'You must drink this.'

'I don't want it,' Alix protested.

'No, no, You must sleep,' he told her. 'And don't worry—I'll stay with you.' He held the glass for her. 'There. Now lie back.'

As he put the glass down, she caught his free hand in both hers, holding tightly. 'I was waiting for you.'

'Yes.'

'Where were you?'

Bertie hesitated. 'Affie's due to go back to sea. We had dinner.'

Alix gasped again, but the sleeping draught was strong and was already easing the pain. She could feel it seeping away. 'As long as I know where you are.'

'I'm here now, my darling,' Bertie said gently. 'Rest.'

As the pain left her, Alix could not keep her eyes open. The tiredness of days swept over her. 'You're so kind,' she whispered, lying back.

Bertie felt her grip slacken on his hand. He laid his other hand over hers, stroking softly, soothing. He did not feel kind, but guilty and self-accusing. Yet even as he told himself he should have stayed with her or come home earlier, he began to feel trapped. The day after, he returned from riding at Windsor to find her condition worse. Five days later, their first daughter was born.

The baby, against all expectations, thrived. Alix did not improve. The pains and the fever increased until her whole body, every joint, ached, swollen and tender, especially her right hip and knee. Her throat was inflamed so that it was torture to swallow and the sleeping draughts gave her only fitful hours of rest. The staff at Marlborough House was electrified when a closed carriage came to a stop at the door and a tall, bearded Scotsman helped the Queen up the steps and into the hall. She had come to find out for herself what was going on. Inevitably, she had again missed the birth and, for a week after it, the Princess's doctors had advised her against visiting. She intended to register the sharpest possible protest at the way of life adopted by her son and his wife, leading to weakness, ill health and disrepute, but all her annoyance was swept away by concern when Dr. Gull nervously confided to her that the Princess was bedridden and likely to be permanently crippled.

Alix had been left with only Lady Macclesfield. Her parents were far away. Bertie had moved his writing desk into her bedroom so that he could spend most of the day with her, but his restlessness and irritability at having nothing to do made her anxious and she encouraged him to fulfil his engagements. The readiness with which he agreed hurt her. No one had told her that the Queen did not know how ill she was.

Victoria was appalled to see Alix so haggard and wasted, gnawed with pain, and to smell the sour, acrid odour of sweat that filled the room. She held her tenderly and Alix laid her head on her breast, crying as she had been unable to do with anyone else, because she thought the Queen had closed her heart to her and she had lost her, the dearest of mothers. In that moment, Victoria forgave Alix for any disobedience or wilfulness she had ever shown, loving her as her own child.

In spite of the Queen's care, Alix's recovery was slow. The days stretched into weeks. Bertie found that his presence hindered the doctors and nurses. He was less and less needed and the great house, hushed and sorrowing, with the smell of sickness creeping through it began to feel like a cage to him. He threw himself into his duties which were really an evasion.

His restlessness became unendurable to himself and his household. It had two main causes. This was a particularly exciting time for him. For once, he seemed to be in favour with the Government. He had succeeded in drawing his mother out of her seclusion to open the current session of Parliament. Adding his persuasion to Disraeli's, he now managed to talk her into laying the foundation stone of the new Hall of Arts and Sciences at South Kensington. Public appearances were a cruel trial for Victoria after nearly four years of isolation from the world. She had almost been overcome by the sight of so many people and the shouts of the crowds at Westminster. She agreed to face the ordeal again only because this was to be a permanent memorial to the Prince Consort, the Royal Albert Hall.

In its way, it was a triumph for Bertie. People had lost sympathy with the Queen's perpetual mourning. In spite of herself, he had saved her popularity for the moment and he hoped the Government would show its gratitude by giving him some real work. He could no longer be satisfied with his position. The engagements, opening schools, attending dinners and charity appeals, he accepted merely to show himself, all the time aware that he had no actual use or authority.

The other cause was the International Exhibition in Paris. The Emperor Napoleon the Third whom he admired and loved was gambling a fortune in an attempt to recover his prestige. He had hesitated before siding with either Prussia or Austria in their war and it was over before he could affect the result. Foolishly, while the peace terms were being negotiated, he had asked Prussia for territory on the left bank of the Rhine as his price for having stayed neutral. Bismarck realised that France was no longer strong enough to enforce the demand and saw no reason why he should share the spoils of victory with a jackal. At the same time, Napoleon had lost his influence in Italy and the French Empire he had tried to set up in South America was collapsing. To prove that France was still a leading nation, Napoleon invited all the crowned heads of Europe to the most spectacular, expensive Exhibition ever staged.

The Queen turned down the invitation automatically. Some years ago she had been captivated by Louis Napoleon, but Albert distrusted his ambitions and she would pay no more official, foreign visits in her widowhood. Bertie was a member of the Commission that organised the British section. Because of that and the efforts he had made to help them, he hoped the Government would authorise him to attend the opening ceremonies in her place.

Benjamin Disraeli was not Prime Minister. Although the leader of his party, he was still not fully trusted. Although he was now in his early sixties and wore sober frock coats instead of the exotic dress of his youth when he had shocked his way to celebrity with his novels and wit and his flamboyant attempts to be elected to Parliament, he had always held office under men less able than himself. But he knew he would not have to wait much longer. He had just pulled off a master-stroke. The Liberals had been defeated in the last election over a Reform Bill. With the Conservatives in power, Disraeli introduced his own, much more radical Reform Bill, giving the vote to householders and working men, and his party was riding high.

Few people enjoyed the appointment as Minister in Attendance on the Queen. Disraeli accepted the extra duties gladly. His task was to tell her what had been discussed in Cabinet and to explain the problems of the day. His personal problem was to win over the Queen, who had always considered him unreliable. He succeeded brilliantly by a combination of overpowering charm and diplomacy. To his surprise, he discovered that the Queen had an acute mind and quick grasp of essentials. Her political intelligence was keen and her advice often remarkably valuable. Besides, if the Government did not have her confidence or tried to force her, she proved she could be disastrously obstructive.

They were standing in the study at Windsor. Victoria still found Disraeli an oddity with his livid complexion, black eyes and dyed ringlets and his mobile, expressive hands, so very Jewish looking. He had a courtly, flowery manner of speaking and she suspected him of wooing her, yet he was never servile and sometimes, even, made her laugh.

'You possess the power, like my late husband,' she said, 'of making problems intelligible, even interesting.'

Disraeli laid his hand on his heart. 'I will confess, Ma'am, that I tremble before an Audience. To know I am about to lay the thoughts of my government before Your Majesty.'

Victoria had been looking at the bust of the Prince Consort by her desk. Her head swivelled sharply. 'I think you flatter, sir.' She had the disturbing feeling that he was mocking her.

Disraeli's hand pushed away the accusation. 'On the contrary—Your Majesty's life has been passed in the constant communion with great men and the knowledge of important transactions. This rare experience must give your Majesty an advantage in judgment which few living people can rival.'

He was so obviously sincere that Victoria relaxed. 'Well—I have certainly learnt by experience.' She was pleased. She sat and motioned him to a chair. Disraeli bowed and took his place opposite her. He concealed his pleasure. It was an infrequent honour to be asked to sit.

He smiled. 'The Prime Minister has asked me to join his congratulations to mine on the birth of your new grandchild.'

'Lord Derby is most kind.'

'I understand the Princess of Wales is delighted that it is a daughter.'

'And once again I missed the birth!' Victoria snorted.

168

'I blame their self-indulgent way of life for her weakness.' She could not hide her irritation. Bertie had written to tell her that the baby was to be named after its grandmothers, Louise Victoria. 'Victoria' *ought* to have come first. 'My son's duty is to set an example to society. But no, he goes where he likes, behaves as he likes—and I suppose, once again he'll blame it on me for not giving him something to do.'

Disraeli absorbed it all with an expression of concern and attention. He had detected a vein of seriousness beneath the Prince's playboy exterior. If it were not exploited, it would be a pity. 'He is very popular, Ma'am.'

'*Was,* Mr. Disraeli. His neglect of his wife during her illness has caused great offence.'

'By all accounts, he has seldom left her side during these last months.'

'And how long will that continue?' Victoria demanded. 'Queen Louise had come from Denmark to stay with her. Let's see what use he makes of that!'

The Exhibition had been open for over a month before Bertie finally realised that neither his mother nor the Government were going to appoint him as their representative. Disraeli could not take the risk of causing offense to the Queen. Bertie discussed it with Alix. She was recovering slowly under her mother's nursing. She was very touched by the number of letters and flowers she had been sent from all over the country, to learn how much people really cared for her, and it made her more sorry for Bertie who had no chance to prove himself. She agreed it was right he should go to Paris. One of the Royal Family had to attend. It was his duty.

The first day she was well enough, her bed was wheeled into the private drawing room and Baby Louise was christened. That afternoon, Bertie left for France.

Paris had never seen such an array of distinguished visitors. Every sovereign in Europe, except Victoria and the Pope, had accepted Louis Napoleon's invitation. The streets were crowded with the coaches of exquisite, jewelled ladies and immaculate gentlemen. At night, the receptions and balls of the embassies and wealthiest families competed with one another in magnificence. The restaurants and nightspots, the pavement cafes, were crowded with the famous and their followers. Offenbach's new musical comedy, *the Grand Duchess of Gerolstein,* poking fun at the vanities and militarism of the tiny, independent German states, drew them to the Variétés. Sarah Bernhardt, divinely passionate, was triumphant in Sardou's 'Fedora'. Celebrated orchestras played. And the Exhibition, itself, was the wonder of the world, presented with all the splendour of the Second Empire.

Bertie arrived to find Paris the centre of the universe, as he had always imagined it. He brought Affie with him and the news that the Prince of Wales and Alfred, Duke of Edinburgh, were here sent invitations flooding into the British Embassy where they were staying. They visited the British Section, the rest of the Exhibition and called on their host. Bertie was moved by the way he was received. Louis Napoleon had been his idol since he was a boy and he felt proud to be part of the throng that honoured him.

The Emperor wept as he welcomed him. He loved Bertie, and his coming put the seal on everything. No one could call him an upstart any longer. He trembled in case anything should go wrong. Already a crazed Pole had shot at Czar Alexander as they drove together. He had only hit the horses before his gun jammed, but it was disturbing. Nothing must interrupt the festivities. Wilhelm of Prussia had come with the Crown Prince and Bismarck. They were like spectres at the feast, sensing the French sympathy for Austria. Still, Bismarck had seen *The Grand Duchess* and laughed uproariously. If only they would realise his desire for peace.

Bertie had never been to Paris purely for enjoyment before. The excited, laughing people, the fantastic decorations, the gaiety stimulated him. Merely to walk in the street made him feel drunk and the Parisians, seeing his open enjoyment, adored him. He was 'un Prince vraiment chic', a born boulevardier. His reputation and exaggerated stories of his exploits in Russia had prepared the way. At Pauline Metternich's superb ball at the Austrian Embassy where the candelabra were galleons of flowers and a huge waterfall cascaded over tens of thousands of roses in the Hall, he met again the ladies who had so enchanted him before, the Comtesse de Pourtalis, elegant and intelligent, the coolly femine Princesse de Sagan, the ravishing Duchesse de Mouchy and the dashing Hélene Standish who amused him by modelling her whole appearance on Alix. The orchestra was led by the incomparable Johann Strauss. As Bertie waltzed and flirted, he was all too aware of his brother-in-law, the Crown Prince of Prussia. Fritz did not want Bertie to stay as it would show too much favour to the Austrians, but the bright eyes and the inviting glances of his partners intoxicated him.

Next day he called early on the Princess de Sagan. She was separated from her husband and lived in a spacious town house in the Rue de Grenelle. She received him in her silk-panelled boudoir, charmingly surprised by his visit and conveniently en deshabille. To be the first choice of the handsome Prince of Wales out of the galaxy of beauties which surrounded him was an overwhelming distinction. They laughed, remembering how, on his journey home from the Middle East, the Empress Eugénie had invited all the loveliest ladies of her court to meet him at Versailles. Only the married ladies, the Princesse stressed, on whose discretion one could rely absolutely. Bertie realised that he had wasted a great deal of time.

Once again his energy became a byword. He went to the races and dined in the fashionable restaurants, often with one of the reigning demi-mondaines. He was captivated by the passionate Sarah Bernhardt. In one scene in her play she wept over the dead body of her lover. Only Bertie's friends in the audience were aware one night that the motionless figure on the bed to which the divine Sarah poured out her anguish was the Prince of Wales. His reputation grew. It was inevitable that he would go to the hit of the season, *The Grand Duchess,* at the Varietes. It's star, Hortense Schneider, was the toast of Paris. Everyone talked of her pout and wriggle, her delicate naughtiness and her teasing Alsatian accent. She was courted by the Kings of Sweden and Portugal. The Czar and one of his sons, Vladimir, quarrelled over her. The Khedive of Egypt showered her with presents. Bertie was in a stage box with the Marquis and Marquise de Galliffet and the Duke and the Duchess of Sutherland. He saw a plump honeyblonde with baby blue eyes. She did not have much of a voice and her dancing was limited but she used her eyes and voice and body to perfection, coy and titillating, amusing and appealing. She was irresistable.

In the second interval, the manager led the gentlemen through an iron pass door to the side of the stage and the star dressing room. Hortense was changing. She leapt up in confusion, clutching a silk peignoir round herself. When the Marquis introduced Bertie, she curtsied, murmuring breathlessly, 'Votre Altesse Royale . . .' As he complimented her and excused himself for disturbing her, still all she could murmur was 'Votre Altesse Royale.' The aura which Bertie had begun to carry around him flustered her. She saw his smile and his unhidden admiration and it was as though the kings and czars had never been. The gentlemen accepted glasses of champagne and she retired behind a screen to finish changing.

Bertie sat at the end of a plush sofa near her dressing table. Her little pet dogs, Amour, Minou and one, she blushingly told him, called Vicky jumped on his lap and tried to drink his champagne. He felt excited himself. The smell of powder and patchouli reminded him of Nelly, yet this charming creature was nothing like her. She was more deliciously feminine than the Princesse de Sagan with none of the intensity of Bernhardt. The breathy, laughing voice behind the screen and the rustle of clothes created an atmosphere of intimacy. The sides of the long dressing table mirror were angled. From where he sat, he caught occasional flashes of movement in the end panel, the curve of a bare pink shoulder, a glimpse of curving indented back. He tried not to look too conspicuously. It was only when the figure in the mirror turned and smiled, one hand on the full breasts, the other touching a round, polished hip, that he remembered it was she who suggested he sit here and understood that the display was only meant for him.

After the theatre, he excused himself from dinner with the Galliffets. The events of the previous days had been so tiring. They sympathised and smiled. Le Grand Seize, the private dining room in the Cafe Anglais, was in use but swiftly vacated for the Prince and his special guest. The decorations were gold and dark red, the lighting subtle. The waiters were trained to be invisible and to enter only when summoned. In a silken gown the colour of Tokay, the skirt fluffed out with layer upon layer of scented petticoats, Hortense was bewitching. The intervals between courses became longer. Next day the whisper ran that the fruit and none of the sumptuous desserts had even been touched.

Bertie came home to find Alix much improved. She was still weak and her legs were painful and stiff but she could be wheeled out into the garden to catch the sun. She envied him his trip to Paris with all its splendours and he promised to take her as soon as she was well enough. He brought the Queen greetings from everyone he had met and reported to Disraeli several rather intriguing things he had noticed, the interest of King Wilhelm and Bismarck in the fortifications of Paris, the reluctance of Napoleon to mention Mexico and the delayed arrival of the Emperor of Austria. Disraeli was impressed. Rumour had suggested that the Prince intended to return to Paris at the end of June for the prizegiving. At his age he would have done the same himself. He urged the Prince, however, to return at least for one day in July when there would be an army review in Hyde Park. Bertie was unwilling to commit himself but finally agreed, as Disraeli was so insistent. He had only really come back now to reassure himself about Alix and to go to the Derby. The race promised to be especially exciting this year. Henry Chaplin's Hermit was running and Bertie had backed it £100 each way through Carrington.

When he drove to Epsom Downs in his carriage on the day, the crowds were unusually silent. He was used to being cheered and it disconcerted him. He put it down to the weather, unseasonably cold with showers of sleet. It did not occur to him that stories of his neglect of Alix were destroying his popularity. The pleasure of entertaining a host of his friends in the Royal Box pushed it out of his mind. Their excitement mounted as they heard that Chaplin had staked an incredible sum on his own horse. The informed knew that most of the betting against him was led by the Marquis of Hastings. Not content with stealing Harry's bride, he was now determined to cripple him financially, driven by some unstable, guilty jealousy. Freddy Johnstone, the racing baronet, confided to the prince that he was worried about Hermit's chances. The horse had had a haemorrhage at its trials and should have been scratched in case its lungs were damaged. Bertie spoke to Chaplin who assured him it was only a broken blood vessel. Still, the parade in the paddock seemed to confirm the worse fears. Hermit's coat was uncut and the experts wrote him off. The odds were 66 to 1 against him.

The going was bad because of the weather. In the Royal Box, the gentlemen sipped brandy and sheltered the ladies who huddled in carriage rugs for warmth. The big race had them all on their feet, the sleet and cold forgotten. Hermit held his own, then challenged the leaders in the last flying, breathtaking furlongs to win by a neck. Bertie had done very well and Harry had won a fortune, much of it from his rival. It was only later they learnt that Hastings had wagered over £120,000 against Hermit and completely ruined himself.

Disraeli saw the Queen again on her return from Balmoral. People had hoped that her few appearances meant her period of intense mourning was over, but she refused to make any more. Discontent at her retirement grew and added to it were ugly rumors about her and John Brown whom she found more and more indispensable. Her courtiers disliked his familiarity. They did not see why the Queen should insist on a Highland ghillie accompanying her everywhere, promoting him, turning a blind eye to his drinking, leaning on his arm, using him as her confidential messenger, driving with him alone and laughing at his rough humour. The natural inference was that they were lovers. Disraeli did not believe it, yet something had to be done. Cautiously, he introduced the subject of her seclusion as they sat in her study. It was imperative that she returned to public life. Victoria had been describing the utter peace she felt in Scotland. She stiffened.

'I do what is humanly possible. I thought my grief was to be respected?'

'The Prince of Wales—' Disraeli began.

'No! Before you ask,' she snapped. 'I will not give him an official post! He cannot be trusted to control his opinions, let alone those of his wife!'

Disraeli had not experienced one of her instant rages, although he had been warned of them. He was too much of a diplomat to let his alarm show.

'Dear Madam—I would not presume to dictate what your relations should be with the Heir. On the contrary.' His voice was soothing. His liquid eyes begged for her trust. Victoria regretted her outburst at once. 'No, the real problem is that there is shortly to be a great military review in Hyde Park, at which the presence of the Sovereign is considered essential.'

With the quick loss of her anger, Victoria was left weak and upset. 'I thought *you,* at least, would understand, Mr. Disraeli. I am not strong enough to attend any more functions without the support of my beloved husband.'

She rose to end the Audience. Disraeli rose, too, and bowed as she moved away. 'Such a pity,' he murmured. 'Particularly, as Her Royal Highness, the Princess of Wales, should be well enough to attend.'

He saw the Queen stop and her head rise. 'Alexandra . . . ?'

'And the Prince is returning from Paris specially for the occasion.'

Victoria turned slowly to him. Her eyes had narrowed. 'How can he be there?'

Disraeli shrugged. 'He holds the rank of Field Marshal. It is not in our power to prevent him.' He disliked using crude cunning, but circumstances justified it. With the rise in agitation against the Queen, the only assets the Royal Family had at the moment were what remained of the Prince's popularity and the enormous love the country bore for his Princess. He could see from the Queen's appalled expression that he had used the right bait.

'But—if he goes, he will be taken as representing me!'

Disraeli bowed. 'That is why I suggested that, if Your Majesty did find yourself well enough to attend, it would give the people a chance to demonstrate that their loyalty is due in the first place to you—as Queen.'

He had read her correctly. In spite of her love for Bertie and Alix, she could not resist the opportunity to put them in their place.

'Yes . . .' she breathed. Then repeated more definitely, 'Yes.'

Disraeli bowed again gratefully. Now she had pledged herself, he would publicise it and make sure she could not change her mind. He only hoped that no outside circumstances would change it for her.

Chapter
11

The unending party that was Exhibition Paris still continued and Bertie stepped back as if he had never been away. This time he did not stay at the Embassy where the Ambassador had grown more and more rigid with disapproval. He had rooms booked for himself and his equerries at the Hotel Bristol. Several friends had promised to join him and Paris welcomed him back. He headed straight for the Theatre des Variétés and through the iron pass door to the perfumed dressing room where the welcome was sweetest.

He accepted an invitation to a Strauss soirée. He had heard Johann Strauss with his own orchestra in Vienna. On the night of the Princess Metternich's ball, the maestro had been off form, leading a French Orchestra. 'This evening, with German musicians, a combination which intrigued the Parisians, all the magic returned. Strauss, with his black hair and burning eyes, conducting with his bow and his violin balanced on his hip, enkindled the fashionable audience. They had loved his music before but now, hearing it played as it should be they surrendered completely. Bertie and some others had heard of a new waltz of his which had been a failure when it was performed as a choral work in Vienna. They could not believe that anything he wrote could fail and called for it. It was 'By the Beautiful Blue Danube'. From the first thrilling notes to the last chord, the audience was mesmerised. Those who were dancing stopped to listen and the applause at the end was a storm that shook even Strauss. He had been convinced by the lukewarm reaction at its first performance that it was not one of his best. The waltz was asked for again and again. It became the song of the Exhibition and the greatest musical success in history. Johann's father had played the music at Queen Victoria's Coronation Ball as Bertie reminded him when they met. He invited him to London as soon as he was free and Strauss accepted. Whenever Bertie heard the Blue Danube again, he thought of it as his own waltz.

He had a delicious, amusing late dinner with the Mouchys, the Pourtales, the Standishes and the Princesse de Sagan. Afterwards, he had a moment's unease. He escorted Jeanne de Sagan home and, as they relaxed, she told him of a tiny secret. She had been separated from her polished, civilized husband for nine years. The difficulty was that she was going to have a child. While Bertie desperately thought of what could be done, she assured him that everything was arranged. It was unthinkable that he should be caused any embarrassment. She had discussed it with her husband who was in complete agreement, the Prince of Wales must be protected. For a while, the de Sagans must seem to be reconciled. She regretted charmingly that it would have to be sooner and appear to be genuine to avoid future scandal.

Bertie was deeply grateful. The worldliness and tact of the French aristocracy was an education after the puritanical strictness or crude, flagrant amours in England. He recognised that his own society had much to learn from the Continent. Meanwhile, the delights of Paris and the Exhibition continued.

The bombshell came on the first of July. That day had been designed as the climax of the Exhibition, with Napoleon presenting the prizes to the exhibitors in front of all the crowned heads and the Emperor Franz Josef of Austria. The afternoon before, news arrived from Mexico. In his attempt to spread French influence to America, Napoleon the Third had sent an army to crush the Mexican republic and establish an empire. He had set the Archduke Maximilian, Franz Josef's brother, on the throne. His choice was planned to link Austria, France and the American continent together but troubles at home and in Europe forced him to recall the French army, although the Mexicans had risen in revolt. Stupidly, Maximilian decided to stay on. His beautiful wife, Charlotte, the daughter of Uncle Leopold of Belgium, went mad with fear. The news was that he himself had been shot by a rebel firing-squad and Mexico proclaimed a republic again under the Indian lawyer, Juarez.

Napoleon suppressed the news and went ahead with the prizegiving. But Franz Josef did not come. He declared full court mourning for his brother. The concept of a pact between France and Austria to resist the rising power of Prussia died with the execution. The story of what had happened filtered through to the audience of kings and princes who watched, stunned, as Napoleon continued with the full programme of the ceremony. Afterwards, they began to leave for home. Napoleon could not keep up the pretence and cut short the elaborate entertainments he had planned for the following weeks.

He persuaded many of his visitors to stay on, amongst them Bertie who had no need to return to London now. Victoria had followed Franz Josef in ordering Court mourning. The military review was cancelled.

Bertie stayed in Paris till the last possible moment, sensing that, as in Russia, this experience would be unrepeatable. He had still not had his fill of Hortense and he knew that, once he was gone, her other lovers would take his place at once. He suspected the gnomelike, shortsighted Offenbach himself was one of them. He had discovered her. She was disarmingly candid about it.

'I don't sing too well and I'm no ballet dancer,' she laughed, 'But Jacques says it's a small theatre and it's more important they have someone to look at than to listen to.' Bertie reminded himself that he had no right to be jealous. It was another lesson he had to learn. He thought of his feelings for Alix and decided that this infatuation did not affect them. He no longer had pangs of remorse or struggled against his inclinations, yet he would not do anything to compromise his marriage. The ladies of Paris had completed his education.

In the days that remained, when he was not riding with Hortense nor lunching with Sarah at the Maison Dorée, he confirmed his new friendships and discussed foreign affairs with the guests of Napoleon who still remained, the ministers who created their countries' policies. He was attentive and charming and absorbed a great deal before he had to say au revoir to the Variétés, the Café Anglais and the mansion on the Rue de Grenelle.

Disraeli and the old Prime Minister, Lord Derby, discussed the letters they had from the Prince of Wales. He sent them interesting comments on Russian intentions and had created a bond with the young King of Belgium. Not so valuable were his warnings about Prussia. He appeared to believe that Bismarck planned to attack France, whereas their information was that he had had very cordial meetings with the Emperor Napoleon and even given him helpful advice. Most useful of all was the information that the Khedive of Egypt and the Sultan Abdul Aziz of Turkey were both keen to visit England.

That created difficulties as the Queen refused to entertain anyone but the wives of foreign rulers who were her friends. People grumbled openly because they had seen the lavish hospitality given to the Prince abroad.

'If France did them proud, why can't we?, they say. They think she's mean, failing in her duties,' Derby complained. 'They've no sympathy for her any more. She's an intelligent woman. Can't she see it?'

Disraeli shrugged. 'She refuses to believe it.'

'Agitation—Republican Clubs springing up. More and more people ask, what use is she?'

'If they knew her, they could not help but admire her,' Disraeli said. 'Well, I fancy I can persuade her that the visits are necessary politically.'

'If anybody can, it's you,' Derby chuckled, relieved. 'You have a way with her.'

'But she won't receive them,' Disraeli told him. 'We'll need the help of the Prince of Wales. He'll have to make the arrangements.'

Derby was dubious. 'Do you think he's up to it?'

'He must have learnt how these things should be done. From something his mother said, I gather our Prince Hal is eager for responsible employment.' Derby looked even more dubious. Disraeli shrugged again. 'Of course, we could find him something else. Now that Canada's become a Dominion, we might make him Governor-General.'

Derby stared at him, horrified. Then laughed uncertainly. Dizzy's eyebrows were raised, his lips faintly curved. It was one of his little jokes.

Bertie was relieved to find Alix's improvement had continued. She was still far from well. She could only move, slowly and painfully, with the aid of walking sticks and her hearing had been affected so that she was partly deaf, but she had recovered her spirits and was determined to get better. Her only real sorrow was that she could not help him properly. They both realised that the visits were a challenge for him. The guests of England could not be treated less magnificently than they had been in Paris or incalculable damage would be done.

Bertie stage-managed everything, supervising every detail of travel, protocol, receptions, dress and accommodation. With the expertise he had gained from his foreign travels, he showed himself a master at organisation, devising exactly the right arrangements and the most suitable entertainments. In the absence of the Queen he acted as host to the Khedive, Ismail Pasha, who regretted that the Suez Canal was not being constructed by a British company but assured him that it would always open to his country's ships. Two days later, came the more important visit of the Sultan. Because of the Queen's objections, Ismail Pasha had been put up at Claridge's Hotel. Backed by Disraeli, Bertie insisted that Sultan Abdul must stay at Buckingham Palace. Together, they also persuaded her to entertain him to lunch at Windsor and to attend the highlight of the visit with him, a naval review at Portsmouth. Bertie's main achievement was that here, although the Sultan was the Caliph of Islam, he managed to prevail on his mother to make him a Knight of the Garter. The day ended with an illumination of the fleet. Sultan Abdul left in tears, vowing eternal gratitude. Assured of British friendship, he was prepared to resist Russian pressure in the Black Sea.

The Government acknowledged that the success was Bertie's. No one could imagine where he had learnt his faultless diplomatic technique, certainly not from his parents. No one had taught him his command of pageantry and his amazing ability to weave an atmosphere of goodwill. He had always had charm, acute observation and a retentive memory. Now he had presence and authority to go with them. He was ready to emerge as a national leader. Victoria had seen Bertie's emergence and the deferential way in which her royal guests had behaved to him. She suspected the Government of bringing him forward. She ordered that no more royal visits were to be accepted and forbade Bertie to receive anyone officially without her express permission. He must not be assumed to speak for the country and for her, not while he was so clearly in Louis Napoleon's pocket and biased against Prussia, favoured revolutionaries like Garibaldi and flattered Turkey only so that his wife's brother could sit safely on his Greek throne.

Bertie went to lunch with Disraeli and his wife, Mary Anne, at their palatial country home at Hughenden, which the Chancellor kept up out of his earnings as a novelist. Mrs. Disraeli was twelve years older than her husband, once pretty, now frail and shrivelled, but Disraeli flirted with her as if she were a young girl.

She confided to Bertie, 'Dizzy married me for my money. But if he had the chance again, I believe he would marry me for love.' They were delightful together.

After lunch, while she and Alix rested, Disraeli and Bertie left the others and walked in the garden. It was a warm July day and Bertie felt almost contented. His mother's reaction had not surprised him. He had hoped, however, that this once she might have realised he could be useful, even have given him some praise. He sensed that the Chancellor was sympathetic but he was always so damned cagey. Disraeli thought what a pity it was, a deplorable pity that the Prince's talents were being wasted. He had meant to use the military review in Hyde Park to illustrate to the Queen how she needed a second-in-command as loyal as her son. The boy would never fight her. Politically, it was ideal. Yet if she refused his employment continually, he might lose the taste of work altogether and concentrate on pleasure. What a misuse of such energy. He mentioned the review and his plans as they walked.

'However—unfortunately,' he shrugged, 'the best laid schemes of mice and men—'

'There can't be another one for some time,' Bertie said. 'Not while she has declared Court mourning for the Emperor Maximilian.'

'I almost wish he had waited another month before getting himself shot,' Disraeli murmured. He stopped, leaning on his cane, and seemed to be contemplating the large clusters of creamy-white flowers on a hydrangea shrub at the side of the path. Bertie was partly intrigued by his wry cynicism, partly repelled. Did anyone ever know what he really thought? As though answering him, Disraeli said, 'May I speak frankly?'

Bertie tensed. 'I would welcome it.'

Disraeli was still gazing at the flowers on their high, arching stems. 'I depended on the warmth of her people's greeting to transform the Queen. On the other hand, you and Princess Alexandra could have been enthusiastically received, at her expense.'

'Alix might have been,' Bertie said.

Disraeli looked towards him, taking his point. It was a relief to discover that the Prince knew he could not rely on his own popularity. Much of it depended on his wife and he would be circumspect.

'I am glad I have some idea, at last, of your real feelings, sir.' His mobile face creased in a smile. It was puckish and winning and Bertie could not help smiling back. They walked slowly on down the path.

'I, too, am waiting in the wings, and have been for much longer,' Disraeli told him. 'I was considered unreliable—and I am a Jew. Even to enter politics in England was foolhardy.'

'You may be Prime Minister soon.'

'Perhaps. But it cannot last. The Tory Party is weak at the moment. We have done too much, too quickly. However, one day I may be more secure and then, I promise I shall do what I can for you.'

Bertie paused. 'And until then?'

'You must be more tactful with your mother.'

Bertie felt himself flush. He wanted help and advice, but he was not used to being talked to like this by anyone apart from his nearest relatives. His whole upbringing urged him to break off the conversation.

Disraeli waited, again not looking at him. He heard the distant laughter of the group playing croquet on the lawn and the distinct thwack of the mallet. He turned to the Prince who was waiting also, tense. He had not taken offence. Good.

Disraeli's hand lifted in a gesture of explanation. 'I am speaking as I would wish to be spoken to. You must not appear to enter into competition with the Queen.

It is the one thing she cannot stand. You must do, or seem to do, whatever she wishes. And to gain her trust, you must first of all heal the breach in your own family.' Bertie was listening intently. He nodded for Disraeli to go on. 'There are many causes. Chief of them is the violation of Denmark. I respect Princess Alexandra's feelings, yet you must try to be objective. It will not be easy for you. But it is something only you can do—and Prussia is too powerful to be offended unnecessarily.'

A few weeks later, Alix's doctors recommended her to try the healing baths and waters in one of the German spas. Bertie chose Wiesbaden, three miles from the Rhine in Hesse-Nassau, famed for its hot springs. They were accompanied by their three children, Sir William Knollys and a lady-in-waiting. Bertie brought his equerry, Christopher Teesdale, Charles Carrington and twenty-five servants.

Wiesbaden was a favourite and stylish watering place with wide promenades, excellent hotels, parks and a famous casino. Alix was reluctant to come here, as Nassau was now part of Prussia, but it was a countryside she had loved since she was a child, not too far from Rumpenheim, and the agonising stiffness in her legs had not eased. She could only hobble slowly, leaning on her sticks. Perhaps the mineral springs would help. And Bertie had assured her that as it was an informal visit, they would not be expected to see anyone. She made sure of that. She would not pay courtesy calls on the Prussians.

During the day, while she had her treatment, Bertie and Carrington looked in at the casino, shot on the estates of local landowners or went riding. They quickly exhausted the possibilities of Wiesbaden but Alix showed signs of improvement and Bertie curbed his restlessness. When she was able, they met often in the afternoons for tea in the Kursaal.

Alix like the spacious room with its wide windows opening on to the terrace, its fountains and the little string quartet playing beyond the palms. It was part of the ritual that they all drank a glass of mineral water from the fountain after tea. She was watching Carrington as he collected a tray of glasses from the attendant. Like Bertie he was dressed in bright summer clothes. Much more attractive than Sir William, who always wore a sober frockcoat as if he were in London. She was sitting with him, Bertie and Tessdale at a table near one of the windows. Poor Sir William. He had been directed by the Queen to give her son a lecture on the evils of gambling and Bertie was irritated with him. It was quite funny, really. In their own fashion, they each had an air of suffering. She smiled to her lady-in-waiting. She had regained her beauty apart from a slight pallor and the high-necked, light dress with a patterned bodice and sleeves showed the slimness of her figure. She had adopted the bustle style gladly, with the skirt looped up and draped at the back, easier to manage than the circular crinoline.

Carrington set the tray of glasses down on the table. The contents were tinged with brown and slightly effervescent. 'Here we are.'

'Foul stuff,' Bertie growled.

'Drink it up, Bertie,' Alix told him. 'If it's good for me, it's good for you, too.' It might help him to lose weight, she thought. He was eating far too much and too quickly. No wonder he kept putting it on. She knew his friends had nicknamed him 'Tum Tum'. Sometimes she called him it, herself, when they were alone. She had to laugh because he got so annoyed.

Carrington sat and passed out the glasses. 'I don't see why people come all the way to Germany to drink soda water.'

'I don't see why people come to Germany at all,' Alix said. She could see Bertie stiffen and laughed. 'All right, darling, It makes the Queen happy—and that's worth the inconvenience.' Bertie relaxed and smiled. He guessed she had said it for Knollys' benefit. It would go in the Comptroller's weekly report.

The others were all sitting, holding their glasses. It was an effort to take the first sip. Alix raised hers and smiled. 'Skaal!'

'Oh, very well,' Bertie grumbled. 'Skaal.' As he drank

the bitter liquid, Alix stopped, looking behind him. He turned and saw his sister Alice coming towards them. Although she was only twenty-four, the strain of the past year and the annexation of her husband's country had told on her and she seemed older. Each time he met her on this trip she sermonised about the need to appease Prussia. He questioned that, but agreed that Vicky and Fritz needed help. While they supported their country, they were opposed to Bismarck's methods. Still, he begged her not to raise the topic in front of Alix and, whenever she appeared, he was nervous.

He rose as she reached them and kissed her cheek. 'Alice, my dear . . .' The other men had risen and were bowing.

Teesdale held a chair for her as she sat next to Alix. She smiled. Alix inclined her head slightly. Her smile was reserved. She knew that Alice and Louis now upheld the Prussian side of the family.

'Well, well,' Bertie exclaimed heartily. 'What a pleasant surprise!'

'I had to come to see you,' Alice said. She turned to Alix. 'No one could tell me if you were better.'

Alix thawed a little and smiled. 'Much better. I can even walk by myself—on four legs.' She held up her ebony sticks which leant against the table and Alice laughed.

'Oh, I'm so glad. Have you heard from Vicky and Fritz yet?'

'No, no, I expect they know it's just an informal visit,' Bertie put in before Alix could reply.

'They say your sister and the Czarevitch are coming,' Alice went on.

Alix smiled. 'Yes, they should be here by this evening.' She had not seen Minny since her marriage and was keen to meet her husband.

Alice was puzzled. 'This evening? I thought they'd be bound to stop at Potsdam.'

'Here now, I'm forgetting my manners,' Bertie said. 'Let me get you some of this magic potion. Charlie, tell Princess Alice how much good it's done you.'

As he rose and headed for the mineral water fountain,

Alix giggled. 'Bertie! . . .' He turned, frowning. 'I hadn't noticed—your trousers . . '

The trousers of his beige, linen suit had been carefully pressed flat with the seams sticking out sharply at the sides. He smiled, pleased she had noticed. 'I had them ironed like that. I hate them when they're crumpled.'

'But it makes you look fatter than ever!'

He drew himself up. 'I thought it might start a fashion,' he said huffily. He walked towards the fountain, self-conscious, very much on his dignity. He could hear Alix and his sister laughing. The others knew better. At any rate, it had changed the subject.

Bertie had rented a house in Wiesbaden for two months. That evening, he waited in the main reception room with Carrington. They were in evening dress. Carrington could tell that the Prince was preoccupied.

Bertie stubbed his cigarette out. 'Deuced awkward, Alice turning up like that,' he murmured.

'And now the Czarevitch Alexander,' Carrington said. 'Is that more complications?'

'Sacha? No, no.' Bertie chuckled. 'I used to think the Russians were all devilish clever till I met him. Alix's sister can twist him round the proverbial. No, they've only come for a family funeral at Rumpenheim.'

'Does that mean the rest of the Danes will arrive?' Carrington asked.

'I suppose so.' That was what troubled Bertie, the whole Danish contingent assembling inside the country that had attacked and defeated them. The ormulu clock on the mantelpiece chimed. 'Since Alix got those sticks she's more confoundedly late than ever!'

'Here she is,' Carrington told him.

The footmen were opening the door to the hall but, instead of Alix, it was Minny who came in. Now the Czarevna. Grand Duchess Alexander, she was dressed in high fashion. Her pastel evening gown was from Paris. Her hair was piled in an elaborate chignon and round her neck was a collar of diamonds from which hung tiny loops of matching pearls. Triumphantly married, she was more attractive and vivacious than ever. The

187

huge, lumbering Czarevitch Alexander followed her in shyly.

'Minny!' Bertie exclaimed, delighted. 'Sacha!' Minny ran to him and kissed him. 'We were to meet at your hotel.'

'So we were,' she said, laughing at his surprise. 'But I knew Alix was bound to be late, so I thought we'd save time.'

Bertie presented Carrington who saw at once what he meant. The young Czarevitch was patently dominated by his spirited wife.

Minny left them as soon as Alix came in, leaning on Knollys. They greeted each other ecstatically, kissing, not letting each other speak.

'Oh, come and sit down,' Minny laughed.

'I couldn't believe it when I got your message,' Alix said. Minny helped her towards the sofa. 'No, here, the piano stool will do.' They sat down side by side and took each other's hands. 'It's been so long!'

'Well, Sacha—' Bertie said.

Sacha nodded to Bertie, pleased. He liked to see Minny happy and his brother-in-law was one of the few people he found it easy to talk to. 'Have a good trip?'

'. . . Good,' Sacha said after a pause. His English was limited.

'Minny looks well.' Sacha smiled 'Still, you won't be enjoying the break as much as us. All those people to meet.'

Sacha shook his head. 'No people.'

Bertie hesitated. 'Surely you had to call on the King and Queen of Prussia?'

'We were going to,' Sacha nodded. 'Then Minny had a letter from Alix, advising us not to, so we refused.'

Bertie was concerned. He could see the news had disturbed Knollys too.

If that story got out, the Prussians would claim that England was intriguing against them. Bismarck already controlled the Chancellery. He could use the story to destroy the 'English Party', led by Vicky and Fritz, who were fighting for rule by a democratic Parliament instead of dictatorship by the King and the army.

Alix and Minny were telling each other their news, asking questions, laughing like schoolgirls, absorbed in each other.

'I was sorry to miss the wedding,' Alix lamented.

'It was good of you to let Bertie come,' Minny said, and laughed. 'He made a great hit. Especially with the ladies of St. Petersburg.' Alix smiled and Minny turned to call to Bertie. 'Quite a few wish to be remembered!'

'All right, Minny,' Bertie said. It was not something he cared to have discussed.

Minny had a sudden thought and clapped her hands together. 'Do you have to stay in Wiesbaden? Mother and Thyra are coming to Rumpenheim, and maybe Willy. There's plenty of room. Why don't you join us?'

'Could we Bertie?' Alix asked, excited.

He was already considering. He had been searching for a reason to get away for a short break but had not wanted to leave Alix on her own. 'Yes . . . It would do you good to spend some time with your family. You'd enjoy it.'

'You'd come, too.'

'For a day or two,' Bertie said. 'Charlie and I have been thinking of going to the races at Baden, just to take them in.'

'Baden?' Knollys repeated, surprised.

Bertie glanced at him. 'Why not?'

Knollys was embarrassed. He lowered his voice. 'Her Majesty has expressly asked you not to visit Baden, sir,' he reminded him. 'The company there is fairly disreputable.'

'Hang it all, man—' Bertie declared indignantly. 'I'm twenty-six, not twelve!'

Alix did not wish Bertie to be disappointed and irritable, and she longed to see Rumpenheim again. 'That's all settled, then,' she said.

Minny laughed and kissed her.

As they prepared to go in to dinner, Carrington murmured to Bertie, 'Are we really going to Baden, sir?'

'Might be safer if we all get away from here,' Bertie told him. He was becoming worried again. 'Though

I'm not sure it's wise to leave Alix. Anything can happen when that family gets together.'

Bertie saw Alix to Rumpenheim where her relatives were gathering in the old house. He left Knollys to look after her and to keep an eye on Sacha. The Czarevitch was very impressionable; this group with their violent feelings against Prussia might egg him on to do something foolish.

He went on to Baden with Carrington and Teesdale. The horses ran for them and they met some beguiling company. All in all, it was a highly enjoyable detour. They returned to find Alix and most of her family in Wiesbaden. When they arrived back, she was holding court in the Kursaal at one of the largest tables, surrounded by Minny and Sacha, her mother, Queen Louise, her younger sister, Thyra, and her brother Willy, now King George the First of Greece. They were arguing over whose country they were all to visit first, very gay and animated. Willy had become a roguish-looking, handsome, young man with a drooping moustache. He jumped up welcomingly as Bertie and Carrington came to them. They were both very relaxed and both now wore their trousers with razor-sharp creases down the front. It was slimming and elegant.

Alix noticed at once. 'Oh, Bertie,' she exclaimed, 'that's much better!'

He was very pleased. 'Thank you, my dear. Yes, I think this *may* start a fashion.' He kissed her and bowed to Queen Louise. 'Mama.' He shook hands with Willy and smiled round the table. Knollys had risen beside Sacha and bowed shortly. Evidently he still disapproved of Baden. Bertie sat beside Alix. She had colour in her cheeks and her eyes sparkled. 'It's good to see you, my dear,' he said. 'You look quite like your old self.'

'Oh, I am nearly,' she smiled. 'I only need one stick now. Did you have a good week?'

'We didn't do too badly.' He caught Willy winking to Carrington and chuckled. 'Well, Willy—how does it feel to be a king?'

'I'm getting used to it,' Willy said. They laughed. 'It took a little time,' he confessed. 'Mother and Father didn't tell me what was going on. I was on my way to class one morning, geometry. And there I saw it—on the newspaper wrapped round my sandwiches—"Prince William of Denmark elected King of Greece".'

They all laughed and Minny asserted, 'Willy's the sort of person who should be a king.'

'I wouldn't mind him calling on me at any time,' Alix agreed.

For a second, the Danish group seemed to hold their breath. Minny laughed softly.

Bertie smiled. 'What do you mean?'

There was a short, strained silence. Alix sipped the glass of water in front of her. Knollys coughed. 'During your absence, sir,' he reported, 'the King of Prussia wrote to Her Royal Highness, offering to call on her whenever it was convenient.'

It was the development Bertie had been waiting for. He smiled. 'When is he coming?'

'He is not,' Alix said flatly. 'I told him I would never receive him, in any circumstances.'

Bertie was stunned. 'You told him . . . ?'

'I didn't send the reply, sir,' Knollys said quietly. Alix swung round. 'Not in that form, Ma'am. It was too blunt.'

'How dare you?' Alix stormed. 'How dare you?!'

'Knollys is right' Bertie told her. 'You must meet him.'

'I am not well enough.'

Bertie looked round the table. None of them could meet his eyes. He guessed what had happened. Days of agitation and memories of the war, and Alix the one who had the courage to make a stand. But she was wrong. Queen Louise had the wisdom to see it, the power to influence Alix.

He spoke to her very seriously. 'Mama—Your Majesty—you know what this will mean. If he has offered to meet Alix, she must receive him.'

'No!' Alix said firmly.

'Of course, not,' Minny approved.

Queen Louise hesitated. It was against the grain but Bertie was probably right. 'Perhaps', she faltered, 'perhaps you should, Alix . . . really.'

'Never!' Alix vowed. She pushed herself to her feet, fumbling for her stick. The others rose in consternation as she limped painfully towards the exit.

King Wilhelm was in Frankfurt with Queen Augusta. Bertie hurried to pay his respects and to explain that Alix had not recovered sufficiently to come with him. The King repeated gruffly that he had offered to come to her, in person. Bertie had written to his mother to excuse Alix, praising her patriotism. She replied tersely that King Wilhelm knew Alix was well enough to listen to the band in the park and to entertain her friends. Another telegram arrived, asking the Princess to state a day and time for the King's visit. Bertie was faced with a diplomatic crisis. It was not of his making, but he would be blamed for it. Because of the Danish feud, relations between Britain and Prussia were now threatened and depended entirely on his actions.

He held a conference with Alix and her family in the library of their house at Wiesbaden. His sister Alice came from Darmstadt to second him. She told Alix that the King had heard she was much better and had taken great offence.

Alix was bitter. 'I should have known you would support him.'

Bertie could see that Alice was hurt. No one had been more injured by Prussian arrogance than she had. Nor done more to lessen it. If she could forgive, so could Alix.

'Alice and Vicky and Fritz are working to help the moderates to keep control in Germany,' he explained to them. 'All the good they have done from inside will be destroyed. They beg you to set a date and a time.'

Alix was unyielding. All she remembered was the anguish of those months when she had her first child, her father's defeat and the ravaging of her country.

'See him again yourself, if you must,' she said.

'If I offer to meet him again without you, it would be taken as a deliberate insult,' Bertie objected.

His conviction began to influence some of the others. Willy nodded. 'He's right, Alix,' He did not flinch when Alix looked at him.

It was the first real break in the opposition. Bertie was encouraged to ask the others. 'Will you see him, Sacha?'

'No!' Minny snapped.

'Let Sacha speak for himself,' Bertie proposed.

The Czarevitch was embarrassed. He admired Bertie and did not wish to be involved in a crisis, but he could sense Minny glaring at him. 'I do not think so,' he said, almost apologetically. 'In any case, he has not asked to meet me.'

Minny turned on Bertie. 'Why are you crawling to those Prussians?'

Bertie fought to keep his temper. He bowed to Alix's mother. 'Your Majesty? Remember what I have said.'

Queen Louise could not look at either Alix or Minny. She knew that her husband would submit, as he had before, to necessity. 'Well—if he does call . . . ,' she sighed, 'I shall meet him . . .'

Her daughters were horrified. 'You cannot!' Alix asserted.

'She is wiser than you,' Alice said.

Alix swung to look at Bertie. Instead of backing her, he had turned half her family into cowards, licking the hands of their oppressors. She felt betrayed. He was watching her anxiously and his expression of care and solicitude angered her irrationally.

'It is a question of common sense,' he said patiently.

'It is a question of feeling!' Alix hissed. Her intensity startled them. Bertie seemed frozen as she went on her voice growing louder. 'I shall never forget what happened to my country! Crawl if you must, but I shall never forgive—never—.'

'That is enough!' Bertie roared. His voice crashed through the library. Minny and Thyra who had begun to mutter were shocked into silence. He had always been unfailingly courteous to Alexandra, understanding, and no one here had ever seen him in a real fury. It transformed him. Even the way he stood was regal and commanding. 'It is your duty to put your personal feelings behind you! It is time you all realised *who* I am and *what* I am. The others may do as they please but you, Madam, will behave as my wife! You will receive the King of Prussia.'

In the silence that followed, Alix stared at Bertie, white-faced and rigid. For a long moment, no one moved, then she turned and limped out of the room on her stick. Alice gasped. Queen Louise and Knollys made to follow Alix, concerned.

'Knollys!' Bertie rapped out. The Comptroller paused and bowed. The Prince spoke clearly and explicitly. 'You will send a telegram to the King inviting him for breakfast tomorrow morning.'

In the morning, Carrington waited with Knollys in the reception room. Carrington wore a frockcoat and Knollys the full dress uniform of a British General. They were both serious and disturbed.

Carrington looked at his watch. 'They should be here any minute.'

'Yes.'

'He should be satisfied if the Prince of Wales and the King of Greece meet him at the station.'

'I doubt it,' Knollys said.

The situation was more than embarrassing. It was explosive. Rather than bow to the Prussian King, the Czarevitch and Minny had left the previous evening. And Queen Louise had gone with them, in spite of her promise. Only Willy had stayed to help Bertie. Beneath the careless facade, he was a fairly astute, young man.

'What will Princess Alexandra do?' Carrington asked.

Knollys looked at him stonily, without replying. No one knew. Alix had gone to her room and stayed there, seeing no one.

They came to attention as she entered the room with Alice and her lady-in-waiting. They saw she had dressed in black, as a sign of mourning for her defeated homeland. It accentuated the ivory paleness of her skin. With the stress, she limped heavily on her stick.

Carrington bowed. 'Good morning, Ma'am.'

Alix inclined her head slightly. She moved slowly to take up a position facing the door.

'Your Royal Highness looks pale this morning,' Knollys said and regretted it at once at the Princess looked at him.

Alix appeared steady and controlled, but her knuckles glinted white as she gripped the head of her stick. Her voice was low. 'I am being forced against my will and my conscience to meet this man. Though I cannot promise what my reaction will be when I see him.' She spoke as though to herself.

Her head rose as the door to the hall was thrown open and Wilhelm strode in. He was a stout, authoritative man of seventy with a bristling moustache and whiskers. He wore a plaid cape over his travelling clothes. His gentlemen followed him in with Bertie and Willy. His eyes surveyed the room and gleamed with satisfaction as he spied Alix waiting for him. Knollys and Carrington bowed. Alice and the lady-in-waiting curtsied deeply. Alix remained tense and erect. She could see Bertie behind the King, watching her.

Wilhelm made straight for her and stopped in front of her. It was an eternity to Bertie. The King had been monosyllabic at the station and in the carriage, scowling. Then Alix bowed slightly. When she straightened, she seemed even taller and more queenly. She held out her hand.

Wilhelm raised her hand and kissed it, impressed. 'I cannot tell the inestimable pleasure of meeting Your Royal Highness,' he said in his rumbling, guttural accent. 'I was disturbed by reports of your illness.'

'They were exaggerated, sir,' Alix replied evenly.

Wilhelm smiled. 'But not the reports of your beauty.' He bowed gallantly and passed on to speak to Princess Alice.

Bertie glanced at Willy and moved in to Alix, immensely relieved. She was still tense. 'I can't say how grateful I am,' he told her quietly. 'The Queen will be very pleased.'

Alix's eyes were lowered and she did not look at

195

him. 'I did not do it for your mother,' she breathed. 'Nor your country. I did it for you.'

Bertie wanted to touch her but had to step back as King Wilhelm turned and offered Alix his arm, to lead her into breakfast. She took it without hesitation. Wilhelm chuckled, gratified by his success, and led her towards the door. The backs of all who watched her straightened as they saw her walk by the King's side, tall and gracious, with scarcely the trace of a limp.

Chapter
12

Victoria was pleased with Bertie. He had shown that he could control his own and his wife's feelings for the sake of the country and the family. Dear Alix's heart was so warm it often heated her head, but he appeared to be overcoming his fatal rashness.

It was a grudging approval and he knew he had to turn it into real trust. Without that, she would never let him share in her work. He schooled himself never to argue with her nor oppose her decisions in anything political. It might take a year, even two, but he was determined to convince her she could rely on him. He made himself accept her rulings on everything, except his private life. That was his own and there he applied the lessons he had learnt in France. His nearest friends, the Marlborough House set, and the wider circle of wealthy members of society who formed his special empire realised that, for them, the law was absolute discretion. The one sin he would not forgive was the washing of linen in public.

He supported his friends loyally and wanted to be sure he could rely on them in turn. He was hospitable and open-minded. They must be, too, and ready to welcome him for an evening or a weekend at the shortest notice. He would not stand bores nor people who tried to use him. The men had to be interesting, active, urbane and generous. The ladies had to be generous, atttractive and amusing. He offered them entry to the most pleasurable and exclusive group in the world. No unmarried girl could belong, except as decoration, and no young wife who had not already given her husband an heir. The complications could be embarrassing. Infidelty had been common in society before, in an age when many marriages were arranged deliberately for family or financial reasons. The Marlborough House set raised it to an art. No compulsion was used. The Prince had an air of controlled power and experience which few women could resist. He was appreciative, kind and tactful. The pretty Lady Aylesford and the mettlesome Lady Filmer were especial favourites but he spread his net wide to avoid jealousies.

Through it all, Alexandra moved serenely, sure of Bertie's affections and increasingly devoted to her children. Her painfully stiff right leg and the irritating deafness which had not abated after her illness made her shy of meeting strangers. She did not object to Bertie going to parties or paying visits on his own but people wrongly interpreted her pallor and staying at home as a sign of sadness and turned against Bertie for ill-treating her. Attacks on him became more frequent in the papers and the popular magazines sneered at his highliving and idleness.

Early in the New Year, the ailing Lord Derby resigned and Disraeli was summoned to Osborne. During the hours in the train to Portsmouth and on the ferry across to the island, he held his exultation down. In the severe study, under a portrait of Albert who had considered him unreliable, the Queen asked him to form his first Government.

As he bowed low and kissed her hands, he murmured, 'In loving loyalty and faith.' Victoria was deeply touched. When his supporters congratulated him excitedly on his return to London, he shrugged. 'Yes, I have climbed to the top of the greasy pole.' Only his wife knew what it really meant to him. At the triumphant reception given for him at the Foreign Office, Mary Anne was escorted by the Prince of Wales and Disraeli had Alexandra on his arm. Like Bertie, he was true to his friends.

Disraeli was not deluded. He knew that his Government could not last. Gladstone had taken the leadership of the Liberals and shaken them back to life, in a way Disraeli had not yet been able to with the Tories. But he had time to bring in some measures which were needed and to do something for the Prince. He had already decided what it would be.

For years agitation had been mounting in Ireland, some of it directed at independence, most of it only at the English Church and the unfair laws of land ownership. Recently it had become more violent because of the Fenians, a subversive organisation formed in America out of Irish ex-patriots, aimed at the overthrow of the British Government in Ireland. Caches of arms had been found in Dublin, and a bomb factory. The violence had reached Britain, most hideously in an explosion at Clerkenwell Prison. In an attempt to free two 'patriots' who were inside, Fenians set off a barrel of gunpowder against what they thought was the wall of the exercise yard. Twelve people were killed, one hundred and twenty injured and the damage to the prison and houses around irreparable. The people of Ireland were horrified by such acts of brutality. The majority, who were loyal, felt degraded and despised. To show them they were not cut off, her Ministers had urged the Queen to visit Ireland, but she refused.

Disraeli's plan was for the Prince of Wales to pay an extended state visit and for him to rent a country home within reach of Dublin. It would give him a knowledge of Irish affairs and could lead to his appointment as Lord Lieutenant. Bertie accepted the idea eagerly. He saw that Dizzy was killing two birds with one stone and took up the challenge. It needed all their powers to convince the Queen but finally she consented. The announcement caused a renewal of agitation.

Many of his friends were worried for his safety and

warned Alix. Even when he called on Harriet Mordaunt as a relief from serious conversation, she begged him to be careful. As usual the servants had instructions they were not to be disturbed. He had laid his hat and gloves on the floor by his chair as a sign that he did not plan to stay long. It was a chilly, late afternoon and Harriet sat on a Chesterfield near the fire in her sitting room. She wore a frilly, peach-tinted afternoon dress which suited her little girl look. She was only twenty and had been married for two years to a man much older than herself, Sir Charles Mordaunt, a stiff, humourless politician. Bertie had known her since she was a child. She had no children. In fact, she had had two miscarriages, so an affaire was out of the question, but she was very provocative. And knew it.

'Now then, Harriet,' he said, smiling. 'Who's been frightening you with this nonsense?'

'Fweddy Johnstone.' She bit her lip.

Bertie laughed. 'Oh, well . . . You believe 'Fweddy' when he gives you a tip on a horse, but on nothing else.'

He rose and moved to sit beside her. His weight on the deeply sprung sofa made her slide closer and her knee touched his. She giggled softly and bit her lip again. He was so very strong and the spicy odour of cigar tobacco that came from his was so masculine. She always felt excited when he was with her. She hoped he could not tell.

Her hands were lying loosely in her lap. Bertie took hold of one of them and squeezed it gently, leaving his hand there. The light pressure of his knuckles against her made her shiver.

'I wouldn't go to Dublin if I thought there was going to be a bomb under every seat, would I?' he murmured.

'No,' she whispered.

He raised her hand and kissed the tips of her fingers. 'So you mustn't worry.'

She shook her head. 'Will you write to me—so I know you're safe?' She asked. 'Pwomise.'

He chuckled. 'Very well. And I'll come and see you again when I get back.'

The fears for his safety increased rapidly when the news came that Affie had been shot in the back by a Fenian sympathiser. Prince Albert was at a fete in Sydney, New South Wales, raising funds for a Sailor's Home. The bullet missed his spine and turned round the ribs to the front of his body. Miraculously he was not killed but there was a great loss of blood. The Australian crowd nearly tore his attacker to pieces.

Alix refused to let Bertie go alone. He had been so loving to her after Wiesbaden and she was going to have another child. She told him that her mind was made up. She would not let him face danger without her. When the Queen hesitated, Disraeli pointed out that it would be a double risk but, if successful, would also double the effect. The Queen gave in, suspecting that Alix would have gone with or without her consent.

In the event, this first visit of the Prince and Princess of Wales to Ireland was like their entry into London. On their arrival at Kingstown, the Princess was presented a white dove as a symbol of peace and affection. The Prince banned armed soldiers from his escort. He would have no troops in the streets of Dublin. The Irish people saw that he trusted them and admired his courage. They heard that the Princess was only just learning to walk again. They saw her stand through presentations, move in procession to St. Patrick's Cathedral where the Prince was made a Knight of the Order of St. Patrick, dance gaily through balls at the Exhibition Hall and Castle and they loved her. For ten days they showed themselves openly everywhere, at Phoenix Park and Puncheston Races, at Trinity College to unveil the statue of Edmund Burke and the Catholic University. The Irish took them to their hearts and, when the visit was over, begged Bertie to stay or at least leave the Princess behind. 'God bless her pretty blue eyes. She must have been born in Kerry.'

Disraeli was jubilant. Their success had exceeded anything he had thought possible, but he had reckoned without the Queen. To set Bertie up in Ireland would be like giving him his own country and diminishing her. The Irish people did not need him to be reminded of their duty. If he had a home in one of the Irish countries, he might prefer it to Abergeldie or beloved Balmoral and she would never see Alix and the children again. She rejected outright the idea of his buying a home there and took care that he had no further connection with Ireland.

Disraeli was too busy fighting to keep his Government in office and Bertie had learnt not to protest. He knew he could have followed up his success in Ireland, but he was not allowed to. He went, instead, to Paris where Jeanne de Sagan had had a son and Hortense helped him to forget. He returned and threw himself into the pleasures of the Season. Alix was the only one who understood. When she watched him dancing, flirting and roaring with laughter as he and his friends raced on teatrays, used like toboggans, down the stairs of Marlborough House, she wanted to weep for him. Sooner than anyone expected, she had her second daughter, Victoria Alexandra.

Although it was over a year since her illness, she had still not fully recovered. Her leg was weak and she limped badly when she was not forced to hide it. Her hearing was worse. She tired very quickly and was often upset by the dreadful rumours about Bertie. People seemed to be shameless in the stories they make up. Once or twice he had even been hissed at the races.

Bertie saw what was happening, but his restlessness had reached a stage when he could not stay at home with his family, which would have restored his lost popularity. The other remedy was work, but he could no longer count on Disraeli, whose Government was facing a crisis. Gladstone was demanding that the state visit should be followed up by concessions, that the Anglican Church should not be the official religion of Ireland.

Bertie met his friend Lord Hartington one night at Evan's Music Hall. He had gone there with the witty Lord Cole and Charlie Carrington. Hartington was a leading Liberal, a shambling, sleepy-eyed man with a straggling beard. If he had the energy to match his intelligence, he would have been at the head of his party.

They found him in a box with Catherine Walters, the famous Skittles, who had once been his mistress. He had since gone back to the Duchess of Manchester but Skittles was still a close friend. She was the only professional courtesan in London who matched the Queens of Paris. In her twenties, with a slim but voluptuous figure and a classic beauty, she first advertised herself by driving a smart phaeton drawn by two gleaming chestnut horses through Hyde Park. The lovely Anonyma in her skintight riding habit who handled her spirited horses so superbly became the darling of the young Guards officers and the most expensive whore in town. For a girl from the backstreets of Liverpool, she had done very well. Much of her charm came from her angelic face which contrasted with her accent and uninhibited freedom of speech.

'I dunno why Harty came here,' she told them. 'He ain't interfered with me an' he's slept through 'alf the patter.'

Bertie laughed and kissed her hand. They sat at the rear of the box and watched the singers through half-drawn curtains, but Skittles was more amused with her flow of gossip and stories.

'I remember the night the Markis, Hastings, let the rats out of the Cremorne,' she was saying. 'What a bloody scramble! A whole sack of sewer rats it was, in the middle of the dance floor. Then 'e an' his pals put all the lights out! You should've 'eard the screamin'—"They're at me garters!"'

As they laughed, someone banged on the partition from the next box. Hartington waved a languid hand at Skittles to keep her voice down.

'Oh, buzz,' she pouted. 'No, I'm sorry 'Astings is dead. Only twenty-six, mad bastard.'

Cole nodded. 'I was with him one day when he bet five hundred on which lump of sugar a fly would land on first. And he won.'

'He lost to Harry Chaplin, though,' Bertie murmured.

'Good thing, too,' Carrington agreed.

'Never got over that Derby,' Skittles said, and sighed. ' 'Ere, did you hear tell of the one about the miss who confessed to her Da that she had a bun in the oven? Well, I'm buggared, he gasped. Oh, La', she said, ain't we an unfortunate family!'

Bertie roared, then caught his mouth as the banging came again from the neighbouring box. On the stage George Leybourne was singing 'Champagne Charlie is me name, Champagne Drinkin' is me game.' Hartington knocked back to promise they would be quiet and they settled down, still chuckling, to listen.

Bertie leaned towards Hartington who lounged in his chair, his eyes partly closed, and asked his confidential opinion of the Government. 'Dizzy can't last the year,' Hartington assured him. 'Then we'll be in, sir. You can lay to that.'

It made Bertie decide. In the political climate and with the increasing number of attacks on him in the Press, he was better out of the country. He had thought of taking Alix on an extended trip abroad. They had been invited to Egypt and Turkey. She would miss the English winter and the cruise would restore her to health. Victoria would not let them take the baby, but the three older children could go with them as far as Denmark. They would leave as soon as he had carried out his last public duty of the year, to lay the foundation stone of the new University of Glasgow.

Alix had longed to travel with him, to the East and further. To her, it was the most exciting thing that had happened since their marriage.

She was not disappointed. The holiday was a second honeymoon that lasted for six months, a crowded, magic time with every day different, every day something new and fascinating. As well as their usual suite, the Princess had her favourite lady-in-waiting, Mrs. Grey, and the Prince took Carrington and the Hon. Oliver Montagu as an additional equerry. Montagu was a dashing young officer in the Royal Horse Guards whose gaiety and charm earned him an open invitation to Marlborough House.

Bertie kept his promise and the first stop was Paris. Like him, Alix adored the lightness and elegance of the city at once. And saw with pride that here he did not walk in anyone's shadow. Everyone treated him like a king. Black-bordered letters came, telling her not to mix with French society, not to buy expensive dresses, not to visit the Emperor's court at Compiègne. They were politely acknowledged, and ignored. It was not an official visit, but their presence made it one. Fashionable Paris fought to entertain them. The beautiful Princess de Sagan, the Comtesse de Pourtalès and the Duchesse de Mouchy were especially honoured to meet Alix. The Emperor Napoleon gave a ball for her at his sumptuous palace at Compiègne and her victory was complete. All the ladies wore their most magnificent dresses, resplendent in diadems, necklaces, pendants and bracelets encrusted with gems. Alix shone amongst them by the simplicity and exquisite taste of her gown and the restraint of her jewellery. She had developed a graceful, gliding walk to disguise her lameness and her colouring was exquisite. Only the glorious Empress Eugénie herself could rival her, and she was twenty years older.

They spent Christmas at Copenhagen simply with Alix's parents. Then, on Victoria's insistence, after a tearful farewell from the children, they went to Berlin. They were reconciled to Vicky and Fritz and King Wilhelm made Bertie a Knight of the Black Eagle. At the banquet which followed, they dined with Bismarck. Then on to Vienna, where Franz Josef's court was as formal as Berlin. Bertie and Alix brought life to it. Strauss played for them. They went on sleigh parties and the lovely, sad-eyed Empress Elizabeth showed Alix her beloved horses in the Imperial stables. People noticed how curiously alike they were but, while Elizabeth was intellectual and cold like a statue, Alix was warm, implusive and alive. The speculation had always been, which was the most beautiful—the Empresses of France and Austria or the Princess of Wales. Having seen all three. Carrington and Montagu had no doubt.

From Trieste, the royal party sailed at last for Alexandria and a welcome out of the days of Haroun al Raschid. Ismail Pasha, Khedive of Egypt, in gratitude for their hospitality in London, spread the treasures of the Nile before them. Bertie knew what to expect but to Alix it was bewildering, the colours and scents, the exotic flowers and native costumes, the majesty of the Pyramids and the fantastic luxury of the Ezbekiyeh Palace in Cairo which was made over to them for their stay, their chairs covered with gold and their beds of solid silver. Acrobats and dancers waited in the gardens all day to entertain them as they went in or out. They saw the Procession of the Holy Carpets and the start of the pilgrims for Mecca, and Alix visited the Khedive's harem, to Bertie's envy.

They were joined at Cairo by the Duke of Sutherland and other friends. They journeyed down the Nile in a fleet of blue and gold steamers trailing barges of wine and provisions. Bertie and Alix slept in their own dahabiah towed by the leading steamer. They had weeks of calm and perfect weather, where Alix rested or sketched or rode her white donkey to the ruins of great temples, Luxor, Edfu, Abu Simbel. Their guide was Sir Samuel Baker, the explorer. The Queen wrote to say she did not consider him a suitable companion but, with him, Bertie hunted hyenas and shot his first crocodile. The slow passage of the river to the cataracts and back to Cairo passed like a mirage.

Before going on to Turkey, they inspected the unfinished Suez Canal with its designer, Ferdinand de Lesseps. The Empress Eugénie was to inaugurate the canal when it was completed but the Prince performed the first ceremony, the opening of the sluices to let in the waters of the Mediterranean.

In Constantinople, they were given the Palace of Saleh Bezar on the Bosphorus. The Turks marvelled at Alix, 'A Princess of cream and honey'. Not to be outdone by Egypt, the Sultan Abdul Aziz had the palace completely redecorated with European furnishings, sent them jewelled gifts every day and an orchestra of eighty-four musicians to play for them while they dined. He even gave a banquet for them at which the terrified members of the Court were allowed to sit for the first time ever in his presence. They were so overwhelmed with receptions and sightseeing that some days later, pleading tiredness, Bertie sneaked Alix out through a back door of their palace and they wandered, gratefully unrecognised, through the bazaars and covered markets.

On the way home, they broke their journey to visit Willy and his new wife, Olga, in Athens, hunted boar in Albania, travelled in a leisurely fashion through Italy and arrived again, as they had promised, in Paris where Louis Napoleon held another ball to mark the end of their holiday.

The children were thrilled by horrific stories of the crocodile their father had shot and Alix showed them photographs of the black, bushy-tailed sheep which was being sent to Sandringham as a pet. It had been brought on their Nile steamer to be butchered, but had slipped its tether, wandered up to where Alix was sitting and eaten out of her hand. She would not let anyone harm it.

Bertie quickly caught up on the political scene. He knew that Disraeli had been defeated in the elections and that Gladstone's Liberals were solidly in power. Granville and Hartington were both in the Government so at least he had some connections. What his relations would be with Gladstone, he could only guess. Certainly not the trust and cooperation he had begun to establish with Disraeli. He wrote a report for Granville at the Foreign Office, telling him of the Emperor Napoleon's eagerness for a renewed alliance between France and England and pointing out that it was the surest way to stop the dangerous ambitions of Prussia from threatening either of them.

As soon as they had settled their household, they took the children to Windsor to visit the Queen. They were both nervous. Victoria had written so many letters of protest and complaint during their trip, about their extravagant hospitality and showing themselves to too many people.

'Everyone remarks on how simply *I* live,' she had said but, in the delight of having them and her grandchildren with her, all her irritation vanished. She thought Alix had never looked better.

'Yes, I only have a slight limp now. My leg is quite strong again,' Alix assured her.

Victoria smiled, then said sharply. 'Georgie, eat your cake properly!'

They were at tea in the sitting room. The Queen was talking to George, who was nearly four, a mischievous, irrepressible little boy. Next to him, his attractive, five-year-old brother Eddy sat much more sedately. Eddy was too quiet, Alix thought often. Lenchen was with them. She had not managed to escape after all. The Queen kept her and her husband in constant attendance.

'I had a letter from Vicky saying that you left a very favourable impression behind you in Berlin,' Victoria said. Bertie remembered the agonising formality and the patronising deference of Bismark. Alix remembered the cold antagonism of Queen Augusta. They both smiled. 'Yes, I'm very pleased with you both,' Victoria went on. 'These past two years you have behaved in an exemplary fashion.'

Bertie was relieved. 'Thank you, Mama.'

'I was particularly pleased by your reception in Ireland. I had great doubts at the time. It was not without risk.'

'They would have preferred to have seen you,' Bertie told her.

'Perhaps one day.' She smiled. 'Have you heard about Mr. Disraeli? Such a devoted man, a good man. When he was forced to resign I offered him an earldom, but he refused it in order to fight on in the House of Commons. I wanted to give him something to show my gratitude. Do you know what he asked for? A peerage for his wife.'

'Oh, how charming,' Alix said. She loved old Mrs. Dizzy.

'I thought so, too. Well, she is now Countess of Beacons-field.' She turned to Bertie. 'Mr. Disraeli speaks most flatteringly of you.'

'He is very kind,' Bertie said evenly.

'He believes that it is, perhaps, time you were brought on.' Bertie was very careful not to let anything show. Her head swivelled quickly and she snapped. 'George, stop that! Stop it at once!'

207

Georgie was jigging about in his chair, eating his madeira cake with his mouth open to embarrass Eddy. 'What do you think you are doing?'

As Georgie looked at the Queen, she frowned, imperiously. He opened his mouth and made snapping movements at her, unabashed.

Victoria glared at him. 'Georgie! You are not behaving like a little gentleman. More like a little dog. And doggies don't sit at the table, but underneath it. Go under the table.'

'Mama—' Alix protested.

'Under the table,' Victoria repeated implacably.

Obediently, Georgie climbed down from his chair and crawled under the tablecloth out of sight. There was an uncomfortable silence. Bertie coughed and Lenchen looked at her plate.

'I think maybe that was a little hard, Mama,' Alix said quietly.

'Nonsense,' Victoria declared. 'You are far too lenient. It's time you hired a proper governess to discipline them.'

'If children of that age are too severely treated,' Bertie objected, 'they become shy and only fear those they ought to love.'

Victoria snorted. 'We never indulged any of you. And it has had no ill effect.' Lenchen smiled secretly to Bertie across the table. Their mother had not taken his point, and never would. Remembering the strictness with which he had been brought up himself, Bertie was the most indulgent of fathers. He glanced at Alix apologetically. He could see she was having to restrain herself.

Victoria sipped her tea. There was a commotion under the tablecloth and Georgie crawled out from under it, stark naked.

'Georgie—' Lenchen gasped.

Victoria glared down at him, scandalised. *'What* are you doing?'

'Woof woof!' Georgie barked.

Bertie began to chuckle.

'What are you doing?' Victoria demanded severely.

'You said I was a little doggie,' George told her. 'And doggies don't wear any clothes. Woof, woof!'

Bertie and Alix were fighting not to laugh at Victoria's disbelieving expression.

As Alix started to rise, Lenchen choked out, 'It's all right, Alix.' Unable to look at her mother, she scooped Georgie's clothes up from under the table and carried him to the door.

'Woof Woof!', Georgie called back over her shoulder as they went out.

Victoria watched them leave, her mouth pursed, her eyes wide. She turned slowly. 'Woof woof,' she muttered. Then her mouth opened and she roared with laughter, reaching for her napkin. Bertie, Alix and Eddy joined in. 'Woof—oh, dear gracious . . . Oh, dear dear . . .' She wiped her eyes. 'Children are a joy. I never want my home to be without grandchildren.'

She patted her cheeks again with the napkin and shook her head. As their laughter quietened, there was a knock at the door and John Brown came in.

'Excuse me, Ma'am,' he said gruffly. 'The Prime Minister's arrived.'

Victoria's smile vanished at once. 'Oh . . . That dreadful man,' she sighed. Bertie was surprised. She folded her napkin. 'I sometimes think he's half crazy.'

'He's devoted to you, Mama,' Bertie assured her. 'And I'm sure has a sincere desire to serve you.'

'So you say.' The Queen's fingers tapped on the table. 'It seems to me a defect in our much famed Constitution to have to lose an admirable government like Mr. Disraeli's for no question of any importance or any particular reason. Merely on account of the number of votes.'

Bertie smiled.

'What?' she snapped.

Bertie paused. 'It must seem very odd.'

'Very well,' She nodded to John Brown. Bertie and Alix rose as she pushed herself to her feet. Before Bertie could move around, Brown was beside her and she took his arm. 'Half the time, I don't even understand what Gladstone's talking about,' she complained. 'He speaks

209

to me as if he was addressing a public meeting.' Leaning on Brown, she stumped out into the study.

Bertie never thought he would envy a servant. He had hoped to be asked to come with her, at least to meet the Prime Minister. It had not even occurred to her. He ruffled Eddy's hair. 'Come on. Let's all go for a walk.'

The days when William Ewart Gladstone was the handsomest man in Parliament had gone, yet he was still tall and vigorous, with a fine head like an old Roman Senator. Serious, with a brilliant mind, admired by Albert for his high moral character, he should have been Victoria's favourite politician. But he had never learnt how to handle her. Unlike Disraeli, he did not know how to flatter nor when to be simple. He could tell that he antagonised her with his obsession over the need for reform, especially on the Irish question, yet he had to continue to convince her.

He was standing foursquare on the carpet in the study, facing her. 'The condition of the people of Ireland is a perpetual reproach to Britain,' he insisted.

'What can I think of people who shot at my son, Alfred, Duke of Edinburgh, while he was handing over a cheque for charity?'

'It shows that some of the extremists cannot simply be appeased.'

'Yet that is your policy!' she retorted. 'And while we are on this—the visits of the Prince of Wales to Ireland and the Middle East have involved him in heavy expenses. Could Parliament not vote him more money?'

Gladstone thought of the recent objections to the amount given to the Royal Family already. He braced himself. 'Ah—the House of Commons has no intention, or disposition, to grant him any addition. Of course, if Your Majesty were to delegate some of your official duties to him . . .' He saw her stiffen and look away. He knew that she deplored her son's way of life and saw an opportunity to make a profitable point. 'Without that, his mode of life can only appear indolent.' He smiled. 'The real answer, however, and the one to which

I would lend the highest approbation and support, is for Your Majesty to undertake these visits yourself.'

The choice of argument was unfortunate and ended the Audience.

During the summer, the Prince and Princess gave an enjoyable series of garden parties at their house by the river at Chiswick, even some for the children, and everyone was pleased to see how attentive he was to her. With Alix able to take her place beside him, he devoted more time to her and the rumours died down. Towards the end of the year, she had their third daughter, Maud. Only the Queen grumbled. It was their fifth child in a row and she had missed the delivery of every single one. She began to doubt if it was accidental.

Alix had never felt closer to Bertie. The only activity from which she was excluded was his new club. When he was lighting his cigar one day in the morning room at White's, a steward had the impertinence to remind him that smoking was not permitted. Bertie promptly founded his own club, the Marlborough, nearly opposite his own house in Pall Mall. The accent in the new club was on comfort and lack of restrictions. His friends were members automatically. He drew up the rules and vetted the applications from all the others who flocked to join. As well as the aristocracy, he chose men from industry and business, the arts, the sporting world and politics, both major parties. As honorary members, he included selected foreign diplomats. At one stroke, he had created a congenial stronghold for himself and a meeting place for men of many different talents and professions. He could bring people together to discuss and settle differences. With this cross-section, he could find out easily what was happening in the country, the new developments. Without being obvious, he could let his own opinions and wishes be known.

In spite of all his efforts and carefulness, nothing had come from his mother. He had met Gladstone socially many times but there was a barrier between them. He realised that, quite simply, the Prime Minister disapproved of him. Yet he needed him on his side. The Liberals had started on a massive programme of reform. Bertie was aware that the new spirit of democracy could not be stopped. It had its extremists in the Republican Societies but, on the whole, he was in favour of it. Some of the members of the Marlborough Club, like Hartington, were in the Cabinet. He welcomed the Bill to make education compulsory. He let it be known that he would give his support to controlled progress, and waited.

It was after Christmas that the Prime Minister called at Marlborough House, a purely social visit to welcome them back from the country. Bertie and Alix sat with him in their private drawing room. He found them charmingly informal after the discomfort of Windsor where the Queen had never once invited him to sit. It was never easy for Gladstone to relax, yet he surprised himself by talking quite freely. Much of it had to do with the Princess's naturalness, but the Prince, too, was unexpectedly knowledgeable. His observation of conditions abroad was acute. Except for this continuing suspicion of Prussia. Gladstone assured the Prince that Bismarck had frequently said his only aim was stability inside Germany. There was no threat to anyone else. He brought the conversation back to the never-ending problem of the Queen's seclusion. The people's patience with her was exhausted.

'You must be aware of the number of Republican Clubs springing up, sir?' he said.

Bertie smiled. 'Oh, yes. Some of my best friends are Republicans.' Alix laughed but Gladstone did not understand. 'The time to worry,' Bertie suggested, 'is when they stop singing 'God Save the Queen' at the end of the meetings.'

Gladstone realised that the Prince was being humorous. 'I am inclined to take it rather more seriously, sir,' he observed stiffly.

Bertie was lighting a cigarette. 'If we take it seriously, Mr. Gladstone, the danger is that it may become so.'

Gladstone considered him. The remark was a little more astute than he had expected.

'Why did you really come to see me?'

The question startled Gladstone. He had come almost against his will, as a forlorn hope. Hartington had urged him to take the Prince into his confidence. The Prince was smiling to him. Gladstone was not at ease himself and did not notice the tension behind it.

'I-I find myself almost unable to communicate with the Queen,' he confessed awkwardly. He was committed now and, as the Prince nodded, went on, 'And yet in these days, with more and more power coming into the hands of the Executive, it is essential. I feel she resents me. She fights the Government's decisions.'

'So I believe.'

Gladstone was encouraged. 'I wanted to ask you if you would use your influence—'

'With the Queen?' Bertie cut in. He laughed and flicked his cigarette into the fire. 'Don't you know I have no influence with my mother? If I had, do you think I would be content to live as I do? That the height of my ambition is to open bridges and lay foundation stones?'

He had spoken more bitterly than he meant. Gladstone stared at him. There were years of disappointment in that voice. In public he always seemed so content and self-satisfied.

'Have you really pressed her to let you do more?' he asked. The Prince was silent. Gladstone saw the swift glance of compassion the Princess gave him. 'Forgive me,' he murmured. If the Prince were really serious, his position for some years must have been intolerable. He could see at once how, with all his contacts, co-operation between them could be very valuable.

'I have been remiss,' he murmured. 'Perhaps we can help each other.'

He was quite sincere. Bertie had been depressed. He had worked hard for this meeting, only to find that Gladstone was as powerless with the Queen as himself. His hope revived, but it was slender. He smiled faintly. 'Others have tried, Prime Minister. But I'll certainly do what I can for *you*.'

'Thank you, sir,' Gladstone said. He rose and bowed. 'I've taken up too much of your time.'

213

'Not at all,' Bertie assured him. He and Alix rose.

Alix had always liked Gladstone. Now that he was friendly to Bertie, she liked him even more, but the Queen had warned her strictly against becoming too intimate with party politicians.

'We have often thought of inviting you,' she said, 'but were afraid it might be misunderstood.'

'I should have been honoured,' Gladstone declared. He was completely charmed by Alix. She was the very model of what a Princess should be.

She took his arm and they moved towards the door. 'Perhaps you could bring Mrs. Gladstone to visit us,' she suggested. 'When the rebuilding's finished at Sandringham.'

'We are completely at your disposal, Ma'am,' Gladstone said.

Bertie let her see him out. He stood for a moment after they had gone, thinking. He was grateful for Alix's natural diplomacy. Gladstone had clearly responded to it. Things had gone well after all. Most important, Gladstone was sympathetic. He would still have to convince him that the faults of his youth were behind him, but that would not be too difficult. He felt the beginnings of excitement and turned as the door opened again.

He had expected Alix but it was Francis Knollys, the General's son. Francis was a very clever, likable young man who was shortly to join the household as the Prince's secretary.

He bowed. 'Sorry to barge in, sir.'

Bertie smiled. 'You're always welcome.'

'I may not be this time, sir.' Bertie could see that he was worried, with a suppressed urgency. 'You've heard about the Mordaunts?'

Bertie nodded. 'Yes, Harriet's had a baby.'

Knollys paused. 'Her husband's going to divorce her.' Bertie stared at him, incredulously. 'Apparently, the child was born blind. With the shock, she thought it was a punishment and confessed to Mordaunt that she's been unfaithful to him. With several men—all friends of his.'

214

'Good God . . .' Bertie breathed. 'And he's going ahead with it?'

'I'm afraid so,' Knollys said. 'She told him she'd committed adultery often, and in daylight—with Lord Cole and Sir Frederick Johnstone.'

Bertie was appalled. They were both close friends. 'Do they know what they're doing?' he demanded. 'It will mean social ruin for all of them!'

Knollys could not look at the prince. His voice was very low. 'The third man she confessed to adultery with . . . was the Prince of Wales.'

Chapter
13

As soon as he had had time to think, Bertie called Alix into the drawing room. He told her quite simply what had happened. She believed him completely when he swore it was not true. Harriet's family, the Moncrieffes, were neighbours of the Queen at Balmoral. Before she was married, Harriet had visited them and Alix had been friendly with her.

'How could she make up such things?' she wondered.

The news of the divorce case swept through London, and that Mordaunt had found a valentine and letters from the Prince of Wales in his wife's bureau. It was dismissed as fantastic. In any case, the Prince would be protected. Then the shock came. Serjeant Ballantyne, Sir Charles Mordaunt's counsel, had advised against citing the Prince as a co-respondent, but he was to be summonsed as a witness. That could be just as dangerous. Bertie knew that, whatever else followed, he must be the first to tell the Queen. It was the hardest thing he had ever had to do.

John Brown showed him into the study at Windsor, where Victoria was working at her desk. She was pleased to see him. He had been behaving so well recently. As the story came out, she became more and more alarmed.

'A witness?'

'I have been sent a sub-poena.'

'To appear in court? A Prince of the Blood . . .' She was horrified. 'It has never happened before in history!'

'I must not stand on privilege,' Bertie said firmly. 'There's no getting out of it.'

Victoria's hands clenched as the implications rushed in. 'Do you realise what this could mean? . . . Do you?! It has taken thirty years to restore confidence in the Monarchy—and you could destroy it in a week!' Bertie had dreaded her reaction. He stayed silent. Victoria laid her hands on the desk. Her fingers drummed. 'Gladstone thinks I do not know of the disturbances in the country, that I do not heed them. I am supposed to be proof against all.' Her head swung up. 'But now you, who are nearest to me, have given these radicals, these agitators, ammunition they can use to mount an attack on the security of the Throne!' Her voice was grating, her skin mottled with anger.

'I have not been accused,' Bertie said haltingly.

'All that people will remember is that you were called to a court of justice to answer for your conduct!' Victoria snapped. All her fears, all Albert's fears were coming true again. She looked at his bust which stood beside her. Its gaze was calming and all-forgiving, so wise. She forced herself to be practical. 'Well—how bad will it be? What will happen?'

'I shall be cross-examined on my relationship with Lady Mordaunt.' Bertie kept his voice level but this was what he most feared. Ballantyne was a brilliant barrister.

The Queen's eyes were fixed on him. Everyone knew that Harriet Mordaunt had become mentally unbalanced after the birth.

'Merely on account of what she said in hysteria?'

Bertie's throat was dry. 'I wrote her some letters.'

216

He could almost feel his mother's eyes. 'I found her amusing.'

Victoria was rigid with disbelief. 'I should have thought that even you—even you! . . .'

'They are harmless,' he assured her.

'Then why does she accuse you?'

Bertie hesitated. 'I have no idea.'

'I have begged you to be careful. But you have never listened!' Victoria began angrily. She stopped herself. He looked so lost and defenceless, like when he was a little boy and Albert had beaten him for playing instead of learning his lessons. When she went on, she was quieter and surprisingly gentle. 'Oh, Bertie . . . Bertie, Bertie. You are what you are . . . Of course, you are innocent. You have no need to tell me. But try to remember that your life is like a city set on a hill. Everywhere you go, everything you do, is known—and people delight in believing the worst of *us*.'

Gladstone had discussed the case with his wife, Catherine, an outgoing, warmhearted woman. He had taken an almost personal liking for the Prince and Princess. This business was an illustration of how vulnerable they were. His wife encouraged him to give what comfort he could.

He was amazed by Alexandra's reaction. 'Pray do not waste sympathy on me, Mr. Gladstone,' she said, smiling. 'Some women may enjoy playing the role of the injured wife, but I do not. I completely believe my husband. All *my* sympathy is for that poor girl.'

Bertie found them sitting together by the fire in the drawing room. He tensed when he saw Gladstone, expecting a veiled lecture.

Instead, the Prime Minister bowed and said, 'I came to express my indignation at this sorry affair. That a Royal Prince should be dragged into the witness box! It's unthinkable.'

'I confess I do not relish it,' Bertie admitted.

Gladstone shook his head 'The worst of it is these scurrilous articles in the Press. Unfortunately, the outcome of the case does not matter. The mere fact that you have had an intimate acquaintance with a young, married woman can only be damaging.'

Bertie glanced at Alix. Gladstone meant to be kind, but he had little tact. 'But you must attend the court,' he went on. 'There is nothing I can do to prevent it.'

'I don't want you to,' Bertie answered. 'If I do not appear, the public will judge me guilty—unheard.'

Gladstone bowed. He had never doubted the Prince's courage.

Bertie felt far from courageous. He had no illusions about Cole and Freddy. They had obviously broken the code. His own conscience was clear. He had not actually slept with Harriet. His friends appeared confident when they were with him, but they were worried about the cross-examination. There were more ways to amuse oneself with a willing and pretty woman than by simply going to bed, and he was not capable of lying under oath.

In the court, the excitement quickened. Mordaunt was vindictive and wanted everything brought out. A parade of servants testified to private meetings when Sir Charles had left for the House of Commons. Hotel staff told of a room Lady Harriet had taken, where Johnstone and the Prince had both come to see her. Coachmen reported secret visits by Cole to the Mordaunts' house in the country. The Prince was not on trial but Ballantyne insinuated his guilt and the corruption of his example. The people packed on the public benches waited eagerly for the final revelation. They were robbed of it.

The defence maintained that Harriet was unfit to plead. Her own father stated that, although her baby's blindness had proved only temporary, she was now deranged. Doctors confirmed it. The excitement swelled again as Bertie came to the stand to be questioned by the defence. The court had been against him but found themselves responding. He said he had known Lady Mordaunt since childhood and admitted visiting her alone. She was also a friend of his wife's. The notorious letters were produced and found to be innocuous, describing a hunt, asking after her health, announcing the birth of his own daughter. When asked if there had been any criminal act between himself and Lady Mordaunt, he answered emphatically, 'Never!'

There was loud applause from the court. To Mordaunt's fury, Ballantyne saw no excuse for a cross-examination. In spite of the contention that she was still sane when she made the confession, the petition for divorce failed on the grounds of Harriet's insanity.

The trial had been almost an anti-climax. Bertie's friends congratulated him. Alix kissed him and said she was proud of the way he had stood up. To show their faith in each other, they went to the Olympic Theatre. The audience buzzed with anticipation. When Alix came into the Royal Box, they rose and cheered. As Bertie appeared behind her, the cheering faltered and turned to hisses and boos. Bertie seemed not to hear. He bowed, expressionless, and sat facing the stage. Under the ledge of the box, Alix gripped his hand tightly.

What Gladstone and the Queen predicted had happened. All the goodwill that Bertie had won back was wiped out. He had been cleared in the witness box but not by the public. The members of the older, stricter aristocracy were outraged. The middle and working classes were amused or shocked by the revelation of scandal in high society, but they all combined in attacking him for neglecting Alix. He was hissed and catcalled wherever he showed himself, at best greeted with frigid silence. The Queen was glad that he had been legally vindicated but, almost with relief, decided that her Prime Ministers had all been deluded. Bertie was imprudent and not to be trusted.

He recognised that he had paid a bitter price for his personal freedom. Despite all his care and obedience to his mother, a few hours of diversion with Harriet had ended his hopes.

Alix was not as lively as usual in the weeks following the trial and everyone sympathised with her, exerted themselves to amuse her. Young Oliver Montagu was desperately in love with her. For a time, he had almost hated Bertie and had tried to stay away but he could

219

not live without seeing her. Bertie understood. Amongst all their set he was the most honourable. He had joined in the private supper parties and bawdy nights at the Cremorne, but his love for Alix transformed him. He became acknowledged gradually as her squire and asked for nothing but to watch over her.

One night they were having one of their parties at Marlborough House. Francis Knollys was turning the handle of the mechanical piano for Alix and Montagu and some of the others to dance. He was smiling as Carrington told him the story of the Prince's row with Freddy Johnstone.

'Freddy had looked on the grape rather too closely,' Carrington said. 'He was weaving about in the billiard room at Sandringham where we were having a last game before bed. So the Prince tapped him on the shoulder and said, "Freddy Freddy, you're very drrrunk". Freddy turned round, tapped the Prince on the stomach and said, "Tum Tum, you're verrry fat!" It was weeks before the Prince would even let him apologise.'

Carrington left him laughing and followed the sound of shouts to the main room used for receptions. The Prince was standing on one of the circular sofas in the middle of the room, right up on the raised, central pedestal, holding a glass of champagne. Charles Beresford was prancing about on the seat. Because of Carrington, he was known as Charlie B. A handsome, curly-haired young naval officer friend of Affie's, he was Irish and full of pranks and devilry, the licensed jester of the set. His impudence was famous, like his telegram, "Can't come to dinner—lie by post". He was prancing to avoid Lord Aylesford, Sporting Joe, who had treed him and the Prince on the sofa. Other friends stood round the walls laughing and shouting encouragement to Sporting Joe who was blindfolded and on all fours. He was only allowed to use one hand for grabbing. He knew he had caught someone. Beresford became too daring and Aylesford hooked his ankle, bringing him down. He crashed on top of Aylesford and they rolled over on the carpet together. The crowd moved in, applauding, and cheered as Bertie jumped to the seat and the floor without spilling a drop from his glass. Aylesford pulled off his blindfold and Beresford helped him to his feet.

'Joe was too fast for you,' Bertie chuckled.

'I sacrificed myself for my Prince,' Beresford said and bowed low. As they laughed, Bertie sprinkled some drops of champagne on the top of his head like a baptism.

'He's pinched your privilege, Xtopher!' someone shouted.

Christopher Sykes, a courtly, droll-faced man, stood waiting with a bottle of champagne to refill Bertie's glass. Everyone looked at him. When he saw the Prince smile expectantly, he raised the bottle and poured it over his own head, the champagne trickling down his face.

'As Your Royal Highness pleases,' he said benignly. It was his party piece, ever since Bertie had once poured a decanter of brandy down his neck.

Laughing, his arm on Xtopher's shoulder, Bertie led the way back to the drawing room. He found Alix talking to Montagu and Louisa, Duchess of Manchester. Hartington was half asleep in the chair beside them. He really looked a mess in his dilapidated evening dress. He started to get to his feet but Bertie waved him down.

'Lottie,' he said to the Duchess, 'can't you get Harty to change his tailor?'

'I've given up trying,' she sighed. 'I think if he wore a decent suit I wouldn't recognise him.'

As they laughed, Alix drew Bertie aside, 'I'm sorry. I'm going to have to go to bed,' she said quietly.

It was not like her and he was puzzled. 'Are you all right?'

'Just tired. Forgive me. Don't let me break up the party.' She smiled to the others and Oliver Montagu saw her to the door.

With the Princess gone, the other ladies had permission to leave. Slowly the party reduced until there were only the unattached men who could not leave before the Prince. He led them across the road to the Marlborough. They knocked for the Porter and played bowls in their shirtsleeves in the alley behind the Club until four.

221

He was chuckling when he got home. He, Carrington, and Beresford had won hands down against Sykes, Aylesford and Sporting Joe's best friend, Lord Blandford. As he went into his dressing room, he noticed the light still on in the bedroom. He looked in and saw Alix sitting by the open window. Dawn was coming up over the park beyond the trees. She was in her nightdress, her hair loose on her shoulders.

'I thought you'd be asleep,' he said, surprised.

She turned to him. In the soft glow of the gaslight, her face was pale.

'I'm leaving, Bertie,' she said quietly. For a second, he felt his whole body stop. 'I am returning to Denmark and taking the older children.'

His mind was racing and he could not think what to say. '. . . When?'

'As soon as possible.'

He moved closer to her and he could see the strain. 'I hadn't realised,' he muttered. 'Of course, you must have been hurt.'

Her head turned away from him. 'It's the way people look at me. They are all so kind. I can't stand being the object of pity.'

He had almost forgotten how lovely she was. Sitting here, half in the moonlight, there was no one more beautiful. The thought of losing her was unbearable.

'I swear I did nothing,' he told her. 'You said you believed me.'

She looked directly at him. Her eyes were steady, her voice calm. 'This time,' she said. The rumours, the stories, the hints and evasions had all fallen into place for her.

He was not sure how much she knew. That she knew anything was bad enough. Her calmness frightened him. 'Alix . . .' He stopped. 'How long will you be gone?'

'I don't know,' she said.

When Alix left, the house felt desolate. Bertie realised he had always needed to know she was there. That it was his own fault made it worse. He was very much afraid she did not intend to come back.

He wanted to follow her, at least to get away to the country, but he could not. The long-awaited riverside roadway on the Thames, the Victoria embankment from Westminster to Blackfriars, was due to be inaugurated by the Queen. She had been advised that if John Brown was in his usual place in the carriage, sitting behind her, there might be ugly demonstrations. Every since Brown had leapt from the carriage and beaten down a madman who tried to shoot her, she would go nowhere without him. If people would not accept her most devoted servant, they would not see her. She withdrew her consent, pleading ill health, and deputised Bertie to take her place. He opened the Embankment with his sister Louise. The crowds were restrained but he could feel their hostility. As soon as he could afterwards, he left for Sandringham. The new house was nearly finished, large enough to take them and their children and staff as well as unlimited friends. Its size and emptiness depressed him even more and he returned restlessly to London.

Gladstone brought him the news that put an end to his waiting. It was startling. In self-defence, Louis Napoleon had declared war on Prussia.

'Your analysis was perfectly correct,' Gladstone admitted. 'Bismarck was plotting to encircle France. The Emperor Napoleon had to act to protect himself.'

Bertie was elated. 'The Prussians can't hope to stand against the French Army! Once and for all, they'll be taught their lesson.'

'Let us hope so,' Gladstone said. He smiled. 'You may also care to know that the Queen is concerned about your sons being in Europe, when the situation is so uncertain. She has ordered Princess Alexandra to come home.'

Alix loved the new house at Sandringham, from the moment she saw it. Nothing was too grand or overpowering. Some of the bedrooms were as small as hers and Minny's had been in the Yellow Palace. The private apartments were more cosy than regal and the public rooms were full of light and air. It was a rambling house, full of surprising, little corners. From outside, it looked very solid and its wide terrace, high windows and old-fashioned gables and chimneys gave it the appearance of a red-brick, Elizabethan mansion.

She had been very reserved when he came to Denmark to fetch her. She had not known, herself, whether she would go back with him and was grateful that he made no demands on her. Then one day, as they walked in the park at Bernstorff with Eddy and Georgie running ahead of them shouting, she had caught him looking at her and his look was so wistful and humble that she had cried and told him she had only been waiting for him to come for her. When he started to make promises, she stopped him. She had learnt not to ask too much. They had been like lovers again, delighting in each other. She was hardly back in England again before she discovered she was going to have another child.

She had just taken Mrs. Gladstone on a tour of the new house. The Gladstones had come down for their first weekend visit and proved to be very good company. Alix took to Mrs. Gladstone straight away. She reminded her so much of her mother and she told her so.

Mrs. Gladstone smiled. 'Oh, I don't see myself as a Queen, Ma'am. I've quite enough to do, taking care of my Willy.'

Alix laughed. She was not used to thinking of the Prime Minister as Willy. She took her arm and led her into the sittingroom. 'And you like our new home?'

'It's perfect. And so comfortable already.'

'That's the most important thing, isn't it?' Alix agreed. 'It's good to have somewhere away from London. We can stay here, in the country, far from everyone and everything.'

'Not if my Willy had his way, I'm afraid,' Mrs. Gladstone said. 'You may be in Dublin Castle.'

Gladstone was walking with Bertie on the terrace. With typical thoroughness, he had checked the Prince's record and was astonished by the amount of public duties he already performed, but .scattered piecemeal throughout the year, undirected. His vitality and talents must be harnessed, properly, he had decided. Of course, the Prince was mainly interested in foreign affairs. On that his record was impressive, too. What had seemed like prejudice against Prussia had been shown to be a remarkably accurate forecast.

'The recent news from France is very grave, sir,' he said.

'I don't want to know the world any more if Louis Napoleon loses,' Bertie muttered. Napoleon had been like another father to him, a kinder, more indulgent father. When he was a boy, he had longed to live with him and Eugenie.

'Bismarck's outsmarted us all, I'm afraid,' Gladstone admitted. 'France is what he was after all along. Denmark and Austria were only the opening gambits. He kept the Emperor Napoleon appeased only until he was ready. Then forced France to start the war so that Southern Germany would join him without having to be asked.'

Bertie nodded. The German States between Prussia and France had been brought into the war automatically. The French successes at the beginning had never been followed up. While they were disorganised, Bismarck's strategy had been drawn up for years and his armies smashed through the French, splitting them and making any unified counterattack impossible.

'I know the leaders of both sides. Could I not be sent with letters?' Bertie asked, troubled. 'You've said yourself, this war is senseless. Could we not urge them to arrange an armistice?'

'I'm sorry, sir,' Gladstone said. 'Our Government is pledged to non-intervention. If we had agreed mutual aid, as you suggested, it would be another matter.'

'Then Bismarck would not have dared to attack.'

Gladstone nodded. The Prince was right, but one must accept realities.

The next few months were agony for Bertie and Alix. The enemies of Alix's homeland whom she longed to see humbled won victory after victory. Bertie thought of the fields filled with dead. The new breach-loading rifle used by the Prussians slaughtered the French. He implored his mother to intervene before too much destruction was done. She ordered him angrily not to be partisan, while she herself approved of the Prussian victories. She regretted the bloodshed but welcomed the collapse of the French whom Albert had considered untrustworthy and immoral. Bertie found it hard not to say what he felt, especially about Vicky. At the start of the war, his sister's letters from Berlin had been frightened and complaining of the terror of France. Now they were triumphant and boastful. Crown Prince Frederick William led one of Prussia's armies. She wrote to say she was sure Bertie must be envious because Fritz was allowed to be a real soldier and live a useful life.

Napoleon was captured after the battle of Sedan. The Government which had cheered the start of the war deposed him and set up a Republic. The Empress Eugenie escaped from the fury of the mob with one lady-in-waiting and found an English yachtsman at Deauville who braved a storm to carry her to safety in England. No one knew what to do with her. Bertie offered her his house at Chiswick. The Government protested and Victoria rebuked him for his 'presumptous indiscretion'. Eugenie thanked him for his chivalry and took a small house in Kent.

With the former Emperor imprisoned near Cassel, the Prussians besieged Paris which held out in spite of incredible privations and lack of ammunition for month after month. Bertie and Alix asked permission to send food to the children of Paris. It was refused. In January of the following year, Paris surrendered. The day before, King Wilhelm the First was proclaimed Emperor of United Germany by the Crown Prince, Bismarck and all his generals in the Hall of Mirrors at Versailles. He was now Kaiser.

In the early spring, Alix gave birth to their last child. It was the brother Bertie and she had wanted for the boys. They called him John. Like Eddy, he was very premature.

Victoria blamed Alix's hostility to Prussia. She had been too emotional. She was dear and loving but had never learnt to govern her feelings, as was her duty. So once again no warning had been given and nothing prepared. All her censure turned to pity overnight. The day after he was born, the baby died. Alix and Bertie were heartbroken. He was the child of their meeting in Denmark. They buried him quietly at Sandringham.

As much as Bertie regretted the downfall of Napoleon the Third, Victoria had welcomed it, but she began to think she had been mistaken. The fall of the French Monarch encouraged the Republican Movement to demand the abolition of the Monarchy in Britian. Riots and demonstrations were frequent. Republican Clubs became more active and widespread as the people saw less and less use for the Queen. She had only appeared in public a handful of times in over ten years, and only in London. If she travelled anywhere, it was in a closed carriage. When she did not have to be at Windsor, she hid herself away at Osborne, or Balmoral. Placards were posted outside Buckingham Palace, saying 'vacant. Desirable Property to let', 'Vacant. These commanding premises to be sold, in consequence of the late occupant's declining business'. And stories spread about her relations with John Brown who now called her 'Woman' and never left her side. It was said they were secretly married or that he was her medium and spoke in trances to Prince Albert. 'Mrs. Brown is mad,' they whispered.

Bertie spent as much time as he could with Alix, to help her recover from the loss of her child for which she blamed herself. He did not forget his other friends. The family home of the lovely Comtesse de Pourtales was in Alsace which had been annexed by Germany. When she visited London and could not come to a reception at Marlborough House because she was in mourning, he sent her a gold bracelet with pearl teardrops, inscribed 'Les Larmes d'Alsace'. But the public saw little of him and complaints about his idleness and extravagance became vicious. If the Queen would not appear, people demanded, why did he not do his duty and take her place? Was he more interested in food and fancy women? Did he surround himself with rich Jews like the Rothschilds because they paid his gambling debts?

Gladstone spoke to his colleagues in the Cabinet before leaving for Scotland to see Victoria. 'I say again—perilous times,' he emphasised. 'The call to abolish the Throne, that once merely threatened, now thunders in every city in these islands. Yet the Queen refuses to alter her way of life. She is no longer a subject of veneration. The Prince of Wales could take her place but he is still denied public office and his conduct called into question. The entire trouble is that the Queen is invisible—and the Prince of Wales not respected.'

Gladstone arrived at Sandringham after his return from Balmoral where he had put his proposals for the Prince of Wales' employment to the Queen. It had been a frustrating journey. Victoria had been too unwell to decide anything. He found Princess Alice staying with her brother for a few days. She had won admiration for founding and equipping a hospital in Darmstadt and nursing many of the wounded in the war herself. She had become much more independent and freethinking.

The Prince was grateful for Gladstone's efforts to help him. He had discussed Bertie's character and interests and drawn up his plans with great precision, covering a wide field. He suggested that the Prince should be given responsiblity either in the army, science and the arts, Ireland, foreign affairs or charitable, philanthropic work.

'Personally, I favour the idea that Your Royal Highness should spend part of the year in Ireland,' he told him. 'But I shall continue to urge Her Majesty to agree to one of the proposals as soon as possible. It is a more dangerous time politically than for many years. There is violent protest that the Queen will neither appear nor let herself be represented.'

'I have talked to her about it,' Alice said. 'She won't believe it's bad for her, bad for Bertie, and for the country.'

'And . . . there are these vile insinuations everywhere,' Gladstone said. He was embarrassed, but they knew what he meant.

Alix nodded. 'She should never have brought him down here.'

'He is her most faithful servant,' Alice protested.

'The fools who complain don't see how good he is for her. She needs him.'

'Unfortunately,' Bertie grunted. He loathed John Brown and resented his rudeness and familiarity with his mother. Yet he understood women well enough to see why his mother needed him. Her nature was strongly passionate and affectionate. Although, after his father, she would never marry again, she still needed a man to rely on, to stimulate her, one who could manage her, preferably if he was strong, handsome and independent. That Brown was her servant made it perfectly safe. She would consider it unthinkable to have sex relations with him. Undoubtedly the feelings were there, but she surpressed them. Undoubtedly, too, John Brown realised it and played on them. He was devoted to her but he enjoyed the privileged position it gave him.

'I know she cries Wolf,' Alice said, 'but this time she has really been very ill. Brown has had to carry her, lift her into bed.'

'She has been unable for months to see her Ministers. How long can it go on?' Gladstone asked. He turned to Bertie. 'The Government intends to press hard to persuade Her Majesty to permit you to deputise for her.'

'I'll accept whatever she agrees to,' Bertie promised. 'But, as always, she won't listen.'

It was more than a family matter now, Gladstone knew. More serious than any of them realised. 'She may have to,' he said gravely. 'When there are even some members of Parliament who call for her deposition.'

As the reality of what the Prime Minister was saying struck him, Bertie felt a rush of protectiveness towards his mother. At the same time, the prospect that he would be called to replace her came nearer. He had always thought he would feel elated, but his mind was suddenly empty. He had a wave of nausea as though he was going to faint. The others were watching him. He had to sit down.

'Are you all right?' Alice asked.

The nausea was passing. He laid his head back. 'Just

depressed,' he muttered. 'I can't sleep these days, ever since we came back from Lord Londesborough's.'

'He's been having dizzy spells,' Alix told them, concerned.

Alice moved to him and felt his forehead. His skin was sallow and he was sweating. 'You must send for a doctor,' she said.

Dr. Gull arrived that evening. Bertie was restless and irritable. If his mother was unwell and under attack, he wanted to go to her but Gull made him stay in bed.

When he had examined him, Gull came back into the dressing room where Alix was waiting anxiously with Alice and Lady Macclesfield. He closed his bag and set it down. The Princess looked so fragile herself that he was reluctant to tell her.

'Well, doctor?' she asked.

'I'm very much afraid . . . that the Prince may have typhoid.'

Alix caught her breath.

For a moment none of them could speak. Alice was the first to think practically. 'How soon will it develop?'

'I believe very soon.'

'We must send for Dr. Jenner,' Lady Mac said urgently.

'No!' Alice snapped. 'Ten years ago his incompetence killed my father.'

Bertie's fever increased and he was soon delirious. Alice took charge of the nursing with Lady Mac. The Queen sent Jenner and another specialist. Alix hardly left his side. She slept on the couch in the dressing room. The children were sent to Osborne.

The first bulletins issued were cautious but alarm swept through the Prince's friends and soon the whole country knew. The very word, typhoid, in connection with the royal family was frightening. People remembered the ordeal of the Prince Consort's death. In a few days, the bulletins left no doubt that his son's life was in danger and the drama was heightened when Lord Chesterfield, who had been one of his fellow guests at the house party, died in agony from the same disease.

At night, only a candle burned in Bertie's room and voices were hushed. He was in constant fever and any noise or shock could bring on acute delirium. He lay, panting and muttering to himself. Alix sat by his bed, leaning forward, straining to hear. Her exhaustion had brought back her deafness worse than ever.

'They're at me garters!' Bertie said loudly and laughed, although his eyes were closed. 'Get them—get them away ... Hastings—you mad, mad bastard! ...' Phlegm slurred in his throat and he coughed. 'Je vais plonger, plonger, plonger ...' he gasped. 'Do you want me to leave? Really? ... Let them sneer. I'll be damned if I'll lick ... lick their boots!'

Alix looked round as Alice came to her and touched her shoulder. 'Come away, Alix,' she said softly.

'No—'

Alice saw how wasted she was with care and watching. 'Dr. Gull says we must not go too near him nor disturb him.'

Alix rose slowly. Bertie's muttering went on, ceaseless. 'I can't—can't make out what he's saying,' she whispered. Not to be able to hear his voice was almost worse than anything.

Alice had spent hours with her brother. During some of his ravings, she had sent the others out of the room. 'It's best not to try,' she told Alix. 'Come and rest. You haven't slept for days.'

'I can't.'

'Just for an hour.' Alice led her out to the dressing room and Lady Macclesfield took her place.

The Royal Family began to gather at Sandringham. Affie was the first to arrive, then Lenchen and her husband. They brought news of the anxiety of the country. More and more people were gathering every day when the daily reports were posted up outside Marlborough House and the Mansion House. They, themselves, waited in the sitting room, for Alice or the doctors to come down, afraid to go to bed.

Alfred thought it essential their mother should be told just how serious it was.

'She is too weak,' Lenchen protested. 'She cannot travel just now.'

They broke off as Alice came in with Lady Macclesfield. Lady Mac shook her head.

'He's just the same,' Alice told them. One of the ladies-in-waiting could not stop herself from crying and Alice looked at her sharply.

"We must leave it to Providence,' Lady Mac sighed.

'Providence? There's no such thing!' Alice's voice was bitter. 'There's nothing.' Lenchen was upset for her. She wanted to ask how she could live without belief, but she froze, staring beyond Alice at the door she had left open.

The Queen, still in her black hooded travelling cape was limping in, supported by John Brown. She was shrunken and ailing, but her eyes were sharp as she looked round them.

'Where is he?' she said. 'Where's Bertie?'

A fretted Chinese screen was set up in Bertie's room and by day Alix and the Queen sat watching him through it, holding each other's hand. At night, Victoria slept alone on a mattress on the floor by her son's bed. Alix prayed by a chair in the dressing room or in a little church at Sandringham. Throughout the country and the colonies the churches kept virgil. It was as if everyone could hear that ragged, tortured breathing as he fought for life.

Bulletins now had to be posted at police stations, post offices and all public buildings. Reports were sent hourly to the newspapers. The waiting crowds, who had hissed Bertie two months before, filled the streets and squares, silent, stunned by the thought they might lose him, that Alexandra would be widowed and the Queen lose her heir as she had lost her husband. It was something beyond reason and politics and it went deeper as the December day they all feared came closer.

All the family were now at Sandringham, except Vicky and Fritz. Even Louis had come from Hesse. They were gathered with their mother in the drawing room. The doctor had insisted on Bertie being left alone, but Alix would not leave him. Knollys came with a statement for the Queen to see. She nodded, agreeing it.

'The demand for news is insatiable, Your Majesty,' he told her.

'They know it is the Anniversary,' Victoria said. The crisis had come during the night, just like Albert. It would go on to the end. She had given up hope.

'Ten years ago, to the day, from Father's death,' Alice said.

'But that doesn't mean—' Affie began. he stopped as Lenchen signed to him.

'It is fate,' Victoria muttered. 'We must accept it.'

They were silent until Dr. Gull came to them an hour later. He bowed gravely and said, 'I am very much afraid, Your Majesty, that the end is near.'

The screen had been removed and the Queen joined Alix by the bed. Alice moved to stand by the doctors, Gull and Jenner. The others filled the dressing room. Bertie was in delirium, restless, haggard, and sweating. He kept muttering the same sentence over and over.

'I'm not your boy . . . You've broken . . . Did I— did I forget your birthday? Broken your vows . . . Oh, yes. When I'm King? . . . When? No, no, no . . . I'm not—not your boy . . .'

Alix stood, too tired to pray, gazing at him. Beside her Victoria tensed as Bertie's words became quieter, then faded away and ceased. His ragged breathing slowed down until it could no longer be heard. He sighed and lay still and quiet, motionless. Alice turned away. Alix held out her hand and Victoria took it, holding it tightly.

Gull hurried to the bed and felt Bertie's neck, then the pulse at his wrist. He glanced at Jenner and to the Queen, bemused. It hardly seemed credible. 'The fever is gone,' he whispered. 'The crisis is over.'

Alix looked at Victoria. She had not heard Gull but saw from Victoria's eyes what he had said. She collapsed against the Queen and Victoria held her, crying too with thankfulness.

In the slow months of convalescence, Alix would let

no one but herself nurse him. One of their first visitors, when Bertie was well enough, was Gladstone.

He found the Prince in an armchair in the sitting room by an open window. It was a fresh spring day. He was still pale and weak and wore a heavy dressing-gown with a rug wrapped round his legs. Alix stood behind him with her hand on his shoulder as the Prime Minister told them of the nation's rejoicing. He was more animated than they had ever seen him, alive with enthusiasm.

'Words cannot express it!' he reported. 'People wept in the streets. The excitement—the affection everywhere, for both of you.'

'Thank you,' Bertie murmured. Alix's hand squeezed his shoulder.

Gladstone could see they were moved. 'Through reaction to your illness, sir, the whole nature of radical politics in Britain has changed. For all practical purposes, the Republican movement has simply ceased to exist.'

In his weakened state, it was more difficult for Bertie to hide his emotions. 'Strange—' he said after a moment, 'that what proved too much for so many brilliant men should have been achieved by a few feet of infected drains.' He managed to smile.

Gladstone smiled back. 'The country insists on an official Thanksgiving Service at St. Paul's. I think I can assure Princess Alexandra and yourself of the most sincere demonstration of affection ever received.'

Bertie glanced up at Alix. She spoke for them both. 'It will mean a great deal.'

'I am deeply indebted to you, sir, and hope shortly to be in a position to prove it,' the Prime Minister said. He had kept the best news to last but could not wait any longer.

'I am confident that I can persuade my Government to create you for an unlimited term—Viceroy of Ireland.' He waited, triumphantly, until his words had their full effect, then went on. 'You would spend the winter months in Dublin and the summer at Buckingham Palace, deputising for Her Majesty.'

Bertie's hands gripped the arms of his chair. 'Will the Queen agree?'

'The arguments are incontestable,' Bladstone said. 'It will give you valuable experience in kingship. And could go far to settle discontent in that unhappy land.'

'Would it be welcomed in Ireland?' Alix asked, as intent as Bertie.

'I have never been so certain of anything,' Gladstone smiled. 'It is a master-stroke.'

Chapter

14

The service of National Thanksgiving was the most stupendous show of love for the Royal Family since the wedding. Victoria had been flatly against it, but Alix convinced her that, while it was wrong to parade their private feelings, the public had shared their grief and had a right to share their joy.

It was a mild, dry day and the Queen wore a dress of corded black silk and a black feathered bonnet with white flowers. Opposite her in the open carriage was Bertie in a scarlet uniform with Alix beside him in dark blue satin and a velvet polonaise trimmed with sable, beautiful and radiant. Eddy, in his kilt, sat between them. The Queen saw how weak Bertie still was, older, his hair thinning, and her smile to him was so tender that the dense crowds wept as they cheered all along the route. She had never seen the streets so decorated, so hung with banners and shields and pennons. For once she did not tremble at the swarms of people and her whole spirit lifted to the singing and the shouts of 'Long live the Queen!', 'God Bless the Prince of Wales!' as the royal cortege moved towards St. Paul's.

Inside the Cathedral, special banks of seats and

galleries had been built to take a congregation of thirteen thousand, the nobility, foreign representatives and officers of State, led by Gladstone and Disraeli. The service was long and emotional. As he stood for the National Anthem that ended it and bowed to the congregation, Bertie felt deathly tired. It was his day and he had been almost overcome by the welcome of the crowds. Alix took his arm and he leant on her, leading the procession down the nave to the great west doors. As he came out on to the portico, the thousands jammed into the yard and the streets beyond surged forward in a tumult of cheering. It was only broken for a moment when the Queen stepped forward. In the breathless pause she raised Bertie's hand and kissed it and the tumult became a continuous roar.

Immediately afterwards, Bertie and Alix left for three months holiday in Italy, where he could rest and recuperate. During it, he thought seriously about Gladstone's five-point plan. His passion was foreign policy and he would really have liked to be a kind of roving ambassador. Before anything else, however, he wanted to be attached to the various Government departments in turn, so that he could learn the inner workings of each. He was particularly interested in the India Board. But he knew he would probably have to accept whatever was arranged for him. Hartington, who was Secretary for Ireland, said that Gladstone now considered a just settlement of Irish problems and the finding of employment for the Prince of Wales the most important challenges of his career. Clearly, he would see the two as linked. Bertie remembered his mother's rejection of the earlier less sweeping proposal for him to serve her in Ireland but, through the Prime Minister's urging, that would most likely be the one she decided on. She had been so affectionate to him since his illness. All the possibilities were exciting.

Gladstone came to spend the weekend at Sandringham when they had returned. He looked worn and tired, walking with the aid of a stick.

When they were alone together at last in the study, he said, 'I have been in constant communication with

236

the Queen over these last months, sir. I have to tell you—the reception at the Cathedral on the day of Thanksgiving proved to her the people's unshaken loyalty to the Throne . . . which she feels she cannot lessen by sharing it with anyone else.' He was sick at heart and had difficulty in going on. 'She has utterly rejected the Irish plan—and any others I may present.'

Bertie was numbed. 'Did she say what she had in mind for me?' he asked tensely. Out of all the proposals she must have agreed to at least one.

Gladstone leant heavily on his stick. 'Her words were—any encouragement of his constant love of running about, and not keeping at home or near the Queen, is seriously to be deprecated.' Bertie turned away. For a moment, he could not see. His fingers touched some papers on his desk, a report he had written on his private meetings with the Pope, the King of Italy and the President of the new French Republic. He realised it would be filed away, unused, as he had been.

Gladstone could give him no comfort. 'She has ordered that any further discussion of these matters between us must be conducted through her.'

Bertie thanked the Prime Minister sincerely and suggested that he rested till dinner. After he had gone, he walked along the corridor, down the stairs and across the hall, out through the front door and across the terrace, heading for the park. He walked blindly, not knowing why nor where he was going, desolate. He heard shouting and the rush of feet coming nearer. He turned and saw Eddy and Georgie running towards him. He held his hands out and when they ran up and caught them, he laughed, spinning them round. With his arm round one on either side, he walked on, making himself smile as they told him how the bushy-tailed black sheep had butted Eddy and how Georgie had jumped on his back and ridden him round the paddock.

Alix's hearing never recovered properly. She often had to guess what people were saying. It made dinners and receptions embarrassing sometimes and she much preferred to be at home where she could laugh and tell people to speak up. She liked her new woman-of-the-bed chamber, General Knollys's daughter, Charlotte, although she was dreadfully plain, because she spoke well and clearly. Charlotte and Oliver Montagu became her closest friends. When Bertie was to busy, they went everywhere with her.

She enjoyed living quietly at Sandringham with her sons and three little daughters. She liked to bath the babies herself, feed them and tell them stories. She liked it best of all when Bertie was with them and they played noisy, chasing games together, or picnicked with the children in the park. She was quite content never to leave Sandringham and did not mind that Bertie was away so much on business. She understood that usually this meant he was being entertained by his friends. If he told her what he was doing, she was pleased. If he didn't, she never asked. Much of the year they spent together and they were happy; she knew instinctively that, as long as she did not try to cling to him, that would never change. She thought frequently of Lottie Manchester, when Harty had deserted her for Skittles, without warning. Up till then, he had taken tea with the Duchess every afternoon at four. One day, after more than three years, he reappeared in his seat opposite her, again without warning.

'Two lumps as usual, Lord Hartington,' Lottie said, as though he had never been away. Alix did not think she had quite that coolness, but it was an example to remember. Though she sometimes cried, it was only when she was alone.

Society had missed the Prince's leadership. When he assumed command again after his illness, they were astonished by his vitality. His restlessness drove him like a demon. Francis Knollys, as his secretary, became indispensable. In London, he filled Bertie's days with meetings and appointments, important or trivial, it did not matter so long as there was constantly something to do. Bertie needed little sleep. Even when he did not go to bed until five, he was up again by seven.

At all times of the year, he accepted invitations to

his friends' country houses, either for himself or with Alix, if they did not clash with a public or family engagement. As a host, he was lavish and hospitable. He expected the same as a guest, superb meals and wines, entertainment arranged so that every minute of the day was occupied, indoors and out. A list of the guests was sent to Knollys beforehand and Bertie gave his approval or made his additions and, more rarely and catastrophically, his deletions. Hostesses hired the most famous singers and musicians, to entice him and surrounded him with the prettiest, most amusing women they could find. He saw an actor wearing a tattered coat but liked the cut of it. He asked the tailor's name and the tailor became the rage. He could dine with a punctilious Archduke or drink whisky in a turf-covered Highland cottage with the crofter, yet he was always the Prince.

Gladstone still worked tirelessly for him, antagonising the Queen more and more. His Government was under fire. He had pushed through reform after reform, all the measures which for years had seemed to him glaringly necessary. But the country had had enough of reform. The world was changing too rapidly. Disraeli led his New Conservatives into the attack, denouncing the Government as 'exhausted volcanoes'. He sensed the depth of the renewed loyalty to the Throne and the people's longing for stability. Most important, he remembered British reaction to the triumphal march of the Prussian army through Paris. International politics were dominated by the demands of the German, Austrian and Russian Empires. Britain with her possessions, dominions and dependencies had the largest empire ever known, though not in name. Nothing could happen in any area of the world without affecting her interests, yet she seemed to have no influence any more. Gladstone's careful pacificism and non-intervention was out of touch with the mood of the people. They had seen the collapse of France and Napoleon the Third dying in exile in his small house in Kent and all their sympathies were with the Prince who had been prevented by the Government from attending his funeral. Was fear of the Kaiser and the new French Republic to be allowed to stop

239

him paying his last respects to a friend? They did not like the implications and responded eagerly to Disraeli's crusading Imperial policy.

Disraeli's fervour also delighted the Queen. She had missed the humour and excitement of working with him. When his wife died, her letters to him were genuine and touching, creating a deeper bond of sympathy between them. He was one who could understand her sorrow.

While he was in St. Petersburg with Alix for Affie's wedding to the Czar's daughter, Marie, Bertie had a letter from Disraeli informing him that he was once again Prime Minister. Gladstone, ill and despondent, retired from politics. Disraeli, older, wheezing with asthma, limping from gout, travelled to Osborne to kiss the Queen's hands. She was so pleased that, for a terrifying moment, he thought she was going to embrace him. He called her his Faery Queen and she sent him the first primroses from her gardens.

Disraeli came to Marlborough House shortly after the Prince's return. Bertie liked Gladstone as a man, in spite of his lack of humour, but Disraeli intrigued him. Gladstone was, morally, very correct but women were as essential to Disraeli as to Bertie.

'I am fortunate in serving a female sovereign,' Disraeli smiled.

'She admires you extravagantly,' Bertie told him. 'While I have had no chance to earn her respect.'

Disraeli could tell what he wanted. It was very difficult. 'Ah—there is much I wish to do in the time left to me, and I should like to do something for you, sir. Yet I must move carefully. If I lose the confidence of Her Majesty, I shall achieve nothing.' Bertie nodded. 'However, I shall continue to suggest that your capabilities have been underestimated and, whenever possible, send you despatches and keep you informed of the Government's plans. It will be, of course, just between us.'

'I'm deeply grateful,' Bertie told him.

Disraeli smiled. 'And if I might advise—any extension of your contacts with foreign courts and politicians would be most valuable. Not merely for information, but for

240

them to know that, whatever happens, there is one person here they can trust. Apart from that, I'm afraid you will have to make your own opportunities.'

On their way to Copenhagen that year, Bertie insisted that Alix come with him to Potsdam to stay with Vicky and Fritz at the rococco Neues Palais, for their eldest son's confirmation. Young Willy had grown into a handsome, straightbacked boy. Bertie read a letter to him from his grandmother, Queen Victoria, and afterward they talked. He could see Vicky becoming worried as the boy, eyes shining, described the Prussian army's victory parade through Berlin after the war, the delirium of the people.

'So many flowers, Uncle Bertie,' he said. 'All you could see of the marching columns were their bayonets.' Willy was completely obsessed by soldiers. To him, war was glorious. It distressed Vicky. She and Fritz had rejoiced at the victory and realised, too late, that they had helped to turn Germany into a rigid, militarist state. Alix was glad she had come. She felt sorry for Vicky, closer to her than she had for many years.

With Alix in Denmark, Bertie went with the smallest staff possible to Paris. The rebirth of the city was unbelievable. There were no signs left of the siege. Under Thiers and the new soldier President MacMahon who had crushed the commundards, France was alive again. Bertie had to steer a finely-judged course between the leaders of the Republic and the old leaders of society, without forfeiting the respect of either. He was triumphantly successful. At the mansion on the corner of the Esplanade des Invalides and the Rue de Grenelle, a magnificent ball was given to welcome him back. Wigged and uniformed footmen lined the curving stairs. By the bottom step, the Princesse de Sagan curtsied and received him as maitresse en titre.

Some of his intimate male friends held a superb dinner for him in the fondly-remembered Grand Seize, the private dining room, in the Cafe Anglais. The dessert was the exquisite Cora Pearl, naked except for a velvet collar, served up on a gigantic silver platter.

From Paris, he went on a royal progress through the chateaux in the valley of the Loire. It was not Republican nor Second Empire. It was managed as in the days before the Revolution by the remaining Princes, Dukes and Marquises of France. He dined, danced and hunted from Esclimont to Chantilly. Only one slight upset marred the festivities and its telling, oddly enough, added to his celebrity. The young Marquise d'Harcourt, who appeared to be surrendering to him, whispered that she would leave a rose on the handle of her bedrooom door. 'So that you will know which it is.' When everyone was asleep, he crept along to the room with the marked door. In bed, he found the ugliest scullerymaid in the chateau waiting for him.

Having pleased the Royalists, on his return to Paris he reaffirmed his friendship with the French branch of the Rothschilds, the Barons Alphonse and Gustave, and won over the Republicans by hunting with the President, Marshal MacMahon.

Back in London, he saw the days stretching emptily ahead. Disraeli was grateful for his comments on German, Russian, and French intentions and, in return, fed him titbits of information. But there was no way in which he could use them. He had to do something positive, somthing spectacular.

He was working one day with Francis Knollys in his study at Marlborough House. Francis was checking through his list of appointments with him, but he could not concentrate.

'There is a visit to Birmingham on the third,' Francis said. 'The mayor, Joseph Chamberlain, is a bit of a Red, so he'll have to be handled carefully.'

Bertie nodded. He thought he might call on Randolph and Jennie Churchill. He'd been very taken with Jennie Jerome, fresh and attractive, like so many American girls seemed to be, fun to be with and not coy. He'd really done Randy a favour there, introducing him to Jennie. They'd just had their first child and might appreciate a visit.

'Sorry, Francis,' he said. 'I've got the fidgets. I'm going out for a little.'

As he crossed the hall, Alix came in from outside with Oliver and Charlotte. She handed her cape to Charlotte and hurried to him. 'Darling, you should have come with us.' She kissed his cheek. 'It was marvellous! Wasn't it, Oliver?'

'What was?' Bertie asked.

'The Exhibition of Native Arts. But so perfect. Especially the things from India—the ivories, the carving! Oh, I'd love to go there. Wouldn't you, Charlotte? All those kings and princes. It must be wonderfully exotic, and none of us has ever been.'

'Except Affie,' Bertie smiled. 'And all he did was get drunk.'

'Now you're laughing at me,' Alix protested. 'You can't wait to get away and I wanted to tell you about it.'

'A little later, my dear. There's something I have to discuss with Francis.'

A few months later, Disraeli arrived back nearly speechless at Downing Street after an Audience with the Queen. He sent for Lord Salisbury, his most trusted, junior colleague.

'I have just had an extraordinary experience,' he said. 'It seems that our Prince Hal has informed his mother that I have suggested, with the full approval of Her Majesty's Government, that he should make a state visit to India.' Salisbury was Secretary for India, and, normally, self-possessed. His mouth opened and closed, then opened again. It explained why the Prince had taken such an interest in his department recently.

'Did he discuss it with you, Prime Minister?'

'Only in general terms. The use of such a trip, and the expense.'

'What did the Queen say to him?'

'She gave her consent, since it was my suggestion.'

Salisbury gaped at him. It was inconceivably embarrassing. 'What are we going to do?'

Disraeli shrugged. 'Write and tell the Viceroy, I suppose.' As Salisbury's mouth opened again, he laughed. 'Well, I did tell him he'd have to create his own opportunities. And it may fit in tolerably well with something I have in mind.' The Prince's idea was that a visit by the Heir Apparent would show the Queen's distant subjects that they were not forgotten and prove to the rest of the world the existence of the British Empire. A brilliant move, if it were successful.

'The problems of organisation!' Salisbury protested. 'Think of the cost—the travelling staff the Prince and Princess will need.'

'Apparently, he has it all worked out already, in considerable detail,' Disraeli said. 'And for some unaccountable reason, has not yet told his wife he is going.'

Bertie was with Carrington, Randolph Churchill, Lord Blandford and the attractive Lady Aylesford in the hall at Sandringham. He had become friendly with Churchill, a rising young politician, brilliant and witty, with a sweeping moustache and rather pale, bulging eyes. He preferred him to Blandford, his elder brother. They had had an excellent dinner after a good day's shooting and the party was just beginning.

'You don't mind if I tell them, do you sir?' Churchill said. Bertie shook his head, smiling. 'Well—the Prince and Princess were on a tour of Coventry with Hartington and the Duchess of Manchester. The Mayor was showing them around and kept insisting that Harty Tarty should see the municipal bowling alley. Finally they reached it. Harty Tarty looked round, grunted, 'What's so special about it?' and the Mayor was very surprised. 'Oh,' he said. 'His Royal Highness asked me to be certain to show it to you, in tribute to your Lordship's well-known love of skittles.'

Carrington collapsed back against the wall. Edith Aylesford squealed and grabbed Blandford's arm.

As they laughed, Alix came from the sitting room. She was white and tense. 'Is it true?' she demanded. 'Bertie, is it true?' He led her away from the others quickly. 'You know I've longed to go there for years, ever since we were in Egypt! How could you think of going without me?'

'We can't talk here, Alix.'

'Don't you want me with you? Don't you trust me?'

Bertie had known how hurt she would be and had delayed telling her as long as possible. 'Alix, try to understand. It's something I have to do on my own.'

There was loud shouting behind them and Lord Aylesford shot out of the sitting room on his hands and knees, blindfolded. Beresford and Christopher Sykes followed him, whooping and whacking him with rolled-up newspapers.

Blandford was standing with Edith Aylesford. 'Joe certainly has an amazing penchant for being beaten about the rump,' he murmured.

Edith nodded. 'Yes, poor old thing.'

Alix did not understand. She appealed to Disraeli who, by now, was as keen for the visit as the Prince and would not let anything upset it. He could not help her. In desperation, she went to the Queen who would not even listen. She would not allow ladies to accompany the party. The climate and the conditions were too dangerous.

'It is my right to be with my husband!' Alix protested.

Victoria restrained herself. 'You will not speak to me of "rights". Your *duty* is to stay at home with your children. I remember Albert once saying to me—I love you far too much to let you do what would do you harm—and there's an end of it.'

Alix wept and clung to Bertie as they said goodbye at Calais. As a consolation she had been allowed to take the children on a Christmas holiday in Denmark, but it was small comfort.

Bertie travelled overland to Brindisi with his accompanying staff and servants to pick up the naval escort and the converted troopship *Serapis* that was to take them to India. He was very depressed by the parting from Alix and hated to leave her behind, but he knew his mother. If he had tried to demand permission for both of them, she would have cancelled the whole visit. As it was, he had to fight to include some personal friends in his suite. He brought Carrington and Beresford for fun, Sutherland for hunting and Sporting Joe Aylesford to organise the pig-sticking and polo.

He did not revive until they reached the Suez Canal. His friends were relieved. After all the anticipation, the start of the trip had been very sombre. In Egypt, the Prince decorated the Khedive's son, Tewfik. In his letters home, he confirmed to Disraeli that Ismail Pasha seemed to be in difficulties. Egypt was on the edge of bankruptcy. As they steamed out of the Red Sea and on to Aden, the heat became unbearable. They slept in hammocks outside their cabins. The Prince had authorised less formal dress for the evenings and his staff were grateful. In place of tails or uniform, he devised a short, dark jacket worn with black trousers and a black bow tie, which he named 'The *Serapis* style'. The others called it a smoking or dinner jacket.

From Aden, they sailed in dead calm across the Indian Ocean to Bombay, once barren rock and now a huge commercial metropolis, where the *Serapis* steamed into the harbour between lines of saluting men-of-war with Bertie at the poop in the full uniform of a Field-Marshal. His visit had caused immense interest; fortunes had been spent in preparing his welcome and decorating every city and town he was to see. As well as the leading British officials, the landing stage held hundreds of chiefs and sirdars, Hindus, Parsees, Mohammedans, come to show their devotion to the throne. On the five-mile-road to Government House, there were flowered arches with 'Welcome A.E.' and 'God Bless the Prince of Wales'. The enthusiasm of the hundreds of thousands who lined the route in every variety of costume and colour was only a sign of what was to follow.

Bertie enjoyed the pomp of the British Administration. It appealed to his love of ceremony and spectacle. Unlike many of the officials, however, he treated the native rulers with respect and courtesy. At his first Durbar, he sat on a silver throne before a panel of crimson velvet topped with his Prince of Wales feathers in silver, and a crimson carpet embroidered with the royal coat-of-arms stretched halfway down the Audience Hall in front of him. Seats for his staff were on the left and for the native rulers on the right. As each jewelled, turbaned rajah, maharajah, rao, gaekwar and nawab was presented, he rose, came to the edge of the carpet, shook hands and led him to his chair of state. Giving them the respect due to them, he won their love and loyalty. The gifts they presented for him, Alix and the Queen were staggering in their magnificence, from ropes of diamonds and rubies and pearls to solid gold cannons. The mood of the vast crowds which followed him changed, as they came to know him, from affectionate curiosity to wild adoration. He was the visible spirit of the Raj, a symbol of what had been promised but never fully achieved. He wrote angry letters to the Queen and Lord Salisbury protesting at the arrogance of some of the British political officers to the princes and chiefs to whom they were attached, demanding better treatment.

He visited Poona and entered Baroda in a silver-gilt howdah. He hunted in Ceylon and shot his first wild elephant after a hectic jungle chase, torn by bamboos and bitten by leeches. He cut off its tail; Beresford jumped on to it as it lay on its side and started to dance a hornpipe. The vast beast had only been stunned. It shook him off, lumbered to its feet and charged off again into the jungle where it vanished. They sailed on to Calcutta, Benares, Lucknow, Agra and Delhi, Fetes, receptions, races, polo, banquets, troop reviews, hunting, balls, investitures, and Durbars, the Prince was indefatigable. The Duke of Sutherland left for home, exhausted.

It was in Lucknow he had the news that Britain had bought a controlling interest in the Suez Canal from the bankrupt Khedive. In order to buy the shares Disraeli had borrowed four million pounds from Bertie's friends, the Rothschilds, on no security but trust.

'Right under the noses of the rest of the world,' Bertie smiled to Francis Knollys, as they celebrated the diplomatic coup.

'It's what you most wanted, sir' Francis said.

'I told him, if we didn't own it, we'd be forced to take it,' Bertie laughed. 'Good old Dizzy.'

In the fourth month of the tour, the chief tiger hunts began in Nepal, on a scale that had not been seen since the Moguls. The ruler of Nepal provided one thousand riding elephants and ten thousand soldiers to act as beaters when they crossed the Sardah River. The camp built for the Prince covered several square miles. On the first day's shooting, he killed two man-eaters.

He was in an exceptionally good mood, standing on the verandah of his tent with Carrington and Beresford after dinner. He lit a cigar, listening to the drums and the wail of reed pipes from the Nepalese soldiers' lines in the distance. Francis Knollys was adding a splash of soda to their brandies.

'Brandy Pawnees,' Bertie reminded Carrington and they laughed.

'Poor Mr. Bartlett,' Carrington said. 'He's still trying to find out who let the armadillo loose in his tent last night.'

Bartlett was the official zoologist attached to them. The camp had been wakened by terrified yells from his tent when he thought a tiger had crept in.

'Dreadful thing to do to anyone,' Beresford observed, inscrutably. 'Don't you think so, sir?'

'Quite, Charlie B,' Bertie said. They smiled to each other.

They looked round as Lord Aylesford came towards the verandah. He had asked to be excused dinner. 'Feeling better, Joe?' Bertie smiled.

As Aylesford came into the light of the lamps hanging on the verandah, he stood blinking. He looked ill and disturbed. 'There was a letter waiting for me,' he muttered. 'From Edith—my wife. She tells me she's going to run off with Lord Blandford.'

The others were shocked. 'Blandford?' Carrington exclaimed, disbelievingly.

'He's left his wife already. Apparently, he's been—been living with Edith ever since we came away.'

'God Almighty . . .' Beresford gasped.

'What're you going to do, Joe?' Bertie asked gently.

'Don't rightly know, sir. Hate the idea of divorce—but I can't forgive her.' He sounded lost. 'Blandford was my best friend.'

'I'd shoot him,' Beresford said strongly.

'Probably would if he were here now,' Aylesford said. He was just managing to keep himself in control. 'Do I have your—your permission to return home, sir?'

Shortly after, the Prince had a long telegram from Randolph Churchill, saying he had persuaded Edith and his brother not to elope by pointing out that a scandal of this type would destroy them both socially. He asked the Prince to influence Aylesford against insisting on a divorce.

Bertie discussed it with the others. They thought Aylesford had a perfect right to make his own decisions. He agreed. It was a private matter and he decided not to become involved in any way in another public scandal. He continued the weeks of hunting which were reported day by day in the Indian newspapers, with increasing awe at his courage, endurance and sheer physical power. On his return through Allahabad to Bombay, he was greeted like a hero-king and the waving crowds cried out and sobbed as the *Serapis* and her escort set off on the long voyage home.

Disraeli was delighted by the overwhelming success of the Indian visit. It has been followed with the keenest interest in Britain and shown the Russians that their ambitions in the sub-continent were hopeless. It had also given him the necessary impetus to put through his Royal Titles Bill, a vital part of his Imperial policy, creating the Queen Empress of India.

Victoria was more pleased with Bertie than she could remember. The reports from the Viceroy and the many letters she had had from the native princes had all been highly gratifying. Some already addressed her as Queen-Empress. She liked that. It had a sound to it. She could hear Disraeli's voice as he spoke it, thrilling, emotional, confirming Britain's position as first among nations. She was very glad that Bertie was out of the country while this unsavoury scandal was taking place in his circle and agreed that he was correct not to take sides. She grieved at the distress of her dear friends, the Duke

249

and Duchess of Marlborough, the parents of Lord Randolph Churchill and the disgraced Blandford.

Alix was as excited as the children that Bertie was coming home and longed to see the shiploads of treasures he was bringing.

'Elephants, tigers, even leopards,' she told Charlotte Knollys as they sat in the drawing room at Marlborough House.

Charlotte smiled. 'Quite a menagerie, Ma'am,' She repeated louder, 'A menagerie.'

Alix laughed. 'Exactly! It's all gone so splendidly. Except for this wretched Aylesford business. Such a pity. I'm so fond of them all.' Charlotte nodded. 'And now I hear Randolph is running around telling everyone that it's Bertie's fault for taking Joe with him and throwing them together.'

'Ridiculous,' Charlotte snorted. 'He actually believes it.'

'I expect he's only trying to protect his brother,' Alix sighed. 'Still, I suppose I mustn't receive any of them—not till it's all settled, anyway.'

'Certainly not, Ma'am,' Charlotte said, shocked.

A page in a dark blue jacket and black trousers knocked and came in. He bowed. 'Lady Aylesford is downstairs, Ma'am, and asks if she may see you in private for a few minutes.'

Alix smiled, delightedly. 'Thank you. Do ask her to come up.'

Charlotte gazed at her in astonishment. 'Do you think it's wise, Ma'am?' she asked.

Alix laughed. 'Well, why not? I like her very much. I didn't even know she was in London.'

Charlotte rose. 'You'll wish to see her on your own,' she said. 'I shall be in my room.' She curtsied and left.

Alix was puzzled. Charlotte sounded so disapproving. She realised why a moment later when Edith Aylesford was shown in. With her deafness, she had completely misheard the name. Lady Aylesford was accompanied by Lord Randolph Churchill and a tall, elderly man, Lord Alington.

'It's very kind of you to see me, Ma'am,' Lady Aylesford said. She was embarrassed and showed signs of prolonged strain.

Alix was not sure what to do. She hoped her dismay did not show and realised that Edith must have been desperate to break convention like this. No other house in London would accept her but, having made the mistake, Alix could not send her friends away again.

She smiled briefly. 'Do, please, take a seat, Lady Aylesford,' she said.

Churchill stepped forward. Of the three, he was the most tense. He bowed. 'I trust you will forgive the instrusion, Your Royal Highness. We are here at my suggestion.'

Alix acknowledged his bow and waited.

'You must know of the involvement of my brother with this unfortunate lady,' he said.

'I do,' Alix answered, 'but I am afraid I cannot discuss it, Lord Randolph.'

'I merely wish to point out the irrevocable destruction of their lives and the harm to society in general if Aylesford goes ahead with his plans for divorce.' When Alix tried to speak, he went on, 'There are other grave matters affecting the case. I beg you to ask his Royal Highness to advise Aylesford against proceeding.'

'You know I cannot do that,' Alix said evenly. She was trying to be considerate. She could see that Lady Aylesford and Alington were uncomfortable. 'Lord Alington, surely—'

Churchill cut in on her again, sharply. 'Alington is only here to witness what I have to say!'

Alix drew herself up. He had gone farther than even friendship could allow, but Churchill was beyond caring. Always highly strung and impetuous, the threat to his brother made him forget all civility.

'The Prince *must* listen!' he insisted. 'I'll do anything to prevent this being made public—and I have the power to do so!'

'Churchill—' Alington protested.

Lord Randolph was in an intense, excitable state. He would not stop. 'You may not be aware, but the

251

Prince has written Lady Aylesford over the past years a number of letters,' he told Alix. 'Intimate letters. They are in my pocket. I warn you, if this case comes to court, the Prince will be called to give evidence and the nature of these letters, if published, would ensure that he will never sit on the Throne of England!'

'Randolph, please!' Lady Aylesford pleaded. 'Ma'am—'

'No,' Alix said firmly. 'I shall not hear any more.' She moved to the fireplace, and pulled the bell cord. She had been desperately hurt but would not show it. She was dazed and unable to think clearly but she forced herself to stand erect and regal, dismissing them. She looked only at the portrait of Bertie and herself with the children on the far wall.

Lady Aylesford curtsied nervously. Alington bowed and retreated to the door. He was upset and incensed with Churchill for involving the Princess so brutally.

As the door opened, Lord Randolph bowed curtly. 'I shall, of course, inform Aylesford and the Prince that I am aware of their attempt to ruin my brother. And that I shall not hesitate to use the letters if necessary.'

Chapter
15

Alix went straight to the Queen. Victoria was furious. Not with her or Bertie, but with Churchill. Merely to prevent his brother and his mistress from being ostracised by society, he had threatened the Prince of Wales. And to involve Alix was unforgivable. She contacted Disraeli at once.

The Prime Minister had heard of Randolph Churchill's boast that he had the Crown of England in his pocket and thought what a fool he was, rash and vindictive. He was sitting at the desk in his office, his painful leg supported on a footstool. He winced and shifted it carefully. The worst was that this mixture of flirtation, social pride and simple adultery could lose the Prince all the popular goodwill he had won back. These letters had already convinced his mother again of his indiscretion. They were possibly suggestive, certainly indiscreet and familiar, and phrases used out of context could be very damaging. Disraeli wanted the Prince to have a responsible part in national life, yet if he were implicated in another divorce case, who would take him seriously as a public figure? He must be told the facts immediately. Disraeli only hoped he would keep his head.

'Take a letter to Cairo,' he told his secretary. 'Sir, and Dear Prince—'

Bertie tore open the letter marked 'Most Private', impatiently. 'About time, too,' he growled.

He was staying in the ornate Gezireh Palace in Cairo, enjoying the hospitality and gratitude of the Khedive. It was there he had read in the newspapers of his mother's new title, Empress of India. He was still smarting that he had not been told officially after he had prepared the ground for the announcement. It was not what he had a right to expect. As he read the Prime Minister's letter, Francis Knollys saw him flush with anger and heard him mutter to himself, 'Monstrous . . . Blackguard!'

Bertie rose abruptly and strode to the window. He stood for a moment, raging. He could only think of the insult to Alix, her pain and distress. 'Get Carrington and Beresford in here!' he roared.

Beresford was dishevelled from playing tennis. Carrington had been asleep on the terrace. When they arrived, Bertie told them quickly and tersely what had happened. 'And I thought of him as a friend,' he finished harshly.

'It's nothing less than blackmail,' Carrington said.

'Well, I'm not going to give in to it,' Bertie promised them.

'What will you do, sir?' Knollys asked.

'There's only one way to treat someone like him,' Beresford said.

'You're right,' Bertie argreed. 'He glanced at Carrington. 'Will you stand by me?'

'Of course, sir.'

Bertie turned to Beresford. 'As soon as the yacht's ready to sail, she'll take you to Brindisi. Get to London as soon as you can and tell Churchill I'll meet him anywhere on the coast of France, and to bring his pistols and seconds.'

Knollys was troubled. 'Is it wise, sir?'

'I don't care if it's wise or not!' Bertie declared angrily. 'He's insulted Alix and I won't let him get away with it.'

The Queen never ceased to amaze Benjamin Disraeli. They played their elaborate game of compliments and confidences, each enjoying it as much as the other, and he thought he could foretell her every reaction. Yet she constantly surprised him. The Heir Apparent was to fight a duel with a noble Member of Parliament and she fully approved. She had not forgotten that Prince Albert himself had made duelling illegal in England over twenty years ago but her romantic nature was fired by the sentiments behind the challenge. To her, it argued strongly that her son was totally innocent in the whole affair. She backed the Prince's determination to defy Churchill and not to interfere in the Aylesford case.

Disraeli had a crowded schedule in the Commons and a peasants' rising in the Balkans was being used by Russia as an excuse to threaten Britain's ally, Turkey, with war. It was a dangerous international situation, complicated by reports of Turkish atrocities. Now, as well as everything else, he had to make Churchill see reason before too much harm was done. His secretary had just shown Lord Alington and Lord Randolph Churchill into his study. Alington was nervous and apologetic, Churchill taut and hostile.

'You are my political leader, sir,' Churchill said, 'but this is a question of my family honour.'

'That honour can hardly be enhanced, Lord Randolph,' Disraeli commented, 'by insulting the Princess of Wales and fighting a duel with the Prince.'

Churchill stiffened. 'I have said I shall go to any lengths to protect my brother's name. As for the Prince, I have refused his absurd challenge.'

'I am relieved that you realise a duel with the Heir is out of the question.'

'As he knew when he proposed it,' Churchill sneered. 'It was a safe gesture to make.'

'It appears you are determined to add insult to insult,' Disraeli murmured. 'I must tell you the Prince maintains that the matter is entirely between Lord Aylesford and your brother and that the Queen advised him to return to London. By turning this into a personal quarrel between yourself and him, you can only cause the greatest possible scandal without achieving your object.'

'He should have thought of that before he ordered Aylesford to divorce his wife!' Churchill said hotly. 'And he can suffer the consequences.'

'The contents of your pockets may not be as valuable as you suppose,' Disraeli warned him.

'We shall soon find out,' Churchill replied. 'I shall not retract. Now—if that is all, Prime Minister . . . ' When Disraeli nodded, Churchill bowed stiffly, and stalked to the door. How noble he thinks he is, Disraeli reflected and how petty.

When the door closed, Alington began to blurt out a full apology. 'I had no idea it would . . . My only thought was to help poor Lady Aylesford.' Disraeli was still considering Churchill, of whom he had once had high hopes. Not any more, since he was capable of being so irrational. Yet he could do an impressive amount of damage and might rob the Prince's return from India of its triumph. He was glad Princess Alexandra was to see her husband first, and alone by his request. At least, their marriage might be saved. Lord Alington was still apologising. ' . . . To save her from a terrible future, you see.'

Not to be spoken to by other ladies, nor made love to by other gentlemen. How terrible, Disraeli thought wearily.

'Thank you, Lord Alington,' he said. 'If I could have it in writing?'

Alix went out in the pilot's cutter to meet the *Serapis* as it turned in at the Needles towards Portsmouth. She was very silent and composed.

Bertie waited for her in the state room. He was grateful that she had come alone as he asked. When he saw her, he did not know what to say, how to begin. Then she made it unnecessary by running to him and, as she kissed him, he knew that she understood and had forgiven him.

'I love you, Alix,' he said. 'I'd have done anything to prevent you being hurt. You do believe me?'

'Of course, my darling,' she whispered. 'I'm so proud you would have fought him because of me.'

'I can't give in to them. You do see that?'

'Everyone does—Mama, Mr. Disraeli,' she assured him.

'Everyone except the public,' he said. 'What do they say?'

Alix hesitated. 'They were all so eager to welcome you back.'

'But no one's sure any more?' He kissed her. 'Well, there's only one way to find out.'

They reached London less than an hour before the curtain went up at Covent Garden on *Un Ballo in Maschera*. They changed quickly and drove to the theatre. The curtain had been held. When the audience saw Alix come into the Royal Box, they rose and applauded. When Bertie appeared beside her, the applause faltered, then turned into a standing ovation that lasted for many minutes. It was repeated in every interval and at the end of the performance. To each person in the audience, and in the country, the Prince had made the British Empire a reality. The letters in Churchill's pocket were worthless.

Within a day, Aylesford discontinued his proceedings for divorce. He separated from Edith quietly and she went to live with Blandford in Belgium. Randolph Churchill found that the doors of London were closed to him. By threatening the Prince and insulting the Princess, he had destroyed his own social and political life. Realisation came late. He wrote a letter of apology to the Prince and took his wife and baby son, Winston, to live with Jennie's parents in America until the storm had died down.

Disraeli was gratified that it was over, yet he was sorry for the Prince. There was nothing to follow the trip of India. It was an isolated victory and had not ended his private war. The Queen would not hear of his being given any official diplomatic work.

'We have no confidence in his prudence, Mr. Disraeli.'

'The Prince of Wales's private affairs are almost as troublesome as the Balkans,' he sighed.

His Secretary, Corry, was packing the secret despatches from Turkey in their boxes. He smiled. 'Shall I send copies of these to Marlborough House, sir?'

Disraeli hesitated. Titania was possibly correct. Prince Hal was too warm-hearted, too prone to take sides. Besides the very qualities that made him so useful and successful could be spoilt if he were fed ready-made information and turned into a professional.

'No, no,' he said. 'No despatches for the present. I'll write him a little note from time to time, to let him know as much as is good for him—and to point him in the right direction.'

Disraeli was well over seventy and no longer well enough to stand the strain of daily debates in the House of Commons. He did not feel so urgently needed either, since his great opponent Gladstone had retired. He entered the House of Lords instead, as Earl of Beaconsfield.

When Bertie welcomed him there, Disraeli murmured, 'I am dead. But in the Elysian Fields.' Shortly afterwards, the reports of the massacre by the Turks of thousands of Christians in the Balkans were confirmed and Gladstone roared out of retirement to denounce Britain's ally. The Czar increased his pressure on Turkey. Disraeli and the Queen supported Turkey, knowing that Russia's

257

ambition was to control the eastern end of the Mediterranean and the entrance to the Suez Canal. Disraeli would not go to war unless Britain's neutrality were violated but he sent the Mediterranean fleet to prevent Constantinople from being occupied.

Bertie agreed with Disraeli. For years he had warned that while Czar Alexander had granted reforms at home, emancipating the serfs, improving the judicial system, he was determined to increase his empire. He backed the Government's action and, in return, Disraeli sent him little pieces of information just before they were released as news. For a while, Bertie was happier than he had even been, until he realised that he was sent nothing that was secret, nothing that was still to be decided. At the same time, his younger, invalid brother, Leopold, boasted that their mother had given him a key to the despatch boxes so that he could help her with her confidential work. His first instinct was to rage at them and demand recognition of his position, but it had happened too often. He was tired of climbing mountains only to find higher ones beyond. Being candid with himself, he admitted that it was too late for him to accept discipline, an office routine. He could only work in his own way. All he could do was maintain and extend his own sources of information and let the Queen and the Government know that he was willing to help, whenever he was needed.

Most of the time, he was happy with Alix but he could not bear the quietness of the life she enjoyed for long and she did not expect him to. His days became a round of ceremonies, functions and an increasingly unsatisfying, ceaseless search for amusement.

He was infatuated for a few months with an American girl, a Miss Chamberlayne from Cleveland, Ohio, who was visiting Europe with her parents. Alix understood. The sexual side of their marriage had never been the most important to her, and she knew he was driven by the demon of his restlessness and vitality which had no outlet in work. She alone could not satisfy him. Alix annoyed him considerably by always referring to her as 'Miss Chamberpots'. They met her in Homburg and

258

he followed her to Cannes, where he charmed both her and her parents. They were highly flattered that the Prince should take such an interest in them. Miss Chamberlayne was beautiful. She was also sensible, virtuous and impregnable. She returned, intact, to the Mid-West.

Bertie resumed his friendship with Sarah Bernhardt. She had developed from a passionate girl into the finest tragic actress of her age. He publicised her first appearances in London and she conquered the English stage as she had the French. He enjoyed the company of actors and invited his favourites to Sandringham, not to perform but as guests. He recognised that he had a great deal in common with them. He admired Sarah sincerely. Their friendship was real and intimate. He resented the snobbish attitude of some members of society to her and let it be known that if they would not invite her, they would not see him.

When she had to return to the Comedie Francaise, he was low-spirited for a time. Alix had been unwell again and her doctors recommended she should rest in a warmer climate. She went to stay with Willy and his wife in Greece. His sons had gone off to the Naval College at Dartmouth. He was worried about Eddy. The boy was sluggish and dull. Alix couldn't see anything wrong with him, though the only one who could rouse any animation in him at all was Georgie. Still, he missed them. He was left with nothing to do and no close companion. The Season had just begun and his hostesses would fill their dining tables with beautiful women for him to flirt with, the same ones trotted out every night, immaculately beautiful. The professional beauties, aristocratic and inaccessible, who were applauded when they rode in the Park and whose photographs were sold in shops and used as postcards.

'Dammit, Francis, I can't even talk to one of them without the whole world saying I'm in love with her,' Bertie growled. He was finishing changing to go to the Opera. He had trimmed his beard to a shorter, more pointed style, more distinctive. He had put on weight again after all the exercise in India but he carried it well.

Francis Knollys smiled. 'Which one is it tonight, sir?'

'My sister, Louise, and her husband,' Bertie said. 'Not so pretty but at least she has some conversation. God, how some of those women bore me!'

'You haven't forgotten you've been asked to a party at Sir Allen Young's sir?'

The Prince's valet helped him into his tail coat. 'No, I told him I might look in after the Opera. Depends how I feel.'

Sir Allen Young was an Arctic explorer. He was popular and gave splendid parties at his elegant house in Stratford Place. It was nearly eleven when his butler brought him word that the Prince had arrived.

'Sorry I'm late, Allen,' Bertie said. 'The piece went on for ever.'

'Did you enjoy it, sir?'

'One of those Wagner things the Princess likes. If I'd known, I'd have taken some sandwiches.'

Young laughed. 'Well, you're just in time for supper, sir.'

'Good Lord, you haven't waited for me?'

They had climbed the stairs and reached the main reception room. It was full of fashionably dressed people. There was a murmur of excitement and they formed themselves into two straggling lines down the room to the doors of the dining room at the end. Bertie paused, smiling to them, then walked down between the lines. He nodded or greeted the people he knew as he passed. Ahead of him, he saw Lord Lonsdale and Sir William Gordon-Cumming standing on either side of a younger couple. The man was plump and goodlooking, the young woman had golden-brown hair and was astonishingly attractive. When he reached them, the men bowed and the girl curtsied. She wore a plain black dress with a very slight train, the front of the skirt ruched up to ribbon bows at the sides, the bodice square-cut, tightly fitting and three-quarter length sleeves, almost moulded to her figure.

Bertie nodded. 'Lonsdale—Bill.' Cumming was a

friend of his, an officer in the Scots Guard, a prickly, boorish man but a fine huntsman.

Allen Young said. 'Your Royal Highness, may I present Mr. and Mrs. Edward Langtry, from Jersey.'

As the young woman curtsied again, she smiled. Bertie could not think why he had regarded her as merely attractive, she was stunning. Her eyes were a soft blue, her skin like white silk. Of course, he had heard of her. She was the latest of the professional beauties. While he had been occupied with Sarah, she had stormed the town. Millais, the painter, had done a portrait of her holding a lily in time for the Royal Academy. A pun of her name—The Jersey Lily. His brother Leopold even had a sketch of her pinned above his bed, until the Queen spotted it. She had climbed on a chair, pulled it down and torn it up.

Bertie gave one of his deep, rumbling chuckles. 'From the Channel Islands, eh? Do any sailing?'

Langtry flushed. 'I have a yacht, sir.'

'Good, good,' Bertie smiled. 'We'll have to have a race sometime.' He nodded and passed on.

Lillie was excited. In the month she had been in London, she had only seen the Prince at a distance. Meeting him had fulfilled all her ambitions but one.

Emilie le Breton, Lillie, daughter of the Dean of Jersey had married her husband largely on the strength of his yacht. He had seemed worldly, rich and experienced. The yacht turned out to be nearly all he had and his worldliness was supremely disappointing, both in bed and out. He was dull and penny-pinching, but she was determined to see London and had talked him into coming for the season. The black evening dress was the only one he had bought her and she had no jewellery. The very simplicity of her dress caught on and, from her first appearance, they had been deluged with invitations. Photographers had begged her to sit for them and her photographs already sold better than all the others. Her debut had been an instant triumph. She had many, many admirers. Some of them so generous they were irresistible, the Earl of Lonsdale, Lord Ranelagh, Sir George Chetwyn and the others.

Her husband was surprised and gratified by all the attention she received. There were carriages stopping at the door of their little house in Mayfair all day, even Royalty. The romantic Crown Prince Rudolph of Austria followed up each visit with masses of flowers, the young King Leopold of the Belgians was so determined to see her alone, he called in the mornings at nine o'clock. Langtry couldn't stand all the small talk and left Lillie to it. The only thing that disturbed him was that, when it was Royalty calling, he was not allowed into the room unless invited. He was not often invited.

After the Prince has passed, Lillie was surrounded again by gentlemen who eased past her husband until he found himself on the outside of the group. Lillie kept peeping round them to see what the Prince was doing. He was chatting to Allen Young and the lovely Mrs. Cornwallis-West at the end of the room. He was shorter than she had imagined and quite pudgy but his voice was deep, and he looked as if he could be fun. She hoped she had made some sort of impression on him, but she was not sure. After all, he had his pick of the loveliest women in Europe, the richest, noblest and most brilliant. Not like her, with her one little black dress. She tried to listen to what Lord Lonsdale was saying.

It was only when Sir Allen Young came to her and bowed that she had her answer. The Prince had asked for the honour of taking her into supper and she knew that the last of her ambitions was going to be fulfilled.

The Langtrys sitting room in their rented house in Norfolk Street was quite small but it caught the sun in its net curtains and all the flowers she was sent turned it into a bower. Lillie made sure that her husband went out to one of his clubs and would be gone till it was time to change for dinner. She had been excited all day. She was wearing her one afternoon dress, of layered plum muslin, with silk panels. She had had to mend one of the seams herself after a visit to Prince Rudolph's. He had offered to buy her a whole shopful to replace it, but she was not yet certain her husband would agree.

When the clock on the mantlepiece struck four and was echoed by the jangle of the doorbell downstairs, she could feel her heart pounding. As the Prince of Wales laid his hat, gloves and cane beside his chair, Lillie told her nervous maid to serve tea and then that they were not to be disturbed.

Bertie had been unable to concentrate on anything since he woke. She had been the first thing he thought of, her smile, her candid eyes, her golden-brown hair lying in a thick knot on the nape of her slender neck, her profile which was just saved from being classic by the slight snub at the end of her nose. Her laugh was artless and infectious. She had kept him amused all through supper and, afterwards, when they danced, she had been light and warm in his arms. She was not full-fleshed like so many others but supple and yielding. He suspected her figure was her own, her slender waist and the high-peaked mounds of her breasts not pulled in and forced up by whalebone. As she moved to sit across from him on the wide sofa, the gentle sway of her hips and the fluid bend of her waist confirmed it. Just to know that there were only wafers or tarlatan and silk between her lustrous body and the air was exciting. He did not remember ever having felt such an uncontrollable reaction.

Their conversation was formal after the ease of the previous night. She thanked him for calling and he said, if not the first, he was determined he would not be the last to welcome her to town. He asked her if she would care to ride with him for an hour in the Park later.

The maid brought in a tray with tea, cream and sugar. As Lillie poured, she was glad of her foresight. She had chosen Moreton Frewen, a handsome not very rich sportsman as her first lover, in her first week in town, because she knew she would have to learn how to ride. He had taught her willingly and given her a present of the horse she used, Redskin. She would always be grateful.

The maid left them and the Prince talked about riding, yachting and mutual friends. Although he was completely relaxed and smiling, she could feel the power of him from where she sat. Once, she had laughed and discounted all the stories told about him. No one man could have had so many adventures. She did not disbelieve any more. He lit a cigarette but his eyes did not leave her. They took in the surge of her bosom, and the long, flawless sweep of her hips and legs, so clearly revealed under her clinging dress. She knew instinctively that it would be wrong to play the coquette with him.

Lillie had always thought him very dignified, but he was warm and natural. Within minutes, she felt she had known him for years. It was a way he had of creating an atmosphere of intimacy. He was telling her of a weekend he had spent with the Duke of Sutherland during a State Visit of the Shah of Persia.

'A monstrous little man,' he chuckled. 'When we were going, he looked back at Sutherland and said—"Too grand for a subject. You'll have to cut off his head when you come to the Throne."'

Lillie laughed and clapped her hands, rocking back on the sofa. She stayed leaning back, her hands by her side. The Prince stubbed out his cigarette and rose. For a heart-wrenching moment, Lillie thought he had reached the end of his allotted time and was leaving. As he smiled and came towards her, she realised that leaving was the last thing on his mind.

Riding in the Park with the Prince was like reaching the summit of the fashionable world. All the gentlemen bowed, the ladies curtsied as they passed. When they paused to speak to anyone, a crowd gathered. Lillie sat, straight and smiling, knowing that they were looking at her. She glanced at Bertie and her throat caught at his quick, answering smile. How could she ever have thought of him as 'pudgy', she wondered. He was strong and solid and he had held her like he managed his Arab horse, as if it were part of him. She had never known anyone who made her respond like he did, so eagerly and openly. She had only lent her body before, never given herself fully. She was dazed by how perfect they had been together. And knew that he felt the same.

Moreton Frewen was standing by the railings with

Bill Cumming. They saw the stir of interest in the people in front of them as the Prince trotted towards them with Mrs. Langtry beside him on her chestnut, Redskin.

'Fine-looking horse, that,' Cumming drawled.

'Yes. I gave her the brute,' Frewen muttered. Cumming could tell he was jealous and did not blame him. Frewen shrugged philosophically. 'Rudolph of Austria was hard enough. But who can compete with Wales?' He bowed as they passed, and muttered to Cumming. 'Anyway, lilies can be dreadfully boring when they're not planted in a bed.'

In a few weeks, everyone knew that the Jersey Lily was the mistress of the Prince of Wales, the first to be acknowledged publicly. When she appeared at a ball or a dinner, guests stood on chairs to catch a glimpse of her. Her portrait at the Academy had to be roped off. She could not shop or walk in the Park for the crowds who besieged her, friendly and curious. Few men condemned Bertie. He was doing just as they would if they had the chance. The ladies copied Lillie's hairstyle and her new dresses, many new dresses, set the fashion. The hostesses were relieved, because they no longer had to find partners to amuse the Prince. Lillie went everywhere with him. At country house weekends, husbands and wives were placed carefully in separate wings and the Prince's room was always near Mrs. Langtry's. Mr. Langtry grumbled and protested a little to his wife but enjoyed the hospitality and not having to pay her bills. At first he was invited along for form's sake, but he gradually faded from sight and left Lillie alone in London. She moved to a splendid, new house in Hampstead. To the town's amusement, it was in Alexandra Road.

When Alix returned from Greece, she found Bertie besotted with the most beautiful woman, next to herself, in London. Many people had been afraid of her return, many anticipating it maliciously, but she disappointed them. At home, Bertie and she treated each other as they had always done and, when they were out together, she had his full affection and attention. She was even glad he had found Lillie. His awful restlessness and irritability were gone. It was far better to know he was with her, than to wonder always which of the many ladies they met had seen him during the day or would see him later that night. She did more than accept Lillie, she made her a friend. It was never once mentioned between them what relation they stood in to each other. Only Charlotte and Oliver Montagu knew how difficult the first weeks after she came back had been. The Princess had looked forward so much to being with her husband again, to find that his thoughts were taken up with another woman. They saw the inner battle with jealousy and it was worse for them because there was nothing they could say to help. Alix felt their sympathy and loved them more for not putting it into words. They were even dearer to her, and Oliver became her constant escort. He sat with her, danced the first dance after supper with her, she took his arm when they walked and they laughed together like lovers. There was a strong sympathetic bond between them, yet he had never kissed her, never held her except when they were dancing. Their friendship consoled her. To Montagu it was a sweet torture and he longed many times to tell her his real feelings, but he understood that if he even hinted at them, their intimacy would be broken. She would never be unfaithful to her husband, even in thought.

Alix befriended Lillie to disarm rumour and to conquer her own jealousy. She was glad she had. She found they had the same vivacious boisterous sense of humour and parties, when Lillie came north for the shooting or to Cowes for the yacht weeks, were gayer. Apart from Alix, she was the only one who dared to play practical jokes on Bertie, tipping icecream down his neck or putting a live lobster in his bed. At a weekend party, she overheard one of the ladies whispering to a guest that she would leave a plate of sandwiches outside her door as a sign that her husband was not with her. Bertie and Lillie sat in their room, eating the sandwiches, and laughing as they heard the footsteps prowl up and down outside. Even the Queen gave in to curiosity and let her be presented at Court. Lillie was terrified when it was her turn to curtsy and kiss the hand of the dumpy figure in black with the expressionless face under a widow's cap. Victoria gave no sign of interest whatever, but she left the Drawing Room shortly after. She had only come to see Lillie.

Bertie seemed to be absorbed in her. Disraeli wondered if he had lost all taste for work. If so, it was a pity, though hardly surprising. In the most positive way, Bertie showed him he had only been waiting for the right opportunity.

The presence of the British Fleet at Constantinople forced the war between Russia and Turkey to an uneasy armistice. At the peace conference which followed, the Congress of Berlin, where the major powers settled terms between the two enemies, Disraeli had the supreme diplomatic success of his career. He virtually excluded Russia from the Mediterranean, ensured reform inside Turkey, independence for Bulgaria and Serbia and acquired the island of Cyprus for Britain, to guard the Suez Canal.

Bertie had been in Paris, as President of the British section of another International Exhibition. Instead of staying, he had come back to London to be with Lillie, and was amazed when Lord Salisbury, now Foreign Secretary, advised him not to return for the close of the Exhibition. France was enraged against Britain, seeing the occupation of Cyprus as a direct threat to French interests in Egypt. Their agreement to the whole peace treaty was in doubt and the situation between the two countries became explosive. Bertie immediately travelled to Paris and invited to lunch the most influential and rabid republican leader, Leon Gambetta, whom he had met only once before. They lunched at the Cafe Anglais and talked till the evening: Gambetta, one eyed, anti-monarchist, a brilliant statesman, and the Prince who represented everything that he most strongly opposed. He was shaken by Bertie's depth of knowledge, his grasp of international politics, and was completely won over.

At the end of the conversation, Bertie asked him why they had abolished the aristocracy in France.

'In England,' he told him, 'we take the most distinguished men in industry, science, literature and so on,

267

and make them noblemen. So our nobility remains a genuine aristocracy.'

'With you that is possible, for some time still,' Gambetta conceded. 'But not with us. Here the old Dukes would not be willing to rub shoulders with the "Duke of Industry". As a Republic, we can have only one aristocracy, that of science and merit. It declares itself without any need of titles.'

Bertie laughed. 'You are a real Republican, Monsieur Gambetta.'

'Allow me to admit, sir,' Gambetta smiled, 'that I consider it logical that you, for your part, should be a Royalist.'

Gambetta persuaded the French Government into accepting Britain's possession of Cyprus and the friendship between the two countries was restored. Disraeli thanked Bertie officially and made sure the Queen heard how delicately and skillfully he had prevented a serious crisis.

Disraeli had not dared to risk his intimacy with the Queen by championing her son. He was determined, however, in his next term of office, to use him more actively and officially in foreign affairs. But at the election which followed, it was home affairs which concerned the public and Gladstone's oratory swept the Liberals back into power. Disraeli regretted he had not done more for the Prince, as he had always intended. It was now too late. He retired to Hughenden, to his books and memories.

Hartington was leader of the Liberals and, for a moment, it looked as if one of Bertie's closest friends would be Prime Minister. When he spoke to him at the Turf Club about forming a Government, Harty Tarty shook his head. It was too much effort. Besides, the country wanted Gladstone now that he had come out of retirement. The Queen declared she would abdicate sooner than accept that awful man again and his radical ideas. Bertie persuaded her, with difficulty, that Gladstone was passionately loyal to her and that she had no other choice. She was forced to give in.

She received Gladstone standing, in an unheated room.

She told him that she hoped he could gain her confidence. One stipulation was that he should not alter the foreign policy set by Disraeli. Another that his Ministers must be forbidden to have any private and intimate communication with the Prince of Wales. All Bertie was to be allowed was Lillie.

Chapter
16

They were years of turmoil. Sultan Abdul Aziz was deposed, murdered and replaced by his brother, Abdul the Damned. Under Disraeli, Gordon was made Governor of the Sudan and, in South Africa, the Transvaal was annexed. There was war in Zululand, the first defeat of the British troops avenged by the rout of the Zulus at Ulundi and their King, Cetewayo, brought to Balmoral to be pardoned and lectured by Victoria. There was war in Afghanistan, ended when General Roberts occupied Kandahar and Kabul, new violence in Ireland and a bloody, indecisive rebellion of the Boers in the Transvaal. Ismail Pasha of Egypt was deposed and succeeded by his ton, Tewfik, but discontent seethed at the joint control of the country by the French and British.

And they were years of tragedy. Bertie's brother, Leopold, endured agonies from haemophilia. Princess Alice's son died from the same disease. She had become Grand Duchess of Hesse, caring for and adored by her people. Her whole family was struck down by diptheria. Although she nursed them herself, her favourite daughter died. Bertie had gone with Alix to Windsor for the annual service on 14th December commemorating the day of the Prince Consort's death and his own recovery. They had just risen and were dressing for the service when

Victoria came to them with a telegram announcing Alice's death that very morning.

Alix cried, 'I wish I had died instead of her.' In his own distress, Bertie comforted his mother.

Czar Alexander was assassinated in St. Petersburg and Bertie and Alix went to his funeral, staying with Sacha and Minny, now Czar Alexander the Third and Czarina Marie Feodorovna, surrounded by troops and police in the Anitchkoff Palace. Inside a few months, Disraeli died and his wish was honoured, not to lie in Westminster Abbey but beside his wife at Hughenden. In his final illness, he corrected the proofs of his last speech in Parliament.

When his doctor protested, he said, 'I will not go down to posterity talking bad grammar.' Bertie attended his funeral and primroses from Queen Victoria lay on his coffin.

Bertie had taken Alix to Denmark. Normally, family holidays at Fredensborg and Bernstorff bored him out of all patience but Sacha was to be there with Minny, and Willy with his wife, Olga. It was too good a chance to miss.

He was out walking with his two brothers-in-law, to let their wives talk. In Russia, Sacha was accompanied everywhere by guards protecting him from assassination, and the freedom of movement in Denmark intoxicated him. They walked for miles and eventually found themselves lost.

The landscape of ditches and fields were completely featureless and each had a different idea of which direction they should take. At last, to Bertie's relief, a high-wheeled cart came along, driven by a local farmer. Bertie hailed him in passable Danish, and asked him the true direction to Fredensborg. It turned out the farmer was heading that way and he offered them a lift, a round-faced, pleasant man. As they jogged along in the back of the cart, he asked if they were visiting Denmark.

'Yes, we are,' Sacha said, and added politely, 'I am

Czar Alexander of Russia and this gentleman is the Prince of Wales.'

The farmer tugged slightly at his reins but, otherwise, did not react. He glanced back at Sacha and Bertie, after a moment. 'I see,' he said. He nodded to Willy. 'But you're Danish, aren't you, sir?'

'I used to be,' Willy smiled. 'Now I'm King George of Greece.'

The farmer nodded again. 'Uh-huh,' he said. He drove on a few yards in silence. 'Do you know who I am?' he asked.

All three shook their heads.

'Napoleon Bonaparte.'

They were still laughing when they came into the salon of the palace at Fredensborg.

Alix and Minny were waiting for them. The two sisters loved being together for these short holidays. Distance and politics separated them so often. For Minny, especially, it was rare now to be able to relax with no fear of bombs or bullets. She envied Alix. Olga had already gone to change for dinner but the men insisted on resting first. When they told Alix and Minny what had happened and how the people in the village had cheered to see them in the cart, they laughed, too.

Minny said, 'Just how it used to be in Russia.'

Sacha stopped smiling. 'Yes,' he agreed. 'It is good to feel free.'

Bertie was saddened by the change in him. He was no longer gauche and charming. He had become imperious and his eyes were hard and suspicious.

'Surely you can make it like it was,' Bertie suggested. 'You have the power. A ruler should not hide himself from his people behind security police. To win their love, he must show them he trusts them.'

'My father trusted them,' Sacha said quietly. 'They called him the Liberator. And they killed him.'

'I'm sorry,' Bertie apologised. 'I spoke out of turn.'

'No, no, you are probably right.' Sacha shrugged. 'But it's already too late.'

'Any concessions now would be taken as weakness,' Minny explained. 'You are fortunate in England.'

271

'I would rather be a bricklayer there, than Czar of Russia,' Sacha muttered. 'Besides, you rule the seas. You do not always have to consider Germany.'

While he was changing, Bertie thought over what Sacha said. He had meant that any weakness, any unrest in Russia would be exploited by Bismarck. His army was a constant threat and he used suspicion between nations as a means of increasing Germany's influence. Despite the friendship of Bertie and Sacha, there was no treaty between their countries. As he led Alix down to dinner, he told her that he intended to visit Vicky and Fritz on the way home. At first she objected.

'We'll only go to Freidrichshof's,' he promised her. 'They used to be our dearest friends. And remember—the Kaiser is an old man. Soon it will be Fritz's turn.'

Crown Prince Frederick William had built Friedrichshof in the style of an English country house to please his wife. Apart from the tile stoves, everything about it was English, its gardens, decoration, and furniture. It could be Kent or Sussex, Alix told Vicky.

'I'm still my mother's daughter,' Vicky reminded her gently. Vicky had grown older with care, her hair greying. 'Fritz always respected that. Indeed, it has cost him much. Because he took my views, he lost his father's trust.'

'And Monsieur Bismarck's,' Alix added.

'That man—that evil man,' Vicky said bitterly. 'He has even turned our son against us.'

'Young Wilhelm?'

'He knows we will end the power of the army one day. Sometimes I think he hates us. My own son.'

They were in the sitting room of the house, crowded with heavy, comfortable furniture, the surfaces cluttered with photographs and mememtoes like Windsor and Sandringham. The teatable was laid with the ritual sandwiches and scones and jams and cakes. Alix had often resented Vicky and regarded her as an enemy. Now, all her sympathy was roused and she realised that Vicky's role had been very difficult. They looked round as Bertie came in with Fritz. Fritz had aged, too.

He was heavier and plagued by an irritating cough that sometimes left him breathless.

'We were remembering before you were married,' Bertie told Vicky, smiling. 'When Mama would never leave you alone. And I agreed to chaperone you.'

'You were very wicked,' Vicky reproved him. 'You went out into the corridor as soon as she'd gone.'

'It was the first time I really kissed you, Liebling,' Fritz chuckled and kissed her cheek. Bertie and he took seats at the table.

'It feels like last week,' Vicky told them. 'And it's all so long ago. Even your wedding.'

'Oh, don't . . .' Bertie protested. 'D'you know something I realised? On my next birthday, I'll be the same age as Papa when he died.'

'He'd be so happy to see us now,' Vicky said. 'It was his dearest wish.'

Alix touched Vicky's hand. 'We should never have got out of touch. I am glad we are friends again.'

Fritz coughed. 'All those days are over, Alix. God willing, forever.' Vicky knew he had discussed the future with Bertie and they were in agreement. She smiled to her brother across the table. Fritz was looking at his plate. 'I used to think your father's ideas were impractical. But Bertie explained it to me. There can be no peace without trust. With trust between two nations we can help each other to build and create, rather than to destroy.' He nodded, remembering the carnage his own army had wrought Denmark and Austria and France. All for glory. 'We must lead the way. Soon—perhaps very soon—the major powers will be joined together in a family alliance that nothing can break.'

The door opened and a young man came in. He was slim and handsome, with the beginning of a moustache, wearing Hussar's uniform. He clicked his heels and bowed.

'Ah, the English tea,' he smiled. 'How delicious!' It was Prince Wilhelm.

'Willy!' Vicky exclaimed, surprised.

'A flying visit,' Wilhelm laughed. 'I heard my favourite relations were here, so I rode over.' He bowed. 'Uncle Bertie. Aunt Alix, how wonderfully beautiful you look.' He took her hand and kissed it.

'Willy, Willy, I scarcely recognised you,' Alix smiled.

Bertie agreed. His nephew carried himself like the model soldier. He stood arrogantly poised. His under-developed left arm was disguised by the uniform and he kept his thumb tucked in his belt. As he joined them at the table, he was smiling and affable but Bertie could not help thinking there was something malicious behind it.

'You recognise the uniform, don't you, Uncle Bertie?' he said. 'You are a colonel in our Hussars.'

'Yes, I am,' Bertie chuckled. 'Though I doubt if I look as slim in it as you.'

They laughed and Wilhelm acknowledged the compliment gracefully. 'You probably look best in British uniform. I'm surprised you can resist the chance to wear it.'

'What do you mean, Willy?' Fritz coughed.

'When such great events are happening.'

'What events?' Bertie asked, suddenly wary.

Wilhelm looked at him with mock innocence. 'Didn't you know ? . . . I was sure your Government could tell you first. Yes—the British fleet has bombarded Alexandria.'

The news was true. Gladstone hated war and his sympathy with the Boers had caused the rising in South Africa. He sympathised also with the Egyptian wish to be free of foreign domination but a rebellion of army officers, led by Colonel Arabi, a nationalist fanatic, was aimed to establishing a dictatorship and began with a massacre of Europeans. The French Government was obsessed by fear of Bismarck and feared to weaken their defences by sending troops out of France. They opted out of their responsibilities and withdrew the French fleet from Alexandria. Arabi placed heavy guns all round the harbour to pound British shipping and Gladstone had finally no option but to order in the fleet.

The bombardment against an almost impregnable position was successful and Lord Charles Beresford, who had gone back to the Navy, became a national hero by running his gunboat, the *Condor,* under the noses of the shore batteries and leading a landing party to strike the main Egyptian guns. The taking of Alexandria was followed up by a military expedition to protect the Suez Canal and put down the revolt. Many of Bertie's friends left at once. Oliver Montagu asked for permission to go with the Household Cavalry. Bertie gave it gladly and went himself to see Gladstone. The Prime Minister understood. The Prince had been checked at every attempt to serve his country at home. Holding the rank of Field-Marshal in the Army, he would feel humiliated if he did not go on this Expedition.

The Queen was helped into the Study at Windsor by John Brown. She was perfectly aware of why her son and the Prime Minister had asked for an Audience. And quite implacable.

'No. No,' she declared. 'It is unthinkable that the life of the Heir to the Throne should be risked.'

'You let Arthur go!' Bertie protested.

'He is not the Heir. In any case, your brother is a serving officer.'

'His Royal Highness could act as a member of the Staff,' Gladstone suggested.

Victoria's eyes widened. 'That is even worse, Prime Minister. To go merely as an observer? It would be even more humiliating. No, no.' She turned to Bertie. 'I appreciate your gallant desire for active service and to share the dangers of our soldiers, but you must abandon the idea.'

Against the Queen's absolute veto, there was nothing Bertie could do. Montagu mentioned in his letters that conditions in the army hospitals in Egypt was disgraceful. He had to content himself with campaigning for improved medical facilities.

At first, Bertie could only think of his mother with anger, but it turned to pity. He had heard that she had a fall down the steep stairs at Windsor and took his sons to see her when they came back from their three years training voyage in the Navy. She was carried into the sitting room in John Brown's arms and laid on the sofa, shrunken, twisted with pain. The fall had brought on a series of agonising rheumatic attacks which crippled her and made her unable to sleep. Brown, too, was unwell. His face was swollen and inflamed and he shivered as he adjusted the knitted shawl round her shoulders.

'I'll wait in the corridor,' he said.

'No, no,' Victoria smiled. She patted his hand. 'I have my boys to look after me. You go and rest.'

'Aye, I'll do that. If ye're sure,' Brown said. He nodded to the Prince and his two sons and went out.

'He doesn't look well, Grandmama,' Eddy drawled. He was tall, handsome and lethargic.

'No, he's not, Eddy,' Victoria said. 'He caught a chill last week, hunting all night for a prowler in the grounds. One of those Fenians our Mr. Gladstone is so fond of.'

Bertie was alarmed. 'Did he catch him?'

'No, he got away. And poor Brown's been ill ever since. It's so inconvenient, just when I need him.' She rallied and smiled. Bertie could see it was an effort but she would not let her infirmity spoil her grandsons' homecoming. 'So you're to stay in the Navy, Georgie?'

'Yes, Grandmama,' George said. He was shorter than his elder brother, as quick and intelligent as Eddy was slow, a popular and successful cadet.

'And you're to go to Cambridge, Eddy. Will you like that?'

'Shan't like being away from Georgie,' Eddy said, after a moment.

'No. But you'll work hard and make us all proud of you, won't you?' She knew how worried Bertie and Alix were about their backward elder boy. Still, he was goodnatured and had perfect manners. 'Now, come along, both of you, and give your old Grandmama a kiss.'

Victoria was determined to recover quickly. She had to be ready to do battle with Gladstone, who was learning the lesson of Egypt and agitating himself over further reforms in Ireland. However, her recovery was delayed for months by the most dreadful, unexpected blow. A few days after Bertie's visit, her son Leopold brought her the shattering news that Brown was dead. She had not even been with him, her friend, her truest, and most loyal servant. No one could appreciate what he meant to her. The strong, dependable arm, the ready sympathy and blunt humour, the picnics at her little cottage near Balmoral when he had brought whisky instead of tea and she had rediscovered the joy of laughter, the security of knowing he was there beside her, behind her. 'Just leave it to me, Woman. I'll take care of it.' Gone, all gone.

The revolt in Egypt did not last long. Arabi's army was smashed at Tel-el-Kebir and the country occupied. Because of the Queen's suffering, Bertie had to deputise for her. As he celebrated the victory, he heard that Bismarck had said of him that his love of uniforms was only matched by his fear of gunpowder. For months, only Lillie could lift him out of his depression.

Lillie had taken up a career. The collapse of her husband's finances and her own extravagance made it essential so that she would still be accepted in society. She had had a daughter, of whose paternity there was little doubt. Bertie would have supported them both but she was too astute not to realise that their affaire could not last for ever. She decided to become an actress. Squire Bancroft, a leading manager and friend of the Prince, gave her an undemanding part in a well-tried play. Bertie's patronage ensured that each performance was sold out and she was launched. She was not a very good actress, but she was popular and, with experience, she improved. Amongst her many admirers was Mr. Gladstone.

The Prime Minister found her at Marlborough House with Princess Alexandra one afternoon when he called to see the Prince. The Prince was at his club and Gladstone happily accepted an invitation to stay. It was a pleasurable experience to be entertained by the two most beautiful women in London and he could not decide which he most admired. On the whole, perhaps, the Princess, who seemed to grow lovelier as she grew older. Her colouring and bone structure were exquisite and she looked as young as her daughters. He pointed out that half the women in town appeared to wear her hairstyle, swept up to a mass of small curls on top, while the other half wore Mrs. Langtry's knot, and they laughed.

Lillie thought that Gladstone was sweet. Well past seventy but still vigorous and with wonderful eyes. He sent her books of commentaries on the Scriptures and had even given her the private code to put on the envelope if she ever wanted to write for his advise confidentially. She could not resist teasing him.

'Mr. Gadstone, I hope you will not think this idle curiosity,' she began.

'Mrs. Langtry?'

Lillie paused as though faintly embarrassed. 'Well—I hear that you have the most extensive acquaintance in London with . . . 'fallen women'.'

'Fallen women. Yes. They are known as prostitutes.'

'I'm sure Mrs. Langtry knows that,' Alix said.

Lillie glanced at her. Sometimes the Princess's artless remarks were a little too naive to be believed. But Alix only smiled ingenuously.

'The object is to rescue them,' Gladstone explained. 'Every night when I am not at the House, I go out to the Haymarket on the streets of Piccadilly, armed with a small stick in case of attack, and meet one of them.'

'Every night?' Alix asked, surprised.

'For the last forty years, Ma'am. Yes, I used to wait until a woman approached me. These days, I simply go up to the first likely one I see and ask her to come home with me.'

'I don't think I should listen to any more.'

It was only when Mrs. Langtry laughed that Gladstone understood the Princess was being humorous. He chuckled.

'When they do accompany me, they find my dear wife waiting. I always choose the most destitute. We give her food and a bed for the night and try to persuade her to give up her degrading profession.'

'Are you often successful?' Lillie asked.

'Not so often as I would wish.' Glandstone smiled. 'But one or two over the years have been saved and that makes it worthwhile.'

Alix and Lillie were touched. 'I trust you will be

278

careful, Mr. Gladstone,' Alix urged. 'Some might misinterpret your motives.'

'Many have, Ma'am,' Gladstone affirmed. 'Yet the Lord's work is there to be done.'

'Is he converting you?' Bertie asked from the door. He came in with Carrington and Sir Charles Dilke. Dilke, a tall, bearded man, was a Radical member of Gladstone's Cabinet. An able politician and a forceful speaker, he was heavily backed as a future Prime Minister if he could overcome the Queen's distrust. He had been an ardent Republican.

Bertie signed to Gladstone not to rise. 'The answer is yes,' he said. 'I'd be delighted to accept.'

Lillie smiled to Gladstone. 'What's this? Have you been keeping secrets?'

'I've been asked to be a member of the Royal Commission on the Housing of the Working Classes,' Bertie told her. 'Sir Charles is Chairman and Lord Carrington is on the board with me.'

'Oh, Bertie, how splendid,' Alix said.

'A job well worth doing, sir,' Gladstone stressed. 'I think you'll find it rewarding.' He noticed Mrs. Langtry sway in her seat. She looked deathly pale. He rose, alarmed. 'Mrs. Langtry—'

Lillie had hoped that no one would notice. The strain of rehearsing and performing, combined with her hectic social life, was exhausting. Bertie took a step towards her, but stopped himself in time. 'I'm so sorry,' she panted. 'I'm feeling a little faint. I think I should, perhaps go home.'

'Are you sure you're well enough?' Alix asked, rising.

'Oh, yes, I shall be fine, Ma'am. I'm really very sorry.'

There was an awkward pause as Lillie rose, unsteadily. Obviously Bertie could not accompany her and one of the other men should offer.

As they hesitated, Alexandra saved the situation. 'Lord Carrington, will you ring for your carriage?' she asked, taking Lillie's arm. 'I shall see Mrs. Langtry home.'

The men bowed as Alix led Lillie out, supporting her. They left a delicate silence behind them.

A remarkable lady, the Princess, Gladstone thought.

'I hope she'll be all right,' Bertie muttered.

'Too many late nights, I expect,' Gladstone said. Dilke smiled inwardly. Bertie glanced sharply at Gladstone, but the old man was guileless. It was damned embarrassing. He only hoped no one saw Alix going into the house in Hampstead. Afterwards, she told him how nice she thought it was, what a comfortable drawing room with its plaster cherubs, and the mural of the triumph in India, who could have suggested that?

When Carrington came back in, Bertie said, 'Now look, gentlemen, I don't want to be just a figurehead on this Commission.'

'Of course, not, sir,' Dilke agreed. 'But the fact that it has your prestige may mean that we'll get something done at last.'

Bertie knew that it was an exceptional opportunity. Things were moving for him again. Because of the Queen's precarious health, Gladstone was supplying him secretly with essential information so that he would be ready to take over. He would be working with Dilke, a valuable partnership for the future. Most important, it was a chance to take a meaningful part in home affairs.

'I sincerely hope so,' he said. 'I have heard that the poverty and bad conditions in some of those slums are indescribable. That's the problem—I have no first-hand knowledge. How could I have? And I want to know what I'm talking about.'

Dilke was impressed. Gladstone murmured, speculating. It would certainly stop the critics from claiming the Prince was being used for political purposes. Young Churchill would be sure to make that point, otherwise. Lord Randolph had still not made peace with Marlborough House but he had fought his way back up the greasy pole to become one of the leading Conservatives, and Gladstone's most stinging opponent.

'If I might make a suggestion,' Carrington offered.

'It should be possible for you to tour some of the streets in, say, Clerkenwell or St. Pancras. You would have to be disguised, sir, of course—to make it authentic.'

A few days later, Bertie and Carrington, dressed as workmen, drove to Clerkenwell with Dr. Buchanan, the Chief Medical Officer of Health. A police cab was sent to protect them. As they walked down the filthy, slum streets, Bertie turned off into an alleyway. The police escort advised him strongly against it. He sent them away.

Carrington and Buchanan guided him through alley after alley, pestholes with sewer rats scuttling openly in piles of slops and refuse. The stench was stifling. Drunks lurched past them and pinched, listless children, squatting barefoot and ragged in doorways, gazed at them with blank incurious eyes. A woman screamed in one of the houses. An old man, threadbare, his lips and nose encrusted with sores, retched in the gutter.

'We'll try in here, sir,' Buchanan said. Bertie followed him into a reeking passage and upstairs to a door. Buchanan pushed it open. Inside, the room was bare of furniture. On the floor, an emaciated woman lay shivering on a pile of rags. Three gaunt children, nearly naked, huddled against her for warmth.

'Oh, God . . . Oh, dear God,' Bertie muttered. He had come prepared and took a handful of gold sovereigns from his pocket.

'Please, sir—no!' Buchanan whispered urgently. 'The others would tear us to pieces before we got out of the alley.'

'I had no idea,' Bertie said. 'No idea such . . . How is it possible in our country—in my country? . . . ' He saw now why Gladstone, Dilke, even Disraeli, had called for reform.

When they reached the wider streets again, Carrington hailed a cab to take them on to Holborn. The driver refused, unless they paid him first. They picked up a junior medical officer to show them round. He did not know who Bertie and Carrington were and laughed as

281

he pointed out some of the most sickening sights they had ever seen.

The week after, the Prince's speech in the House of Lords, impassioned but reasoned, described what he had witnessed. He had proved with the workers' houses on the Sandringham estate that decent housing could be provided economically and he demanded immediate and drastic action. The speech won him an ovation and no one questioned his right to sit on the commission. Not even Churchill.

All Bertie's main contacts were now with the Liberal party. He recognised that this was limiting and also that, just as Dilke was a future Prime Minister, so was Lord Randolph. He agreed to meet him again at a dinner given by the Attorney-General. Churchill represented the kind of dynamic, progressive Conservatism with which Bertie was in sympathy. Their friendship was renewed and valuable to both of them, politically and personally. Most pleasurably, it brought the gay and diverting Jennie back into the orbit of Marlborough House.

After months of hearings and evidence, the Commission's report was ready. Bertie signed it with Dilke and the scholarly Conservative leader, Lord Salisbury, who had also been convinced by its findings. He championed Gladstone's Third Reform Bill and announced his intention of voting in its favour. His friend, Lord Rosebery, a young, prominent Liberal, came to him with Gladstone. They told him it was impossible for him to vote.

'In Heaven's name, why?' he demanded. 'I supported the Commission, signed the report, and believe in this Bill!'

'Nevertheless, sir,' Rosebery said, 'under the Constitution—'

'Hang the Constitution!' Bertie stormed. 'I want to declare my position and rally support. If I don't, the House of Lords will throw it out.'

'No one regrets it more than I, sir,' Gladstone assured

him. 'Yet, constitutionally, it is impossible. The Crown must be above politics, always.'

'Always . . . ,' Bertie repeated, some hours later. He had been to see Lillie in her latest play at the Haymarket, taken her to dinner at the Cafe Royal and was now sitting on the bed in her sumptuous bedroom in Hampstead. He was still brooding.

Lillie was at her dressing table, brushing her hair. It hung loose in a glossy, golden mane nearly to her hips. She laid down the brush and swivelled on the stool to look at him. All she wore was a cambric chemise and rose silk, openwork stockings, moulding her sleek legs and thighs. Under the mist of the chemise the soft shapes and tones of her body glimmered.

'I'm sorry, my dear. I've been poor company, I'm afraid,' he muttered. He had been depressed all evening and even she had been unable to cheer him up. He grunted. 'They won't let me rule, or fight, or work. I can't even vote!'

'Oh dear,' Lillie said innocently. 'What will they let you do?'

'As he looked at her and saw her faint smile, he rumbled into laughter.

Prince Otto von Bismarck was a noticeable figure in his white and gold uniform at the Kaiser's birthday ball in Berlin, thick-bodied and powerful. His face was commanding, with full, flowing moustache. When he chose, the sharp eyes under the bald scalp and beetling eyebrows twinkled and his smile was disarming. It revealed nothing of his thoughts. He was smiling now, considering the dancers in the royal quadrille.

Crown Princess Victoria was partnered by her brother, the Prince of Wales. Wales—sometimes Bismarck thought him a posturing dandy, sometimes the only other person who understood international politics. Often when his agents approached the key members of some foreign government, they found the Prince had been there just before them. It paid to be careful with such a man. How fortunate his mother gave him no real power.

Crown Princess Vicky—her mother's daughter, as she said. Bismarck had difficulty even in being polite to her. The problem was that Kaiser Wilhelm seemed indestructible, but he was eighty-eight and, at any moment, his pacifist son could become Emperor. Not a prospect Bismarck relished. His whole policy was based on keeping all power and government in the hands of the Kaiser and the military elite. As the Kaiser, guided by his English wife, Frederick William would bring in a free parliament and, by restricting the army, reduce Germany's claim to lead Europe. The web of Bismarck's schemes would be broken. He had made the Kaiser's authority absolute, himself. He could not oppose him.

He smiled to see Wales's son, Prince Eddy, dancing with Alicky of Hesse. The sleepy-eyed Eddy was popular but no comparison with his cousin Wilhelm, the hero of the young officers, the Kaiser's favourite and Bismarck's protege, a true Hohenzollern. The thought of the day when Eddy was on the throne of England and Wilhelm ruled Germany made Bismarck chuckle, the lion and the lamb. But first would come Bertie. With him ruling England, his brothers-in-law in Germany, Russia, Denmark and Greece, his cousins in Belgium, Portugal and Spain, the treacherous Italians and the mincing, womanising French would all dance to his tune. Bismarck prayed to the God of Iron for a miracle, and that the Widow of Windsor would live for ever. His smile became a scowl. He had just seen that the Crown Prince's daughter was dancing with the handsome Prince Alexander of Bulgaria. The girl had fallen in love with him, but there could be no marriage. Bulgaria had quarrelled with Russia, whose friendship Bismarck was cultivating. He had made it perfectly clear they were to be kept apart.

When the quadrille ended. Bertie led Vicky into the long, marble gallery at the side of the ballroom. Fritz was sitting where they had left him. He was tired and tormented by the constant raw pain in his throat.

'How many years has it gone on now?' Bertie asked him, worried. 'I wish you'd seen an English doctor.'

Fritz smiled. 'If it would please you. Anything to cure this.'

'It would have to be when we visit Mama,' Vicky said. 'It would cause resentment here.'

'Do you have to be so careful still?' Bertie asked them, surprised. 'Well, not for much longer.' He smiled as he saw Prince Wilhelm coming towards them.

Wilhelm was immaculate in his uniform, a short, frogged jacket and skintight breeches. His moustache was precise, waxed upwards at the ends into arrogant spikes. Like Bismarck, he had little respect for his parents and he had been taught to distrust his uncle. Vicky's smile to her son faded as he bowed coldly.

'I regret having to interrupt a family conference,' he said, 'but you may not be aware that my sister is dancing with Prince Alexander.'

'She's old enough to choose her own partners, Willy,' Fritz coughed.

'They make a charming couple,' Bertie agreed.

'Quite possibly,' Willy snapped. 'But an engagement between them could throw Russia into the arms of France! I realise that might be looked on favourably by . . . other matchmakers.'

'Don't you see—' Bertie began.

'I cannot discuss it further,' Wilhelm said, he turned to his parents. 'I have come to inform you that the Kaiser has ordered Prince Alexander never to see her again.'

'You mean Bismarck,' Vicky corrected.

Wilhelm looked at her briefly and turned away.

'Willy . . .' Fritz growled, warningly. 'You'll treat your mother with respect, do you hear?'

Wilhelm paused, then bowed stiffly.

'By the way,' Bertie said mildly. 'I think we'd better forget about that invitation for you to visit Sandringham this year.'

Wilhelm lost his stiffness at once. 'But I—' he faltered. 'I wanted very much to come.' For a second, he sounded like a hurt boy.

'If you came, you'd have to call on the Queen,' Bertie explained. 'And since she's very much in favour of the marriage, I don't suppose she'd wish to see you.'

When Wilhelm left them, Bertie could see that Fritz and Vicky were upset. 'Don't worry,' he assured them. 'You saw how keen he was to come to England. At heart, he's one of us.'

'Only part of him,' Fritz said heavily. 'He is torn.'

'He loves us, but he is afraid that love is weakness,' Vicky sighed. 'Sometimes I'm so sorry for him. And I keep remembering when he was quite small, playing with the soldiers of the Guard. His nose started to bleed but he would not let them staunch it. He said—'I want all my English blood to run out".'

The turmoil continued. The Government's fatal delay in sending a relief column to rescue General Gordon in Khartoum lost them the support of the Queen, the Prince and the people. At the same time, led by his conscience, Gladstone came to the decision that the only solution to the unrest in Ireland was Home Rule within the Empire. The Bill he tried to introduce split his own party and lost him the election. Sir Charles Dilke's political prospects were ruined for ever by a sensational divorce case, where he was accused of seducing both a woman and her married daughter.

Out of the ruins of his political friendships, Bertie still had Churchill. A brilliant Chancellor of the Exchequer in the new Conservative Cabinet, and leader of the House of Commons, he was visibly challenging the cautious Prime Minister, Lord Salisbury. With the active group he formed around him, he stung and prodded the older Conservatives towards reform of the economy. His success was watched with fascination and his admirers laughed when he flamboyantly threatened to resign if his suggestions for the Budget were not accepted. With masterly political acumen, Salisbury accepted the resignation. Lord Randolph Churchill's career was finished. His impetuosity, as Disraeli foretold, had destroyed him. Bertie was left with no intimate friend in power. It was only in their fall that Dilke and Churchill learnt to appreciate the Prince's friendship. He continued to back them, even though the Queen told him to break off all communication.

The passion had gone out of his affaire with Lillie. By mutual consent, the exclusive nature of their relationship ended. With the excitement her name now produced, she had had an unrivalled success in America, where she was now to spend much of her life. Through all her romances and scandalous adventures, Bertie was always there if she needed him.

Slowly it dawned on the country, and the world, that Victoria had reigned for fifty years. For over half of them she had been a widow. She had ridden out storms of protest, deaths, wars and upheavals and imposed her own unwavering standards on three-quarters of the globe. The indomitable little old lady in black had gradually become the most revered person in the world. It came as a surprise to her and she found the countless gifts and letters and demonstrations of affection infinitely touching.

Bertie arranged all the pageantry of the Golden Jubilee. He was proud of his mother and the love she inspired, and he founded the Imperial Institute in South Kensington to commemorate it. At the climax of the celebrations, forty-four carriages bearing Kings, Queens, Princes, Princesses, Grand Duchesses and Rajahs from Europe to Japan went in procession from Buckingham Palace to Westminster Abbey. Bertie led a mounted troop of sixteen princes as the escort for the Queen's landau, in which Victoria sat with Vicky and Alix. They had not been able to talk Victoria into wearing her Crown or robes of state. On a day of perfect sun, she rode to the Abbey in a new dress and a white lace bonnet with diamonds. She was moved by the exultation of the crowds and glad that the Abbey was so crowded she had not been able to see Mr. Gladstone.

Afterwards she said, 'What a proud day this would have been for my beloved husband.'

Next to Bertie, the most popular man in the procession was Fritz, handsome and erect with his golden beard and the Prussian eagle on his helmet. He had now utterly lost his voice but the doctors had told him all he needed was rest. A banner across Whitehall on the day read "Good Sovereign. No change required". Fritz saw how it disheartened Bertie, although he loved the Queen. Through Vicky, he assured him that the time was coming when he would be more than his mother's master of ceremonies. Together, they would bring peace to Europe.

Sooner even than they expected, Kaiser Wilhelm died and Fritz and Vicky became Emperor and Empress of Germany. Bismarck tried to suggest that an Emperor who could not speak should not be allowed to rule, but he was silenced. The reign of Kaiser Frederick William began, full of hope and promise.

It ended ninety-nine days later. A telegram arrived, telling Bertie that Fritz had died of cancer of the throat. It was signed by Kaiser Wilhelm the Second.

Chapter
17

The party at Marlborough House was in honour of Eddy being made Duke of Clarence. As an officer in the Hussars, his dash and stylish appearance masked his sluggish mind. From his starched collars and the meticulous inch and a half of shirt sleeve at his wrists, he was known as 'Collar and Cuffs'. He was a complete contrast to his quieter, more serious brother, George, who was absorbed in his career in the navy. After his own experience, Bertie had encouraged them to take up a profession. Both he and Alix hoped the responsibility would be good for Eddy, but the only things that seemed to interest him were clothes and girls.

The party was gay and the ballroom crowded with their friends. Waltzing with his wife, Mina, Lord Charles Beresford wondered how long she would make him suffer. He concentrated on her, smiling into her suspicious eyes, knowing the violent scenes that would follow if he even glanced at Daisy. Mina had found out all about their affaire, and, although he had sworn it was over, kept raking it up, reading his letters, ferreting his thoughts. He had to account for every minute he spent away from her. The agony was that he could hear Daisy laughing as she danced with the Prince, the free, silvery laugh that was so much a part of her. He remembered her laughing, galloping beside him in her scarlet coat as they led the hunt, young, naked and laughing in the summerhouse at Easton, daring him, the hero of Alexandria, to be afraid that anyone might come. His wife's eyes questioned him, her face, garishly made up under her yellow wig, set and suspicious. He had aged, himself, in the last years his curly hair thinning in front. But he was still handsome and impetuous.

He smiled. 'The Princess is looking remarkably lovely tonight, don't you think, my dear?'

Alix was dancing with Oliver Montagu. Slim and radiant, no one could believe Bertie and she had already celebrated their silver wedding. While he was greying and putting on more weight, she seemed younger every year. Oliver was her ideal partner, light and gay. Over his shoulder, she could see Bertie with Lady Brooke. As the waltz ended, they stayed together and Bertie was clearly agreeing to something, smiling and pressing Daisy Brooke's hand. She had just the fair hair and blue eyes he always admired.

'It's not beginning again,' Alix breathed. 'Not all over again? . . .'

'What, Ma'am?' Oliver asked.

Alix started. She smiled. 'The music. I can't hear it when they play too softly.' She took Oliver's hand and led him across to where Prince George was talking to a pretty girl, Julie Stonor. Eddy had joined them and was flirting with her. It was unfair. Georgie was shy in company and Eddy was taking the girl over. She could tell straight away he had been drinking too much. 'Eddy, you are very naughty,' she protested. 'You have ignored me all evening.'

'Oh—sorry, Motherdear,' he smiled. 'I was just circulating.'

'I think it's your head that's circulating,' George said. They laughed.

Rosebery and Christopher Sykes came to them and bowed. Rosebery was good-looking, with a strong, blunt jaw, an intellectual with a sense of humour.

'We're hoping you'll settle an argument for us, Ma'am,' he said. 'We cannot decide which of us is to have the honour of being your next partner.'

'Neither,' Alix told them, laughing. She slipped her arm through Eddy's.

'I'm going to dance with my soldier-boy.' As the music started again, Eddy led her out on to the floor.

From the side, Francis Knollys smiled as he saw the Beresfords begin to dance again, too. Such a display of fidelity from Charlie B. was phenomenal. He looked over at Lady Brooke. She had her beautiful back to the dancers and was talking to the Prince and Arthur Sassoon. Knollys wondered idly who would replace Beresford. Daisy was far too attractive and highspirited for her husband, a pleasant, undistinguished man, over-addicted to shooting. The Queen had once considered her for her son, Leopold, but she had flatly refused him. That took courage. He turned, just in time to see snobbish Sir William Gordon-Cumming cut Maurice Hirsh, the Prince's Financial Adviser, Jewish like Sassoon. Poor Baron Hirsh, Knollys thought, he gives millions to charity and no one will speak to him but the Prince. He sighed. Cumming was heading towards him.

'Sometimes when you come here you think you've wandered into a damned synagogue,' Cumming scowled. 'Isn't Wales going to play any cards tonight?'

Alix was laughing as she spun with Eddy. He had a wicked charm and used it even on her. She pretended to scold him. 'I'm sure the army's teaching you bad habits. It's high time you were married.'

'Ah, but where would I find someone as lovely as you, Motherdear.' He smiled, and kissed her cheek.

When Frances, Lady Brooke, known as Daisy, called on the Prince of Wales next afternoon as they had arranged, she was very timid and appealing. He was touched that she had come to him for help. He had known about her affaire with Beresford and that it was over. Mina had just had a daughter. Daisy sat, blushing and twisting her gloves, as she told him how she had, foolishly, written to Beresford when she heard his wife was to have a baby, an impulsive, passionate letter. She did not understand even why she had sent it, but Mina Beresford had opened it. Now she had given it to her solicitor, to hold in case her husband was ever unfaithful again. Poor old Charlie B, Bertie thought. That was why he had given up his post at the Admiralty and was going back to sea—to get away from it.

'I'm so afraid,' Daisy faltered. 'She's unreasonable, capable of anything. I'm so afraid she'll use it against me. She's threatened me.'

'It's your letter, Daisy,' Bertie said. 'Why don't you ask for it back?'

'I—I wouldn't know what to say.' She hesitated. 'And if it got out, it would hurt Brookie so much.' She glanced up at Bertie, biting her full, lower lip. Her eyes were trusting, a soft, melting blue. Her face was a perfect oval, her hair piled up to cluster in delicate, fair curls. She smiled to him tremulously.

Bertie took her hand. 'All right, Daisy,' he promised. 'Leave it to me. I'll see what I can do.'

George Lewis, Lady Beresford's solicitor, was surprised and flattered when the Prince of Wales called on him late that night and made no difficulty about showing him the letter. It was even more passionate than Daisy had admitted. With regret, Lewis explained that he could not let him take it, technically a letter once sent belongs to the receiver, nor could he destroy it without Lady Beresford's permission. He agreed it was deplorable, but he had to obey his client's instructions.

As soon as possible, Bertie called on Lady Beresford. She was indignant that he had been involved and suspected that her husband and his mistress were using the Prince to weaken her hold over them. She refused to give up the letter.

When Bertie came to see Daisy, he made certain that her husband had gone to his club. For greater privacy, they talked in her boudoir, a warmly feminine, little room, with her writing desk and cushioned daybed. At first, Daisy was disappointed, but he reassured her. All Lady Beresford wanted was to avoid a scandal. With Charlie B going off to the Mediterranean for two years, she would leave the letter safely buried in Lewis's office. To make certain she did, he would keep a light pressure on her. All Daisy had to do was keep out of her way until she had cooled down.

As his deep, confident voice reassured her, Daisy felt more relaxed than she had for months. She had been desperately worried at the thought of becoming common gossip, and hurt by Beresford's weakness. Now she had as her champion, the leader of society. She still remembered how thrilled she had been when she first met him and the Princess. She knew all about Lillie Langtry and the others. She had tried to flirt with him once but he had been far more interested in Jennie Churchill. She had even felt envious when he took Jennie off with him afterwards for a holiday in Baron Hirsch's castle in Austria. To be one of his intimate friends, to be his favourite, made one the most envied woman in the fashionable world, next to the Princess. His reputation as a lover was unequalled. She had often felt a tingling excitement when his eyes had just met hers for a moment in passing. They seemed to say they could tell exactly what she would be like. Daisy suspected she might surprise him. Others had been surprised by her abandon, her total, joyous delight. No, she told herself, if he took me it would not only be for a week or a month. I'd leave him no need for any others. He would never leave me.

They were sitting on the daybed, close and confidential. Bertie had been conscious all the time of her perfume. Her high-necked silk day dress, lavender overlaid with lace, clung to her incredibly slender waist and emphasised the fullness of her hips. Bertie had been hoping to comfort her and to help Beresford, but he knew he would like to see Daisy again, now their friendship had become more personal. As he framed the words to arrange another meeting, he suddenly noticed the heightened colour of her cheeks, the slight dilation of her nostrils, the unmistakeable tension. The tip of her tongue touched her lips quickly and she leant back against the cushions heaped at the head of the couch.

'I don't think you should have any more trouble, my dear,' he said. He paused. 'Provided you're quite sure you've finished with Charlie B.'

'I have forgotten him,' she answered quietly. Her eyes had been lowered. She raised them and looked fully at him. 'You've been so kind,' she murmured. 'How can I ever thank you?'

Daisy was a revelation. As a mistress, she was thoughtful, generous as he was, capricious but yielding and always ready. Bertie had been tired of the unending round. The cruel death of Fritz had affected him deeper than anyone but Alix realised. All his plans and hopes had seemed to be wiped out. He was still only his mother's master of ceremonies. Even now that Leopold had died, tragically young, she would not let him work with her. Alix was absorbed in her children. Louise had married, but she kept Toria and Maud with her at Sandringham most of the year, enjoying their companionship to the point of possessiveness. Bertie took refuge in horse and yacht racing and almost compulsive gambling. But Daisy revived him. She brought back a zest which had gone from his life. In return, he cherished and protected her. On the lists of dinner and party guests sent for his approval, if he saw Lady Beresford's name, he stroked it out and wrote in Lady Brooke. Hostesses soon learnt not to invite Mina when they had the Prince and Daisy.

While Bertie recovered his vitality and Daisy became accepted as his constant companion, Lady Beresford's jealousy tormented her. The best parties were those given for the Prince. Not only was she excluded but she saw her rival exalted. She complained to her husband. Beresford had hoped the matter was over. He had begged his wife to destroy the letter. When he discovered that the Prince had also wished it destroyed, after reading it, he became enraged. His anger was unreasonable and caused partly by jealousy. The Prince not only knew his secrets but was Daisy's lover. He was leaving London to take up his command in the Mediterranean. He went first to Marlborough House.

Bertie was working in the study with Francis Knollys. When Beresford was announced, he rose from his desk to meet him, pleased that Charlie B had come to say goodbye. When he held out his hand, Beresford ignored it.

'I am told that you have interfered in a matter that concerns only myself and my wife,' he said.

Bertie let his hand fall. He considered Beresford, seeing that he was taut, barely holding himself under control. 'Well now, Charlie,' he said evenly. 'I think we'd better sit down.'

'I prefer to stand . . . sir,' Beresford told him. 'I demand an explanation!'

'Demand?' Bertie stiffened.

'You have interfered in my private affairs.'

Bertie was trying to keep his temper. 'I acted to prevent unnecessary harm being done, to help both Lady Brooke and you.'

'You needn't tell me why you interfered. I know you well enough for that,' Beresford sneered.

'Beresford—', Knollys warned urgently.

He paid no attention. His jealousy and hurt pride tore down his control. 'Not content with amusing yourself with Daisy, you try to ruin my wife socially!'

Bertie was angry now, too. 'If your wife feels excluded, she knows the remedy,' he snapped. 'Francis, will you show Lord Beresford out.'

'I'm not leaving until I'm ready!' Beresford shouted.

Bertie turned away. He heard Beresford take a step after him and looked back. Beresford's fist was clenched and raised. 'You're a blackguard, sir,' he stormed. 'A blackguard and a coward!'

'I should advise you not to strike me,' Bertie said, very quietly. He was icily calm. He made no move to defend himself.

Beresford's fist wavered and lowered. Through the haze of anger, he realised how close he had been to throwing away his career. Bertie had saved him from being cashiered.

'You'll make it up to her . . . ,' he muttered thickly. 'You'll make it up . . . or you've not heard the end of it.' He turned abruptly without bowing and stalked out.

Bertie found that he was trembling. He moved to the couch and sat. There was a moment's silence. 'I believe he would have struck me, Francis,' he murmured.

'I believe he would have, sir,' Knollys echoed. He was still shaken, himself.

'It's that Irish temper . . .' Bertie had been dazed. Beresford had once been his most intimate friend. He stood up. 'Well, I'm damned if I'll let anyone speak to me like that—or if he can force me to see his wife. It's a good thing he's going back to sea. He'll have a chance to think better.'

'Do you remember the name of his new ship, sir?' Knollys asked. Bertie looked at him. 'The *Undaunted*.'

Alix was very excited. One of her fondest dreams was coming true. Eddy had given her so much anxiety. They had tried several times to find him a wife, without success. He had turned them all down except his beautiful cousin, Alicky, the daughter of Princess Alice. She was far too intelligent and it was she who refused him. Alix, indulgently, tried to blame that for the life he was leading. She knew she had not heard the worst, but his drinking and indiscriminate womanising had become notorious. Now everything had changed. He had fallen in love with the Count of Paris's daughter, Hélène. There were difficulties. The girl was Roman Catholic, and Eddy, as heir to the Throne of England after his father, could never marry a Catholic, yet Alix was too keen to see him settled and happy to care.

She had gone to stay at Mar Lodge in Scotland, the home of her married daughter, Louise, Duchess of Fife, who was expecting her first baby. That was another excitement. Alix could hardly believe she was going to be a grandmother. She was waiting in the garden. When she saw them coming towards her, Eddy, tall and handsome, his arm around the tiny, exquisite Hélène, she could tell at once he had proposed. She kissed them both and bundled them straight into a carriage, to go to Balmoral.

Eddy and Hélène were very frightened as they stood before the Queen, who could not resist young lovers. When Hélène promised to change her religion, she kissed her and consented to the engagement.

Bertie could see the difficulties more clearly. They were not only religious. Hélène's father was the Pretender to the Throne of France. The French would react violently, both the Bonapartists and the Republicans. Not to mention his nephew, Wilhelm, who would see it as a plot. Bertie was more than ever concerned about him. He was insufferably arrogant, callous to his mother, surrounding himself with new advisers, while he boasted flamboyantly about 'the irresistible expansion of the German Empire'. Even Bismarck was worried. Bertie was positive something was going to happen there soon. He put it out of his mind as he watched his hosts prepare the card table.

He was in Yorkshire for the week of the St. Leger race. Usually he stayed with Christopher Sykes but, this year, Xtopher was in financial difficulties and he had helped him by accepting an invitation from Arthur Wilson, a shipowner, to stay at his house near Doncaster. The house, Tranby Croft, was comfortable and it was a large party, including his friends, Xtopher, Lord Conventry, General Owen Williams, Reuben Sassoon and Sir William Gordon-Cumming. Even so, it had been disappointing. Daisy should have been with him but, at the last moment, an uncle of hers died and she had to attend the funeral.

Luckily, Bertie had brought his counters with him and they were able to spend the evenings after dinner playing his favourite game, baccarat. Bertie was bank, playing against the others. The stakes were not too high, yet enough to be interesting. With brandy, cigars and good company, it was fairly enjoyable. The only constant winner seemed to be Bill Cumming.

Bertie chuckled. 'You've the luck of the Devil tonight.' He did not notice that five other people, including their hosts, were not playing but watching Sir William.

Cumming had bet five pounds on Lord Somerset who was playing against the Prince. He leant over to see what cards Somerset was holding, his hands loosely clasped. Somerset had a natural, a nine and a court card. Cumming's fingers opened and he dropped three more red £5 counters on to the table.

When the Prince paid him, he said, 'There's another fifteen, I think, sir.'

'Oh—sorry, Bill,' Bertie smiled. 'Pay him fifteen, will you?' General Owen, who was paying out for him, passed Cumming another fifteen pounds.

The watchers saw him repeat the same manoeuvre in later coups, adding counters or sliding them away. In all, he won over two hundred pounds.

When General Williams and Lord Coventry confronted him with the accusation later that might, Cumming, normally a haughty, insolent man, went to pieces. As a colonel in the Scots Guards and a personal friend of the Prince, he saw his life ruined. At first, he strongly denied it, then he asked them for their advice.

'What—what do you think I should do? I must—you must let me talk to the Prince,' he begged.

Bertie was as shaken as the others when they told him. He could not believe it, but they questioned the witnesses and there was no doubt that Cummings had been cheating. He was sorry for his old friend and warned him not to make it worse for himself.

'We have no desire to be unnecessarily hard on you,' he said.

General Williams and Lord Coventry wrote a statement for Cumming to sign, the traditional method of handling such cases. It said that, in return for the silence of all concerned, he would promise never to play cards again as long as he lived. Cumming protested that that would be admitting his guilt. If he were not allowed to play cards and the Prince dropped him, everyone would ask why; nevertheless he signed. Bertie and the others countersigned and Cumming left the house. The unpleasant business was over.

Alix was deeply upset. After all her hopes, Eddy's marriage to Hélène could not take place. She had seen how hurt they had both been when, after months of discussion, the negotiations had ended. She had never understood when Bertie had tried to explain the objections to her.

They were in the sitting room at Sandringham. Eddy had just left to rejoin his regiment. 'I'm sorry, my dear,' Bertie told her, 'but if neither her father nor the Pope will let her change her religion, there is nothing more we can do.'

'Eddy is heartbroken,' Alix protested.

Privately, Bertie doubted if it meant as much to their son as to Hélène. Nothing concerned Eddy for long. It was becoming more of a problem. He turned as Francis Knollys came to them. He seemed perturbed.

'I'm sorry to interrupt you, sir,' he said. 'But I thought you ought to know. I've just heard a rumour about something that happened at Tranby Croft.'

Bertie had never wished to hear the name again. 'What kind of rumour?'

'Well, sir—it's pretty vague. All that's being said is that you were playing . . . an illegal card game for money, and that someone was accused of cheating.'

Alix was concerned. 'What's this about, Bertie?' she asked.

'Nothing. Nothing, my dear.' Unless the rumour were stopped quickly, Cumming was finished and it could turn into a nasty little scandal. 'Nothing important.'

As a former colleague of Disraeli, the Queen normally found Lord Salisbury very soothing. He was a shaggy, heavily-bearded, serious man. Today, however, the Audience was disturbing.

'How is this possible, Prime Minister?' she demanded. 'My son assured me that everything had been done to protect this Gordon-Cumming.'

'When the rumour got out—as it was bound to do, Ma'am—it appears Cumming decided his best method of defence was attack. He has brought an action against the people who originally accused him of cheating.'

Victoria frowned. 'But it could have all been decided by a military court of enquiry.'

'Unfortunately, Cumming's solicitors appealed against that.' He hesitated. 'The most regrettable aspect is that His Royal Highness's attempt to save Cumming from public disgrace has been seen as condemning a man without a fair trial. People are saying that he was forced to sign this document purely to prevent an unpleasant scandal involving the Prince of Wales.'

In the court, it almost appeared as if Bertie were on trial. Enormous public interest had been roused and all the old rumours of his gambling debts were revived. Bertie spoke briefly and straightforwardly. He was called merely as a witness, but Cumming's counsel, Sir Edward Clarke, turned the whole defence of his client into an attack on the Prince's way of life.

Bertie sat expressionless, listening as Clarke thundered in his summing up, 'Furthermore I would suggest, my Lord, that previous instances have been known of men, men of courage and dignity, who were prepared to sacrifice themselves to support a tottering throne or prop up a falling dynasty. It is my contention, it is my belief, my lord, that, at Tranby Croft, Sir William Gordon-Cumming was victimised to save the honour of a prince who encouraged habitually an illegal game—who had jumped recklessly to a wrong conclusion on bad evidence!'

The Queen was horrified by the amount of publicity given to the case. Although Cumming was unanimously found guilty and discharged from the Army, it was Bertie's popularity which suffered most. The Puritans lashed him. He was condemned in the Press and from the pulpit with no opportunity to defend himself. The Secretary of War had to apologise on his behalf in the House of Commons. The Kaiser even wrote to his grandmother to protest that Prussian Hussars should be involved in a gaming scandal.

Victoria sat at her desk in her study at Balmoral. Her eyes had been troubling her and she found it easier to have books and newspapers read to her rather than strain at the small letters. Her Indian secretary, Abdul Karim, had just finished a newspaper report which quoted Clarke. The words, 'a tottering throne', still hung in the air. They were most offensive, and inaccurate. Once again, Bertie had been betrayed by unsuitable friends. She did not blame him personally, knowing the facts, but she decided that he must make an effort to restore his prestige. He must write at once to the Archbishop of Canterbury, openly, denouncing gambling. She felt certain Lord Salisbury would agree. Even the Leader of the Opposition, Gladstone, was at least *morally* sound.

Gladstone had no more success with the Prince than Salisbury.

'I will not write such a letter,' Bertie maintained. 'It would be the worst kind of hypocrisy.'

Gladstone was now over eighty. His hair was pure white, wispy on the crown of his head and curling thickly at his neck. He walked, slightly bent, with a stick, but his eyes were still alive and keen.

'My hopes were, sir, that it might improve your position with Her Majesty.'

'I doubt if anything can alter that, William,' Bertie said. 'My position is simple. I abhor gambling. But it is as absurd to describe as gambling a harmless game of baccarat, played by rich men for stakes they can comfortably afford, as to consider a glass or two of champagne at dinner as intemperance.'

Gladstone smiled very briefly. 'I scarcely think that statement would serve the purpose the Queen had in mind.' He sighed. 'Such a pity, when Her Majesty and I are in agreement for once.' He bowed and Knollys saw him to the door of the study.

Bertie would like to have pleased the old man. 'If

it'll do any good I'll announce I'll play no more baccarat,' he said. 'Only bridge.'

Gladstone looked back and smiled. He nodded and went out with Knollys. Bertie slumped in his chair. He thought of how shocked he had been that night to learn that Cumming had deliberately and contemptibly cheated him. Under the cover of that righteous pose, how many other times had he cheated? Yet thousands of people now saw Cumming as the hero, the victim. The whole business had been hurtful and exhausting. He was tired of being criticised and misrepresented. One thing he was determined on. He would not lie, crawl or pretend to be what he was not, to win back popularity. He was human, not a saint, nor a paragon like his father. They'll have to take me as I am, he though, or not at all.

Francis came back to the door. 'Lord Rosebery, sir. He's been waiting some time.'

Bertie was relieved to see someone who would not moralise. 'Hello, Archie,' he smiled. 'Come and cheer me up for Heaven's sake.'

Rosebery bowed. 'I wish I could, sir.' He hesitated. 'The Prime Minister had asked me to tell you he's had a . . . somewhat hysterical letter from Lady Beresford.'

'What on earth about?'

'Since she is no longer invited to Marlborough House, she is no longer asked anywhere. Apparently, she had been so distressed that she and her husband are threatening to make the details of their quarrel with Your Royal Highness public.'

Bertie was incredulous. 'He's still with his ship, isn't he?'

'Lord Charles has applied for urgent home leave, sir.'

'I thought the whole damn thing was forgotten!' Bertie exploded. He rose and strode to the window. That damned letter again. Daisy had been hurt enough. People were whispering that it was she who had given away the story of Tranby Croft. The Babbling Brooke, they sniggered. And now the Beresfords. 'What do they think they'll achieve?'

'I'm told they are demanding an apology and an undertaking that you will receive Lady Beresford.'

Bertie swung round to look at him. 'I'll be hanged if I shall!'

Rosebery was embarrassed. 'I'm afraid there's more, sir. Lady Beresford had had a pamphlet written, describing the quarrel . . . and your relationship with Lady Brooke. She is prepared to make good her threat and publish it.' Bertie's mind was racing. 'The Prime Minister feels that, coming so soon after Tranby Croft—'

'Yes,' Bertie muttered. 'Yes, yes.' He had understood the danger at once. He could not, he simply could not believe that Beresford had changed so much. Like Cumming, and Churchill before him. What happened to people? Denied friendship in his youth, he saw it as something sacred, to be cherished. For a moment, he wondered if his father had been right, that the only chance for him was to be alone, to have no one close and trusted. He remembered Carrington, and Sykes, Francis Knollys, Jeanne de Sagan, and would not accept it. 'No,' he said. He looked at Rosebery. 'Beresford ended our friendship. I shall not receive his wife.'

There was a knock at the door and Oliver Montagu came in, without waiting. 'I'm sorry to interrupt, sir.'

'We're busy, Oliver,' Bertie said.

Montagu was serious. 'I'm sorry, sir. But I think you ought to see Her Royal Highness.'

Bertie found Alix in her private sitting room. She was standing at the piano, looking at a photograph of Eddy. He waited for her to speak.

'I've been to talk to May's parents,' she said. 'They are willing.'

Bertie relaxed. He had not known what to expect. At least, this was something settled. Eddy had been behaving disgracefully. He was totally irresponsible. The only hope for him was to be married to an intelligent, quiet girl who might steady him. The ideal choice was Princess May, daughter of the Duke and Duchess of Teck, who lived in England. Alix had been to sound them out.

'May is a sensible girl,' Alix said. 'She will do as her parents wish.'

'Good,' Bertie smiled.

Her voice was level. 'I heard today about a pamphlet that was read out at someone's dinner party.' She turned to him. Her apparent lack of emotion and the suddenness of it had taken him by surprise. 'I stood by you these last months—but this is different.'

'Alix—' He could see now that she was distressed.

'No, Bertie. I will not be an object of pity again. I will not support you for the sake of Lady Brooke. I am leaving.'

In the months that Alix was gone, the Prince's popularity was lower than at any time since the Mordaunt scandal. People suspected that she was punishing him. At the end of her holiday in Denmark, when she went to join Minny and Sacha in the Crimea instead of coming home for his fiftieth birthday, the fear grew that she did not mean to return.

Bertie was not certain himself, but he could not leave London to follow her while Mina Beresford's hysteria had reached a point where she was capable of anything and her husband wrote screeching, irrational letters to the Prime Minister. Salisbury was amazed by them. A sensible man, who went out little in society, he saw the ridiculous side of it immediately. The Beresfords had rejected the Prince's friendship violently and now they were demanding to be treated as friends again or they would ruin his reputation. Salisbury found himself embroiled with the Queen, Marlborough House, solicitors and the Beresfords and their relations. His sympathy, such as it was, was with the Prince. As he struggled to find a solution, he would gladly have consigned them all to the Devil, except that another royal scandal could cause a national crisis.

As before, it was her family that brought Alix home. George collapsed with typhoid. At the very mention of the word, she hurried back to Sandringham to be with him. As Bertie and she watched over him, they were drawn together again. Alix understood that she

303

could not change him and it was enough to know that she would always come first in his life. Bertie loved her. He also knew he could not change but, without her, he had felt as though part of him was missing. On the day George began to recover, Eddy proposed to Princess May and was accepted.

She arrived to spend Christmas with them at Sandringham and they saw at once how good she would be for Eddy. She was a self-contained, fair-haired, attractive rather than beautiful. Her personality was warm and, in spite of her reserve, she fitted into the family perfectly. Alix adored her. Not least because she lived all her life in England. She had never liked the thought of her boys marrying the inevitable German Princesses. Bertie welcomed her, too. He could see the effect she was having on Eddy already. For almost the first time, he was beginning to think before he spoke. He was courteous and considerate to her. They made a striking couple and Bertie hoped they would really love each other.

It made a settlement of the Beresford quarrel imperative. Lord Charles had arrived in England, his wounded pride turned to hatred. Pride in its most petty form, social pride, was behind it all, Salisbury told Bertie when they met to discuss it. He had been negotiating with Beresford ever since he returned.

'It is remarkable to me that honour should be considered less important than an invitation to tea.' Salilbury was very grave. 'The Beresfords appear to have lost all reason. They now demand, in addition, the exclusion of Lady Brooke from Court.'

Bertie controlled his anger. Even Alix had made no such condition. Daisy was not asked to Sandringham which was their private home. That was the only restriction on the relationship.

'It is out of the question,' he said.

'I must tell you, sir, that Lord Charles has arranged to meet the Press. He intends to give them details about certain incidents in your private life, known to him from the past. He will not listen to reason.' It was almost beyond Salisbury's understanding. He knew that victory over pride had to come from the Prince. 'I'm afraid that Your Royal Highness will have to go some way towards meeting his demands.' He saw the struggle in the Prince, the hurt at the new betrayal, but Bertie finally yielded.

Lady Brooke would temporarily not be invited to Court. The petty quarrel that had nearly become a major scandal was resolved. When he saw Eddy and May together, he knew he had made the only possible decision. He was happy the last two years were over.

The parties at the beginning of the New Year to celebrate the engagement were the gayest anyone could remember. May and her parents stayed with them at Sandringham and the wedding was arranged for February. During the day, the ladies discussed plans and details, while the men went shooting. One afternoon, they noticed that Eddy was falling behind. He had a bad headache and had hoped the fresh air would clear it but, as they walked it became worse. By the time they reached home, he was shivering and pale. Alix made him go to bed and sent for the doctor, who diagnosed influenza.

The next day was his birthday and he insisted on coming down for his presents. He was so weak that he had to go back to bed. He was sweating heavily and his breathing was laboured. Inflammation of the lungs had set in and the doctor sent him for a specialist. Alix and May took turns sitting with him in the small bedroom he had since he was a child. They read to him or just sat quietly, keeping him company. He was cheerful but his condition suddenly became so much worse that the specialists would not let May see him, only Bertie and Alix. He was raving and delirious, fighting for breath as the inflammation turned to pneumonia. Stunned, Bertie wrote to the Queen but the letter was too late.

Alix would not leave Eddy. She sat by his side through the day and the night and the next day, wiping his forehead and cooling his temples with ice, as he raved on and on. At the end of the second day, Bertie forced her to take some rest. The specialist had told him that there were no signs of improvement. They had scarcely left Eddy's room when they were called back. He was still talking but no one could make out what he said. The doctor, the specialist and the nurses could do nothing more for him.

Alix knelt beside him. The shock and the suddenness made her almost hysterical but she forced herself to be calm, although she could not stop her tears. 'Eddy, my darling . . . Eddy . . .' she whispered, but his eyes saw nothing. Bertie stood behind her, gazing at his son. He tried to pray, to ask for a miracle like the one that had saved him. May came to stand beside him and, one by one, George and Toria and Maud until the little room was crowded.

All at once, Eddy's eyes opened wide and he stared at them. 'Something too awful has happened,' he said, his voice quite normal. 'My darling brother George is dead.' George sobbed and Bertie put his arm round his shoulders. At the door, the parson from the church at Sandringham was reading the prayer for the dying. 'Who is that?' Eddy asked. 'Who is that?' He repeated the words over and over, his voice growing fainter until he sighed very quietly and lay still.

Bertie's heir and the child of Alix's heart was dead.

Chapter
18

Sympathy for the Prince and Princess at the death of their son put an end to the years of criticism. The nation mourned with them when Albert Victor, Duke of Clarence, was buried at Windsor.

It was many many months before Alix came out of black and she never again wore bright colours. She returned to Sandringham shortly after the funeral with her daughters, Toria and Maud, as if to hide herself there from the world. But Bertie could not be inactive. When the first grief was over, he desperately needed work. His son's death had drawn his mother closer to him again, but she had not changed her opinion. While she disapproved of his way of life, she would not trust him. He threw himself into the business of his estates, the school, charity and hospital boards, Marlborough Club and Imperial Institute which had been neglected. He arranged for his unsuccessful racehorses to be moved to a better training stable and approved plans for a new racing yacht, the *Britannia,* to outclass all others. By the close of the period of mourning, all his energy and vitality were restored.

During the years of scandal, many things had been neglected. He knew he had to rebuild his contacts abroad. All Europe's alliances were shifting under the impact of his nephew, Kaiser Wilhelm. Bismarck had discovered, too late, that he had created a monster. Wilhelm saw no need to consult him since he had younger, more flattering advisers and, when Bismarck protested, summarily dismissed him. It sent shockwaves round the world. France and Russia had been kept apart and distrustful by Bismarck's cunning. To Wilhelm's consternation, the first result was that they made a firm treaty of alliance, upsetting decades of careful diplomacy. He felt isolated and set himself out to become popular, to take his uncle's place as the leader of European Society. While the Prince was distracted, he nearly succeeded, but he could never forget that he was an Emperor, even in private.

Bertie's friends in Paris and Homburg welcomed him back. When he strolled into the crowded Moulin Rouge one night, en garcon, La Goulue was dancing the can-can in a froth of teasing white petticoats and black stockings.

She screamed with delight, ' 'Ullo, Wales! Tu vas payer mon champagne?' and waggled her impudent backside.

Bertie waved his hat to her, chuckling, and ordered champagne for all the orchestra and dancers. Within weeks, everyone was wearing the wide check material of his suits and playing the new game he had taken up, lawn tennis. He had regained his position effortlessly and shown Wilhelm there was no contest; he returned to London in time to congratulate his old friend Gladstone on winning the General Election.

To the Queen's amazement and horror, she had had to accept the People's William, the Grand Old Man, as her Prime Minister for the fourth time, at the age of eighty-three. He travelled to her study at Osborne to kiss hands. The Queen limped in, bent, on her stick. Gladstone limped painfully towards her on his. He bowed and waited for her words of congratulation or welcome.

'You and I, Mr. Gladstone,' Victoria said, 'are lamer than we were.'

He had lost none of his fire. He could still argue all night in debate and make a two-hour speech, standing, the next day. He was well aware that this was his last chance to push through the legislation he believed in and, in his first months, invited the Prince to be a member of a Royal Commission on the aged poor, on practical ways of providing relief. He sensed that having purposeful work to do again would help him.

'Thank you, William,' Bertie said. 'I'm very grateful.'

'Grateful, sir?' Gladstone was indignant. 'It should be just one appointment amongst many! I consider the deliberate misuse of Your Royal Highness's talents one of the tragedies of our time. In my view—' He stopped himself and waved the words away. 'Well, I believe we both know to what, or whom, I refer.'

Bertie smiled. 'I believe so. If I can do anything else—'

They were walking towards the door of Bertie's study. Gladstone paused. 'I'm glad you reminded me, sir. You know that Lord Rosebery's wife has died. He was a brilliant Foreign Secretary—and could be so again. Yet, in his grief, he refuses office.'

'I'll speak to him,' Bertie promised. 'Although I have every sympathy with him. Since my son's death, I have begun to understand how grief can make everything else seem unimportant.'

Bertie's first concern was Alix. She had retreated further and further into her mourning. It was lengthened in the

308

most cruel way. Bertie had seen how she clung to seclusion at Sandringham, like his mother at Osborne and Balmoral. She had to be drawn out of it before it became permanent and unchangeable. He had asked Oliver Montagu to help. They had persuaded Alix to spend a holiday at Mar Lodge with Louise, and Oliver went with her. His devotion consoled her. They walked, he taught her salmon fishing and his companionship brought her back to life. But he had not been well for some time and his doctor advised him to spend the winter months in Egypt, for its mild, dry climate. A few weeks after arriving in Cairo, he was dead. A brave and gentle man, he had love her for over twenty years and Alix loved him, too, for his kindness and thoughtfulness.

She spent more and more time every day sitting in the room in which Eddy had died. It was dangerous. When Rosebery came to visit them at Sandringham, he saw how worried Bertie was that the Princess would become like the Queen, a recluse whose life had ended with the death of others.

'I wish I could help, sir,' he said. 'As you helped me.' He had thought all his ambition had died with his young wife. 'I didn't want the Foreign Office. I didn't want anything, but to be alone. I'm glad you made me accept.'

'It's the most important ministry, Archie,' Bertie said. 'It needs the best man.'

Rosebery smiled. 'That remains to be seen, sir.' They were sitting over their drinks by the fire in the drawing room. Rosebery took a narrow leather case from his pocket and placed it on the table between them. 'By the way, I thought you might like this.'

'What it it?' Bertie asked. He opened the case. Inside, there was a small gold key. He looked at it, mystified, then at Rosebery.

'It was made specially for you father, sir,' Rosebery told him. 'It is the key to the Foreign Office despatch boxes.' All foreign reports and policy decisions were sent in those boxes to the owners of keys. 'I know it has not been the practice, but I would like you to have it.'

Bertie would have no more need to rely on guesswork. He would be as fully informed as the Queen. He lifted the gold key from the case and his fingers closed on it tightly. His eyes were wet.

'I—I cannot find the words to thank you.'

Alix sat on a plain wooden chair by Eddy's bed. His uniform and the clothes he last wore hung on a hook by the door. His brush and comb lay on the locker as they had, untouched for over a year. The morning light picked out a Union Jack which was draped on the bed. Alix was dressed in black, silent, motionless.

She stirred when there was a knock at the door. Rosebery came in. He bowed. 'Forgive me for intruding, Ma'am, but I wanted to pay me respects before returning to London.'

'You're not going back so soon?'

'I must, I'm afraid.'

Alix saw how he looked round the room with its precious relics. 'I feel very close to him here. Of course, your dear Hannah—you must miss her, too, and understand.'

'I do, Ma'am. There is not an hour when I do not think of her,' he said quietly. He hesitated. 'May I say something?'

'Please.'

'At first, when she died, my instinct was to hide. Being alone, I could still see her clearly and imagine her near.' Alix smiled. 'But I realise now I was mistaken.'

Alix was puzzled. 'Mistaken?'

'Yes, Ma'am. Forgive me—I make no comparison of what we have both suffered. I only mention mine to show my heartfelt sympathy. Great grief seeks its refuge in seclusion, and such as I might seclude ourselves without notice. But Your Royal Highness cannot.' Alix looked away from him. 'Nothing, after all, can recall the past, but it should be the shrine to which we retire at times, not the cell in which we live.'

Alix nodded very slightly.

'I'm afraid I practise very badly what I preach. But there are so many who love and need you. They hope, as I do, that the memory of the affection in which you are held by the people of this country may persuade you to come among us.'

When he fell silent, Alix still sat looking away. She sighed once, softly. 'Thank you Lord Rosebery.'

His new prominence distressed George. Since Eddy's death, everything was different. He was the younger brother, happy to stay in the navy, marry eventually and live a useful, quiet life on the fringe of greatness. Now, he would one day be King; everything he did and said had a new importance. He had been created Duke of York, the leading man in the country after his father. He had loved Eddy and the thought that he was taking his place tormented him. He had still not fully recovered from the illness that brought Alix home and it made him more vulnerable. He was grateful to his father, who treated him more like a friend than a son and helped him through the first bewildering months.

Bertie worried about Georgie. It disturbed him to see his confidence so weakened, although he understood why. He was sorry that for a time the only remedy was bound to lower it further. He told Alix one evening as they discussed a cruise she was planning. She had come back to life, realising that, although she had lost her dearest child, the others still needed her. She had decided to take George on a convalescence cruise to Greece.

She looked at Bertie in astonishment. 'May? . . .' she repeated.

'She would be a good wife for him.'

'It's not possible!' Alix protested. 'She was to marry Eddy. She is his.'

'Think, Alix,' Bertie said gently. 'What kind of life would you condemn her to?' Alix was silent. 'He must marry, and she is almost one of us already. After all, it's happened before. Your own sister married Sacha when his elder brother died. They married out of duty. Look how happy they are now.'

Alix could not argue. And George knew he had little

311

choice. May had been chosen as the ideal wife for the future king. Not only did he have his brother's place, he was to have his bride. When he returned from Greece, he proposed. They were married in the Chapel Royal and he brought her to live at York Cottage, in the garden of Sandringham House.

May had always accepted that any marriage for her would be arranged by her parents. She had grieved for Eddy who was gay and handsome but already she had known George longer and shared suffering had made them friends. She would rather have been further away from her adoring mother-in-law, yet Alix helped her to turn the uncomfortable, little cottage into a home. May was glad that George was shy and thoughtful like herself. The first months were difficult but, in learning to live together, showing each other kindness and understanding, their affection became love.

Daisy's husband accepted her continuing friendship with the Prince philosophically. A charming man, he saw how much pleasure it gave her and, as his life was not disturbed, had no complaints. In fact, he found the friendly company when the Prince came to stay with them at Easton Lodge most enjoyable. It was her money that kept them going and she had given him three children. It would be unreasonable to ask for more.

She was the most enchanting and exasperating mistress. She gloried in her position and laughed at her exclusion from Court. After all, she did not have to go to London. The Prince and his inner circle came to her. He came so often that she had a private railway station built near her house for the royal train. Her parties were the most amusing, the most lavish, and all arranged for Bertie. She sometimes shared his trips abroad, went with him on visits to their friends, came to Cowes to cheer him when his new yacht, *Britannia,* won race after race, but her greatest joy was to have him in her own home where they did not need to be formal with each other, to keep outsiders guessing about their intimacy.

Enchanting, Bertie thought. But exasperating. He had come down to Easton for a few days to relax after his work on the Commission. It had been absorbing and tiring. He sat up and reached for a cigarette. Daisy had got out of bed, splendidly naked, her loosened hair heaped on her shoulders and hiding her face as she rummaged among papers in a drawer of her dressing table. The curve of her back was flawless, the sweep of her haunches emphasised by her slender waist.

'Here it is,' she said, and turned, holding a sheet of handwritten figures. She scooped her hair away from her face and threw it back. Her full breasts danced. 'This shows how much they can make. I've tried to be realistic.'

'My darling Daisy,' Bertie protested. 'It is not realistic to discuss it at three o'clock in the morning! Can't we leave it till tomorrow?'

She came to him and sat on the side of the bed. 'I want your advice.' She had begun a needlework school for the daughters of poor tenants. They had made the lingerie' for May's trousseau and she was thinking of opening a shop in Bond Street to sell what they produced.

'If you bought one less dress or gave one less party,' Bertie said, 'the money you'd save would be more than they'll earn in a year.'

Daisy's startlingly blue eyes opened wide. 'It would be degrading to them, just to give them money. What they need is a chance to earn it.'

'I agree, but—'

'And you're smoking,' she said. She took the cigarette from his mouth and dropped it into an unfinished glass of champagne on the nightstand.

'What the Devil—!' he spluttered.

'You'll wake the servants. . . ,' she warned him, smiling. 'Don't I smell nicer than tobacco? Anyway, it makes you all breathless, and you're putting on so much weight.' She climbed on to the bed and sat, straddling him. As he chuckled, she flicked the sheet of paper away. She laughed and bounced on him as if posting on one of her hunters. 'It's so much more fun with the light on.'

313

Gladstone had been true to his principles. Although his Government's majority was very small, by the force of his oratory and personality he had pushed a bill through the House of Commons to give Home Rule to Ireland. It was thrown out by the House of Lords. It was the end of his years of struggle. There was nothing more he could do and the country waited for him to resign. He came with his wife for the weekend to Sandringham. They had been many times and were now dear friends. They reminded Alix of her own parents and she insisted on tucking Mrs. Gladstone up in bed the first night herself. Gladstone sat in the smoking room with the Prince and Francis, now Sir Francis, Knollys.

'It is true, sir,' he sighed. 'I cannot continue. I can do no more for that unhappy land.'

'You have done much, William,' Bertie said.

Gladstone shook his head. 'Never enough, I am afraid. I tendered my resignation to her Majesty this morning.'

'Did she accept it?' Knollys asked.

'With the utmost cheerfulness.' Gladstone could still see the Queen's delight. She had given him not one word of thanks for sixty years of noble service.

'I am truly sorry,' Bertie told him. The country can never pay its debt to you. Nor can I.'

"I thank you, sir.' Gladstone forced himself to be matter-of-fact. 'I believe she will ask Rosebery to take my place, although he will be in the House of Lords and must leave the Commons to Asquith and Campbell-Bannerman.' He smiled. 'Still, I know he'll have your support.'

Bertie regretted that the last of Gladstone's brilliant Ministries had ended in failure, but he welcomed Rosebery as Prime Minister with his experience at the Foreign Office. International affairs had reached a dangerous level of tension. The scramble for new territory begun by Kaiser Wilhelm in his ambition to extend his possessions had brought the major powers into conflict with the British Empire, its Colonies, Dominions and Protectorates. In Africa, China and South America, they intrigued to undermine British influence and contested the strips of unclaimed land. There was no way they could expand except at one another's expense. France's alliance with Russia, and Germany's with Austria and Italy formed two blocs that jockeyed each other for supremacy. Britain stood outside, secure in the mastery of the seas, envied by them all. The chief danger was the Kaiser's conceit and rashness.

Wilhelm was insufferable. When he came to Cowes every year for the yacht racing, he was escorted by warships of the German Fleet and strutted the decks of his imperial yacht, the *Hohenzollern,* in the uniform of a British Admiral. Bertie had talked the Queen into giving him the honorary rank as a gesture.

'To wear the same uniform as Nelson,' Wilhelm smirked. 'It makes one feel quite giddy.' He was tormented by jealousy of Bertie's reputation as a sportsman and when his yacht was beaten by the *Britannia,* stormed at the unfairness of the handicaps, and insisted that the whole regatta be reorganised.

He lost no chance to score over his uncle, treating him with a mixture of affection and concealed contempt, but could not go too far. Not until he had won back Russia from its alliance with France and did not need the friendship of Britain.

Bertie much preferred his gentle Russian nephew, the Czarevitch Nicholas, Minny and Sacha's son. Nicky brought his beautiful, reserved fiancee, Alicky, to ask for the Queen's blessing on their coming marriage, as Alice's daughter, Alexandra of Hesse was very dear to Victoria. While she stayed at Osborne, Bertie took Nicky to Sandringham to be spoilt and petted by his Aunt Alix and teased by his cousins. The comfort and freedom, were just as he remembered from when he came on holiday as a boy. His own father had been stern and he confessed shyly how he had longed to live with his aunt and uncle in England.

Bertie had been sorry for him and indulged the guarded, hesitant boy, who was so like George. Even now the resemblance was amazing. He had little real contact any more with Sacha who had changed beyond recognition. Driven on by unrest in Russia, he had become a harsh, despotic Czar, crushing freedom of thought and religious toleration, persecuting Jews and ruling by fear. Bertie still met him sometimes in Denmark but, even there, Sacha's police surrounded him. The old holidays where they laughed and talked freely were gone. Russia was inflamed with hatred and envy of Britain, and no diplomat could change it. Bertie promised Rosebery that if he ever saw a chance, he would take it.

Only four months after Nicky's visit, shortly before his wedding, Alix had a telegram from Minny, telling her that Sacha was dangerously ill in the Crimea and begging her to come. Bertie left with her at once but by the time they reached Yalta, Sacha was dead. Nicky was distraught and Bertie took charge of him. Minny was in such despair that Alix was afraid to leave her and even slept in the same bedroom. They were still as close as they had been when they were girls. Alicky came to join them and the long ritual of the Imperial Russian funeral began. They travelled slowly with the embalmed body of the dead Czar by train to Moscow for funeral services in the Kremlin, then on to St Petersburg where they followed the coffin through crowded, silent streets, past the painted mansions, across the river Neva to the tiny, baroque church in the fortress of St Peter and St Paul where all the Czars since Peter the Great had their tombs. Sacha's body lay with its face exposed, in the light and heat of thousands of candles, for seven days of ceremonies and masses. By the end, the stench of the body which had not been embalmed until three days after death, was no longer stifled by the incense and the smell of burning wax. Bertie noticed it growing as he came to support Nicky at each day's mass. It makes an obscenity of death, he thought. At the climax of the final, four hour burial service, he and Alix took their place with the family to kiss the dead man's putrefying lips. It was an ordeal.

The whole family stayed together in the Antichkoff Palace and, while Alix comforted her sister, Bertie did what he could for Nicky, now Czar Nicholas the Second. He had seen the tears in the streets and the love the people had for him.

'To be a Czar is glorious, but to be a just Czar is more important. It is not too late. Trust your people,' he told him.

He was like a father to him and Alicky and when Nicholas married his beautiful, golden-haired Alexandra in the chapel of the Winter Palace, Bertie signed as a witness. For that day official mourning was set aside but, in spite of the splendour, there was no gaiety. Minny, dressed in white, the Dowager Empress Marie Feodorovna, wept and clung to Alix. It reminded him irresistibly of his own wedding and he was concerned for them. They were in love and deserved to be happy. Minny was so possessive that she would not even let them leave her for a honeymoon, not even to move to one of their other palaces. She did not consider how embarrassing it was for them to come down to breakfast with the whole family on the first morning. He could see trouble for Nicky. Alicky was as strong-willed as his mother and he would be torn between them, loving them both. Bertie used all his tact and charm to help them and when he had to return home, left Alix behind for two months as a companion for Minny.

His success was complete. People had seen his care of their young Czar and the whole Russian attitude changed. Inside three weeks he had ended twenty years of suspicion and hostility to Britain. As he drove to the station in the uniform and shaggy greatcoat of a Russian colonel, all St Petersburg turned out to cheer him and Nicky wept as they said goodbye. When he reached London, the Government was waiting to thank him and Rosebery wrote, 'Never has Your Royal Highness stood so high in the national esteem as today, for never have you had such an opportunity. That at last has come and has enabled you to justify the highest anticipations, and to render a signal service to your country, as well as to Russia and the peace of the world.' He had been able to work again in his own way.

The Kaiser was furious. He had championed the wedding himself, because Alicky was a German princess. He had meant to use it to regain his influence in Russia and now his fat, philandering uncle had beaten him.

He arrived at Cowes with his two newest warships as escort. One of them he had named the *Worth* after the victory in the Franco-Prussian War twenty-five years before. On the anniversary, he made a fiery, warlike speech on the *Worth,* celebrating the battle. It was meant to impress and humiliate his uncle through his love of France. Bertie was offended but so, also, was the entire British and French Press who criticised Wilhelm sharply for his bad manners. It infuriated him further. He was not used to criticism. The thought that his uncle's yacht would also beat his in the Queen's Cup race became intolerable. When the race started, he refused to join in, claiming again the handicaps were unfair and designed to make sure that the Prince of Wales would win. He summoned the Prime Minister, lectured him on the failings of his foreign policy and sailed huffily back to Kiel. Not for the first time, Bertie wondered if his nephew was unbalanced.

He was angered by Wilhelm and annoyed with Daisy. She was no consolation. On the death of her husband's father, she had become the Countess of Warwick, even richer than before and more recklessly extravagant. But a strange thing had happened. After the most spectacular banquet and ball of her career, four hundred guests at Warwick Castle dining and dancing in Louis the Sixteenth costumes, with Daisy as Marie Antoinette, she had read a scathing attack on her irresponsible extravagance in a radical journal, the *Clarion*. She had stormed up to London, found the offices of the *Clarion* and confronted the editor. How dare he say she was indifferent to the miseries of the poor! Her ball had given work to hundreds. The editor destroyed her economic argument in an impassioned speech that lasted for two hours. She emerged, dazed, her vague philanthropism turned into a kind of half-understood socialism. Like a revelation she suddenly saw how she could become a power for good behind the throne, a Joan of Arc. Her mission was to lead the Prince on to the true path.

His response was disappointing. 'My darling,' he told her over and over, 'the one thing you know I cannot do is belong to a political party. And certainly not an extreme radical one.'

'But you believe in progress,' she pleaded. She would not give in and brought it up whenever he was off guard. 'If only you would come to one of our meetings.'

It was not what Bertie wanted to hear when he kissed her. He would have taken her more seriously if her beliefs had affected her own extravagance. What he needed was distraction. His success in Russia had elated him. With a close friend as Prime Minister, his advice was asked and he had been better informed than ever before, but Rosebery's government had been defeated in a snap election and the ageing Lord Salisbury trudged back into Downing Street. He was his own Foreign Secretary and did not need the Prince's assistance. And he still had vivid memories of the Beresfords and Tranby Croft.

Bertie knew that all Salisbury saw him as was his mother's Master of Ceremonies. Since the Golden Jubilee, Victoria had looked more favourably on the people's need for show, but her age and crippling rheumatism stopped her from appearing very frequently herself. Bertie replaced her, welcoming foreign royalty, Trooping the Colour, riding in parades. He enjoyed the adulation and the cheering, but he would have given all of it for an ounce of responsibility. Even when England was nearly forced into a war, he seemed to be the last to hear of it.

In South Africa, both the Cape Colony and its neighbouring Republic, the Transvaal, owed allegiance to the Crown. Dutch Boers controlled the Transvaal, although the majority of its inhabitants were British.

'Cecil Rhodes, Prime Minister of the Cape, sent a Dr. Jameson with four hundred odd mounted police on a raid into the Transvaal,' Salisbury told him, 'hoping to incite a revolt against the Boer Government.' He had been summoned to Marlborough House. He felt distinctly uncomfortable as the Prince stared at him. 'His intention—his hope, sir, seemed to be to turn the whole southern tip of Africa into a federated British dominion.'

'But the raid failed?'

'He underestimated the strength of the Boers. Jameson was forced to surrender.'

'And why was I not told?' Bertie exploded.

'I can only assure you, sir, it came as a complete surprise to all of us. Rhodes acted on his own initiative. He will, of course, return to this country for an official enquiry.'

'My nephew, the Kaiser, will use it. Already, I hear he has sent a telegram to Kruger, the President of the Transvaal, congratulating him on preserving his "independence".' His tone was biting.

Salisbury coughed. 'I believe so, sir.' He normally saw the Prince in public, smiling and affable. He had seen him concerned and fighting to preserve his dignity against scandal. He had never felt the power of command before, so rarely used. It was unnerving.

'Very well, Prime Minister.' Bertie moved back behind his desk. 'But in future I'd appreciate it if you kept me a little better informed. It's surely not too much to ask that I should know about what's going on in a British colony before the Kaiser.'

Bertie had watched the rising in the Transvaal, where the Boer Government treated the British settlers farmers and miners like inferiors, allowing them no vote and no share in the running of the country. They had begged Rhodes for protection against persecution, and conflict was inevitable. Wilhelm would take it as the chance he had been waiting for, to weaken British influence. His telegram to Kruger had been a concealed offer of aid. If Her Majesty's Government did not support Rhodes, they would be faced with the most dangerous situation for many years. Bertie urged them to remember that if he had been successful, he would have been given a hero's welcome.

Cecil Rhodes was censured at Westminster and forced to resign.

Victoria was laughing to herself as the handsome, bearded Abdul Karim helped her down the stairs at Balmoral. This was a special day and it had begun splendidly, so many letters and telegrams. Then when she was dressed and sitting in her wheeled chair with Abdul in attendance, little David, George's son, had come in, walking so well already for two years old.

'Gangan,' he shouted, 'Get up! Get Up, Gangan.' He had taken her hand and tried to draw her out of her chair. When she would not move, he pointed to her and said to Abdul, 'Man pull it.' Man pull it . . .

Her legs were so painful. It was humiliating to have to hobble down the stairs like this with everyone watching, but it could not be helped. Abdul could have carried her, like Brown used to. But like dear Brown, everyone was so jealous of him and she wanted no upsets on this day. Not with Nicky and Alicky come to show her their first child. Not today, when she had reigned one day longer than any other British sovereign before her.

The hall was bright with the tartans of the guests. The walls hung with shields, swords, weapons, and antlers from the deer Albert had shot. In the morning, Bertie had waited with Nicky, Alicky, George and May and their staffs. When Victoria was helped into her chair and rolled into her place at the end of the room away from draughts, they congratulated her in turn and Bertie led the cheers.

Dear Bertie . . . His heart was so good. Tonight, there was the music of the pipes and the guests whirled in reels and quadrilles. Victoria wore her purple velvet dress with a sash of Balmoral tartan and laughed, holding Alicky's hand, as they watched the Russian suite trying not to trip in the unfamiliar steps of the reels.

Bertie stood near them with Nicky, resplendent in Highland dress. He had arranged the whole visit of the Czar and Czarina, the special train and torchlight processions, the hunting parties and balls. Nicky admired his uncle excessively and already felt as though the Queen were his own real grandmother. It was the climax of their meeting in St Petersburg, the return visit that showed the world that the new friendship between their countries was genuine. Bertie had supervised each detail, to make the visit perfect. At the right time, after the first celebrations, talks could begin on a formal alliance.

'It was kind of you to let Aunt Alix stay in Denmark with Mama,' Nicky said.

Bertie smiled. 'Well, they're good for each other. And it keeps your Mama out of your hair for a while, eh?' Nicky smiled back. He had ceased to be surprised at how well his uncle understood his problems. He looked at his wife.

Victoria was saying to her, 'Up till now my grandfather, George the Third, held the palm but today it has passed to me.'

Alicky nodded. 'We are all very proud of you, Grandmama.' She wore a dress of gold satin and a coronet of diamonds.

She really is very beautiful, Bertie thought, but there's iron determination under that reserve. She has all Alice's intelligence without her tenderness. George was standing next to the Queen and Bertie looked from him to Nicky as the piper began to play a *schottische*. The resemblance between them was even more striking now they had both grown the same light beard and moustache.

'Well, now, which of you two handsome young men is going to ask this lovely young lady for a dance, eh?'

'I'd like to see you dance, Alicky,' Victoria approved. 'Your mother was a very graceful dancer.'

As Nicky and George hesitated, each waiting for the other, Bertie smiled. 'Too late, too late. With your permission, Mama.' He bowed and held out his hand to the Queen.

Victoria shrieked with sudden laughter. 'What me? . . . No, no, no.' They laughed as she patted Bertie's hand and pushed it away.

'I'm so disappointed, Mama,' Bertie chuckled. He bowed to Alicky. 'Well, what do you say, my dear? Will you give your old uncle the pleasure?'

Alicky smiled and rose. 'I'd be delighted, Uncle Bertie.'

Victoria clapped her hands as he swept Alicky off

into the *schottische*. 'He's more like a boy than either of you.'

'He certainly has more energy,' Nicky agreed. He felt exhausted after these days of hunting.

'You mustn't let him tire you out,' Victoria said. 'We still have to talk, you know.'

The next day's shooting was partly spoilt by rain and a piercing wind. Most of the game was frightened away by the army of Russian plainclothes police that scoured the ground around them as they walked. Nicholas would not leave them behind. By the time they came back to the castle, Bertie was more concerned than ever about his nephew. His mother, the Dowager Empress, seemed to be making all his decisions for him and insisted that his father's way had been best, to rule from strength. His wife agreed with her, although it appeared to be the only thing they agreed on. Between them, the young Czar was being crucified. He was obviously troubled and badly in need of advice.

Lord Salisbury had arrived and was waiting in the Hall with Francis Knollys. 'Did you have good sport, sir?' he asked.

'Not bad. Could have been better,' Bertie told him. He smiled at Nicky. 'It's all those blundering detectives. We don't need them in Scotland, you know.'

Nicky was tense. He had been tense all day. 'Mama says they are necessary.' He bowed. 'If you will excuse me, I must change out of these wet clothes. I have to see Her Majesty in half an hour.'

As Nicky and his gentlemen hurried up the stairs, Bertie was puzzled. 'What's this? Is it an official meeting? I wasn't told about it.'

Knollys hesitated. 'No, sir. The Queen is meeting with the Czar and the Prime Minister at six o'clock.'

'We are to discuss the relations between our two countries and the situation in Africa,' Salisbury confirmed. 'The next two days will be taken up with talks.'

'I see,' Bertie muttered. It was inconceivable but he already sensed it was true. 'And I have not been invited to attend?'

Salisbury was silent, embarrassed. 'I'm afraid not, sir,' Knollys said quietly.

Bertie could feel George and the others watching him. Not to be invited, to smile and play host while the talks were held in private, was the cruellest humiliation. It destroyed his prestige with the Czar at a stroke. He could not let his hurt and anger show.

'Well, it's not iimportant,' he said abruptly. 'I was thinking of leaving tomorrow in any case, for the races at Newmarket. Now I think I'll change for dinner. Come along, George.'

When they had gone, Knollys turned to Salisbury, urgently. 'You are making a serious mistake!' Salisbury stiffened. 'Forgive me, Prime Minister, I know that by now I should be used to it, but I'm afraid it still makes me angry.'

'The decision to exclude him was not mine,' Salisbury explained. 'The Queen insisted.'

'The Prince is much loved in Russia, and by the Czar. He is the strongest link we have,' Knollys said. 'Yet once again when he could be of real service, he will not be at the council table but at the races!'

Salisbury nodded. 'Yes. His advice would be invaluable.' It was a statement he had never expected to hear himself making, but he had remembered Gambetta and the Khedive and Ireland. Now Russia. The Queen was half crippled, half blind, nearly eighty, but as firmly in control as ever.

He sighed. 'What can I do? Until Her Majesty decides otherwise, I'm afraid it will always be the races.'

The races were more than a consolation. For years Bertie's racehorses had been an expensive disappointment, but the new stables and the young stallion Persimmon, fiery, almost impossible to train, brought him victory. No one thought he had much chance against Leopold de Rothschild's St. Frusquin at Epsom and when Persimmon took the lead and thundered past the post to win the Derby in record time, the first royal win for a century, the spectators screamed with excitement. Bertie, Daisy and their friends were on their feet in the box, cheering. Two days after leaving Balmoral, when Persimmon also won the St. Leger, Bertie became the hero of every man in England. It was irrational, yet undeniable. He had arrived at the track looking strained and depressed but the crowds saw a transformation. The cock of the beard, the smile and jaunty wave of the tall, silk hat as he led Persimmon in had them yelling. 'God Bless the Prince of Wales,' they sang, 'the King of Sportsmen.' My first crown, Bertie thought, and laughed. But it was more than a consolation.

A few nights later, he was in a box at the Empire Theatre of Varieties with Daisy, Knollys, Charlie Carrington and Ernest Cassel, a Jewish millionaire banker, who had taken over from Hirsch as his financial adviser. Daisy had been pestering him to use his winnings from the races for some useful community purpose.

'My darling,' he protested, 'we are here to listen to the music, not a socialist lecture.' He had been talking to Cassel about building a new yacht. The Kaiser in his determination to be first had spent a fortune on a racing cutter of the same style as *Britannia,* only bigger and faster. It was unbeatable.

'There's no chance of your affording another one, sir,' Cassel told him. 'Not unless the Queen or the Government helps.'

'No hope of that,' Bertie said. 'Well, I'm damned if I'll let my nephew turn the regatta into a political arena. We'll sell the *Britannia* and concentrate on the stables.'

'Might be wise, sir,' Knollys agreed.

'Think what a gesture it would be if you used that money to finance a working men's club,' Daisy urged.

Bertie was lighting a cigar. He glanced at her. 'Spare us, my dear.'

'But don't you see? Any of you?' Daisy went on. 'If wealth is redistributed, we can make a new society. We—'

'No one can make a new society, Daisy,' Bertie interrupted impatiently. 'Society grows. It is not made. Now, let us listen to Miss Lloyd.'

Down on the stage, Marie Lloyd was singing. 'The

boy I love is up in the gallery.' Bertie was smiling but his fingers drummed on the arm of his chair. Knollys and Carrington looked at each other. It was an unmistakable sign that he was bored. Daisy was on the way out.

Chapter
19

'Jubilissimee . . . That's what the Home Secretary suggested,' Victoria laughed. 'But the people are calling it the Diamond Jubilee and that is what it shall be.'

Alix was beside her on the sofa in the sitting room at Windsor. She smiled briefly, taut. 'Mama, I wanted to talk to you about Greece.'

Victoria pretended not to hear. She had discovered that partial deafness had its uses.

'Sixty years—no other monarch has ever reigned as long. I did not want too much fuss. The thought of all those Emperors and Kings filling up Buckingham Palace again . . . It's always such a problem where to put them.'

'Mama,' Alix pleaded, 'my brother's country is being attacked by Turkey. His army has been defeated. He has begged the great powers to save him!'

'I could not stand another Thanksgiving Service at Westminster Abbey,' Victoria said. 'It gets far too hot in there. Not enough air. And I doubt I could manage the steps at St Paul's.'

'The Turks only attacked because the Kaiser persuaded them to. Now there is nothing between them and Athens.' Victoria looked at her. 'I came to plead for your help.' Alix had asked Bertie, Salisbury, even Gladstone who told her sadly he had no more influence now he had finally retired.

'No,' Victoria said. When Alix tried to speak, she repeated more firmly, 'No, I cannot intervene. It is not a quarrel in which I wish this country to become involved. If Germany supports Turkey at the peace talks, we shall support Greece. That is all I can do.'

Alix nodded, stricken, knowing it was hopeless.

Victoria spoke again, more kindly. 'I know what it means to you, dear Alix, but try to understand. When one has almost limitless power, one must learn to use it very sparingly. Too much force or interference at the wrong time can turn a small fire into a conflagration, a war that could burn all across Europe. We shall see that a just peace is signed and that is all. Now—' She smiled. 'You will ride with me in my carriage on the day. And I shall not invite Wilhelm.

The mausoleum was cold in the early morning and there was scarcely enough sun to bring the colours in the stained glass windows to life, but the white marble effigy of the Prince Consort lying on its granite slab glowed in the light of small gas jets.

The Queen, lame, hobbling on her stick, limped painfully towards it with Vicky, the Dowager Empress Frederick, supporting her. Vicky had aged beyond her years with wretchedness and pain, but her mother's failing eyesight still saw her as a girl. When they reached the sarcophagus, they stood gazing at the calm face in silence.

At last Victoria sighed. 'I thought to have joined him years ago.' Beside her, Vicky trembled. 'I have been his widow for nearly forty years. There has not been a day when I have not missed him and wished him alive again.'

Vicky's eyes filled with tears. 'Please, Mama—you'll make me cry.'

Victoria smiled to her. 'I had to come here today.'

'Yes, Mama, Your jubilee.'

'Well . . . We'd better go and get it over with.' Victoria looked again at Albert's face, how young it seemed now. Farewell most beloved. Here at length I shall rest with thee, with thee in Christ I shall rise again.

327

In spite of the dark, threatening skies, people wore their lightest clothes, and their faith was justified. As Victoria came out to her carriage at Buckingham Palace, the sun burst through the clouds and they vanished, leaving London bathed in the warmth of the Queen's weather. A telegraphic box was presented to her and she pressed the button, sending her personal message round the world.

'From my heart I thank my beloved people. May God Bless them. Victoria, R. and I.' No one objected any longer to the name Empress. She had become an almost mystical figure, revered as no human being before her in history, The Queen Empress of three hundred and fifty million people.

Bertie had spent months arranging the huge procession, not this time a parade of Kings, but an Imperial festival. Leading all came the Premiers of the independent states of the Empire, each in their own carriage, escorted by his own soldiers, Canadian mounties, lancers from New South Wales, carabiniers from Natal. After the colonial forces marched companies from all races subject to the Crown, Hausas from Nigeria and the Gold Coast, Cingalese, Dyaks, Cypriotes, Malays, Zouaves, Chinamen from Hong Kong in pigtails, red coats and white helmets, with the place of honour given to the turbaned, scarlet coated Imperial Service troops of India, followed by the Princess of India and the envoys of the rest of the world, from the Papal Nuncio in his purple robes to the Princes of Siam and Japan and the emissary of the Emperor of China.

They were spaced out as escorts for the Queen's older relatives and her grandchildren and great-grandchildren, carriages full of little princes and princesses. Then George led a troup of the Crown Princes and Grand Dukes of Europe and Asia and, at last, the Queen in her carriage drawn by eight cream horses. Alix and Lenchen sat opposite her and Bertie in his Field-Marshal's uniform rode by her side.

From every nation in the world people had come to join the millions lining the streets of her capital, to catch a moment's glimpse of the tiny, frail woman in her new, lace bonnet, holding her white parasol, to add to the unending thunder of devotion.

Sixty years since the day of her coronation. As the procession moved in all its pageantry along the familiar route and stopped for the short open air service of Thanksgiving by the steps of St Paul's, Victoria thought of the many dear faces that were gone, the friendly voices hushed. Yet she could not be sad. The homage and pride of her people lifted her heart and when she smiled, that rarely seen, tender smile that transformed her, she looked for a moment like a girl again.

That night, the streets of London were turned back into day as people gasped at the coloured festoons and the garlands of the new electric lights. At ten o'clock, a rocket soared up from the keep of Windsor Castle. Its bursting was the signal for giant beacons to be lit on the hills around and each of them was the signal for other fires, until two and a half thousand of them were burning on high places from Caithness to Land's End and each was a link in a fiery chain winding from Windsor through England, Ireland, Scotland and Wales.

Of all the memories of that day, the one that touched Victoria most deeply was when she had been wheeled out on to the balcony of Buckingham Palace and, in a moment's pause in the cheering, a lone Cockney voice shouted, 'Go it, old girl!' What pride and affection there was in that.

On the silver-painted screen, the small figures seemed oddly unreal, the carriage stationary between the crowds and the massed choristers and bishops at St. Paul's, the Queen lowering her parasol with Alix turning to look as the Archbishop stepped forward, with Bertie beyond, flanked by his brothers Affie and Arthur. The picture was hazy and the figures moved too rapidly, like jerky marionettes, yet it was miraculous to the guests gathered in the drawing room at Marlborough House and the gentlemen managing the Cinematograph equipment were asked to show it again and again.

'Pictures that move,' Alix breathed. 'Like my snap-shots, only they move.'

'A remarkable invention, Ma'am,' Gladstone agreed. With his fading eyesight he had not been able to see much, but he had made out the horses and the Queen.

'They'll have to improve the quality before it is of any real value,' Toria said.

'They're bound to,' Bertie told her. 'I imagine that, in future, all great events will be recorded in the same way.'

'I hope so, sir,' Mrs. Gladstone said. 'What a blessing it will be to those who cannot get about.' She was now well over eighty like her husband.

While the gentlemen checked their equipment and allowed it to cool, Alix led the guests next door for refreshments.

Gladstone moved slowly on his stick. What a stupendous feat of organisation the Jubilee had been, he thought. No one but the Prince could have done it so well and to honour the colonial premiers, that was genius. He could see the Prince waiting for him, smiling. 'I wanted to express my admiration at the success of your Hospital Fund, sir.'

'Thank you, William. Yes, we've collected nearly a quarter of a million pounds already. The income will be distributed to all London hospitals, to provide extra beds and equipment.

Gladstone nodded. 'It will probably be the most lasting thing to come out of the Diamond Jubilee.' And the best, he added to himself.

'The Queen has sent a contribution,' Bertie said.

'You know my opinion, sir,' He had to say it. 'The most valuable gift Her Majesty could give to her peoples this year would be to abdicate in your favour.'

Bertie smiled. 'Not many would agree with you, old friend. I don't think I do, myself.' He took Gladstone's arm to help him. 'No, there was a time I would have welcomed it, a time I longed for it. But I've got used to being her Master of Ceremonies and I'm not sure I even want the job any more. To be honest, I doubt if I'm up to it.'

The weather at Sandown Races was perfect. As he strolled through the fashionable crowd in the enclosure with Alice on his arm, Jack Leslie felt more than pleased with himself. She was an exceptionally attractive young woman, her dark auburn hair piled up under her feathered picture hat, her tan costume overlaid with cream lace, with its slight train, leg-of-mutton sleeves and tight waist showing her rich, hour-glass figure. Witty and amusing as well as beautiful. Her husband, the Hon. George, was an officer in the Norfolk Yeomanry, tall and handsome but a bit of a bore, and Jack congratulated himself on having her to himself for a few hours.

There was a stir of excitement in the people ahead of them and the sound of applause. 'Oh, look,' Jack said. 'The Prince of Wales has arrived. I wonder if he'll come this way?'

'Do you know him, Jacksy?' Alice asked.

'Wales? I've met him once or twice.' He did not wish to give the impression of boasting and added, 'Of course, I'm not one of his set.'

At that moment, the crowd thinned partly and there was the Prince with a group of his friends, full-bodied and imposing in his elegantly-cut frockcoat and glossy top hat. He turned and, seeing them, waved his stick.

'I—I think he wants to talk to me,' Jack whispered, surprised. 'Come on.' He hoped Alice was impressed.

The Prince smiled as they came up. 'Hello there, Jack.'

Alice curtsied and Jack bowed. 'May I introduce Mrs. Keppel, sir?'

'I believe we've already met,' the Prince told him. 'I am colonel-in-chief of her husband's regiment.' Alice smiled. Her eyes were turquoise, sky-blue tinged with green. The Prince's gaze never left them. 'I have a new colt running this afternoon. May I show him to you, Mrs. Keppel?'

'I'd be most interested, sir,' Alice murmured.

The Prince crooked his arm for her and raised his hat. As she took his arm, he looked round. 'Nice meeting you again, Jack.'

Jack bowed again. The Prince's friends nodded and

smiled to him as they passed. Jack nodded and smiled back, and wished desperately that he had taken Alice to the seaside instead.

Victoria sat at her desk in the study at Osborne. A pile of papers and documents were under her fingers, but when she looked at them, she saw only a blur. For years she had been complaining that her correspondents did not use black enough ink and that their handwriting was disgraceful. She finally had to admit that it was herself. Cataracts were spreading in both eyes and she could only read with the greatest strain and difficulty.

Her youngest daughter, Beatrice, was reading the morning paper to her. 'Mr. Gladstone's body was carried into Westminster Abbey by eight pall bearers, among them His Royal Highness the Prince of Wales and His Royal Highness the Duke of York.'

'No precedent,' Victoria muttered. 'There is no precedent whatever for such an action.' She was seriously displeased and would write to Bertie. That crazy, old—wicked, old man. To honour him so.

'Shall I go on, Mama?'

'Go on.'

' "There followed a moving service during which the great man—" ' Victoria snorted. Beatrice paused, then repeated. ' "During which the great man was laid to rest in the north transept of the Abbey close to the grave of Sir Robert Peel. After the committal, while the organ played Mr. Handel's Dead March from Saul, Mrs. Gladstone was seated in a chair at the head of the grave and His Royal Highness the Prince of Wales, followed by the other pall bearers, walked over to where she sat—" ' Beatrice faltered, then read very quickly, ' "And kissed her hand." '

Victoria was rigid. 'He did what?'

' "His Royal Highness the Prince of Wales walked over to where she sat and kissed her hand." '

In the silence, Beatrice looked up from the paper. She saw her mother's eyes staring, her hands trembling as they lay on the pile of documents. With a cry of fury the Queen pushed the documents away and swept everything off the top of her desk on to the floor.

The dinner party Bertie and Alix gave at Marlborough House, a month before the world greeted the twentieth century, was for only a few friends. Carrington, Ernest Cassel, Reginald Brett who had helped to organise the Jubilee and had once been Hartington's secretary, Lord Rosebery and the blunt, forceful Admiral Sir John Fisher.

Francis Knollys sat between his sister Charlotte and the Prince's daughter Toria. He would much rather have been with the vivacious Mrs Willy James or Agnes Keyser, who was sitting next to Cassel. She was a close friend of the Prince, attractive, middle-aged and intelligent. A close friend purely because he could talk to her seriously and relax. Platonic? Unlikely, Knollys thought, but possible. He glanced at the head of the table where Mrs Keppel sat on the Prince's right. That was the best thing to happen in years. An enormous improvement on Daisy Warwick, perhaps not so beautiful but so much more understanding and sympathetic. She obviously loved him for himself, and not for what she could get out of him. And she had apparently even been accepted by the Princess. Two exceptional women.

He looked at the other end of the table where the Princess sat between Rosebery and Jacky Fisher. She was easily the most beautiful woman here, in her fifties she still looked no more than thirty, warmhearted, spontaneous. A little subdued tonight, but then everyone was, with this damned war in South Africa. The news was bad and getting worse.

After the failure of the Jameson Raid, the indecisive policy of the British Government encouraged the Boers in the Transvaal and the Orange Free State to dream of turning the whole South Africa into a Dutch Republic. They had drummed up support in Europe, made a treaty with Holland and attacked the thinly garrisoned British territories.

'To hear my nephew, Willy, you'd think we started it,' Alix said.

'I thought the Kaiser was on his best behaviour during his visit, Ma'am,' Rosebery said, surprised.

'Elaborately so,' Brett told him. 'When he wasn't complaining about the handicaps at Cowes, he was working out plans for the defence of Cape Town.'

Alix sighed. 'He is extraordinary. Do you know, he actually brought a special hairdresser with him—and a hairdresser's assistant whose only job was to wax the ends of his Imperial moustache.' They laughed.

'Well, I suppose we ought to give him credit for coming here at all,' Bertie said, 'when we're so unpopular in Germany. And in France. They're both very hostile.'

Cassel shrugged. 'It's sheer hypocrisy. They champion the Boers against us, merely because they want to take over in South Africa. All they're interested in is the gold and diamonds in the Transvaal.'

'How is the war going, sir?' Alice asked.

'Not well. Not well at all, I'm afraid.' Bertie admitted. 'I hoped it would be over by Christmas, in time for the new century. But we've been pushed back everywhere.'

'It is inconceivable to me,' Fisher declared, 'that a British army could be beaten by a mob of ignorant farmers!'

'There's a lot of them,' Brett answered. 'And they've been planning for years.'

'I had a letter from young Winston Churchill, Jennie's son,' Bertie told them. 'He's out there as a war correspondent. He says they're all skilled guerrilla fighters, with a knowledge of the bush our chaps don't have. Our losses have been very heavy.'

'I'm most anxious to do something to help,' Alix said to Admiral Fisher. 'I am sending out twelve nursing sisters. But I wonder if you could advise me on the possibility of fitting out a proper hospital ship?'

Fisher smiled. 'I'd be honoured, Ma'am.'

The Queen returned from Balmoral to Windsor to be nearer her Government and to inspect the first reinforcements leaving for South Africa. The war had become a series of disasters, with her armies besieged in Kimberley, Mafeking and Ladysmith. Three of her generals were defeated in battle, one after the other in the space of a week, and the casualties were fearful. The Boers were better armed, with heavy artillery from France and Germany, better led and more mobile. There was not one British success to set against the tide of blunders and defeat. After all the pomp and glory of the Jubilee, the parade of the invincibility of the Empire, national pride was shaken and morale began to crumble.

More than half blind, crippled with rheumatism, eighty years old, Victoria summoned up her courage. She would not give in. Her attendants had grown used to seeing her frail and ailing and her new energy astounded them. She crowded her days with activity, reviewing troops, visiting hospitals, writing letters of condolence. When she was not writing, she knitted scarves and gloves. She ordered a hundred thousand tins of chocolate for the men. It was a sign to her Government of how many soldiers she was prepared to commit if necessary.

For once she fully agreed with Bertie. Her Generals had not yet understood the nature of the war they were fighting. If they would not learn, they must be replaced by others who already had experience of this type of enemy, Lord Roberts in Afghanistan and Lord Kitchener in the Sudan, as he suggested. They were the men. And finally they were sent.

When tall, serious Arthur Balfour, Salisbury's nephew and Leader of the House of Commons, came to Windsor to report the Government's alarm at the course of the war, she received him, standing.

'Please understand that there is no one depressed in *this* house,' she declared, firmly. 'We are not interested in the possibilities of defeat. They do not exist.'

The casualty rates rose steadily. Alix used her own money to send out another twenty nurses. Financed by Bertie, Agnes Keyser turned her house in Grosvenor Crescent into a Nursing Home for officers. Amongst all the howls and rejoicing from Europe, Kaiser Wilhelm wrote to Bertie suggesting that the British should accept defeat gracefully as they had done the previous year in the cricket matches against Australia. Bertie reminded him that this was not a game. Defeat in South Africa would threaten the whole existence of the Empire. Britain's rivals abroad were jubilant at the Boer supremacy and becoming more and more hostile. Only the Fleet stopped them from sending in arms and supplies.

The first success came at last. Ladysmith was relieved. The Queen ordered her carriage and drove through the streets of London with no escort or police. The reaction of her people surpassed both jubilees. The possibility of defeat did not exist. From then on, the news became a list of victories, the rout of the Boer armies, the relief of Kimberley and Mafeking and Roberts riding in triumph into Pretoria, the capital of the Transvaal.

Alix was touched that Bertie had come with her. She was travelling to Copenhagen to visit her family but anger and resentment were so violent against the British that he would not let her go alone. He had had to cancel his own annual trip to France for the first time and refused an invitation to Paris because of the ferocity of the French Press.

They had decided to take the direct route through Belgium and their train was just pulling into the Gare du Nord in Brussels. Bertie was sitting next to Alix in their compartment.

She put her hand on his arm. 'I'd have been perfectly safe, you know.'

'No doubt, my dear,' he smiled. 'I just wanted to make sure. I cannot stay, of course. I'll have to get straight back.'

Alix nodded. The war was not over, although the end was inevitable. She knew he was also concerned about the Queen, who had used up so much of her strength. She was so vigorous and alive, one sometimes forgot how old she was. More and more, Bertie was being called on by the Government to attend Privy Councils and take over an increasing number of her duties. The Queen still reserved the right to make all final decisions, but it was now only a question of time. Bertie seemed almost afraid of her dying. Nonsense, he always said, she'll go on for ever. She's indestructible.

When the express train slid to a stop, they saw that a wide area on the platform beyond the royal compartment had been roped off and a line of police were spread out round it. Inside the area, the station master waited with the British Consul and his staff. Further along, passengers were leaving the train, others joining it.

'Well, I think I'll stretch my legs,' Bertie said. He looked from Alix to Charlotte Knollys who sat opposite. 'Either of you coming?'

Just as he began to rise, Francis Knollys came to the door of the compartment. 'Excuse me, sir. I've just had a communication from the British Consul. Because of the possibility of demonstrations, he strongly advises you not to leave the train.'

'Blast!' Bertie snorted. 'What demonstrations? There's no sign of anything.'

Knollys smiled. 'Perhaps he's being over cautious, sir.'

'Like you are with me,' Alix said. She smiled to Bertie and patted the little pug dog on her lap.

Bertie sat back, reluctantly. 'Well, find out how long we're going to be stuck here, will you, Francis?'

As Knollys left to speak to the station master, Bertie looked out of the window. Some ladies were boarding the train at the next compartment but one. A young man in a decent grey suit, wearing a soft hat, passed them. The police paid him no attention. Bertie scarcely noticed him until he suddenly pulled a revolver from his pocket and leapt on to the footboard, clinging to the edge of the window.

He fired and the bullet smashed the glass and ploughed into the cushioned headrest between Bertie and Alix. Charlotte screamed. Bertie rose quickly to cover Alix. The man pulled the trigger again twice, aiming pointblank at Bertie. Both times the gun misfired. As he cursed and fired again, the station master grabbed him from behind and the shot went into the air.

Officials ran to help the station master. They tore the gun from the man's hand and overpowered him.

He was struggling wildly and shouting, 'A bas les tyrans! A bas les tyrans!' in a strange, high-pitched voice.

The little dog was barking and yelping in terror and Alix tried to calm him. Charlotte sat shuddering, holding her mouth with her hand.

Knollys raced back and pulled open the door of the compartment, worried. 'Are you all right, sir?'

'Fine, thank you, Francis,' Bertie said, very steadily. He looked at Alix. 'You, my dear?'

'Oh, yes,' Alix smiled. 'It startled me, that was all. It was so sudden.'

Knollys stared at them in amazement.

'That's the one good thing about these anarchists,' Bertie said. 'They're damn bad shots.'

On the platform, their attacker was still struggling and shouting. His hat had fallen off. When Bertie came to the carriage door and looked at him, he stopped struggling for a moment and gazed up, his eyes crazed with hate. He was only a boy, hardly more than fifteen. As the police dragged him off up the platform, he began screaming again. 'Vive les Boers! Vive Transvaal!'

'Don't let them hurt him,' Bertie said. 'Tell them not to hurt him, Francis.' Knollys hurried off up the platform as anxious officials crowded round the Prince. He looked at them, puzzled. 'He was only a boy. Only a boy.'

As the train pulled up at Altona, they were surprised to see the Kaiser and his staff on the platform. He had come by special express from Potsdam. He hurried on board to embrace and kiss them both.

'I—I came to tell you how happy I am for your escape.' He was trembling as he turned to Bertie. 'If we had lost you—If anything had happened to you, I—I couldn't have borne it.'

When he arrived back in London after leaving Alix in Denmark, dense crowds cheered him all the way from Charing Cross to Marlborough House and the Queen sent him a message of thankfulness for his deliverance. Later, as he lay in bed, he saw again the face of his attacker, boyish but contorted with hatred.

Alice shifted beside him and he glanced at her. Her chestnut hair tumbled over the pillow. The lace nightdress had slipped from her shoulders. She lay facing him and her eyes were closed.

If his gun had not misfired those other times, he thought it would have been my body they brought back from Belgium. And when Mama died, George would have been King. That might have been for the best. I am too old now, fat and tired.

Alice stirred again and her hand moved up to lie on his chest. 'Thank God you're safe,' she murmured. And he saw she had been crying.

The Queen was fading. All the effort of the past year had exhausted her, and she discovered she had not done with sorrow. Her soldier grandson, Lenchen's boy, Christian, died of fever in Pretoria. And Alfred, Duke of Saxe-Coburg, her own second son, dear Affie, died of cancer of the throat, in the same long agony as Fritz. Cruellest of all, she learnt why Vicky had not come to be with her. Vicky was dying, too, of cancer of the spine, the only disease no one could cure. Surely no sins could deserve such punishment? To keep the secret nearly broke her mind. But still she would not give in.

She moved from Balmoral to Windsor and, at last, to Osborne. She went out every day in her pony chaise and sat in the sun with her white Pomeranian, Turi, on her lap, but the brightest days had become cloudy and, by Christmas, the candles on the tree had no sparkle for her. She had difficulty sometimes in speaking and could not be understood, yet she would not let Bertie share any of her power. She was the Queen.

When the spry, whitehaired Field Marshal, Lord Roberts, came home from South Africa, Bertie met him and warned him to be brief with her, but it was as if this was the moment for which Victoria had been waiting. By sheer force of will, she held herself erect and controlled her mind. They discussed the whole course of the war and its probable results and, to honour all the soldiers of her army, she conferred on him an earldom and the Order of the Garter.

Bertie could not settle. Hartington had become Duke of Devonshire and married Lottie at last. He took Alice Keppel to stay with them at Chatsworth for a shooting party, but left to go to Sandringham. For a few days, he found peace there with his family, but although he loved Alix, he could not talk to her of what troubled him. He returned to Marlborough House to wait for the message that he knew would come.

He was in the study with Francis Knollys, who sat near the telephone, trying not to look at it.

'That boy who shot at you, sir,' he said. 'He was a Belgian student, a member of a socialist club. The jury acquitted him. They thought he was too young to have any criminal intent.'

Bertie was lighting a cigar. He coughed. 'I wonder what he'd have to do to earn seven days in jail?'

As Knollys smiled, the telephone rang, taking him by surprise. He rose and lifted the receiver quickly. 'Knollys speaking . . .' When he turned, serious, he saw that the Prince had risen. 'It's Fritz Ponsonby, sir.'

Bertie took the receiver and listened as Ponsonby, his mother's acting private secretary, told him that the Queen had had a stroke and was sinking.

'Thank you, Fritz. I'll come down first thing in the morning,' He hung up. Although it was the call he had been expecting for months, he was numbed. He noticed the cigar in his hand and, as an absurd gesture of respect, stubbed it out. 'Will you ring the Princess, Francis?' He hesitated. 'Oh, and would you ask Miss Keyser if I could possibly have dinner with her tonight?'

The Nursing Home which Agnes Keyser had made out of her house in Grosvenor Crescent was efficient and successful. Many wounded officers had been treated there and to all of them she was known as Sister Agnes. In a way, she was a sister to the Prince. He trusted her calmness and capability and few people suspected how many evenings he spent with her, quietly in her rooms.

'This time it's true, I'm afraid,' he told her. 'This time she's dying.'

'I'm deeply sorry, sir.' Agnes was also concerned

for the Prince. She had seen him tense before and soothed him, but this evening, he seemed lost, almost despairing. She poured the single brandy he liked after dinner and placed it beside him.

'She was a—is a great Queen,' he said. 'That's what frightens me. Ridiculous, isn't it? After so long, when it looks as if it's to happen, I'm frightened.'

'It would be most unnatural if you were not, sir,' she said quietly.

He smiled briefly. 'Everything I've done—even the best things—they've all been spoilt, somehow. She never trusted me, you know, Agnes. She never thought I could do it. I've come to agree with her. I don't think I'm fit to reign.'

Agnes was shocked. 'That's nonsense!'

'Is it? I'm nearly sixty—tired. And so many people expect me to fail.'

'Who expects you to fail?' she demanded. 'Who?'

'Oh—I can see it when they look at me. And those articles in the papers. 'Various incidents in a long career lead us to wonder . . .' You know the sort of thing. I've been thinking . . . perhaps it would be better if I stood aside, and let George do it.'

'You cannot,' Agnes said firmly. 'You must not even consider such a thing.'

'I haven't the sticking power,' he confessed. 'I've lost it. Mama had it, right up to this last year. Nearly blind, unable to walk, it was her will that drove her on. That power to keep on and do what you know is right. I've lost it somewhere along the road—if I ever had it.'

'You mustn't think like that, sir.' Agnes was angry for him. What cruelties had been done to him? 'Every man has doubts. Only a fool is certain all the time.'

Bertie shook his head. 'But I can't change, Agnes. I am what I am. Do they realise that?' He hesitated. 'I keep remembering what my father said to me—"We must think always of our country".'

'Exactly, sir,' Agnes agreed strongly. 'And the country will support you. You are greatly loved.' He looked at her. 'Greatly loved.'

'Am I? . . . Am I really, Agnes?'

341

The January fogs had cleared from around Osborne but the windows in the room were tightly shut against the cold. Victoria lay in her wide bed, her hair, grey and thinning now, spread on her shoulders. The right side of her face was slightly flattened and she lay very still and weak as her doctor, Sir James Reid, took her pulse. Her daughters, Lenchen and Beatrice, stood at the foot of the bed.

'Am I any better at all?' Victoria asked. Her voice was only a whisper.

'Yes, Ma'am,' Reid told her.

Victoria managed a faint smile. 'Then may I have Turi?'

Beatrice fetched the little white dog and laid him on the bed where she could see him, but he was nervous and Beatrice had to hold him.

The Queen's children and grandchildren were gathering at Osborne. Arthur and his wife, Alix with Toria, Louise and Maud, George and May with their children. A telegram had announced that the Kaiser was coming, uninvited. It was awkward. He had gravely upset the Queen by his attitude during the war. Bertie went back up to London to meet him.

Wilhelm seemed subdued, older. 'I have come in place of my mother,' he said.

On the island, he behaved with tact and dignity, staying downstairs with the junior members of the family.

In the bedroom, Victoria still held on to life, although she could hardly see or speak. Randall Davidson, Bishop of Winchester, read her favourite prayers quietly to her. Only a slight movement of her head showed that she was listening.

> So long thy power hath blest me, sure it still
>   Will lead me on:
> O'er moor and fen, o'er crag and torrent, till
>   The night is gone;
> And with the morn those angel faces smile
> Which I have loved long since, and lost a while.

When Bertie brought Alix in, the doctor looked at him, telling him the end was very near.

In the sitting room, the Kaiser waited, apart from the others. When Bertie came to fetch them, he stepped forward.

'I am here purely as my mother's son, Uncle Bertie,' he said humbly. 'I would like to see Grandmama once more before she dies—but if that is not possible, I shall quite understand.'

'Of course you must see her, Willy,' Bertie said. 'I know she would wish it.'

Throughout the house, the servants and staff lined the corridors, silent, and on the island, the mainland and all over the Empire every thought was on that room at Osborne.

The Queen's breathing was very faint and she was much weaker. The Kaiser supported her pillow on her left and Sir James Reid on her right, propping her up. Stricken and grieving, her children and grandchildren were grouped round the bed, Bertie and Alix nearest her, beside Reid. The Bishop's prayers were a quiet murmur beyond them.

Victoria's eyes flickered open and all around the bed tensed as she looked slowly from one to the other, trying to see them clearly. Alix knelt by her holding her hand and the Queen clutched it, gazing at her, but could not speak.

At last she managed to whisper, 'Bertie . . . ?'

Bertie moved closer and leant towards her. He had been holding himself very tightly in control.

Seeing him, Victoria was relieved. She had wanted to tell him something, something important, but she could not remember. And then she did. She wanted to tell him that she forgave him, forgave him for everything. But she could not make her voice speak for her any more and it was too late. As he watched her, she smiled to him, just to him, very sweetly and tenderly, and her eyes closed. Bertie fell to his knees beside her, covering his face, sobbing.

Her other children and grandchildren began to say their names to her, hoping to call her back. The Kaiser

343

and the doctor held her for another two hours until her face began to change, the lines of pain smoothed away and she lay still, as if smiling to someone who had been waiting for her.

The news stunned the world. Not only to the Empire but to nearly every other nation, she was a symbol of something imperishable. She had come to represent a whole way of life and thought. Generation after generation had grown up knowing that she was on her throne, watchful and enduring, her very name expressing order and majesty. No one could believe that she was gone.

It was twenty-four hours before Bertie was acknowledged as King, King Emperor, the master of the greatest power and wealth on earth. It did not seem possible. Even at Osborne, he seemed to be chief mourner rather than Sovereign. Alix refused to be called Queen or let anyone kiss her hand until Victoria was buried. Queen Alexandra, it sounded wrong.

Bertie had to decide what he would be know as. Albert Edward, his mother had insisted. Albert must come first. Bertie decided he could not live up to that name. He chose simply Edward, the name of six previous kings. He was applauded for his humility. But as he listened to the laments, spoken openly around him, 'What will happen to England now? How can we survive without her?' he felt his determination and his courage grow. He had been given no trust, no training and had a vast amount to learn, but he would learn it. His people were lost in mourning. He would give them back their pride and a new joy of living.

A week after the Queen died, the arrangements for her funeral were complete and the small coffin started on its way to the Mausoleum at Frogmore to lie next to the Prince Consort. On foot, Bertie with his brother Arthur, Duke of Connaught, and his nephew, Kaiser Wilhelm, followed the gun carriage on which it lay to the Admiralty Pier at Cowes. Black Watch pipers led the cortege and Alix followed, veiled in black, with Lenchen and Louise. The coffin, draped in a white pall embroidered with a gold cross and the Royal Arms, was carried up on to the quarterdeck of the Royal Yacht *Alberta* and laid on a crimson bier. The *Alberta* had an escort of eight black torpedo-destroyers and ahead stretched a five-mile line of giant warships, moored two and a half cables apart, leading all the way to Portsmouth Harbour. It was a tremendous display of the might of the Empire.

Bertie stood on the deck of the *Alberta* with the royal mourners.

When the Captain saluted him and asked permission to sail, he looked up. The Royal Standard fluttered half-way up its mast.

'Why is the Standard at half-most, Captain?' Bertie asked.

The Captain and the people standing around him, Alix, Wilhelm, Arthur, were surprised.

'Why, sir,' the Captain faltered, 'because the Queen is dead.'

Bertie's eyes held his for a moment, then he said quietly and clearly, 'But the King lives.'

The backs of all around straightened and the Standard with the arms of England, Ireland, Scotland and Wales rose to stream free at the masthead, and the great guns of the warships crashed out in salute as King Edward carried the body of his mother across to his new kingdom.